Look for Brenda Novak's next novel
In Close
available November 2011

BRENDA NOVAK

IN SECONDS

MIRA®

Recycling programs
for this product may
not exist in your area.

ISBN-13: 978-0-7783-1244-4

IN SECONDS

Copyright © 2011 by Brenda Novak, Inc.

For questions and comments about the quality of this book please contact us at
Customer_eCare@Harlequin.ca.

www.MIRABooks.com

Printed in U.S.A.

To Larry and Gloria Morrill—
Thank you for opening your home and your hearts.

Dear Reader,

Last November, when one of my best friends suggested I go with her to Montana to spend a few days with her parents, I agreed. It wasn't like me to take the time. I have a family, tight writing deadlines and lots of travel for speaking and conferences. But I'd never been to Montana. I wanted to see it and believed it would be therapeutic to have some "girlfriend" time.

I flew into Kalispell, which has a tiny but attractive airport, and met Dara there. I was looking forward to a quiet, scenic getaway and that's exactly what I got. I didn't realize that in these modern times, places still exist where there's no cell service for miles, but I have to admit I really like the idea and hope it never changes—it stirs my imagination to think technology hasn't completely tamed the Wild West.

We stayed in the Chain of Lakes area, right on Crystal Lake, which was so beautiful (especially in the mornings with the mist coming off the water) it stole my breath. Even better than the scenery was being able to feel like a kid again as Dara's parents, Larry and Gloria Morrill, took care of us with delicious food, interesting anecdotes about their family history (they now live where they grew up), research help, sightseeing trips and love. I will always remember my stay fondly—and associate that trip with this book. Not only is the story set in a fictional town I've placed not far from Happy's Inn, which is a stone's throw from their house, I started the manuscript while sitting in one of the bedrooms in their home.

I've posted pictures of Crystal Lake and Libby (where Myles works) on my Facebook page (http://www.facebook.com/pages/Author-Brenda-Novak/120794854630624). Please go there if you'd like to see what I saw (and "like" the page). Also, I'd love for you to visit brendanovak.com, where you can sign up for my mailing list, peruse my backlist and future releases and join the many authors, readers and philanthropists who support my annual online auction for diabetes research (my son has this disease). I hold this event at my website May 1 to May 31. So far we've raised over $1.4 million and are continuing the fight. Here's to a cure!

I hope you enjoy Laurel and Myles's story!

Brenda Novak

1

It was the murder that triggered everything. The moment Laurel Hodges—Vivian Stewart as of two years ago—heard about it, everything she'd been through, everything she'd done to escape her past, came rushing back at her. And it happened at a place where she'd felt completely safe only seconds before. She was having highlights put in her hair at Claire's Salon, which wasn't much of a salon, just an add-on to her friend's small home.

Although Claire had grown up here, Vivian had lived in Pineview only since she'd assumed her most recent identity. She'd chosen this town because it had an extremely low crime rate, it was so far from where she'd been before and it was on the backside of nowhere. She'd never dreamed the people who'd been chasing her for four years would think to look *here*. And it'd been a long enough stretch of peace and quiet to believe the terrible years were over. She'd left her old self behind, adjusted, established her fledgling purse-design business and begun to live again. She and her two children—Mia, seven, and Jake, nine—were finally starting to *belong*.

And now, in the blink of an eye, everything they'd created here felt threatened.

"What'd you say?" Lifting the hood of the commercial hair dryer, she leaned out so she could hear. The postman, George Grannuto, had just walked through the doors Claire had flung wide so they could enjoy the breezy June morning while she vented the fumes of the hair-coloring chemicals.

"Pat Stueben's dead," he repeated, handing Claire her mail. "He's been murdered." His face, drained of its usual ruddy color, made him appear years older than he was. Vivian knew his exact age—fifty-five—because she'd attended his birthday party last month. His wife was part of her Thursday-night book group.

Claire, only five foot three or so, leaned on the broom she'd been using to sweep up hair. Vivian had wanted a sassy cut to signify the freedom and happiness she'd been experiencing so often of late. She'd also gone back to being a blonde, which was her natural color. But going so short was a big change. Now she couldn't help staring at the dark brown locks lying on the floor, feeling as if she'd just shed her skin.

"How? When?" Claire brought a hand to her chest. George's words had obviously shocked her as much as they had Vivian. With the disappearance of her mother fifteen years ago and the death of her husband after only a few years of marriage, Claire had had more than her share of bad news. And now this… "Leanne and I saw him and Gertie at Fresh Ketch last night," she said. "They were in the booth next to ours."

Tall and bony, George resembled a cartoon stork delivering a baby when he carried his bulging mailbag down Claire's little dead-end street, and the shorts that went with his warm-weather uniform didn't improve his appearance. They revealed stiltlike legs with knobby knees and varicose veins. But he always wore a smile.

Except today.

"Someone called him," he explained, "wanting to rent one of those cabins he owns over on the north shore. So after breakfast he drove around the lake to show the property—and never came back."

If he'd said that Pat had died of a heart attack, Vivian wouldn't have found it difficult to believe. Pat was no longer as svelte as the picture posted on his real-estate signs. But...*murdered?* That couldn't be. They still didn't know what'd happened to Claire's mother, but no one had ever been *killed* in this tranquil place, not in recent memory. Folks here didn't even lock their doors at night. If the community had more deaths than some, that was because it had more seniors.

The old cloying fear welled up, making it hard for Vivian to breathe, let alone talk. After two attempts to clear her throat, she managed to find her voice. "Who discovered him?"

"Gertie." The clicking sound George made with his tongue was shorthand for "this makes it even worse." "When he didn't come home, she drove over to see what was keeping him. You know how close they are. *Were*," he corrected. "The scene when she walked in was—" He shook his head.

"She got there too late?" Claire asked this question; Vivian was still chasing words around the vortex of panic in her head.

George lowered his voice. "She found him lying in a pool of blood, beaten senseless. He died before he could tell her anything."

The hair on the back of Vivian's neck stood on end. *Beaten senseless?* Who could hate Pat enough to kill him—and in such a violent manner? No one from Pineview. He was popular, jovial, well-liked.

Did this tragedy mean what she thought it might?

"Do they know who did it?" Claire beat Vivian to the question that was uppermost in her mind. It was obviously important to Claire, too, and it wasn't hard to guess why, not with a mother who'd been missing for nearly two decades.

"I don't think so," George replied. "Maybe that would be different if we had cell phone service here, but we don't. And if the sheriff knows anything, he's not talking."

Sheriff King happened to be Vivian's next-door neighbor, so she knew him, at least a little. He wasn't the type to divulge details until he was good and ready, especially if doing so might jeopardize a case. Myles was a by-the-book kind of cop. He was also a handsome widower with a thirteen-year-old daughter. He'd asked Vivian out on occasion, but she'd never accepted. Claire said she was crazy for rejecting him, but she was still trying to get over Rex McCready, her brother's best friend who'd entered WitSec—witness protection—when she did. Besides, she was afraid to get *too* close to anyone who was unaware of her real situation for fear her past would come crashing into her present, just like it seemed to be doing today.

"How do you know all this?" There. She'd found her voice again. She'd also come to her feet.

"My route covers the whole lake." He gestured toward Crystal Lake, even though they couldn't see it from this part of town. Claire's house was artsy, in a hippie sort of way, but it was located on the poor side of Pineview.

Claire started to speak, but Vivian plowed over her. "You were at the scene?"

"I was. So was the coroner, the sheriff, some detectives and forensic techs from the county. Boy, were they were a grim bunch. The sheriff was downright stone-faced."

For good reason…

Heedless of the hair clippings that remained on the floor, Claire set her broom aside. "Is he the one who told you about Pat?"

"No, C. C. Larsen did. When Gertie found him, she ran to C.C.'s to use the phone."

"But C.C.'s house is a quarter of a mile from those rentals," Claire said. Having lived here her whole life, she knew every street, every alley, every empty field and rental cabin. She'd searched them all, at some point, for her mother.

He adjusted his bag to redistribute the weight. "She didn't want to go to another rental for fear of who might be there. You can understand." Wrinkling his nose, he added, "C.C. and I watched 'em cart out the body."

"This is terrible," Vivian muttered, but she wasn't really thinking about what she was saying. She was wondering if the panic intensifying her sadness over Pat's death was justified or simply an echo of an earlier time.

"I *tried* to get a few more details from the sheriff, but…it was useless," George said. "He told me he's 'investigating the incident' and that he'll know more later. He also said everything will be okay. But I don't see how it can ever be okay for Gertie."

The sheriff had answered without really answering.

Brenda Novak

Vivian recognized his "cop-speak" because she'd heard it before. When her stepfather had been shot and killed, the investigators wouldn't tell her or her family anything. Not knowing what was really going on had been almost as agonizing as learning that they were placing the blame on Virgil, her older brother, and prosecuting him, at eighteen, for murder.

"We've got a right to more information than that," Claire complained. "It's our community, too."

George nodded. "I see those shows on TV. I know what can happen when a serial killer gets started. Psychopaths don't quit till someone stops 'em. And this sounds like a psychopath to me. Who else would beat a man to death for no reason?"

"Do you think maybe some drug addict wanted Pat's wallet and he wouldn't give it up?" Vivian grasped at any feasible explanation, hoping the truth wasn't what she feared.

"It's possible, I suppose," George replied. "C.C. told me that Gertie said his wallet was missing. But there was only about fifty bucks inside. Still, a bungled robbery would be better than a serial killer. Imagine someone like that Zodiac fella or—or BTK setting up shop here in the Chain of Lakes."

Vivian *couldn't* imagine it. That was the problem. Claire's mother disappearing fifteen years ago was the only blemish on this town, and most folks believed she'd run off. Pineview, nestled so close to Crystal Lake, was picture-perfect. Safe. Close-knit. Stunningly beautiful. Untouched by the rest of the world. Apart from it, too. As George had said, Pineview didn't even have cell-phone reception.

It did, however, have its first modern-day murder.

"The FBI would descend on us. The media, too." George was expanding on his psychopath theory.

Claire checked the street, probably hoping to see her sister, Leanne, roll toward them in her motorized wheelchair. Crippled in a sledding accident when she was thirteen, Leanne drove it everywhere, even through the ruts on their road. "Maybe Chester over at the paper will get a letter from the killer, taunting Sheriff King."

George staggered under the weight of his bag. "Or someone else will die."

A real-estate agent beaten to death inside his own vacation rental spoke more of rage than a stalking type of murder, but Vivian didn't say so. She preferred to fade into the background, didn't want Claire or George to think she knew anything about the subject. No one here had any idea that her stepfather had been murdered, or that her brother had served fourteen years in prison before being exonerated. They had no idea of the problems that had started upon his release, either. Because all of that had happened to Laurel Hodges, not Vivian Stewart.

"If there's a serial killer running around, the danger is far from over," Claire said, but Vivian wasn't so sure this perpetrator had killed just for the thrill of it. If the violent gang her brother had joined while he was in prison had caught up with her yet again, it could be that Pat had merely gotten in the way. Like that U.S. marshal in one of the places she'd been before. The Crew had slit his throat and left him bleeding out on the floor. They would've killed her, too, if not for—

She couldn't even think of what had almost happened, because it involved her children. The men who belonged to The Crew were ruthless. They'd proven that, hadn't they? They'd also proven that they could get hold of whatever information they wanted. Vivian was convinced that someone in the very agency charged with their protection had been talking. That was the only way The Crew could've found them before, when they were all living in D.C. So they'd left the witness protection program, assumed new identities yet again and separated. Other than Virgil, his wife, Peyton, and Rex, who lived in Buffalo, New York, *no one* knew where she was, not even their handler from WitSec who'd helped them relocate the first time. After all that, what more could she possibly do to keep her small family safe?

Should she have changed her children's names, too? Because children were so difficult to trace—they didn't sign up for credit cards or get jobs or do any of the other things that left a trail—she'd opted to keep their first names. They had a different last name, though, which they understood was because of her divorce. Her new first name, she'd told them, was because she liked it better. Even that had taken them a while to get used to.

"We need to look out for each other, report any strangers we see," Claire said.

"But it's tourist season," George responded. "There're always strangers this time of year, most of 'em young guys who've come to hunt or fish or canoe. And you know how rough some of 'em can look, with all their tattoos and body piercings."

"Then we'll have to keep an eye on *all* of them." Claire glanced at Vivian, anticipating her full agreement, and did a double take. "Oh, my God! We've got to get you rinsed!"

She'd changed her hair. Drastically. Myles King noticed that right off. For one thing, she was now blonde.

That suited her, but he didn't know if he liked the cut; he couldn't see Vivian clearly enough to tell. His neighbor waited just outside the dim yellow glow of his porch light as if she feared he might press her to come inside if she moved any closer. She always approached him as warily as she might a bear or some other dangerous animal.

Why was she so skittish?

He might've guessed that he intimidated her. Police officers got that reaction sometimes. It came with the uniform. But at six foot two, he was only four inches taller. And maybe she was slender, but she was fit. She didn't seem like the type to feel easily threatened.

Besides, he'd been so nice to her! He rolled her garbage can to the curb if she forgot to set it out, mowed her lawn when he mowed his, bought enough fresh strawberries to share (he'd once overheard her telling her son that she loved fresh strawberries). He couched it all as an attempt to be neighborly, and it was—being neighborly to the beautiful brunette, who was no longer a brunette, next door. But nothing he did seemed to break down her defenses. Her kids were always excited to see him, but other than those strawberries or something as small as that, she politely declined every gift or invitation.

His instincts told him he was better off *not* getting involved with her. But he could sense the chemistry between them, and that was what confused him. He'd never forget the time he was working in the yard without a shirt and caught her watching him from where she was weeding her garden. It was as if a lightning bolt had gone through them both, incinerating them on the spot.

He knew desire when he saw it; she was as attracted to him as he was to her. So why wouldn't she let him take her to dinner?

"Can I help you?" Determined not to try any harder than he already had, Myles kept one hand on the door. It'd been a hell of a day. The last thing he needed was to top it off with another dose of sexual frustration.

"Um, yes…maybe you can." She cleared her throat. "I'm afraid my fridge has gone out."

The images of blood and death he'd seen earlier still filled his head, making it difficult to immediately comprehend her words. He'd returned from the scene of Pat Stueben's murder more than an hour ago, but he'd carried the grisly sight home with him. The fact that anyone would beat a good man, a friend to everyone, in Myles's own backyard, so to speak, made him so angry he couldn't think of anything else. "Did you say your *fridge?*" he clarified.

"Yes."

He felt his eyebrows go up. "Okay…"

"It went on the blink a couple of hours ago and… Claire told me you're a better handyman than Byron Jacobs." She flashed him a quick smile. "She said he had to call you when he couldn't fix her stove last month."

She was here for a *favor?* She never darkened his door, except to drag her son away. Jake slipped over whenever he could. The kid liked to follow him around, even help with the yard work, so Myles had been training him to use the weeder, the edger and the pruning shears.

But he wasn't in the business of fixing other people's broken appliances. He'd done Claire a favor. He wouldn't mind lending Vivian a hand, too, but it'd taken him three days to screw up the nerve to ask her if she'd go out on the lake with him two weeks ago. And her response? She had to clean her house—an excuse that was almost as bad as telling him she had to wash her hair.

He opened his mouth to turn her away. He was about to say the food would last until Byron could get to it in the morning. But he couldn't make himself go through with it, which just proved how obsessed with her he'd become. His wife had died of cancer only three years ago—but thirty-six months of celibacy felt a lot longer to his body than his heart. Not only that, this was the first time Vivian had invited him inside her home. From what he could tell, she didn't ask *anyone* in. Except maybe Claire and Vera Soblasky, who occasionally watched Jake and Mia for her.

Curious to see how she lived, he heard himself accept. "Sure. I can come over right now, if you want."

"Marley won't mind?" she asked.

His daughter had a friend over; they were watching a movie upstairs on the big screen in his room. They wouldn't miss him if he stepped out for a few minutes. "No. She'll be fine."

Vivian's face lit up. "Great. Thank you so much."

When that rare smile shot like an arrow to his groin, Myles cursed the testosterone that made him so…*male*. He had single women coming on to him all the time, but he wasn't interested in them. Instead, he wanted this complicated neighbor who'd let him know in no uncertain terms that she wouldn't welcome him even as a friend.

But tonight she needed help. And he was planning to make sure she got it. Apparently even the gruesome murder of an upstanding Pineview citizen couldn't lessen her impact on him. "I'll grab my toolbox and come over."

2

Vivian sat at the kitchen table while the sheriff un-plugged her fridge and tore apart the motor. She hadn't been sure he'd agree to help, but now that he had, she hoped he wouldn't be able to tell she'd sabotaged it her-self. She also hoped the job would take long enough to strike up more than a superficial conversation with him. It hadn't required much effort to cripple her fridge. She'd yanked out a few wires and was afraid he'd simply re-connect them before she could learn anything about Pat Stueben's murder, see if he had any idea who might be responsible.

"Kids in bed already?" he asked as he worked.

"Yeah. They're usually out by nine." He looked better in a pair of jeans than any man had a right to. She tried not to let her gaze drop to the assets those jeans dis-played, but it wasn't easy. She hadn't allowed herself to get this close to a man in the two years she'd been living in Pineview—especially a man who made her so aware that she'd soon be heading to bed alone. Just like every other night.

"What do you do after they're asleep?"

A screw fell to the floor. She bent to pick it up so he wouldn't see the warm blush that'd infused her cheeks.

"Work. The hours from nine to one are my most productive."

"You must not get much sleep. Not with kids who wake up at…what, eight?"

"Or earlier." She rolled her eyes for emphasis.

"Where's Jake and Mia's father?"

He'd spoken conversationally but this was information he and almost everyone in town had been dying to get out of her since she'd moved here. They didn't like how closed off she was; they weren't used to it. But she hadn't revealed any details about her ex so far, and she wasn't starting now. If she didn't give Pineview's good citizens a loose thread to tug on, they couldn't unravel the whole ball. "He's no longer part of our lives." *And that's all I've got to say on the subject.* She didn't add that, but her tone implied it.

"I see." If he was offended by her clipped response, he didn't show it. His fingers brushed hers as he took the screw and her stomach did an inconvenient little somersault. "So once they go to bed, you design purses?"

He smelled like soap. She wondered if he'd come home and showered. Probably. Anybody would want to wash after seeing what he'd seen. She knew because she'd watched two men gunned down four years ago. In some ways, it seemed as if eons had passed since that night. She'd come so far since then, had changed so much. In other ways, it felt like only yesterday, as if the horrifying sights and sounds of those murders were forever etched onto her brain and would stay there, as vivid and constant as the moment it happened.

Myles had stopped to look at her; she hadn't answered. "I do some designing, yes. I also handle orders, do the accounting, check out my competition or look at the photographs for my new catalog." Or, occasionally, Claire talked her into taking the night off and watching a movie. "I've got more than enough to stay busy."

"Your job is unusual for someone living in the wilds of Montana." He put the screw she'd picked up in his back pocket and she had to fight to keep her gaze from lowering to his ass. "How'd you get into designing?"

Although they'd never discussed this—they typically exchanged nothing beyond a few pleasantries—she was fairly sure he'd heard the story through the grapevine. That much of her past she'd already divulged. But if he wanted to make small talk while she waited for an opening to bring up the murder, she had no objections. He didn't seem to think there was anything strange about what had happened to the fridge, thank God. "I entered a contest sponsored by Coach purses and *Vogue* magazine while I was living on the East Coast and—" she shrugged "—my design won."

The interest in his green, brown-flecked eyes felt as good as a long massage. Maybe it was the two glasses of wine she'd drunk to get up the nerve to go next door, but a warm tingle swept through her whenever he looked up or smiled. She missed having a man in her life. She hadn't realized how much.

"Were you surprised?" he asked.

"Shocked." Even that was an understatement. Other than the births of her children, winning that contest was the best thing that had ever happened to her.

"To what do you attribute your success?"

To an intense fascination with fashion and design. To watching every show there was on the topic. To reading all the beauty magazines. To trial and error. She was self-educated, but careful not to miss the tiniest detail.

She had too many handicaps to overcome, she couldn't afford to be halfhearted or sloppy. But exposing the desperation that had fueled her dream seemed too personal. "Luck," she said to make it simple.

"That contest must've opened the right doors."

"It did. Coach asked me for other samples of my work, so I quickly came up with a few."

"They liked those, too?"

"Even more than the one that was selected as the winner."

"You must have natural talent."

With the kids asleep, the clock ticking rhythmically above the sink and the wine circulating in her blood, it was easy to let down her guard enough to enjoy his company. "That's what my boss at Coach said when he offered me a job. Before I went out on my own."

"Had you been to fashion school?"

She laughed out loud. There'd been no time or money for that. "No."

"Where did you go to college?"

Her levity vanished. Inevitably one question led to another. And so much of her past was too painful to talk about, or would be too dangerous to reveal. That isolated her from others, kept her from being able to connect.... "I didn't."

Once again, he paused. "You didn't have the opportunity?"

"No." She jerked her head toward the fridge. "That looks pretty complicated. Have you ever fixed one before?"

Taking the hint, he continued working. "Actually, I have."

"Did they teach you that at the police academy?" She

grinned to make up for her coolness. Prickly wasn't her true nature. It was a learned response, the only way she could create the space and privacy necessary to function somewhat normally.

He changed the head on his electric screwdriver. "Not quite. My father was an attorney, but he was raised by the most frugal individual on earth. Fortunately, he didn't turn out to be quite as tightfisted as his old man, but he refused to hire anyone to fix what we could learn to fix for him. He believed boys should grow up to be self-reliant. And there were four of us, so he had a lot of ready labor." He raised his voice to compensate for the hum of the screwdriver. "He'd find broken garbage disposals, toasters, fans—you name it—at the dump and haul them home just to make us fix them."

"What'd you do with those things after you got them working? Four boys could potentially fix quite a few toasters."

"We'd sell some."

She could picture him in a household of rough-and-tumble brothers. With his charm and energy, she guessed he'd be right in the thick of trouble. "And the others?"

"We'd give them to the poor. Until I got into college, anyway. Then *I* was 'the poor,'" he said with a chuckle. "I survived and paid my tuition by fixing various appliances. And cars. When I turned sixteen, my dad had a tow truck deliver an old clunker for me to rebuild. That was my birthday present." He gave her the crooked smile that had half the women in Pineview swooning over him. "Now I love to tinker."

Trying not to be taken in by that smile, Vivian leaned against the edge of the table. "Is that what you do in your garage late at night?"

She'd often seen the light seeping out from under his garage door. When she stepped onto the screened-in porch in the middle of a dark and silent night, she sometimes heard the whine of his power tools—even though quite a bit of space separated her home from his. Enough for two old sheds and a large garden, and that was just on her side. On his property, an expansive deck and party-type barbecue area took up most of the back and side yards. She'd never known him to use it, though—and she would've noticed since there was no fence. She was pretty sure he'd built it as a gift to his wife. She'd heard from Claire and the other women who liked to discuss the handsome sheriff that he'd finished it shortly before Amber Rose passed away, and then couldn't bear to see it once she was gone.

"I'm restoring an old Ducati," he explained.

"A Ducati's a…car?" When he glanced at her, she couldn't help wondering whether he liked her new haircut. He hadn't mentioned it, despite the fact that it was now as short as his.

"Motorcycle."

Briefly it occurred to her that Jake might have seen it. Was this one of the marvels that drew him next door?

She didn't ask, didn't want to acknowledge her neighbor's massive appeal to her nine-year-old, or all the manly activities and shared interests Myles could offer Jake that she could not. "How long does a project like that take?"

"Depends. I've been at it for six months, but it should've been done already." A dimple appeared in his cheek. "I haven't made a concerted effort."

Maybe there was a reason for that. Maybe he was afraid to finish for fear there'd be nothing left to distract him during those lonely hours. Sometimes she'd slip out, hoping to hear him working so she'd know she wasn't the only one walking the floor while the rest of the world slept. If he wasn't in the garage, she'd occasionally spot him sitting on his porch, drinking a cup of coffee or tea. He'd stay there for some time, even in the dead of winter, staring into the inky blackness. She'd stay, too, until he went inside. She could feel the hole his wife's death had left in his life, knew he missed Amber Rose. But Vivian was too attracted to him, and too afraid of where it might lead, to lend him more support than these secret vigils.

"Are you almost done with it?" she asked.

"Getting close."

"Will you keep it or sell it?"

"Don't know yet."

Vivian was about to bring up the murder, but he spoke before she could. "Are you glad you branched out on your own?"

Cursing herself for not jumping in sooner, she forced a smile. "Definitely."

"Why'd you leave Coach?" He was on his hands and knees so he could reach whatever he needed in the motor.

"I wanted more artistic freedom and control, and that meant establishing a separate brand." She'd also *had* to quit, but she couldn't tell him that. There was no way to keep her job and assume a new identity. "It's a little lonely being such a small enterprise. I have only three employees who run my showroom in New York. But we're starting to grow."

"Did you ever consider using your name, like so many other designers?"

Which name? Certainly not her real one. She had to stay behind the scenes or run the risk of putting her life, not to mention her kids' lives, in jeopardy. She had Colleen Turnbull, her most experienced employee, handle all media appearances. "No, to me Big Sky Bags lent itself to a certain look and a certain feel, which was more in keeping with the type of brand I was hoping to create."

He held up one part of whatever made her fridge work. It wasn't the part she'd damaged, fortunately. "This fridge isn't that old. I'm surprised it's giving you trouble already."

Planning to place the blame on rats or precocious children once he diagnosed the problem, she mumbled something about having bought a lemon and got him a paper towel so could set the part on the floor.

"How long have you been out on your own?" he asked.

"Since forever."

When he twisted around to look at her, she wondered why she'd said that. He'd asked in regard to her business. But she was just so tired of having the same superficial conversations with everyone. She wanted to go deeper, to really *talk* to another human being—to talk to *him*—but she couldn't. She had to watch herself even with Claire. She couldn't trust anyone.

"Care to elaborate on that?" His voice suggested he understood her desire to open up and welcomed the honesty, but she already knew she could say no more.

"No. Sorry. It's the wine." She waved an apologetic hand. "I started Big Sky Bags the minute I moved here."

She could sense his reluctance to let the more personal comment go, but to his credit he didn't pry. And for that, she was grateful. Her brother constantly warned her, in almost every one of his weekly emails, that she couldn't trust anyone. Especially a cop, who had access to far more information than the average Joe.

"Isn't it tough to succeed as a designer when you're so far from New York City and all your competitors?"

It *was* hard. For months she'd been afraid that she'd taken too much of a gamble when she launched Big Sky Bags. But a lot of designers lived west of the Rockies. Like her, they had their showrooms, their PR companies and their ad agencies in New York and their warehouses in New Jersey, but so many things could be done over the internet these days that it worked. Although she'd initially planned on running her business exclusively on the internet, and had been managing in just that way for two years, her designs were gaining popularity among a few influential fashionistas in Los Angeles. In the past three months, several high-end boutiques had begun to stock her purses. She felt encouraged, as if she was entering a whole new phase of her career. It was one of the reasons she'd been so happy recently.

But now, after Pat's murder, she had no idea whether or not she might have to move again, just like before. And she simply couldn't face the thought of it, couldn't deal with the loss.

"It's not as important to be in New York as it once was," she told him. "The internet makes it possible for me to work from almost anywhere. The factories are in Hong Kong, anyway. Once the sample purses arrive, I hire a freelancer to take photographs and load them on my website. Then they go to my showroom, where they're seen by department-store buyers and the wholesale places that focus on more niche markets. I don't have to be in New York to do that."

"It's a long flight if you have to go back there."

She'd already had to go twice this year, once when she'd decided to change her ad agency and once to meet with her PR firm. She didn't mind because it gave her a chance to see Virgil and Peyton, his wife, who were now going by the names Daniel and Mariah Greene. They lived seven hours from the city. But it wasn't easy for Vivian to leave the kids at home. Fortunately, Vera Soblasky, who lived behind the church in town, had been willing to take them in the past. An unmarried retired schoolteacher, Vera worked as a librarian three days a week, but since she had no children or grandchildren, she preferred to spend her free time with Jake and Mia, who didn't have a grandmother of their own. Not one they had contact with, at any rate.

Vera was another reason Vivian couldn't move. She couldn't tear her children away from their "Nana." They'd never forgive her. Then there was Claire, who'd become such a big part of her own life. Claire was always willing to help out with the kids but usually had to work.

"I try to avoid the trip, if possible," she said.

"Here's your problem." He held up the metal piece from which she'd removed the wires. "These are supposed to be attached."

She frowned as if this was surprising to her. "I wonder what could've happened to them. Could a rat have done that?" She felt like a rat just saying this.

"It's possible."

"So…can you fix it?"

He turned the part over. "It'd be easy if this wire wasn't so damaged. It isn't safe with so much of the protective coating gone. But I might have some wire in the garage that'll work."

Rubbing damp palms on her shorts, she blew out a sigh. "That's really nice of you. I appreciate it."

He went home and returned a few minutes later with

a piece of wire, and put the motor back together—which left Vivian scrambling for a way to keep him longer. She hadn't broached the subject of the murder; she was afraid to blurt out her questions for fear she'd give away her true intention in having him over.

"I think we're set," he said when he plugged the refrigerator back into the wall and it began to hum.

"Wow. That's amazing. Thank you so much." The guilt she felt about lying made it difficult to meet his eyes.

"No problem."

"Would you like a glass of wine?" she asked as he packed up his tools.

She'd surprised him. That was obvious from the way he straightened. "Okay."

It'd been so long since Vivian had had company, she felt awkward, out of practice. Her life wasn't conducive to socializing. Even after coming to Pineview, she hadn't entertained. Not a man, anyway. Claire and Vera dropped by every now and then. But she tried not to get too attached. What if she had to pull up stakes and leave?

That question hung over her. Always.

At least she was the only one who had to endure the weight of it. Her children didn't understand why she was so guarded. And she didn't want them to know, didn't want them to become as paranoid as she was. But that left them unprotected from possible disappointment.

"Did you grow up wanting to become a cop?" she asked as she poured chardonnay from a new bottle.

He put his toolbox by the kitchen door, which led to a mudroom on the side of the house facing his property, and took a seat at the table. "Pretty much. My uncle was in law enforcement. He used to come over on the weekends, help me work on whatever project I had going. And while we worked he'd talk about his job. His stories not only fascinated me, they made me passionate about seeing justice done. I wanted to get involved in that fight."

She set his wine in front of him. "You didn't want to be a lawyer, like your father?"

"No. Definitely not enough action in that."

"What about an electrician?"

"I figured that could be a fallback. But I was more interested in police work."

She'd already drank enough wine for one evening. It didn't take much to make her tipsy. But she was so self-conscious. And the alcohol was doing a great job of relaxing her.

One more glass… "If you want action, what are you doing in a sleepy little town like this?"

He studied his wine, swirled it around. "My wife visited here once, with her parents, when she was a child. They spent the whole summer. She'd always dreamed of coming back to live. So once she got sick and the doctors said there was nothing more they could do, I thought it might be the best place for her."

He'd done everything he could, even built her that expensive deck. Claire had told Vivian how, in her last days, he'd carry Amber Rose outside and hold her on his lap so she could feel the sun….

Did it hurt him to talk about his late wife? Vivian wanted to ask, but such personal questions fell into what she'd designated a restricted area. She had to respect other people's boundaries if she wanted them to respect hers.

"Where did you live before?" she asked.

"Phoenix."

She cradled her glass. "That's a big change."

"And yet I love both places," he said with a shrug.

"Will you ever go back?"

His nicked and scarred hands served as a testament to all he did with them. And they were so large they made his glass appear small by comparison. "No. Marley's settled here. She's happy. After she lost her mother, I'd never take her away from her friends. I think stability's important, don't you?"

Very. That was the problem. Thanks to The Crew, stability wasn't an easy thing for her to provide. "But do you think it's as safe here as we once believed?"

Weaving his fingers together, he clasped them behind his head. "You've heard about the murder."

She'd found the lead-in she'd been searching for. But she was afraid she'd given herself away. He could read people so well. She'd seen him do it many times— watched him step in to defuse a disagreement at the Fireworks by the Lake show last July fourth before it could erupt into a fight, watched him steer various inebriated people away from the bar so he could drive them home before they tried to get behind the wheel, watched how gently he deflected unwanted female attention. He kept his finger on the pulse of everything that went on around him, noticed changes and figured out the reasons for them. And inviting him over had definitely been a change. So he had to be wondering. And watching for clues.

"I think most people have heard about the murder," she said. "You know what gossip is like in this town."

"I do, which is why I'm curious…"

When his eyes latched onto hers, she knew he wasn't

going to limit his comments to the superficial and polite. And that made her uncomfortable enough to drain her glass. "What?"

"Why no one ever has any dirt on you."

Her stomach muscles tensed, but she smiled. "You're changing the subject."

"Maybe I am. But I can tell my statement doesn't surprise you. And that makes me even more curious."

"I haven't given anyone a reason to talk," she countered.

"Exactly. You don't flirt. You don't date. You don't sleep around. You don't get involved in church or the school board or the politics of this town."

"I take the kids to church on Sundays."

"That's it, though. You rarely even go out for a drink. As far as I can tell, your social life consists of having Claire over to watch an occasional movie and book group on Thursday nights. You live in the background of a place that's already in the background. Why?"

Oh, God. She shouldn't have had him come here, let alone served him a drink. "I'm too busy with my business and raising my children."

"You don't feel the need for intimacy?"

He wasn't talking about sex but, thanks to the wine, that was precisely where her mind went. By the time her marriage ended, she'd cringed whenever Tom touched her. But her opinion of making love had improved once she met Rex McCready. Giving pleasure was one thing Rex could do right. "How do you know I'm not in a relationship?"

"I'd notice if a man came to the house."

Was he as preoccupied with her as she was with him? She hoped not. For the past several months she'd been absolutely infatuated. He and he alone occupied her thoughts during the long nights when she was too tired to work but couldn't sleep. Claire was starting to pick up on her interest and badger her about why she kept turning him down.

More wine. Right away. Getting up, she retrieved the bottle and poured herself another glass. She offered him a refill, too, but he shook his head. "Maybe I had a bad experience, so I'm hesitant to take the risk," she murmured.

He ran a finger over his lip in a thoughtful gesture. "Bad in what way?"

The anxiety that'd been gnawing at her seemed to have lost its teeth, but she held fast to the rules she'd established for herself when she moved here. She was already too close to Claire; she didn't need to wag her tongue to the sheriff. "I don't want to talk about it."

That should've been direct enough to head him off. He couldn't possibly have missed her "you're treading too close" signal. But the sheriff wouldn't let it go. Not tonight. "What'd he do to you?"

She downed more wine as she searched for a casual response. But even the alcohol couldn't stifle the painful memories. Tom forcing her to have sex with him several times a night whether she was interested or not. Tom heaping on the guilt simply because she craved other people and relationships in her life, especially girlfriends. Tom undermining her attempts to get a job so she'd be completely dependent on him. And then there was the physical abuse, the worst of which she'd blocked out....

When she finished what was in her glass, the sheriff was still waiting, and watching her closely. "He was abusive, okay? I'm sure you've guessed that already. But if you want to hear me say it, I just did."

"Physically?"

She winced as she remembered some of the humiliating things Tom had made her do, how easily he'd been able to manipulate her because of their children. "Yes."

He leaned over and touched the scar where Tom had cut his initials into her arm. "Did he do this to you?"

That had been minor, compared to some of the other stuff. She pulled away. "That and more."

"Where is he now?"

"I don't know. I just hope he never finds me." There were others she feared far more, but she couldn't tell him that. This would appease the sheriff's curiosity; make him believe he understood why she was so withdrawn and secretive. Make him stop questioning her about the past.

"You think he's looking?"

"He could be." She'd had a lot to drink tonight, too much, and wanted even more—anything to further numb the sharp edge of fear—so she refilled her glass.

"I'm sorry," he said. "I wouldn't have pushed. Except…I've tried asking you out so many times."

She didn't want to talk about them. "Sheriff, please."

"Sheriff?"

"Myles, then." It wasn't easy to say his name; it felt too familiar. "In case you haven't guessed, I'm not interested in a relationship."

Instead of getting offended, he leaned forward again and caught her chin so she had to meet his eyes. "Is that right?"

She got the impression he wanted to touch her. Desperate for even this small amount of contact—it'd been *so* long since she'd been with a man—she drew a shallow breath. "You don't believe it?"

"Sometimes the way you look at me is…a bit contradictory."

Gazing at him from beneath her lashes, she attempted to deny it. "I don't know what you're talking about."

"Take now, for instance."

The wine was going to her head. But she welcomed it. She'd had to battle for her life and the lives of her children for so many years that she felt too weary to continue. *"Now?"* she repeated.

"Yeah, now. This very second. If I didn't know better, I'd say you're definitely…*interested.*"

He could've said *aroused,* because she was. The warmth of his body appealed to her, the hard muscle, the completion he could offer, but… "Not in a relationship," she said.

"Then what?" The softness of his voice begged her to level with him, but she couldn't. The fantasies she'd indulged in over the past twelve months stood between them. So did his job.

"N-nothing."

"You know I'd never hurt you the way your ex did, right?" He ran his fingers down her arm, light as a faint breeze.

"Look, you—you don't want to get involved with me," she said, but turned her hand over to reveal the more sensitive skin on the inside of her wrist.

"You're sending me mixed messages again," he pointed out.

She couldn't seem to help herself. Although she was starved for the physical stimulation she'd grown accustomed to during the year she'd spent with her brother's best friend and former cell mate, she couldn't let this go any further. Myles had a daughter. And he'd suffered enough with the loss of his wife. She needed to take that into consideration. She'd hate herself if she brought any more pain and unhappiness into their lives.

"You'll have to trust what I say."

His fingers continued to glide back and forth, creating goose bumps. "What if I prefer what you're *not* saying?"

He didn't realize what he was doing, stirring up such longing. She was so tired and scared she couldn't seem to marshal her self-control. "What do you want from me?" she whispered.

His hand stilled. "I'm thinking yes to dinner would be nice. Any chance we could start there?"

Dinner? That wasn't enough. Not now. Everything she'd been missing, craving, imagining in the dark hours of night was bearing down on her all at once—distilling into a reckless abandon unlike anything she'd experienced before. Nothing seemed to matter except obliterating that aching need. "I have a better idea."

He cocked his head, and she swallowed hard before continuing. "What if we made an…arrangement?"

"What kind of arrangement?"

Her heart felt like a fish flopping around on the sand. "An arrangement that would…last for one night."

When his eyes narrowed, she knew she'd piqued his interest. "The only arrangement I know that lasts for one night is called a one-night stand."

When she didn't tell him he'd gotten the wrong idea, as he so obviously expected, he sat up and blinked. "When a woman turns a man down for dinner as many times as you've turned me down, he pretty much figures sex is out of the question."

That didn't mean it *had* to be. They couldn't have a relationship. But one night wasn't a relationship. It was an escape.

She wet her lips. "Is that a no?"

He took an even closer look at her. "You're serious."

"It's a simple question." She'd knocked him off balance but *she'd* been off balance from the beginning. "Do you want to make love to me or not?" *Don't say no. I can't keep waging this battle alone. Just one night with company in my solitary world. That's all I ask....*

He shoved back in his chair, the small movement a sudden explosion of energy. "Is that a trick question? Because if this is…some sort of test…I mean, if you think that's all I'm after—"

He was searching for pitfalls when there were none. "You don't understand. That's all *I'm* after. One night. Just promise me two things."

Several creases appeared in his forehead. "What?"

Vivian curled her fingernails into her palms. "You have to keep it to yourself—"

"What kind of person do you think I am?" he retorted.

She didn't bother answering, because this next part was the clincher. "And you can't ask me out again. Ever. You can't come over here hoping for a repeat, either. We agree to forget about tonight, act as if it never happened, and we go back to being polite neighbors. That's all. It's a…a time-out for both of us."

Jumping to his feet, he paced to the counter. "Listen, I'm sure it's probably been as long for you as it has for me. I understand how—" he seemed to be choosing his words carefully "—lonely you must be…living the kind of life you've been living, taking care of your kids, working so much and devoting any free hours to your garden.

But…there's a lot we don't know about each other. And we're not the most transparent people in the world."

He was trying to be kind, using *we.*

"I'm not sure having sex is the best way to start a friendship," he finished.

"It's not a friendship," she corrected. "It's a one-night stand, like you said."

"But we're neighbors. We live in the same small community."

She knew it would be awkward afterward, but they could deal with it, put the barriers back up. And if they couldn't, she didn't care. She refused to be logical, to acknowledge the risks. Fortunately, the wine made that easy. Couldn't she just *act* for once, before her self-control regained the upper hand and denied her yet again? How much more sacrifice could life demand? She was thirty years old and she'd had one fulfilling sexual relationship, which had lasted less than a year. "You don't have to explain or justify your decision. You merely have to make up your mind. Do you want me or not?"

When he cleared his throat and adjusted himself, she could tell he wasn't unaffected by the tension crackling between them. "This isn't about *want,* for Christ's sake. If that was the only thing I had to consider, I wouldn't think twice."

"Then *stop* thinking."

"I can't. Taking off our clothes isn't the right place to begin a relationship."

Why was he saying that again? She'd already told him she didn't want a relationship. There was no beginning. Only an end. And she'd let him choose what that end would be.

She gave him a rather tight smile. "I understand. Thanks for fixing my refrigerator."

He went stone-still despite all the energy that seemed to be coiled up inside him. "Thanks? That's it? What about a movie? Bowling? A hike? Boating on the lake? We could drive into Libby if you're afraid someone here might see us and make an issue of it."

Her head suddenly felt as if it weighed a ton; just holding it up became a struggle. She was too weary to continue carrying her usual load, which had been made all the heavier by Pat's murder. And now she knew there'd be no relief, not even for a few hours. "No, but thank you."

"This is crazy," he said. "You want to sleep with me, but you won't go out with me? *Why?*"

"I can't."

"That doesn't make any sense!"

She pressed her palms to her eyes. "Please…go. I—I should never have asked. I wouldn't have, except…" Except she had no other alternative. She felt she had to grab hold of *someone* before she lost all ability to cope. "Never mind. It's no excuse for my behavior, but…I'm tired."

"Listen." The tension threatened to escape his control, but he managed to bridle it. "You've had too much to drink. That ties my hands right there. But…you never know where dinner might go."

"I understand," she said again. "But no, thank you. I had no business asking. I can't even imagine how it must've sounded."

"I want to get to know you better first, use a little caution. We're not eighteen."

"Right. It was my mistake. I'm sorry."

That she agreed with him only seemed to bother him more. "But it's still a no."

"I'm afraid so."

"Fine. Forget it." With a frustrated scowl, he strode to the door, where he turned back and studied her as if he couldn't believe they'd reached this impasse.

She forced herself to look away. "Your daughter's probably wondering where you are."

Cursing, he grabbed his toolbox and left.

The click of the door echoed in Vivian's mind as she sat alone, staring at the wine bottle that had come between her and some restraint.

"Great. I just propositioned my neighbor," she muttered. "And it was the county sheriff." What'd gotten into her? Could she really be desperate enough to make such a fool of herself?

Apparently so. Embarrassment would consume her in the morning. She could already feel a hint of what she had coming, dancing just beyond the fuzziness caused by the alcohol.

Pouring herself the last of the wine, she decided she could deal with that later. First, she had to contend with the cold emptiness that'd settled into the pit of her stomach.

Laying her head on her arms, she looked at the clock on the wall, watching the second hand move slowly from dot to dot. One minute… Two…

She hadn't even gotten any information out of him about the murder. *Shit… Shit, shit, shit…*

Then she remembered the shock on his face when she propositioned him and started to laugh. If she didn't laugh, she'd cry. And what good was crying? There was no one to hear her, no one to help....

As usual.

3

I have a better idea... What if we made an arrangement?... What kind of arrangement?... An arrangement that would last for one night....

Holy hell. Myles had so many hormones coursing through him he couldn't even bring himself to sit down. Leaving the lights off—the darkness gave him a sense of privacy he desperately needed right now—he prowled around his living room, fighting the urge to return to Vivian's. If he couldn't convince her to go out with him, why not take what he could get? Tonight might be his only chance.

But that was a pretty creepy way to look at it. He really didn't want to be that big an asshole. For one thing, she'd had too much to drink. That meant he couldn't.

There were other issues, too. He still felt some loyalty to Amber Rose, hadn't been with anyone since. Then there was Marley and how irresponsible it would be for him, as a father and a police officer, to be intimate with someone he wasn't even dating. And what about Pat? The murder of a Pineview citizen should've been enough to keep him occupied and well beyond temptation. He'd assigned his two best investigators to the case, but he'd have his work cut out for him in the morning, when the press began to call and everyone started demanding answers. He should be getting some sleep. The whole community was depending on him....

But he *wanted* her. There was no question about that. As guilty and disloyal as it made him feel, he'd wanted her almost from the first day he saw her, watering her lawn wearing that pretty summer dress and no shoes. Would one night of hot, sweaty sex be *that* reprehensible?

If he indulged himself, maybe he'd be able to start living again. He felt as if his life had been on pause since Amber Rose died. He'd convinced himself to go out on a couple of blind dates set up by well-meaning friends, and he'd joined a softball team in an attempt to socialize, but he was merely going through the motions, pretending to be whole when he wasn't. Except for the love he had for his daughter and the interest Vivian sparked whenever he saw her, he felt very little passion for anyone or anything—even, to a point, his work.

This might be the answer, might bring him back to the man he used to be.

He imagined taking Vivian to the lake, pictured himself peeling off her swimsuit and bringing his mouth to her breast, and nearly groaned. Allowing himself to dangle at the far edge of restraint was driving him mad—

"Daddy?"

His daughter's voice acted like a splash of cold water in the face. Whipping around, he saw her charging down the steps, heading toward the kitchen. He'd left the light on in there. Her best friend, Elizabeth, trailed after her. Their movie must've ended.

"Yes?"

His answer, coming from the direction it did, startled her. She hadn't expected to find him brooding in the dark.

After hesitating for a moment, she came forward. "Is something wrong?"

A lot was wrong. But he felt as though fifteen minutes with Vivian could fix at least some of it. "No, why?"

"What are you doing here?"

"Just thinking."

When she leaned closer, he could tell she was trying to see him more clearly in the light spilling from the hallway. "Why is your hair messed up?"

Better his hair than his clothes, he thought, and jammed his hands in his pockets. "I must've shoved my fingers through it."

"It looks funny." She nudged Elizabeth and they both giggled. But then she sobered and the worry was back. "Are you sure you're okay?"

That was a question he hoped he'd be more capable of answering in the affirmative tomorrow. "Of course. What's up?"

"Elizabeth and I were wondering if I could stay over at her house tonight."

"No!" The quickness of his reply revealed that he hadn't even considered it. She wouldn't like that, of course, but he didn't care. He couldn't let her stay elsewhere. Not until they found Pat's killer. Besides, her absence would leave him with an empty house, making it that much more difficult not to slip over to Vivian's.

When she summoned the pout he usually couldn't resist, he knew she wasn't going to accept his answer without an argument. "Why not? It's summer. It's not like I have school tomorrow."

He hated to tell her about Pat, but she obviously hadn't

heard. "Pat Stueben was murdered today, Marley. I don't want you going anywhere."

The "please, please, please" part had been coming next. He could tell. But this brought her up short. "What do you mean...*murdered?*"

He put some effort into gentling his voice. "Someone killed him."

She gaped at Elizabeth, whose horrified expression matched her own. "The real-estate agent?" she breathed when her attention shifted back to him. "The guy who sold us this house?"

"That's him."

"Oh, no!" Her hand flew to her mouth. "Now I feel *awful* for making fun of that plaid jacket he always wears...wore."

Her comment might've been comical under different circumstances. Under *these* circumstances, Myles wasn't even tempted to laugh. "It's very sad, especially for his wife."

"Are you sure someone did it? It wasn't an—an accident?"

"I'm sure. A person doesn't get beaten to death by accident."

"So that's why you're pacing around in here."

The murder was part of it; his angst over Vivian was the rest. That lust could take center stage on a night like this made him question his own character.

Marley turned on a lamp. "But...how could someone do such a thing?"

The sexual tension that had held him in its grip was beginning to dissipate. His daughter grounded him, helped him remember what was important. He'd made the right decision coming home. How could he expect

Marley to approach sexual relationships with respect and caution if he didn't set the proper example? "I don't know, but we're going to do everything we can to find the culprit."

"Are *you* investigating it? I thought you had people who did that for you."

"I do, but I'm in charge, so I'm responsible for how it's handled."

Troubled eyes regarded him as she pondered the news. But with typical teenage narcissism, she reverted to what *she* wanted almost immediately. "So why does that mean I can't go to Elizabeth's? You don't think it's safe?"

That wasn't what he'd meant to convey. He didn't want to cause mass panic in Pineview. He simply preferred to have his daughter at home tonight, where he could watch over her. And he wanted to remove the temptation to unleash the anger, disappointment, sexual frustration and myriad other emotions of the past three years on his neighbor. Taking Vivian up on her offer wouldn't have made dealing with their lives afterward any easier. "That's not what I'm saying. I just want to be cautious while my investigators figure out how and why it happened and make sure the same thing doesn't happen to anyone else."

"You think someone *else* could be killed?"

Unless the perpetrator had already moved on. For the sake of everyone who lived in this small town by the lake, Myles hoped the danger had passed. But he also craved justice for Pat and understood how much harder it would be to obtain if his killer had left the area. "I can't even guess. Like I said, we need to be cautious until we know more."

"Oh, my gosh!" She grabbed her friend's hand. "Then can Elizabeth stay here instead?"

So much for being afraid he'd spook her. With a sigh, Myles stretched the taut muscles in his neck. "Sure. As long as it's okay with her parents."

"We'll call," she said, and they hurried into the kitchen.

Despite the opening and closing of various cupboards—Marley digging out a snack—Myles heard Elizabeth on the phone.

"You know that real-estate guy? The one with the fake hair and that old-fashioned jacket? He's *dead*," she told her parents. "Someone *killed* him."

The horror in those words doused the last of the arousal burning inside Myles. He had no business obsessing about a woman who wouldn't even go out with him, not when he had a murder to solve.

And yet he was still up, rambling around the house, long after the girls fell asleep. Never had he missed Amber Rose more. *It's not fair. She should still be here with us.*

But life wasn't fair. No doubt Pat Stueben would tell him that.

If he could…

Vivian woke angry at Myles. It was the only way to avoid the embarrassment that would set in otherwise. After he'd shown a great deal of interest in her over the past year, she'd been nice enough to offer him the physical intimacy he had to be missing—and it wasn't going to cost him so much as a meal. But he'd refused her. She had no patience with a guy like that. What was he, some kind of saint?

"Of course he is," she grumbled. She'd heard what everyone had to say about him—how hard he tried to be a good father, how tender he'd been with his wife. This town considered him their guardian angel, the answer to every problem. He was even more popular than the mayor. But she didn't have the luxury of living in a world where she could welcome the possibility of love. Not without putting the person she loved in danger. Or taking the risk of being wrenched away from him. That was why, in some ways, Rex had been perfect for her. Falling for him hadn't drawn him into her problems. As Virgil's former cellie and an ex–Crew member himself, he'd been involved before they ever met.

Tightening her robe, she tossed both wine bottles in the recycle bin. Pat's murder had sent her reeling, made her reach for an antidote to her pain and fear. But the fact that someone had been killed was all the more reason to keep her wits about her. Especially since Claire would be over soon, wanting to know if Vivian had heard any more about the murder, if the sheriff happened to mention it to her, if she could ask him whether it might have a connection, however remote, to her missing mother. When Myles first came to town, he'd reopened the case as a favor to Claire, but her sister, Leanne, didn't want to be reminded of the past. She'd reacted so badly to the investigation that Claire had asked him to stop.

Movement next door drew Vivian's attention to the kitchen window. Myles had emerged from his house.

Don't look at him!

She didn't want to, but couldn't resist. Tall and commanding in his uniform, he was as gorgeous as ever. She knew Virgil and Rex wouldn't approve of her fascination with a cop. After having spent so much time

in prison, they didn't care for the type of personality
generally attracted to law enforcement. But, as Claire
so often pointed out to her, Myles was different. He was
real, warm, unaffected by the power his office gave him.
That was because he had a natural sense of authority, and
even if he wasn't the sheriff, she felt pretty certain that
people would expect him to take charge—

Wait! Was he looking back at her? Yes! Startled by the
realization, she ducked out of sight and, a few seconds
later, heard his car start.

"Thank God," she whispered as he drove away.

"What's wrong, Mom?" Jake had come stumbling into
the kitchen. Although he was dressed—in swim trunks,
a T-shirt and flip-flops—his thick blond hair stood up
on one side and his eyelids drooped with sleep.

A bit self-conscious about being discovered hiding
behind the curtains, Vivian pasted a smile on her face.
"Nothing, honey. What are you doing up so early?" She
glanced at the clock. "It's barely six."

"Nana Vera is taking me fishing. She'll be here any
minute."

A trickle of unease slid down Vivian's spine. Last
week, when she'd agreed to let Vera take Jake for the
day, she'd had no idea they'd planned an activity so out
of the ordinary. "What do you mean, you're going fishing?"

"Nana Vera said I could do anything I want. Today
is my half birthday." He grinned at the idea of having a
second birthday in one year. "So I picked fishing. I've
never been fishing before."

A twinge of guilt added yet another element to the
chaos of Vivian's emotions. Myles had invited her and
the kids to go out on the lake a few weeks ago, had spe-

cifically mentioned how much her son would enjoy it, and she'd refused.

She didn't feel comfortable with Jake being near the water today, either. She wasn't as afraid of letting him grow attached to Vera as she was Myles. Vera seemed far safer in that regard. She needed Vera's help too badly to avoid letting her have contact with the children, anyway. But she wasn't sure their "nana" was completely reliable when it came to keeping Jake safe so close to the lake. Would she have the physical strength and agility to save him if he fell in?

Or was she being overprotective? He'd be wearing a life jacket, he knew how to swim and no doubt he'd be fishing from the wharf, where so many young men liked to go.

Because of everything that had happened—the release of her brother from prison, his and Rex's attempt to leave The Crew and The Crew's determination to stop them or make them pay—Vivian had a tendency to shield her children too much. That only made her son more determined to escape the strictures of her concern. She could sense him pulling away from her as he grew older, preferring to spend time with Myles and other men, to embrace life without fear or reservation.

But there was so much Jake didn't know, so much she wouldn't tell him for fear he'd have to carry the same burden she did....

"What about your sister?" she asked, stalling while she decided whether or not she'd go along with this.

He selected a box of cereal from the pantry. "It's not her half birthday, so she doesn't get to go."

"Why not?" This came from Mia, who'd entered the kitchen behind him. Still in her nightgown, she looked as tired as Jake. But, in true Mia fashion, she wasn't about to miss out on anything. She seemed to feel as if she should be able to trail after her brother 24/7.

"Because it's not *your* half birthday," he said with sufficient exasperation to tell them both that he was tired of repeating it. "You'll get your turn. I was born first, so I get to go first. You heard Nana."

Her bottom lip jutted out. "I want to catch a fish."

Vivian handed Jake a bowl and a spoon, which he carried, together with his cereal, to the table. "Then ask Nana to take you fishing when it's your turn," he said.

"I'm calling her!" Mia started for the phone on the wall, but Vivian intercepted her by sweeping her into both arms for a hug. She was getting too big to carry, but Vivian couldn't resist. Besides, this day meant a lot to Jake. Vivian felt she had to agree to it or risk driving an even bigger wedge between them.

"We'll let Jake have his half birthday and plan yours, okay?" she said.

Mia opened her mouth to complain, but Vivian spoke before she could. "What are *you* going to do for yours?"

The furrows on her forehead disappeared. "Make a cake," she announced. "And have a party!"

"That sounds like fun," Vivian said. "Will I be invited?"

Her daughter gave her an impish grin. "Will you bring a present?"

Vivian laughed. "Of course."

"What kind of present?"

"Aren't presents supposed to be a surprise?"

As Mia tried to weasel an answer out of her, Jake wolfed down his cereal, set his bowl in the sink and went up to brush his hair and teeth.

Just as Vivian heard the faucet go off, a car horn sounded outside.

"Nana's here!" she called up to him.

Rapid footsteps pounded the old wooden floor in the hallway above as he dashed for the stairs and jumped down them two at a time.

"Have fun!" Vivian said, but she almost couldn't leave it at that. Wanting to warn Vera about all the dangers of the lake—and to make sure she'd heard about Pat Stueben's murder so that she'd be extra cautious—she nearly followed him out of the house. But that was precisely the sort of thing that upset Jake.

Vera was careful with the kids. She'd take good care of him.

"I can't wait till it's my turn." Mia's wistful comment broke the silence that had rolled over them like a fog in the wake of Jake's rushed departure.

Vivian smoothed her daughter's hair off her forehead. "Your turn will come soon enough, sweetheart," she promised. *If* they were able to stick around…

Where would they go if they had to leave? And how would she manage another relocation? She'd been on a rent-to-own plan and had recently signed the contract to purchase her house. She no longer had the government's help and, expecting the coming fall to be her best year yet, she'd invested what money she hadn't put into the house in her business.

Just when she'd stopped looking behind her…

Eager to send her brother an email, to get some reassurance that he, Peyton and Rex were okay in upstate New York and to keep him apprised of what was happening in Montana, she quickly prepared Mia's breakfast. Then, sitting at the desk in one corner of the living room, she went online—and that was when her throat closed as if someone had tightened a noose around it.

It was Tuesday, not Sunday. This wasn't the day she and Virgil usually communicated. But there was a message from him. And it was marked Urgent.

4

Myles went straight to the vacation rental where the murder had taken place. Now that the initial shock was over, and the forensic techs and the coroner were gone, he wanted to examine the scene by himself. He planned to look at it from all angles to see if he could get some impression of the events that'd led up to Pat's death. He also wanted to see if he could figure out a possible motive.

But, early though it was, he wasn't the first person at the cabin. An old dented Porsche 911 sat parked off the narrow road on a thick layer of pine needles. Myles recognized it as belonging to Jared Davis, the investigator he'd put in charge of this case.

"Who'd want Pat dead?" Jared called out as soon as Myles stepped over the yellow crime-scene tape. But he was nowhere to be seen. He must've heard the cruiser and glanced out the open door before Myles came up the walk.

"No one I know," Myles replied to the disembodied voice.

"There's his wife."

"Gertie? She wouldn't have the upper-body strength." He found Jared in the dining room, crouching not far from the blood on the kitchen tiles, notepad in hand. It was cool outside, about sixty degrees, but the temperature would soon climb to eighty. Why Jared would be wearing a trench coat and wing-tipped shoes, Myles had no idea, but the investigator reminded him of the character on the TV show *Columbo,* which his mother used to watch. He even acted like him—a little disheveled and disorganized, often absorbed and seemingly inattentive, although he rarely missed a thing.

"She could've hired someone to do it."

Myles was just as skeptical of that, but Jared continued before he could respond.

"She stands to collect half a million in life insurance. I checked."

Because most murders were committed by family or friends, Jared had classified her as a "person of interest." That was standard procedure, to look close to heart and home. But Myles didn't believe Pat's killer could be Gertie. "You've got to eliminate every possibility, right?"

Jared stood but at five foot eight he barely came to Myles's shoulder. "You don't think it's her."

Myles had made that clear yesterday. "Not a chance. I saw her after she found her husband. She was destroyed. Grief like that can't be faked. Besides, they were happy, always together."

"Maybe she's a hell of an actress. Maybe, when I dig a little deeper, I'll find out she's been embezzling from her husband's real-estate company and he was about to audit the books."

The interior of the house contrasted sharply with the beautiful day dawning outside. Birds sang in the towering trees that shaded the property and the lake lapped gently at the shore only fifteen yards or so from the front entrance. It was a rustic paradise. Pine and moist earth overpowered every other scent, and the forest behind the house created a deep and resounding quiet. Everything about this crime seemed incongruent with its surroundings.

Trying not to let the disturbing sight get to him the way it had yesterday, Myles ordered himself to maintain some emotional distance. He'd grown soft since coming here, had gotten caught up in the idyllic life of a "safe" community. "You're jaded, you know that?"

"I'm just saying. It wouldn't be the first time a wife decided to off her hubby to avoid detection. With humiliation and divorce on the one hand and the answer to all her financial problems on the other…" He let his words fade away.

"She didn't need to embezzle. Pat would've given her any amount. They'd been married for forty years."

"Doesn't matter."

Myles arched an eyebrow at him. "You're jaded, like I said."

"Yeah, well. You spend twenty years working for the LAPD and that's what you get." He shrugged. "You can take the cop out of L.A., but you can't take L.A. out of the cop, not after that long. I plan to check her bank accounts and telephone records, just in case."

"You do that. I'm relying on you to be thorough. Don't waste a lot of time, though. I want to catch this bastard. And the longer you dick around with Gertie, the less chance we'll have."

"I don't dick around when I'm on the job, Sheriff." Jared sounded insulted. He had a tendency to take things literally and to carry logic to illogical extremes.

"I'm telling you not to pursue her exclusively, okay?"

"Of course I won't. I'll follow every lead."

"Perfect."

"You seem uptight," he added. "Is there a reason?"

"Pat's murder isn't reason enough?" Myles retorted, but he knew his agitation had as much to do with Vivian as Pat. He couldn't figure her out. He wanted to feel angry at her for being so unreasonable, but those marks on her arm, the ones put there by her ex-husband, made it impossible to hold her resistance against her. She probably didn't want to give another man any control over her life, and yet her body craved what every healthy adult body craved.

Including his…

"We'll get the guy who did this," Jared promised.

Myles tilted his head as he studied the smeared blood on the tiles, the fingerprint dust, the partial footprints, the spatters on the wall, baseboards and cupboards. In some places, so much blood had been spilled that it hadn't completely dried. Knowing it came from the man who'd sold him his house made Myles sick to his stomach. He'd seen death—car accidents and gang shootings when he worked for the police department in Phoenix—but never such a brutal slaying. And never anyone he knew. "What about Pat's stepson?" he asked.

"Delbert's on my list."

Jared's absolute reliance on logic was usually helpful in an investigation. At any rate, no one else had as much experience with murder. Since Myles had taken over as sheriff, his office hadn't dealt with a crime worse than hunting without a license or holding up a liquor store with a Super Soaker. "Good."

"You placing your bet on Delbert?" Jared asked.

Myles propped his hands on his hips. "I'm not placing any bets."

"So why'd you bring him up?"

"Because he's at least as likely to have killed Pat as Gertie is."

"Except that he lives in Colorado."

"Travel being what it is, maybe he came back."

"I spoke to a few of Gertie's neighbors last night. I guess she and Pat had some sort of falling-out with her son over a vehicle?"

That hadn't been cleared up? Myles had all but forgotten it. "About a year ago, Pat and Gertie lent him the money to buy a new truck. He was supposed to pay them a couple thousand the moment he received his tax refund but he didn't. I remember Pat complaining about it when he came to the station to deliver the calendar he gave out at Christmas, but…I haven't heard about that since."

"I'll see what Delbert has to say," Jared said. "If I can reach him."

"You've tried?"

"Three times. Could be he's on his way here."

Myles walked over to the sliding glass door and found droplets of blood even there. Pat had put up a fight; he'd simply been overpowered. "I'm sure he is," he said. "Especially if he expects to be included in the will. Delbert has always taken his parents for everything he can."

Jared wrote a note about Delbert on his pad with a pencil that'd been broken in half and barely had any lead.

"Is that shitty pencil the best you can do?" Myles asked, momentarily distracted.

Jared held up his hand to examine the pencil stub. "What's wrong with it?"

Myles opened his mouth to say that he could at least carry a decent pen—but snapping at such an inconsequential detail only revealed his stress. What did it matter as long as that pencil put words on paper?

Once again reining in the irritation that'd been lurking ever since he crawled out of bed, Myles waved away Jared's concern. "Not a thing," he said, but Jared was too literal to let it go. He couldn't understand why Myles would mention it if he didn't expect some action to be taken.

"There might be a pen in my car...."

"Forget it." Even if there was a pen in his car, he had little chance of ever finding it. His vehicle was so full of wrappers, receipts and other flotsam, Myles often wondered if it violated the health and safety codes. "What about the call Pat received prior to coming here? Do you know who made it?"

"Not yet."

"Why not?"

Jared blinked at him. "The number goes to the pay phone outside the Kicking Horse Saloon."

The fact that Pineview didn't have cell service wasn't going to help them solve this crime. Here, pay phones were still an important form of communication, which meant that call could've come from anyone. And that particular location, right outside the town's favorite bar, made it unlikely that a bystander would pay attention when someone was using it.

"So you're checking out Gertie and Delbert," Myles summarized. "Who else is on your list?"

"All the hunters, campers, fishermen and recreationists who've come through here the past couple of days."

Myles eyed the blood spatter on the wall. The photographs shot by the forensic techs would be sent to an expert. But it would take time to get the analysis. *Every-*

thing took time.... "How many people do you figure that is?"

"Least fifty."

"That narrows it down."

Jared didn't react to his sarcasm. "We got a partial thumbprint—in blood—on the door handle. That should help. Especially in conjunction with all the footprints."

Except that none of them were very clear. They'd lifted the prints with tape but who knew if they'd show anything useful. "If we find a suspect these things might help. Otherwise…"

"If it's not Gertie or Delbert it's one of the campers."

"Why would a camper call about a rental and then kill the real-estate agent?"

"Sometimes there isn't a reason."

"You think we have a psychopath in the area?"

"It's a possibility."

"I don't know about that. Pat wasn't attacked as soon as he and whoever he was with came into the house. He was murdered in the kitchen—as if he spent some time with his assailant, had a discussion first. If death was the goal from the beginning, there'd be no reason to pretend to be a prospective renter. Not once the killer got inside the house anyway."

"So you're suggesting he knew his attacker," Jared responded.

Which was why Jared kept going back to Pat's family. "There are holes in that theory, too," Myles said. "Anyone who showed up here intending to kill would bring a weapon. This offender used some sort of blunt object. To me, that suggests he grabbed whatever was close at hand." Myles wasn't sure what that was. A rock? Part of a tree branch? A hammer? He was relying on the autopsy to reveal more about the wounds Pat had sustained and what could've caused them.

"But if the murder resulted from a spontaneous act, a sudden flare of temper, why couldn't Delbert be our man?"

"He could. Except that Pat wouldn't have driven over here to meet Delbert. What would be the point?"

"Delbert could've lured him here under false pretenses."

"We just established that this wasn't a planned killing. The evidence doesn't support it."

Jared scratched his chin. "Do you know how hard it is to solve a truly random crime, with no eyewitnesses? If our offender was a visitor to the area, we might never narrow it down."

"Exactly what I'm afraid of."

Putting his pad in his coat pocket, Jared turned to leave.

"Where are you going?" Myles asked him.

"I'm meeting Linda at the Golden Griddle."

Linda Gardiner was the other investigator Myles had assigned to the case.

"We're hoping to come up with a list of people who used the pay phone yesterday when Pat received that call," Jared went on.

The Golden Griddle was across the street from the bar. Anyone there would have a clear view of the pay phone—if he or she happened to look. But that restaurant only served breakfast. "It closes at one. The call came in shortly after two."

"True, but it takes the waitresses an hour or so to clean up. If we're lucky, one of them saw someone at that pay phone while she was getting into her car and can at least give us a description."

If we're lucky. What if they weren't?

They'd have nothing but a body.

5

Heartbroken, Vivian gaped at the screen.

"Mommy?"

She could hear her daughter calling her but Mia's voice sounded small and tinny, as if it came through the dark tunnel of a dream. Vivian didn't react, couldn't react. She was frozen in time and space. It wasn't until her daughter came up and tapped her arm that she was able to blink and look away. And then the many years of practice she'd had hiding her fear and disappointment from her children came to her rescue, and she managed to conceal her reaction to what she'd just read. "Yes?"

Mia's eyebrows knotted. "Why wouldn't you answer?"

"I was concentrating on something else." She wondered if Mia was getting old enough to see through her smile. She would at some point, wouldn't she? Vivian was screaming inside: *This isn't fair! Not again! Not Rex!*

"Oh." With a shrug of her thin shoulders, Mia let it go. Nothing bothered her for long. "Watch me, okay? I'll show you my new dance."

Mia was taking ballet lessons and, much to Jake's chagrin, she often made up her own routines and insisted on performing them, even in public.

Vivian schooled her features into a pleasant expression as Mia leaped and twirled. No music played, but that didn't diminish Mia's enthusiasm. She danced just to move and she did it whenever the mood struck her. Costumes were more important to her than music, but this morning she hadn't bothered to change into the tutu she sometimes wore all day.

Vivian believed her daughter had real talent, but ballet was far from her thoughts right now. The terror that'd begun to advance on her when she heard about Pat's murder raced up to smack her right in the face as the meaning of what she'd just read went through her mind.

Rex is missing...Rex is missing...Rex is missing...

Where? How? Was he *dead?*

No, that couldn't be. She was still in love with him. Maybe. Or maybe she only wished for what could've been. Even if her feelings weren't quite that strong—even if desperation, familiarity and the need for a safe harbor had brought them together in the first place—he'd been a good friend and a talented lover, relief from the loneliness that had plagued her both before and after their breakup.

"Do you like it, Mommy?" Mia sang out.

Vivian's face ached with the effort of maintaining her smile. "Of course. It's beautiful."

Beaming at the compliment, Mia lengthened her performance by stringing other routines together, ones she'd been taught in class that Vivian easily recognized. "Aren't you going to clap?"

Vivian dutifully brought her hands together.

When, at last exhausted, her daughter finished, Vivian clapped again. "Bravo!" she cheered, but trying to staunch her tears only caused the lump in her throat to swell.

Fortunately, Mia seemed satisfied. She ran off to change and brush her teeth, leaving Vivian alone to deal with Virgil's news.

Propping her chin on her fist, she returned to the computer. What could've happened to Rex? Virgil had given her very little information.

Hey, I hate to tell you this, but Rex is missing. Two weeks ago, he mentioned going to Los Angeles to see a woman he met on the internet. I tried to talk him out of it, but he wouldn't listen. He took off on his motorcycle.

Vivian didn't have to wonder how he got off work. From what she'd heard, he was still doing jobs here or there for Virgil but was no longer a partner in their bodyguard company. He'd talked Virgil into buying him out shortly after they moved to Buffalo and had been burning through the money ever since.

I probably wouldn't be so worried except that every time I call his cell, it goes straight to voice mail. I haven't been able to reach him since the day after he left. And I know he wasn't planning on being gone this long. I have a job coming up—told him he could have it. Lord knows he needs the money.

Apparently he wasn't still burning through the money. He'd already finished it. She'd figured it was just a matter of time.

I've reported his absence to the police. They're doing what they can, but I doubt he's a priority.

They're searching for him as Wesley Alderman; I couldn't give away his true identity without adding more risk. I didn't see how it would help, anyway, to divulge the past. He obviously made arrangements to be gone, so they feel he might merely be delayed. And they have other cases they consider more urgent.

So what did this mean? Now that he was broke, had he returned to The Crew, where he could get an endless supply of the OxyContin he craved?

He'd die before he'd give either of us up. I just don't know if we can count on him staying off the pills. And that could change the situation. He hasn't done well since you left. Anyway, I had to warn you.

He'd never done drugs when she was with him. But she'd known they were a big part of his past. Drugs were epidemic to the gang culture he'd embraced at one time. And now he was back at it.

I'll let you know if anything changes. Keep your eyes open.

V.

Vivian's gaze strayed from the screen to the phone on the desk at her elbow. They'd agreed not to communicate by telephone; doing so would establish a traceable link between them. She didn't see The Crew as being sophisticated enough to find and follow that link, but they could've hired a private investigator or someone else to do the tracking. Harold "Horse" Pew and his foot soldiers had certainly found them before. That was why they'd split up, to be cautious. But she had to talk to her brother, even if it meant breaking the rules. She missed him so much, hadn't seen him in two years.

With equal amounts of trepidation and excitement, she dialed the cell-phone number Virgil had given her to use in case of an emergency.

She had a blocked number. Probably hoping it was Rex, he answered on the first ring with a quick and eager hello.

The tears she'd been holding back sprang to her eyes at the sound of his voice. "It's me," she murmured.

"Laurel." He used her real name, then cursed under his breath. "I was afraid you'd call."

She understood why he might not be happy to hear from her, knew he was worried about the risk, but his response stung all the same. Emails couldn't replace personal contact. He had his wife. She had no one. She'd been so happy in D.C. After fourteen years of waiting for Virgil to get out of prison, she'd had family she could both love and trust, only to have him once again ripped away from her. "Don't…"

He seemed to understand that she couldn't tolerate being chastised right now. "Are you okay?" he asked.

"That depends on your definition of *okay.* I was doing great until Pat Stueben was murdered yesterday morning."

"Who's Pat Stueben?" Obviously he'd expected her reaction to the news about Rex, not this.

"A friend."

"I'm sorry."

The concern in those words made her feel a bit better. "He was more of an acquaintance actually—the man who helped me find this house, my—my Realtor." Tears streamed down her face; she hadn't adequately mourned Pat. The possibility that she or one of her children might be next had kept her grief bottled up, along with her fear.

"Hang on a sec." She heard jostling, then a door closing. When he came back on the line, he spoke more loudly. "Okay, I can talk."

"Are you at the office?"

"Yeah."

"How's business?"

"Not quite what it was in D.C., but building."

She remembered when he and Rex had started their bodyguard service, how pleased they'd been with their success. After selling out in D.C., Virgil had reincarnated the business under a different name when he moved to upstate New York. He had Peyton's help now, at least in the office. Although she normally worked in corrections she'd left her job when they moved and didn't plan to return to her career until the kids were older. Even with Peyton there three days a week, it wasn't the same for Virgil. He missed Rex as a full-time partner. But once Rex's mother died and his family blamed him for the grief he'd put her through, he'd gone downhill.

As much as Vivian wished it wasn't so, she was sure their breakup had added to the problems that'd sent him into a tailspin.

Luckily for her, she hadn't been around to see the worst of it. She'd heard about the fallout from Virgil, via his weekly emails. Then, during his more sober moments, Rex had begun calling her again, even though, for safety's sake, he wasn't supposed to.

"What exactly happened to your friend?" Virgil asked.

"Someone beat him to death."

"Why?"

"He was robbed, but…this went far beyond robbery."

"Who did it?"

"No one knows. Not yet. That's why…why I was already nervous when I received your email."

"You think there's some connection between your Realtor's death and our situation?"

"Maybe. That type of thing doesn't happen here."

"Didn't you tell me you have a friend whose mother went missing?"

"Fifteen years ago, and there's never been any proof of foul play. Maybe she simply walked off into the sunset."

"How often does that happen?" he asked drily.

"Often enough." *She'd* done it. Twice. She still wondered what the people at her job in Colorado must've thought when she left. One day she was there, the next she was gone, without any explanation or contact since. She did the same thing in D.C.

"There's no rhyme or reason to Pat's murder," she told him. "He couldn't have put up much of a fight. Word has it his wallet didn't contain a lot. Why would he risk his life over fifty dollars?"

"You've lived there for two years. If The Crew had followed you, they would've acted by now. Don't assume too much."

"It's not just that there's been a murder," she explained, terrible though that was. "It's the violence involved. If you'd known this man… No one would want to kill him. He was in his sixties, sweet, harmless. Then, on the heels of his death, I get the news that Rex is missing."

"Could be totally unrelated. Maybe Rex heard from his father, or one of his 'successful' brothers, and that sent him over the edge. You know how he is."

She did know Rex. She knew what he'd done for her and Virgil in the past, what they owed him regardless of his self-destructive tendencies. "Surely The Crew can't still be after us. It's been four years since you and Rex quit the gang. Surely they've gotten tired of chasing us and turned their attention to other things." She couldn't come out of hiding, couldn't present herself as a target, of course, but did she really have to worry about them searching for her? *Still?*

"That kind of thinking could get you killed."

"I'm tired of running."

"You have no choice."

She eyed the walls she'd painted herself, remembered how important it was that she get the perfect color. These walls weren't ordinary walls. They were *her* walls; she'd planned to look at them for years.

"Why?" she asked, unable to accept his answer. "How long could this grudge of theirs last?"

"After what we did?"

"We did nothing!" Everything Virgil had been through, everything she'd suffered as a result of being related to him, could be blamed on their uncle and mother. Thanks to Ellen's soliciting her brother's help, Gary Lawson had killed Martin Crawley, their stepfather, then let Virgil pay for it. If Virgil hadn't spent so much time in prison, he wouldn't have joined The Crew, or had to get out of it, and they wouldn't have tried to kill her as both warning and retribution.

"That's not strictly true," he said. "When they came after you in Colorado, I told the authorities everything I knew about them. Several of those guys went to prison, and two of the ones already inside were dumped into the federal system and moved because of me."

"You would've kept your word and stayed silent if they hadn't tried to kill me. That's when you decided you owed them nothing."

"Doesn't matter. As far as they're concerned, Rex and I are both traitors. They'd love nothing more than to make examples out of all of us."

"But—"

"Listen, I was trusted by those who held power, put above others who've remained loyal. It humiliated them when I left. And if they can't get to me, they'll go after you again. Especially since they lost some of their own in Colorado. Getting to you would be just as good as getting to me, because they know it would kill me to see you or your children hurt."

"It's just so pointless to keep this going! Revenge is... stupid!"

"To you and me. But there's nothing worse to a gang leader than appearing weak. It's about street cred, taking care of business. That's all they have—their pride in being badasses."

She found it hard not to resent him at this moment, no matter how close they'd always been. If not for him, she wouldn't be in this predicament. But it wasn't his fault. In her heart, she knew that. They were both victims of circumstance and had done the best they could to handle what was thrown their way. "They have to make a living, too. Isn't that hard enough? Doesn't running prostitution rings and—and smuggling drugs and evading police take time and effort? My business is legitimate, yet it takes every ounce of energy I've got."

"If they need money, they send someone to hold up a liquor store. It doesn't take much time. They're profiting off other people's hard work, not their own. Nothing has a higher priority than nursing a grudge and paying off old debts. Especially a debt as personal as this one. Their lives revolve around planning violence, perpetrating violence or taking credit for violence. They won't stop looking for us. At Shady's funeral, Horse swore a blood oath to avenge his death. Rex heard about it while we were living in D.C. Don't you remember?"

Mia had come downstairs to play with her Barbies, so Vivian lowered her voice. The last thing she needed was for her daughter to repeat something she'd overheard to the sheriff or someone else in Pineview. "Maybe we should've stayed in WitSec." Without the program to fall back on, they were walking a tightrope without a safety net. "Maybe there was no leak."

"What are you talking about?"

"Rex is the only one who's contacted anyone from his past," she said. Because he'd been estranged from his family for years, she and Virgil had never expected him to be the one who'd have trouble forgetting the people he once knew. But the emotional issues he had as a result of those old dysfunctional relationships had kept him in a state of limbo, kept him checking back despite the danger, and once he'd found out about his mother's death, he hadn't been able to cope.

Walking away from everything hadn't been easy for her, either. What she'd just told Virgil wasn't strictly true. She'd called her mother a few times. The police had never uncovered the proof they needed to prosecute Ellen for her role in Martin's murder, so she was still in Los Angeles going from man to man. But now that she was getting older and suffering from arthritis and type 2 diabetes, Vivian felt duty-bound to check on her every few months. She'd always used the pay phone outside the bar, however, or a phone other than her own, and been very careful about the information she divulged. After what Ellen had done to Virgil, Vivian couldn't trust her.

"Rex hasn't been disloyal, Vivian. That's crazy. They want him as badly as they want us."

"He hasn't been the same since he heard the news about his mother. He could've made a deal with them, a trade." She didn't really believe this, but she didn't want to believe the alternative, either, and arguing with Virgil helped blow off some steam.

"Stop it."

"He's the only link we have left to The Crew!" Unless their mother had revealed that Vivian had been in contact with her. But that was just too horrible to contemplate. They'd been through enough because of Ellen. Surely, after taking her brother's side all those years ago instead of defending her son, instead of believing in Virgil, Ellen wouldn't let them down again....

"Then how'd they find you in Colorado?" Virgil was saying. "Rex was still with the gang then. He's *told* us someone provided insider information. It took time, but they found us in D.C., and they would've found us again if we'd continued relying on law enforcement to hide us."

He was right, of course, but she wasn't ready to stop playing devil's advocate. "No one in the Federal Bureau of Prisons even knows where we are. That's why I think it has to be Rex."

"It's not! I trust Rex with my life." He trusted him more than their mother—with good reason. Virgil hadn't spoken to Ellen since he went to prison. At least that he'd admit. It wasn't as if Vivian had told him she'd been calling, either.

Problem was, she trusted Rex, too. So what was she

saying? That if someone had to betray them, she'd rather it was Rex than Ellen? She didn't want it to be either one, but she couldn't withstand that kind of rejection from her mother. Better to attribute this betrayal—if betrayal it was—to the drugs Rex used and mitigate his responsibility that way. "You mean you trust him when he's sober, right?"

Virgil didn't respond to that comment, probably because it pained him to doubt Rex. Rex had been his cell mate for nearly a decade. Including their years on the outside, they'd been looking out for each other half their lives. But Virgil was obviously nervous about Rex's state of mind and his difficulty navigating a world that didn't include gang affiliations.

"Horse blames us as the reason Shady and the others are dead and Ink is in prison," he said.

Horse. Shady. Ink. Just the names of The Crew members who'd come after them sent a shiver of revulsion through Vivian. Horse had taken Shady's spot as gang leader, but it was Ink who'd appeared in Colorado. Covered from head to toe in tattoos—even his eyebrows were tattooed into lightning bolts—he was a frightening specter of gang life. His flat, dark eyes added to the unnerving effect he had on her.

She wondered what he was like now, if he'd changed. After months of physical therapy, he'd recuperated enough from what had happened in Colorado that he was no longer confined to a wheelchair. But according to the U.S. marshal who'd helped them get situated in D.C., he was still crippled. Vivian wasn't sure how crippled, but it didn't matter. He was serving a lengthy prison term and wasn't likely to get out before he died of old age. That was what mattered. "Then you believe Rex is...dead?"

"I don't know what to believe!" he snapped, and that was when she understood just how worried he was. He talked as if he had faith in his best friend but he was as scared as she was. Rex could be heroic; he could also be unpredictable, especially when he was using.

"Except that we're not safe from The Crew," she said. "You're convinced of that."

"Completely."

Vivian remembered all the calls she and Rex had exchanged when she first came to Pineview. Their breakup had been so rough that they'd contacted each other numerous times, despite Virgil's edict. And she hadn't gone to a pay phone. During her weaker moments, she'd almost taken Rex back, almost had him come to live in Montana. She would have if he hadn't started using.

Had The Crew found him and exacted their revenge for his part in the deaths of two of their own? Tortured her and Virgil's addresses out of Rex, then killed him? Or had he gone to Mexico with some woman?

More likely he was on a drug binge, holed up in a fleabag motel or lying helpless in a gutter.

The thought of that upset her nearly as much as all the rest of it. If she'd given him one more chance, maybe he could've made it. There were so many times he'd seemed close. But he'd pushed her away as often as she had him.

Bottom line, they weren't good for each other. She'd been caught in a painful cycle of breakup and reunion for eighteen months before she came here, but she was free now and didn't want the past to encroach on her new life.

The question was...would she be able to stop it?

"What do we do?" she asked. "How do we stay safe?"

"The smartest thing would be to move."

"I can't," she said, and realized it was true. She couldn't sacrifice everything she'd established here, couldn't drag her children away from the happiness they'd found. Not again. This was her house, the first possession she'd ever really owned. Leaving it behind would be letting The Crew win even if they didn't find her.

"I feel the same way," he admitted. "It was hard starting over when we moved to New York. The idea of doing it again…" He paused. "And I don't know if Rex is stable enough to go with us. The last move hit him hard."

Because of the timing. That move had come soon after he'd heard about his mother and started using again; that was when they'd broken up for the last time. "What's the alternative?"

He seemed to consider the question. "We'll have to be prepared, I guess. Do you have the gun I gave you?"

"No." She'd been terrified one of the children would get hold of it and there'd be an accident.

"Where is it?"

"At the bank. In a safe-deposit box."

"I suggest you get it out."

She cringed at the thought of having to use it, even though he'd insisted on showing her how and making her practice. "Can this really be happening?"

"As much as I wish I could say no…"

He couldn't. She understood. "I'll get it."

"Great. Let me know what you hear about your Realtor's murder. And I'll do the same if there's anything new on Rex."

She could tell he was about to hang up, but she wasn't ready to let him go. "How's Peyton?"

"Fine."

He would've mentioned in his emails if anything was wrong, but it felt better hearing this assurance from his own lips. "How does she like staying home with Brady?"

"She misses corrections, but she'll go back when the kids are in school. In the meantime, she's enjoying a period of less stress. She's still handling the books at the office, the advertising and some of the scheduling."

"Are you guys ready for the new baby?"

"As ready as we can be. I just hope it doesn't go like last time."

Last time, Peyton had miscarried at seven months, and losing the baby had devastated her, devastated them both. Because of endometriosis, she'd had difficulty getting pregnant at all. And Vivian hadn't been there for any of it. She could hardly believe so much had happened in the past two years. It seemed like only yesterday that she was living in Colorado, a scant five miles from the prison, hoping and praying her brother would survive until he could be exonerated. "It won't," she said. "This little girl will make it."

"I keep imagining her just like Mia." Then he asked about the kids, Pineview, her love life, and she pretended to have one. When the conversation wound down, she said, "Do you ever miss Mom?"

Their mother was a subject they usually avoided. But Vivian felt guilty for secretly keeping in touch with "the enemy." And she couldn't help wondering how Virgil felt about their mother these days. Was he softening at all? *Should* they soften? In a situation like this, was there ever a point when the past should be left in the past?

"No." His clipped tone indicated that he didn't want anything to do with Ellen, and she couldn't blame him. Ellen had ruined his life when she went after her then-husband's life-insurance policy, which she'd received. Whether or not she'd really instigated his murder had never been firmly established, but the fact that she hadn't done more to help police uncover the true culprit, that she'd allow her son to go to prison instead, was unbelievable, unforgivable.

And yet, Vivian sometimes missed Ellen terribly. It wasn't as if she had a father she could turn to. Cole Skinner had gone on his merry way shortly after she was born. She'd heard from him a total of three times in her entire life.

"I don't miss her, either," she lied. Then she told him she loved him and hung up.

"Who was that?"

Mia stood a few feet away. Vivian wanted to admit it was her brother, but that would only spark more questions. "A friend."

A sad expression appeared on Mia's face. "Why are you crying?"

Dashing a hand across her cheeks, Vivian struggled to contain her emotions. What was wrong with her? She was usually stronger than this. "I miss him."

Sidling close, Mia lowered her voice. "Was it Rex?"

She remembered him. Vivian managed to smile through her tears as she hugged her daughter. The Crew had cost her the life she'd built in Colorado and Washington, D.C. She wouldn't let it cost her what she'd created here. She'd go to the bank as soon as she dropped Mia off at ballet and get the gun Virgil had purchased for her—and then she'd defend herself and her children against anyone who threatened them. They had to stop running sometime. "That wasn't Rex, honey, but I miss him, too," she murmured into her daughter's hair.

Mia cupped her face in both hands. "Maybe he'll come for a visit."

And maybe he couldn't....

6

With its high ceilings and marble floors, Mountain Bank and Trust was cold and quiet, peaceful in the sterile vein of most banks. Vivian generally liked coming here. She knew Herb Scarborough, the manager, from sitting next to him and his wife so often at church. He waved through the glass walls of his office in the corner. Then there was Nancy Granger, one of the tellers, who'd recently joined her book group. Nancy flashed her a smile, too.

As childish as it made her feel, Vivian found the bowls of candy on the loan officers' desks as tempting as her kids did, but today she didn't so much as glance over to see what kind of candy those bowls contained. She was in too much of a hurry. Mia's ballet class lasted only forty-five minutes. She wanted to get in and out as quickly as possible, then stow the gun in the trunk of her car until after the kids fell asleep this evening. No way did she want them to see it—or even the small blanket she planned to wrap it in. Why incite their curiosity?

"Hi, Vivian. Can I help you?" Naomi Jowalski, the assistant manager, stood as Vivian approached her desk. Naomi had helped her before, when she'd first come to town and brought in the tightly wrapped bundle that hid the gun.

"I'd like to get into my safe-deposit box, please."

"No problem." She began sorting through the large number of keys she wore on an expandable bracelet. One of those keys unlocked the door leading to the basement vault. "Can you tell me the number?"

Vivian gave it to her and showed her driver's license—the one Virgil had purchased for her on the black market just before she'd moved here. Then she signed in and Naomi led her downstairs to the vault that held a smattering of boxes, some bigger and some smaller than her own. Considering the population of Pineview, the bank didn't need to devote a lot of space to safe-deposit boxes and they didn't. They'd tucked them away in a far corner of the basement and, at the moment, that basement was empty except for the two of them.

"I'll wait right here." Naomi stopped at the entrance to allow Vivian some privacy.

Even as she turned the key, Vivian wasn't too happy about taking the gun into her possession. She couldn't bear to think of what could happen if her children ever found it. But she watched her kids carefully—and just as bad was the thought of being unable to protect them if The Crew showed up. She'd been in that situation before, hadn't she?

"Did you hear about Pat Stueben?" Naomi said.

Blocking the assistant manager's view in case she glanced over, Vivian unwrapped the gun. She'd been in such a rush to get Mia to ballet on time she'd forgotten to bring a bag to carry it in, but she had her purse. Leaving her real birth certificate and driver's license, along with her children's birth certificates, in the box, she put the gun in her bag and locked up. "I did. Tragic, isn't it?"

"Who could beat someone to death, especially someone like Pat?" Naomi asked. "For forty-eight dollars?"

Everyone was wondering the same thing. Vivian had just had a similar conversation with Pearl Stringham, Mia's dance instructor. "No one we know. It has to be a stranger."

"That's what I've been hearing. But still—" she rubbed her arms as Vivian approached "—I get chills thinking about it."

"Certainly makes it difficult to sleep at night." How would Naomi react if she knew what Vivian had been through? What she was fighting so hard to prevent?

"All finished?"

Vivian nodded.

"Right this way, then."

Supremely conscious of the gun in her purse, Vivian followed Naomi up the stairs. Having a lethal weapon empowered her in a sense. But that didn't end the worry. What if she made a mistake? Shot the wrong person? Nana Vera and Claire—not to mention Leah, a waitress from the local diner who'd introduced her to the Thursday-night book group—had a tendency to come by at unexpected times. Occasionally they'd even make themselves at home while waiting for her to return. That was the type of community they lived in....

"Vivian?"

Engrossed in her own thoughts, she'd missed a question. "Yes?"

"Is there anything else we can do for you here at Mountain Bank and Trust?"

"No, thank you."

The assistant manager donned a pleasant smile. "Have a good day."

Eager to hide the Sig in her trunk and get back to Mia's ballet class, Vivian lowered her head and charged through the double doors, only to run into what felt like a brick wall. Bouncing back, she hit the door, which hadn't quite closed, and dropped her purse.

Buster Hayes, six foot four and three hundred and fifty pounds of collegiate football star, had just rounded the corner; she'd plowed right into him.

"Oh, wow! I'm sorry." He steadied her, then bent to recover what had spilled out—but froze when he saw the Sig P220 lying on the concrete between them.

Chrissy Gunther was walking toward the bank at the same time, and came to an immediate stop. "Is that a *gun?*" she gasped.

Vivian scooped it up, along with the rest of her belongings. "Just a little something for self-protection," she muttered, and hurried away.

None of the waitresses at the Golden Griddle had noticed anyone using the pay phone, which left the investigation exactly nowhere.

Head pounding, Myles turned off the lights and propped his feet on his desk. Half of Pineview had called him this morning. Chester Magnuson, over at the paper. Gertie, looking to see if he'd been able to identify her husband's murderer. The stepson, who'd arrived in town and was staying with his mother. Delbert wondered how such a thing could happen in Pineview and wanted to know what was going on with the investigation. Even the mayor had phoned.

Myles needed a few seconds to himself. But the

moment he closed his eyes, Chrissy Gunther came dashing into the reception area, squawking like an old hen. He wished he could ignore her. It was his lunch hour. Surely that meant he could take five minutes. But there was too much excitement in her voice to attribute all of it to her high-strung nature. And no matter how many excuses she trumped up to talk to him, she didn't usually drive thirty miles to do that.

"I have to speak with Sheriff King," she told Deputy Campbell. "Right away. It's important."

Wishing the painkiller he'd swallowed several minutes ago would hurry and stop the jackhammer in his head, Myles forced his eyes open and got up to turn on his light. Although married, Chrissy made a habit of seeking him out. He was pretty sure she didn't understand how he could resist her, despite her marital status.

Deputy Campbell appeared in the doorway just as he reached for the light switch. "Chrissy Gunther is here to see you. She says she might have some information on the Pat Stueben case."

"Really? Chrissy?" Myles could see the little dynamo coming to report that the school principal wasn't allowing her cheer squad to use the gym, even though school was out for summer. Or that the lunch lady hadn't refunded the three dollars and fifty cents that was left on one of her children's lunch cards, and was therefore trying to steal it. To Chrissy, those things would be worth the drive. But her world didn't extend beyond her kids.

Campbell cast a glance over his shoulder as if he wasn't quite sure what to think. He lived here in Libby, not in Pineview, so he didn't know Chrissy, but the look on his face suggested that he could tell she was a handful. "So she claims."

"Fine. Send her in." Perhaps she'd spotted a stranger with blood on his shoes or something. Myles could always hope. No one paid closer attention to the actions and mistakes of others than Chrissy Gunther.

Hoping that whatever she had to say would be worth putting up with her flirtatious smiles, Myles stood to one side as she came bustling past him. "I saw it myself!" she exclaimed before he could even greet her.

He tried to rub away the grit in his eyes, but the stress of the murder, his lack of sleep and preoccupation with his neighbor was taking their toll. "What are you talking about?"

"The gun."

The headache and fatigue instantly disappeared. "What gun?"

"The pistol Vivian was carrying out of Mountain Bank and Trust a few minutes ago."

Hearing Vivian's name added a one-two punch. A gun belonging to anyone else wouldn't have been particularly noteworthy, not unless there was more to go along with it. Montana's gun laws weren't exactly the strictest in the nation; guns didn't even have to be registered in this state, and almost everybody had at least a rifle. But someone like his neighbor toting a handgun out of a *bank?* "Vivian Stewart?"

"I think you're familiar with her. There's just one Vivian in Pineview, right? And I've seen the way you watch her. It's made all the rest of us girls jealous."

Inappropriate as it was for her to include herself in that comment, he ignored the jab. "Are you sure?"

"That you watch her?" She fluttered her eyelashes. "How could I miss it?"

"I mean, are you sure it was her?" He suspected she'd

understood what he'd meant the first time, but he wasn't about to let her draw him into the kind of conversation she obviously craved.

Annoyed that he wouldn't rise to the bait, she propped one hand on her hip. "Positive. And she definitely had a gun in her purse. I wasn't the only one to see it. Buster Hayes saw it, too. All you have to do is ask him."

Myles had no idea what Chrissy was talking about. Maybe Montana had the third-most legal gun owners per capita, only a tenth of a percent behind Alaska. And maybe the prevalence of firearms per capita in a rural county, one with eighteen thousand residents, would be even greater than the more populated parts of the state. But he couldn't see Vivian toting around a weapon. Especially a hidden weapon. For one thing, he'd be very surprised if she had a permit to carry concealed. And she didn't like guns. He'd heard her say so when Jake asked her how old he had to be before he could buy a hunting rifle.

So what did she plan on doing with a pistol? Why would she be attempting to conceal it? And why would she take it to the bank?

He motioned to a chair. "Would you like to sit down?"

Chrissy's ponytail—an obvious hairpiece since he'd seen her without it—bounced as she perched on the edge of the chair.

"I suggest you speak to her immediately," she said.

Myles tried not to notice that the vinyl was only slightly more orange than her self-tanner. "Thanks for the advice. But first, why don't you slow down and tell me exactly what happened?"

Rhinestones embedded in the acrylic of her nails flashed as she fanned herself. It wasn't remotely hot in his office, but the excitement of her errand seemed to be affecting her. "There isn't much to it," she said. "She was coming out of the bank, bumped into Buster Hayes and dropped her purse. That's when we both saw it. She had a handgun in there that fell out."

Myles returned to his own seat. "You're not suggesting Vivian tried to hold up Mountain Bank and Trust."

"Maybe she was thinking about it. Maybe she chickened out at the last minute. Why else would someone carry a pistol into a bank?"

"Did you ask her?"

"I didn't have the chance! The minute she realized we'd seen the gun, she grabbed it and rushed off." Chrissy lowered her voice and widened her eyes for emphasis. "I'm telling you, she was acting *really* strange."

Myles imagined Vivian as she'd been last night. She hadn't behaved like the woman who'd done her best to ignore him over the past few months, to stay out of his way. That signified a marked change, too, didn't it?

Or maybe not. Their feelings toward each other had been changing for some time, growing more intense. On both sides. Until last night, Vivian had hovered on the edges of his life, remaining safely out of reach. But for the first couple of years after Amber Rose died, she could've run naked across his lawn and it wouldn't have raised his pulse by one beat. "In what way?" he asked.

Chrissy adjusted the strap of her blouse, which had slipped off her shoulder. She dressed as if she was one of the cheerleaders she coached—short shorts, skimpy tops and always a bow. "I don't know. Spooked. Guilty."

"So…how do you think this firearm you saw ties in to the murder? My deputy said—"

"It's not every day someone drops a handgun coming

out of a bank!" She put her purse on the floor, leaning forward to give him a clear view down her blouse.

Averting his eyes, he straightened his stapler. "I realize that. But a lot of people own guns around here. And the murder wasn't committed with a firearm. So bear with me. I'm searching for a link."

Her nails clacked as she tapped them together. "Something's up, okay? That's all I'm trying to tell you."

For some reason, Myles liked Chrissy even less than he had before. She wasn't bad-looking, but her personality... He'd heard rumors about how bossy she could be and how poorly she treated her husband. They ran a secondhand shop together, situated near the bank. He'd felt sorry for Mr. Gunther before, when Chrissy came on to him at the annual crab feed or at the bar. But driving all the way out here just because she had a tidbit of information? A tidbit about someone she viewed as a rival for his attention? That made him feel even worse for the poor bastard who'd married her.

"I'll look into it," he said. And he planned to. He'd forgotten to give Marley money to go to the bowling alley with her best friend this afternoon, so he had to drive back to Pineview, anyway. "Thanks for stopping by."

She jumped to her feet. "If you'd like me to go over there with you, I will."

He made a gesture that suggested she needn't trouble herself. "That won't be necessary. But...can I ask you one more thing?"

Her face lit up. "Of course!"

"How well do you know Vivian?"

"Not very well," she confided. "I met her when we both helped out at the school last year—our girls are in the same grade. I invited her to one of my jewelry parties, but she canceled the day before." Chrissy wrinkled her nose. "She's not very social. I don't know what her problem is, but I'm beginning to think she's hiding something."

She *was* hiding something. She was hiding herself and her children. An abusive ex would motivate anyone to keep a low profile, maybe even buy a gun. But he planned to check out Chrissy's report, just in case.

Chrissy hesitated at the door. "Oh, and, Sheriff?"

"Yes?"

"I'm not sure if this is important, but in light of recent events, I think it might be."

"What's that?"

"When Vivian first arrived in town, her daughter told my daughter that she moved here because 'bad men' were chasing them."

Myles came to an abrupt stop. He might've expected "a bad man." But *men?* As in more than one?

Was this a lie Vivian had concocted for the sake of her children? So they wouldn't have to know that it was their father causing all the trouble? "Did she say who those bad men might be?"

"No. But it had to do with someone breaking into their house, someone who was shot and had—" she made quotation marks with her fingers "—'blood coming out all over.'"

Another surprise. He had no idea what it meant, and yet he felt the urge to defend Vivian and Mia. "That could be make-believe, something she saw on television."

"I know it sounds far-fetched. I thought the same thing at first. I mean, not every mother is as diligent about what their children watch as I am. But now I wonder…"

Myles wondered, too. Was Mia speaking about an

actual event? If so, how did this tie in to what Vivian had told him? Was there one man she feared—or more? Did she really have an abusive ex?

And, if so, had she killed him?

Myles stood on her porch. Vivian could see his blurry image through the misted oval glass, recognized the blue of his uniform and knew why he'd come. Because of Chrissy. Buster wouldn't have bothered the sheriff. Buster wasn't a nosy troublemaker like Hope's mother, who was generally known as the bane of the elementary school staff, if not the whole town. Unfortunately for Mia, Hope was turning out much the same. Before school ended for the summer, Hope had purposely excluded Mia from her popular clique.

Frowning, Vivian pushed away from her computer, where she'd been using Gchat to convince Claire that Pat's murder had nothing to do with her mother's disappearance. She'd been answering some of the emails that'd flooded her box over the past twenty-four hours, too. The blue-jean cutoffs and Little Big Town T-shirt she'd donned when she got home wasn't really what she'd choose to wear in front of guests, especially male guests. But she didn't want Mia to know the sheriff had come, didn't want her to overhear the questions Myles might ask. So she got up and hurried to answer before he could ring the bell.

Fortunately, he knocked first, and not very loud. He could probably see her inside the living room, just as she could see him on the porch.

Determined to keep their encounter as brief as possible, she opened the door slightly. "Yes?"

When his gaze dipped to her chest, she knew he'd

already noticed that she wasn't wearing a bra. It'd taken less than a millisecond for her breasts to become his focal point and raise the tension between them. But the tension itself was nothing new. That was why she'd been bold enough to proposition him last night. She'd never dreamed he'd refuse her.

"Vivian." He bent his head.

Forcing a polite smile, she used a similarly formal tone. "Sheriff. How are you today?"

"I've been better."

So had she. For a lot of reasons. The most pressing was Rex. She couldn't stop thinking about what he'd once meant to her, couldn't stop wondering if he was still alive and whether or not she'd contributed to his downfall. Although she'd grown used to living with fear, guilt was new and more difficult to tolerate. Then there was the embarrassment she'd been trying so hard to avoid. With Myles standing less than two feet away, it was virtually impossible to shove the memory of her offer and subsequent rejection into the recesses of her mind.

She considered apologizing for her behavior and blaming it on the wine, but she wasn't one for excuses. The alcohol hadn't changed how she felt, only revealed it. He probably understood that as well as she did. Besides, if he thought she was a tramp, maybe he'd make her life easier by staying away from her and refusing to let Jake hang out with him.

"I'm sorry to hear that." She paused, but he didn't take the opportunity to come to the point of his visit. Instead, silence fell.

"Can I speak with you for a few minutes?" he asked when she didn't invite him in, as he'd obviously expected.

"Of course."

His eyebrows slid up. "Do we have to do it right here?"

Mia would be less likely to overhear if they chatted on the porch. "Why not? It's a beautiful day. I'll join you."

Stepping outside, she closed the door quietly behind her and crossed the wooden planks to one of the rocking chairs she'd picked up at an antique auction last summer. She loved these chairs. Their weathered look fit perfectly with the wide veranda and stark simplicity of her hundred-year-old house. *Her* hundred-year-old house.

But maybe not for long. If she had to go on the run, there'd be no way to make the payments. She wasn't even sure she'd have the money to survive. She'd have to lean on Virgil, and how long could she expect him and Peyton to take care of her? It was possible they'd have to leave what they'd created, too.

"You're not curious about why I'm here?" he asked, trailing after her.

She sat down and pulled her legs up to hide her chest. "Judging by the uniform, it looks official, so...I'm guessing you haven't stopped by for a quickie." She'd thought making light of her blunder would ease the awkwardness between them, but her joke didn't draw the grin she'd been angling for—or any other indication that they could laugh about last night.

Instead, his gaze slid over her bare legs, making her regret the reference even more.

"Forget I said that," she muttered. "It was my way of apologizing for putting you on the spot after you were kind enough to come to the rescue of my refrigerator. That's all."

"It was an apology?"

"That's right."

"Not a suggestion."

She cleared her throat. It *definitely* wasn't a suggestion. "I wouldn't make the same mistake twice."

"How sorry are you?"

"Excuse me?"

"I'm just wondering if you're sorry enough to change your mind about letting me buy you dinner."

Most men would be grinning while they threw out a line like that, but he wasn't. Hugging her knees closer, she shook her head. "More like…embarrassed enough to avoid you in future."

His eyebrows knotted in frustration. "You're not giving us a chance."

And he wasn't used to that. She couldn't name a single unattached woman, at least one anywhere close to his age, who wouldn't drop everything to spend a couple of hours with him. All she heard was, "That poor Sheriff King. How he loved his wife." While it was a compliment, it was almost always spoken with a certain wistfulness that said the speaker would like to be next in line.

Vivian wasn't any different. She felt that same desire to have what Amber Rose King had enjoyed. But that wasn't something she *could* have, not unless she somehow managed to free herself from the past. "Maybe I don't have a choice."

The interest that evoked made her regret saying it. "What do you mean?"

"Nothing. Never mind." She slapped the armrests of her chair for punctuation. "What brings you by today?"

He didn't bother answering. "What are you afraid of?" he asked.

She ran a hand through her freshly cropped hair. A new habit. It still felt so foreign to her. "Nothing I can't handle."

"I'll help if you'll let me, Vivian."

"I know." She smiled sadly. "There's nothing you can do. Just…tell me why you're here."

His lips, normally so full and soft-looking, thinned. "When you were coming out of the bank today…"

Sitting taller, she steeled herself for what was coming. "Yes?"

"You were carrying something."

"Chrissy Blabbermouth told you."

"You thought she wouldn't?"

"I knew she would. She uses any excuse to get your attention. But that doesn't make her interference any less infuriating. What a busybody!"

He had a way of watching her as if he was waiting for an opportunity to peel back another layer. "Believe me, I'm not thrilled by her interest, but this time I'm glad she stuck her nose where it doesn't belong." He placed his hands on his hips. "Why don't we talk about the gun."

Too uncomfortable to remain in the same position, she released her legs. "It's a method of self-defense, right? Surely I'm not the only one who has a gun around here."

Judging by the unrelenting sternness of his mouth, he wasn't going to let her dismiss it that easily. "Do you have a permit to carry a concealed weapon?"

She didn't answer.

"Is that a no?"

Damn… "Everyone carries concealed around here whether they have a permit or not. Unless they're waving it around in someone's face or they're making threats or they're drunk…no one really cares. Or are you going to be a hard-ass?"

"Maybe." He leaned against the railing. "Where'd you get it?"

"It was a gift from a relative."

"You have relatives?"

He was teasing about the way she kept her life under wraps. She acknowledged it with a smirk. "One or two."

"Where?"

"One's in prison, if you must know."

"Which prison?"

He was marking every detail she dropped. So why was she giving him another nugget of information? "That's none of your business."

"Are we talking about a father or a brother?"

She couldn't resist. "Neither."

"Then who?"

"An uncle, okay?" That was far enough removed....

"What'd he do?"

"Something that's destroyed my life and the lives of almost everyone I love."

"And that was…"

Taking a deep breath, she lifted her chin. "Never mind."

"You can't tell me that much and then retreat."

Sure she could; she'd already gone too far. "It's not something I'm willing to discuss."

He was sifting through the possibilities. She could tell by his speculative expression. "That means you had *two* violent men in your life."

"True."

"How does your uncle connect with your ex? Did he shoot him?"

"No."

"The two stories are unrelated?"

"Completely." Except that she probably wouldn't have

married Tom if she hadn't left home so early and been so desperate for a friend.

"Okay, so what were you doing with a gun at the bank?"

They were back to that. "What do you think?"

His scowl told her he didn't understand why she had to be so contrary. "A straight answer might serve you better."

The sun was hot today, but the trees around her house blocked its direct rays, and a gentle breeze, coming off the lake, cooled the air. Rarely did it go above eighty in Pineview. With all the wildflowers in bloom right now—the lupine, the Indian paintbrush, the kinnikin-nick ground cover—it was a beautiful time of year. She loved it here, especially in summer.

"I was getting it out of my safe-deposit box. What else?" she said with a shrug.

"Why today?"

"Why not today?"

"Does it have anything to do with recent events?"

"If by 'recent events' you mean Pat's murder, yes." It had even more to do with Rex's disappearance, and the fact that he knew where she lived and could tell the wrong people if sufficiently motivated or careless, but that was one of those things she couldn't talk about. Over the past four years, she'd gotten so good at guard-ing her tongue she weighed almost every sentence she spoke. The constant vigil was taxing, which must be the reason she was suddenly slipping up. She was so tired of the charade, of the caution and worry. She was also tired of spending so much time alone or on the internet, trying to fill her life with strangers or business associates who posed no threat. Even Claire didn't know who she really was.

"How does Pat's murder affect you?" he pressed.

"Unless you've caught the person who's responsible, it affects everyone, doesn't it?"

He shoved away from the railing. "That's it? You're worried about safety?"

"I think we all are."

"Pat's murder doesn't hold any special significance to you."

"I'm sad it happened."

"That's not what I'm asking."

She ruffled her hair again. As short as it was, she couldn't do any damage. "Then I'm afraid I don't understand what you're after."

"This doesn't relate to your uncle or your ex-husband?"

"No."

"Do you know *anything* about why it occurred? Who might be responsible?"

Guilt stabbed her like a knife to the gut. It was possible she did. If what she feared was true, she should say something. But what if she was wrong? The information she had to offer could derail the investigation as easily as help it....

It was better to wait. Why ruin the life she'd created here, which she was so intent on protecting, if she didn't have to? "Of course not. What makes you think I might?"

He shook his head, "I don't know. Something's up with you. I can't figure out what it is but—"

"I already explained."

"When you told me about your ex-husband."

"That's right."

"And his name is…"

Fresh alarm curled through Vivian's veins. She couldn't give him Tom's name in case Myles used it to dig up her real identity. And yet she couldn't come up with a good excuse not to. "I don't even want to say it."

"Because…"

Shit. She'd thought a quick mention of her abusive ex would put an end to the sheriff's queries, provide an excuse for her secrets, but it'd only made him hungry for details. After two years in this place, she'd broken down and done exactly what she'd sworn she'd never do—she'd shared a specific detail that could, if she wasn't careful, unravel the whole truth.

"Because he's part of my past and I won't revisit those years," she said.

He turned her arm so he could see the scar Tom had left. "Tell me about this."

Thanks to years of healing, the initials her ex had carved with his pocketknife weren't as visible as they'd once been. Even if Myles could decipher them, there wasn't much he could do with *TH.* But the possibility that she could be underestimating him added to her anxiety.

"There's no need to go over it." She pulled her arm out of his grasp. "It's not related to anything."

"Did you kill him?" His eyes seemed to drill a hole right through her.

"Who? My ex-husband? Of course not!"

Lines formed on his forehead. "Then why won't you tell me about him?"

She stood. "Because it has nothing to do with you or… or this town…or Pat's murder."

"Are you on the run, Vivian?"

"No!"

"Then what?"

"I just want to mind my own business, to be left alone!"

He looked disappointed. "Thanks for the trust."

"Why should I trust you? We barely know each other!"

"Is that right?"

"Yes! We—we're neighbors, nothing more," she said, but couldn't quite meet his gaze because what they'd done in her dreams was certainly more intimate than anything that would occur between strangers.

He lowered his voice to a muted growl. "Then why do you find excuses to come outside whenever I'm working in the yard?"

Her mouth dropped open. This was the last thing she'd expected. "I—I don't!"

"And why do you follow my every move when you think I'm not aware that you're there?"

Oh, God... Heat rose to her cheeks. "I don't know what you're talking about."

"The invitation you extended last night didn't come out of nowhere, Vivian. There are plenty of other men in Pineview who'd gladly take you to bed. But, to my knowledge, you've never had any of them over here."

"That doesn't mean I won't!"

"Yes, it does. That's not your style. What happened last night didn't come from wanting to get laid as much as it came from all the hours you've watched me...like I've watched you."

It was difficult to speak with her heart in her throat, but she had to make the effort, had to reel in the emotions that seemed to be exploding between them. "Look, I've already tried to explain. Last night was a—a mistake. One you won't have to worry about me repeating.

I don't know what I was thinking or…or feeling, but… it was just a weak moment, okay?"

"And now you regret it."

"Exactly."

"Would you regret it as much if I'd said yes?"

"Probably more," she admitted.

"That's why I refused."

She narrowed her eyes. If he wasn't going to let her get away with anything, she'd hold him to the truth, too. "That isn't the reason."

"Then what is?"

"You're afraid of me. Afraid of what you don't know."

He ignored the accusation. "About that gun…"

Her stomach muscles tightened. "What about it?" Would he confiscate her Sig? She got the impression he was considering it. But now that she'd made the decision to keep the weapon close at hand, she didn't want to lose the advantage it could give her.

"It's dangerous to have it in the house."

It was more dangerous *not* to have it, which was why Virgil had given her the Sig in the first place. "I'll be careful."

"Do you really need it? I mean…I'm right next door."

With a thirteen-year-old. No way would she get him involved if The Crew came to call. The Crew would kill him *and* Marley, just like they'd butchered that U.S. marshal….

The panic she'd felt as she called 9-1-1 that night a few years ago returned to her mind, along with the memory of the marshal's blood, still warm, as she tried to hold the wound in his neck closed. She couldn't let anything like that happen again. Ever. Which meant she had to control herself and her emotions. "Thank you, but...I can take care of myself."

She'd offended him. He wanted her to rely on him as a lawman, if nothing more, but he didn't argue with her or try to convince her. He nodded once and turned to go.

Unable to stifle the impulse, she followed him to the steps. "So...that's all you have to say?"

When he faced her again, the hooded expression he'd worn since he arrived dropped, revealing raw desire. "Yes. No. Yes. No. You're driving me crazy," he murmured.

She was driving herself crazy, wanting what she couldn't have. "I'm sorry."

"That's all you've got to say?" he said, repeating her line from a moment before.

"Yes." What more was there? She had no choice but to do exactly as she was doing.

"No." He shook his head.

"No?"

"You want to keep your gun?"

Where was he going with this? She slid one arm around the pillar to steady herself. "You know I do."

The emotion that'd burned so bright only a second before disappeared behind a professional facade. "Then go for a ride with me. Tonight at six-thirty. Marley will babysit."

"The kids can't stay here—" she started, but he cut her off.

"Then we'll take them to my place."

Even if The Crew was in town, they'd have no reason to go looking for her or her children at the sheriff's house. Mia and Jake would be safe. But still... Was she getting in over her head?

"What if I refuse?"

"I'll take your gun from you right now."

She swallowed hard. "And if I go with you?"

"You might have a chance of keeping it."

"Might?"

"Depends."

"On what?"

"On whether or not I'm convinced you know how to use it."

This, she hadn't expected. "Excuse me?"

"Bring it with you," he said, and walked away. When he reached his car, he called back, "And dress warm. We'll be taking the Ducati."

7

Myles knew he shouldn't push it with Vivian. She was too dodgy. Chasing someone so mysterious and closed off was asking for trouble. And yet…she attracted him like no one else. He hadn't seen it coming, not initially, at least not the way it was currently playing out. He'd assumed he'd date her, see whether or not it went anywhere, and probably wind up moving on to the next candidate. He had no real hope he could meet someone he loved as much as Amber Rose.

But Vivian wouldn't let their mutual interest travel along that well-worn path. She was so different from anyone he'd been with, so different from the kind of woman he'd married. Amber Rose had been a safe bet. Trusting, warm, sunny. Vivian, on the other hand, was complicated and full of shadows. That made her a definite risk. And he had no business taking a risk at this point in his life. Not with a daughter who'd already lost her mother…

So why couldn't he seem to back away and forget his pretty neighbor?

Because he wanted her too badly. It was that simple. He'd been trying to engage her without climbing in too deep—get to know her better before deciding whether or not to lower his defenses. This was part of the reason, aside from the fact that she'd had too much wine, that he'd refused her last night. But she wouldn't allow him to play it safe. He'd have to jump in over his head if he wanted to get wet at all.

Which was a stupid thing for him to do, right?

Of course. When he presented it to himself like that, he could see the danger easily enough.

He should call her and cancel. . . .

But even as the thought crossed his mind, he knew he wouldn't. Last night had lit a fuse. Now it burned quickly toward detonation and he was actually looking forward to the explosion. For the first time since Amber Rose died, he felt some positive emotion about life in general and his neighbor specifically—excitement, eagerness, arousal, curiosity. If Vivian offered him another opportunity like last night, he'd take it. Even if he wound up mired in regret, at least he'd escape the numb emptiness that had replaced the pain of losing Amber Rose.

He glanced at his watch. Pat's autopsy was scheduled for three. He'd expected to have plenty of time to make it back, but lunch with Marley had taken longer than expected. He'd also stayed at Vivian's too long. He needed to hurry if he wanted to observe the procedure.

The needle on his speedometer edged up to seventy-five as Pineview faded in his rearview mirror. Like his office, the morgue was in Libby, thirty minutes away. But less than five miles down the road, he spotted a vehicle broken down on the shoulder.

Because he was so intent on reaching the morgue, he almost left the driver to work it out on his own. Two men were with the car. But there wasn't any cell service here, so they couldn't call for help, and when he saw one of them limp around the vehicle to reach the engine, he slowed.

The man had an awkward gait, as if one leg was shorter than the other. Maybe the second guy, who was sitting in the driver's seat, wasn't any more mobile and that was why he hadn't gotten out.

Flipping on his lights to warn other motorists to give them a wide berth, Myles pulled in behind the economy-size truck and cut the engine. Then he ran the California plate, only to learn that the computer system was down and had been for the past twenty minutes.

"No big deal," he muttered. These boys just needed a hand. If he got them on their way soon enough he could still make the autopsy.

As Myles got out, the handicapped man leaned around the hood. "Afternoon, Officer."

"Looks like you got trouble." A red bucket of bolts, the truck probably hailed from the early nineties.

"Radiator's busted," came the response.

Camping and fishing gear filled the bed, not unusual for this time of year. The person inside the cab stared at Myles through his open window but stayed put. He seemed young. Not young enough to be the driver's son, but maybe a nephew or brother.

The lame guy leaned heavily on his hands, as if it pained him to support his own weight. Although dressed in jeans, a long-sleeved T-shirt and a ball cap, which didn't expose a lot of skin, what skin Myles could see as he drew closer was covered with ink, even his face. The images of snakes and gargoyles were off-putting enough to make Myles wish he'd been able to run the license plate. He dealt with a lot of tourists, mostly men, some of them pretty rough. But this guy went beyond anything he'd seen since his days on the force in Phoenix. His appearance and lack of relief at the prospect of having help, not to mention the way the fellow behind the wheel pulled his ball cap down and sank lower in the seat, set Myles's cop instincts abuzz.

He immediately thought of Pat's murder and wished he could find out if they were driving a stolen vehicle or had outstanding warrants. "Engine's hot, huh?" he said.

"Too hot to drive without cracking the block." A jug of water sat on the ground next to the speaker. Obviously he'd done what he could to remedy the problem.

Judging by the burned smell, Myles thought it was too late to save the engine. "If that's true, it can't be driven. Why don't I call for a tow? Harvey can come out, pick you up and take you and your vehicle into town."

Tattoo Guy fidgeted with the change in his pocket, then squinted at him. "How much will that cost?"

"Can't say for sure, but I'm guessing it'll be around eighty bucks."

"You hear that?" He banged on the truck to attract his friend's attention. "'Cause of you, we need a tow."

The door cracked open. When the young man poked his head out, dark eyebrows met over vivid blue eyes. "I'm the one who said we had to stop!"

"No, you didn't!"

"Yes, I did!"

"If you need a tow, then you need a tow," Myles interrupted. These two didn't seem to be getting along so well. The boy was definitely sulky and Tattoo Guy barely seemed able to contain his irritation.

"Go ahead an' give 'em a call," Tattoo Guy grumbled.

Myles offered them both a bland smile. "Will do, but

first I need to see your license, registration and proof
of insurance."

Blue Eyes sat up straight. "Why? We haven't done
nothin' wrong."

Because he was outnumbered and had no idea whether
or not these men possessed firearms, Myles kept his
voice and expression calm. He didn't want to spook them.
"It's nothing to worry about." Unless they had something
to hide… "Just standard procedure."

The kid couldn't be older than nineteen or twenty.
Although he didn't seem to have had a shower recently,
and his clothes were wrinkled and dirty, he wasn't bad-
looking. Tall and thin, he had a good build. It was the
furtive air about him, and the sweat popping out on his
forehead, that made Myles nervous.

"Just because our radiator broke?"

His reluctance to provide the requested documentation
rang another warning bell in Myles's head. This wasn't
a situation he wanted to be in, not without backup or
some assurance that these guys were law-abiding citizens. There wasn't much traffic on the road today, which
put the odds even more in their favor. Only one vehicle
had passed since he'd stopped, certainly not enough to
act as any type of deterrent. These men could easily shoot
him, drag his body into the woods and steal his cruiser.

"Like I said—" Myles left his hand by his side so he
could grab his gun if need be "—standard procedure."

"Get it for him," Tattoo Guy barked, as if he made the
decisions.

Tension coiled in Myles's chest. This was the most
anxious moment of any traffic stop—when the driver
reached across the seat to open the jockey box. He could
pull out a gun instead of his registration. That wasn't

something Myles worried about when dealing with folks in Pineview. But these were total strangers.

Fortunately, there was no blast. Easing his stance, Myles breathed an internal sigh of relief as the younger man handed him registration and proof of insurance, all of which appeared to be in the name of one Quentin J. Ferguson.

"And your license?"

The boy lifted his cap and resettled it on his head. "Sorry, sir. Lost my wallet in the river yesterday."

That sort of thing happened often enough, and yet Myles couldn't bring himself to believe it. He turned to the other man. "What about you?"

"Didn't bring any ID. Considering I'm such a cripple, it's better if I don't drive."

Neither man could provide proof of identity? "Why don't we start with your names?" Myles tilted his head at Tattoo Guy, who grinned from ear to ear as he answered.

"Ron Howard."

Myles stiffened. "Like the director?"

"What director?"

Was he for real? No way. This guy knew exactly who Ron Howard was. "How'd you get injured, Mr. Howard?"

"Fell off a ladder while working construction. Hurt my back."

Myles had a feeling he might have to arrest these two. Something wasn't right… "I hope it's only a temporary condition."

"'Fraid not."

The pain seemed real. "Sorry to hear that."

Bitterness contorted his features, making those gargoyles on his face dance. "Yeah, so was I."

"Ron Howard," if that was really his name, was as

fascinating as he was repulsive. With some effort, Myles pulled his gaze away and indicated the Toyota truck. "You the owner of this vehicle?"

"Nope." He angled his head toward Blue Eyes. "His brother is."

"What's your name?" Myles asked the driver.

"Peter Ferguson." He pointed to the registration. "Quentin is my brother. The *J* stands for Joe—" he squinted into the bright sun to read Myles's badge "—Sheriff King." Now that he was on the spot, he'd gone from trying to avoid notice to putting on a show.

Myles wished he could believe what he'd been told. He also wished he didn't have to present his back to these two in order to return to his car. But he couldn't stand there all day. "I'll get that tow truck coming."

The crunch of his boots on the gravel shoulder sounded loud, probably because he was so aware of every step. Pat's murder, combined with the disconcerting appearance of Tattoo Guy and his younger sidekick, had made him skittish, as skittish as everyone else in Pineview. He strained to hear movement behind him, any indication of impending danger, but reached his car without incident.

Leaving the door hanging open so he could get out quickly if necessary, he called dispatch with the plate number instead of entering it into the computer—and was told what he'd learned before—California's Motor Vehicle Division was down.

Shit… "Call me as soon as it goes up," he told the dispatcher.

He used his radio to call Harvey's Tow. Then he stayed in his car, studying the documents he'd been given. The address on the registration indicated the owner of the vehicle lived in a place called Monrovia, California. Was that northern or southern California?

Myles had no idea. He'd been to Disneyland once with Marley and that was it.

"Ron Howard" began to limp toward him. Myles had been stalling, hoping to hear from dispatch before going back to the truck, but there'd been no word in the past ten minutes. Knowing his open door could act as a shield should there be trouble, he stood but remained behind it. "Tow truck's on its way."

"You don't have a bottle of water or somethin' else to drink in there, do you?" "Ron," the tattooed man, asked.

Myles didn't have any food or drink. "Sorry."

A nod acknowledged his response, then "Ron" headed back but got only ten feet or so before doubling over and cursing aloud.

"You okay?" Myles called out.

The guy seemed to be in pain; Myles couldn't help being concerned. "Should I call the paramedics?"

"No, there's…nothing they can…do," he ground out.

"Do you need aspirin or something? I don't have any of that, either, but the tow truck driver might."

"Aspirin won't…make any difference."

"Then you must have a prescription for stronger meds."

"It…fell in the river…with Peter's wallet."

Myles was just about to leave the safety of his car to help the man to his truck when the radio sparked to life. Dispatch was trying to reach him. "Hang on." Ducking back inside, he grabbed the mic. "What have you got for me?" he asked the dispatcher.

"That plate you gave me is registered to Quentin J. Ferguson from Monrovia, California." It was Nadine

Archer. Myles had spoken to her so many times since coming to this area, he recognized the voice.

"Has it been reported as stolen?"

"No, sir."

He looked up. "Ron" had managed to straighten and was dragging his foot as he made his way back to the truck. "Does Quentin J. Ferguson of Monrovia have any outstanding warrants?"

"Not a one."

"When was he born?"

"In 1964." That meant Quentin, Peter's brother, was forty-six, quite a bit older than Peter was. But…it was possible. Quentin could even be a half brother.

When "Ron" climbed into the truck, he seemed to instigate an argument but, given the situation, that didn't strike Myles as unusual. It was hot, they were stranded far from home and one of them was in pain and had lost his meds. "Can I get clearance on a Ron Howard?"

"Also from Monrovia?" Nadine asked.

Myles figured that was as good a guess as any. "Sure, give that a try."

He had to wait a few minutes before she came back on the line. "There are several Ron Howards, but I don't show any outstandings."

"Got it. Thanks."

"Anytime, Sheriff."

"Good to know," Myles muttered as he returned the mic to his radio. Apparently his intuition was a little off today. Maybe. He still didn't like these two.

The men stopped talking the moment he drew close. He sensed some unease, but knew there could be a lot of reasons for that. Perhaps they'd had some run-in with the law in the past. In any case, there was nothing he could do. He didn't have any reason to detain them. He might as well get to the autopsy before he missed it entirely.

"Your tow will be here any moment," he explained as he returned their documents. "I've got business in the next town, so I'm going to head out."

The boy sat taller. "Really?"

"You don't mind waiting alone, do you?"

"No, no problem at all. Thanks for your help, Sheriff."

The man who'd said his name was Ron Howard didn't speak. He merely rested his head against the back window and closed his eyes.

"Your friend going to be okay?" Myles asked.

"He'll be fine," Peter assured him. "It's chronic pain. Nothing anyone can do."

"He should contact his doctor, have him call in a new prescription. There's a drugstore right across from Harvey's Tow."

The boy nodded. "We'll do that. Thanks."

"Good luck," he said, and walked back to his car. He probably would've continued to wait, just in case "Mr. Howard's" condition worsened and he ended up needing emergency care, but Harvey radioed to say he was five minutes away.

He could leave them, couldn't he? As odd as they were, these boys hadn't given him any trouble. He couldn't imagine they'd give Harvey any trouble, either. It wasn't as if he carried money on him. The only thing he'd have to steal would be his truck, but if they were going to do something that rash, they would've tried to take his cruiser.

Relieved to be free, Myles informed Harvey that one of the men had a medical problem. Then he drove off. With any luck, he could still make the autopsy.

8

"Shit, that was close!" Ink muttered as he watched the sheriff leave.

L.J. shoved the gun—which he'd hidden beneath an old shirt—back under the seat. "Good thing I didn't shoot him. What if I'd blown him away like you told me to?"

Ink didn't bother opening his eyes. He'd exaggerated his condition to entice the sheriff out of his cruiser and away from his radio sooner rather than later, since they didn't need any other cops to join him. But he felt pain almost all the time. That was no act. "Then he'd be dead. And there's nothing wrong with a dead cop. I like that kind better than any other."

"I wouldn't cry over it, either. But we can't be stupid, or we'll wind up back in prison. I still can't believe he didn't bust our asses. I was sure he was planning to." He adjusted the rearview mirror.

"Tow truck comin'?"

"Not yet." L.J. started searching for a station that played music to his liking, but Ink couldn't tolerate the static, which was about all they were getting, so he reached over and turned off the radio. His back pain was giving him a headache. When he'd broken out of prison, it wasn't as if he could take the nurse and her meds with him. Now he was trying to manage with the recreational drugs he'd gotten from various gang members who'd helped them once they hit the outside, and what he could buy over the counter.

"What do you think changed his mind?" L.J. asked.

"You mean the sheriff?"

"Yeah."

Wasn't it obvious? "His computer didn't have anything to say about us."

L.J.'s eyebrows slid up. "How could that be? He had us, man."

"He didn't even know our real names."

"What about the plates? We stole this truck a *week* ago."

Ink leaned out the window as far as his back would allow. Mild as the summer was here in the mountains of Montana, this was the hottest part of the day. "Guy we stole it from must not have reported it—or this would've ended very differently."

L.J.'s baby face registered a frown. "I can't imagine the owner hasn't called the cops."

"Maybe he hasn't missed it."

"How do you not miss your own vehicle?"

Where was the damn tow truck? Sitting here baking in the hot sun was making Ink angrier by the minute. Angrier than he normally was. "By having too many to begin with," he snapped. "By having one that's such a hunk of junk you don't give a shit that it's gone. Hell, maybe it's not even his. Maybe he was storing it for his son, who's in the military or away at school or in rehab. You saw where this baby was parked. Way out on the south forty, mostly hidden by storage. I'll bet whoever owns that property doesn't walk there every day. Another week could pass before anyone notices."

Fidgeting was how L.J. dealt with his nervous energy, but Ink had a hard time tolerating the repetitive movement. Actually, it wasn't just the movement that drove him nuts. It was the constant questions. L.J. was so damn green. That was the problem with growing old in prison. The fresh fish soon seemed like mere babies, and yet they all wanted to join The Crew. Ink had promised to sponsor L.J. if he helped him break out, but there was no way he'd follow through. L.J. wasn't worthy.

"So why the hell didn't he sell it if he didn't care about it anymore?" L.J. asked.

Ink shot him another glance. *This* was what he had to work with.

But he'd managed so far. They'd busted out of prison, hadn't they? Of course, it'd helped that, after four years of good behavior, they'd transferred him to a medium-security facility. No one expected someone as handicapped as he was to cause any trouble. And L.J. had gone to prison for possession. He'd only had a year left. No one expected him to bust out, either. If he wasn't trying so hard to impress the leaders of The Crew, who wanted to see Laurel and Virgil dead as badly as Ink did, he probably wouldn't have.

"Are you going to answer?"

The impulse to bash in L.J.'s head nearly overwhelmed him. But he wrestled with it, subdued it. Thanks to his tattoos and his limp, he was too distinctive, too memorable. He needed a front man. So what if this boy had shit for brains? It was probably better that way; he'd never challenge Ink. At least the kid's body was strong and healthy.

Just like Ink's used to be—before Rex, Virgil and his bitch of a sister came along.

"Who gives a rat's ass why he wouldn't sell it?" Ink said. "Quit with the dumb questions, okay?"

L.J.'s voice was sulky when he responded. "They're not dumb questions. You think everything's dumb."

Ink let his head bump against the back window again. "I think *you're* dumb, that's for sure. You're like a five-year-old. The owner didn't report the truck stolen or we would've been arrested. It's that simple. Happy now?"

"No, I'm not happy at all," L.J. grumbled. "You said if I helped you break out we'd have one hell of a good time. But here we are, after almost a week of camping in the woods with no bathroom or shower, sitting on the side of a road in the middle of nowhere. It's a miracle we didn't get arrested by that hick sheriff! If he'd dragged us off, we could've been charged with the murder of that guy you killed. If that ever happens, they'll give us both the death penalty, even though I had nothing to do with it."

Lowering his eyelids, Ink skewered him with a malevolent glare. "You were there, weren't you?"

"Unfortunately." He rubbed a hand over his face. "That Realtor was harmless. He reminded me of my grandpa."

"The old bastard had it coming."

"For saying you had to have money before he'd rent you a place?"

Ink heard the deep rumble of a diesel motor. Cautious to avoid causing himself more pain, he twisted around until he could see the tow truck chugging up from behind. "I offered him some money, but it just wasn't enough. If he wasn't going to give us a place, he had to give us *something*. I wasn't going to come away empty-handed."

"You think anyone else would've let us take the cabin for fifty bucks?" L.J. rolled his eyes. "And you call *me* dumb."

"He didn't have anyone else in there, did he? Fifty bucks would've been better than nothing."

"It wouldn't even have covered the maid service."

A blue placard was affixed to one door of the bright yellow tow truck: Harvey's Tow, 133 North Main, Pineview, Montana. There was a phone number below, then a saying, written in script: "I Will Follow the Good Shepherd."

Ink rubbed his temples. "Great. A religious fanatic."

Harvey, or whoever was behind the wheel, came parallel with them and waved before maneuvering his truck in front of theirs.

"How do you know he's religious?" L.J. asked.

"Just shut up, will ya?"

"What are we gonna do about the gun?"

"What do you think? We can't leave it in the truck. Stick it down your pants."

The diesel engine died, ending the vibration humming through the earth, the vehicles, the air.

"Are we going to ride back with him?" L.J. whispered as Harvey's door opened and two work boots came into view.

"Hell, no. What if someone's reporting that truck stolen right now? And what if the sheriff gets wind of it and radios Harvey? We'll be at their mercy." He shook his head. "Now that we've been connected to this truck, we can't head back with him."

"Great. So…where do we go from here?"

Ink shifted too fast. He had to clamp his jaw shut to cover a groan. "We just beat it. I'll figure out what happens later," he said when he could speak. "Whatever you do—" he drew a ragged breath "—let me handle this."

A large man with tufts of gray hair sticking out from a greasy ball cap and a nose permanently reddened by years of working outdoors came to L.J.'s window and bent to look in. "You need to get out while I hook up," he said.

A man of many words… "Right. Of course." Ink gave L.J. a pointed glance to indicate he should do as the driver asked.

L.J. got out, but it took Ink a bit longer to vacate the cab. He wanted to move without looking like too much of a cripple. He hated the attention his injury drew, which was pretty ironic, considering his tattoos. He used to enjoy the horrified reactions he often inspired. But fear and intimidation were different from pity. Ever since a bullet had damaged his spinal cord, the stares he received made him desperate to stop all gawkers, or punish them, just like when he'd let loose on that Realtor. He'd dismissed the incident at the cabin as if he'd meant to kill the old guy, but Ink still wasn't sure what had made him snap. The disappointment of being told something he didn't want to hear, he supposed. These days that was all it took. His mother claimed he'd been like that ever since he was a baby. But he knew he was getting worse. The injury had screwed up his mind as well as his body.

"Can you see the gun?" L.J. whispered as they watched Harvey go to work.

Ink barely looked. "There's a slight bulge, but it's not really noticeable. Maybe you're just well-hung, huh?"

"I am well-hung." He grinned at the joke but shoved

his hands in his pockets to help conceal the weapon. "So...we let him drive away?"

"That's exactly what we do."

"Then what?"

"We get the hell out of here."

"On *foot?*"

Ink clenched his hands in his own pockets. "Quit whining. Once he's gone, we can hitchhike."

L.J. kicked a pebble across the road. "But I thought you had plans in Pineview. I thought that's why we came here. You were going to take revenge on that bitch that got you shot, remember?"

She'd also spat in his face, which to him was almost as bad. *No one* spat in his face and got away with it, least of all a woman. "You don't need to remind me. I haven't forgotten. I could *never* forget. It'll happen. It just needs to happen a certain way."

"Why?"

"Because if I play this smart, I might get the bastard who shot me—and her brother, too."

"But *hitchhiking?* Seriously? Who's going to pick up someone with lightning bolts for eyebrows? Those tattoos'll scare everyone who drives by."

His Crew wannabe was growing too bold for his own welfare. Ink would've broken his jaw for less, but they had enough problems right now. He'd deal with L.J. later. "I'll hang back in the trees until you flag someone down."

"And then what?"

The tow truck's winch made a grinding sound as it lifted the Toyota.

"We ask for a ride."

"What if they refuse after they see you?"

Ink gritted his teeth. "We blow the driver's head off and take his car. What else?"

L.J. might've argued against more violence. He talked tough but it was mostly an act. He'd vomited after Ink had beaten that Realtor to death. But he didn't have a chance to speak. Finished, the tow truck driver walked over.

"You two need a lift?"

L.J. waited, allowing Ink to respond. "No, thanks."

The man's craggy face showed his surprise. They were far enough from town that he'd expected the opposite answer. "You sure?"

"Positive. A friend's coming to get us."

His gaze shifted to L.J., then moved back. "Why not meet your friend in town? Save him the trip?"

Refusing to reveal his discomfort, Ink cocked one leg to ease the pain shooting up his distorted spine. "Because he doesn't live in Pineview, and he's already on his way."

The tow truck driver scratched under his cap. "What if he misses you?"

"He won't."

He didn't mention how far it would be if they had to walk. If he'd noticed that Ink was handicapped—or tattooed—he didn't make an issue of it. Ink appreciated his "live and let live" attitude. This was a man who knew how to mind his own business.

"Fine by me." He held out a contract fastened to a clipboard. "Just need you to sign this and show up at Reliable Auto this evening or tomorrow morning to see about the repairs."

"No problem," Ink said and scribbled Ron Howard's name.

Harvey—his name was on his shirt—accepted the

clipboard and handed him a copy, then started walking away. But Ink called him back. "Hey!"

He turned before reaching his truck. "Yeah?"

"You don't happen to know a woman who lives in Pineview who's about five-ten, blond hair, blue eyes and has two kids, do ya?"

His eyebrows came together as he squinted against the sun. "Why do you ask?"

"She's my sister, adopted out at birth. I've been searching for her for years. A P.I. I hired, when I could afford that type of thing," he added sheepishly, "told me she lived here. I'd sure like to find her. Can't tell you how much it would mean to me."

"You don't have a name?"

"Her birth name was Laurel Hodges. I know that much, of course. But I don't think she goes by it."

He took his hat off, shoved a hand through his hair. "What does she look like again?"

Vivian sat in her living room, staring at the windows and doors as if she expected someone to try to break in. Jake hadn't returned from the lake yet. Mia was in her bedroom, playing dress-up. And Vivian was supposed to be working. But she couldn't concentrate. Instead, her mind was feverishly developing ways she could defend herself and her children if that became necessary.

But…short of installing iron bars over every point of entry, which was completely impractical given the fact that she had no money, there wasn't a lot she could do. She felt very vulnerable, living alone with her children in a small community, unable to even voice her fears.

Would The Crew come at night as they had in Colorado? Should she have Mia and Jake start sleeping with her?

That'd worked when they were small, but she wasn't sure Jake would go along with it at nine. He was so damn independent, so determined to throw off the yoke of her protection.

Remembering that he was at the lake—and she wasn't fully comfortable with that—she stood and began to pace. Maybe she should see if Nana Vera would keep the children with her for the next couple of weeks until Vivian could determine whether or not she had reason to be worried. She could present it as Nana's Summer Camp, make it sound like fun and pay Vera a small amount for her trouble. If Vera wouldn't accept money, she'd get her a gift as she had in the past.

But what would she tell Vera when she asked for this favor? That she was behind on her concepts for fall and needed the time to work?

Possibly. So then…what about her gun? It was still in the trunk of her car. She could carry it in after her children went to sleep, as planned. But where would she hide it at that point? If she put the Sig somewhere safe, like the attic or underneath the porch, she ran the risk of not being able to get to it in an emergency.

If she *didn't* put it somewhere safe, however, she could lose the advantage she was trying to give herself.

Maybe Myles would take it away and she wouldn't have that decision to make.

Pivoting at the window, she glanced at the phone. She'd already picked it up several times, planning to call the sheriff and cancel their plans for the evening. She just hadn't gone through with it yet. He scared her almost as much as The Crew, but for very different reasons. In her precarious situation, she had no business feeling the way he made her feel. Even if she didn't have some history to hide, she wasn't sure she could take an emotional risk at this point in her life. So what if she was lonely? So what if she craved the support of someone who could be with her in body as well as spirit? She didn't want to get involved with Myles for the wrong reasons. She'd just become healthy again. So had he—if she was right in assuming he was finally over his wife's death.

Cancel. Do it. Let him deal with his issues while you deal with yours. If he chose to push her about the gun, she'd just tell him she didn't feel safe without it. That was the truth, wasn't it?

Certain she'd reached the right decision, she hurried over to the desk, but the phone rang before she could lift the handset. Caller ID couldn't provide her with a number or a name but she answered, anyway, just in case it was Vera or Jake. "Hello?"

"Laurel?"

Virgil. She tightened her grip on the phone. This was the first time her brother had called since they'd left Washington D.C., but the second time she'd spoken to him today. It had to be important. "You've found Rex."

"No."

She ducked her head so her voice wouldn't carry up the stairs. "Something else has happened?"

"Not yet. Maybe it won't. At least, that's what I'm hoping."

An image of Trinity Woods, the young woman who used to babysit for her in Colorado, appeared in Vivian's mind. Trinity had been shot and killed on Vivian's doorstep four years ago, a death Vivian felt she could've prevented if she'd been more assertive about making sure someone warned Trinity. That was when Virgil had just gotten out of prison and The Crew had entered her life. Back then she hadn't known them like she did now and she'd had no idea they'd kill someone completely unrelated to the situation and for no reason whatsoever.

"I don't understand," she said. "Why are you calling?"

She couldn't help the coolness in her voice. The ease with which he seemed to have moved on while she continued to struggle made her angry. Maybe that anger was petty; in fact, she recognized that it was. After what he'd been through, he deserved the happiness he'd found. But in her most difficult hours, when she dragged her isolation around like a ball and chain, she grew too discouraged to be magnanimous and simply wanted to find fault.

"I feel bad about this morning," he said.

"You don't have anything to feel bad about." Despite her rapidly shifting emotions, she knew he'd change things if he could. He was at the same disadvantage she was, merely reacting to forces beyond his control.

"I should've been more prepared for your call," he admitted. "I didn't respond to it the way I would've liked. I was too much of a hard-ass."

"You said what had to be said. What else could you do?"

"That's just it. I feel so boxed in, so…helpless. I want to make the past right for you, for Peyton, for all of us. I can't tell you how much I regret ever joining The Crew—"

"You were only eighteen and fighting for your life inside a maximum-security prison. You had no choice."

There was a moment of silence before he spoke again. "Still, I wish I could reassure you instead of scaring the hell out of you. But I'm afraid the second you drop your guard it'll be like two years ago when…"

He didn't finish, and she knew he couldn't even speak the words. "I understand."

He cleared his throat. "Have you heard anything more about Pat Stueben's murder?"

"No." But if she kept her date with Myles, she might. And that was why she wouldn't cancel, despite her earlier determination to do so. "Do you think we should be more proactive about searching for Rex?" she asked. "Maybe it's not too late. Maybe he needs us, Virgil."

"That's just it. The more waves we make, the easier we'll be to find, and there're children involved." He cursed again. "We can't even be good friends to him."

"Have you tried calling his family? From a pay phone?"

"Of course."

"And?"

"His father and brothers won't talk to me. And his mother is dead. Should I go through the rest of his family tree?"

He wasn't being sarcastic; he was asking a serious question. But contacting any more of Rex's relations would be a waste of time. The rift with his family had driven Rex into gang life to begin with. "No."

"So what else?"

"I guess…nothing," she said. And then she understood. Being helpless was the worst possible experience for a man like Virgil, who tried to take charge of—and fix—every situation. "We just have to wait. And hope for the best."

"You asked me if I missed Mom."

He surprised her with the sudden change of subject, and then didn't give her any time to respond.

"The answer to that question is yes. I've missed her every day of my life since she stabbed me in the back. I wish I could hate her. Sometimes I do. But more than anything, I wonder what was wrong with me that she couldn't love me the way I love my son," he said, and hung up.

Vivian rubbed her face. She shouldn't have asked him about Ellen.

"Damn it…" Where could she turn? She had no idea what she could do to help Rex. She hated the thought that her brother was hurting as badly as she was. And she could no longer justify canceling her evening with Myles.

Jake's voice out in the yard brought her around to face the door. He was home. She could see him charging toward the house and was glad that Vera was behind him, hobbling up to say hello instead of just dropping him off.

"Mom?" Jake flung the door wide only to find her standing about three feet away from him. "Oh, there you are. We had so much fun!"

She wanted to hug him. To hold him close and never let go. But he was wet and didn't smell all that pleasant. And these days he wouldn't tolerate more than a short squeeze. "Did you catch anything?"

"*Three* rainbow trout! They're in the cooler. But I don't know how to gut them and neither does Nana. Do you think Sheriff King's at home?"

Great. Another reason for him to turn to Myles. "Not yet," she said. "But I can go online and look for a tutorial. Want me to do that?"

"Nah, Sheriff King will know how." He glanced toward the stairs. "Where's Mia? I want to show her."

Vivian propped up her smile with a bit more determination. "In her room."

He dashed around her, yelling his sister's name as Nana Vera reached the front door. "He had such a good time," she said, using the doorjamb to help her get up that final step.

Vivian held out an arm to steady her. "I didn't realize you knew how to fish."

She shrugged her bony shoulders. "I don't. But there was a book on it at the library. I read it last week. Then I went down and bought what it said I'd need. Somehow... it worked. Jake and I *both* learned something today," she added with a tired laugh.

Vivian shook her head. "I'm impressed."

"I'm a better fisherman than I thought. But I don't have the foggiest idea what to do with those poor creatures now that they're in my ice chest. To be honest, I wasn't expecting to catch a thing."

"Beginner's luck." Considering the smell, the mess and the revulsion factor, maybe they *should* let her son seek Myles's help. "I'm sure we can get Sheriff King to teach the kids."

Vera adjusted her wide-brimmed hat. She was also wearing long pants and a lightweight yellow jacket to protect her from the sun. "I doubt he'll have time," she mused. "Not today."

"Why's that?"

"He's probably at the autopsy. And who knows what he'll have to do afterward."

"The autopsy's today?" Myles hadn't mentioned it

when he stopped by earlier. He was so careful to keep the details of the case to himself.

"According to Lawrence Goebel."

Goebel was the county coroner. He was also Vera's ballroom dance partner. They went down to the veterans' hall once a month and took a few turns around the dance floor, but a decade earlier, they'd entered numerous competitions. Vivian thought they owned every ribbon that could be won in this region. She'd once asked Vera why she'd never gotten romantically involved with Goebel—they made such a handsome couple—and Vera had whispered that she and Goebel were both interested in the same man. To their mutual disappointment, that man had recently married a third party. "What does he have to say about the murder?" Vivian asked.

"Pat was killed by blunt-force trauma."

Vivian raised a finger to indicate silence. Jake was bringing Mia down to see his prized fish. Although the children would hear about the murder eventually, Vivian didn't want them to be frightened by the more gruesome details—probably because of the images that still haunted her.

Only after they'd brushed past and run outside did she resume the conversation. "What kind of blunt-force trauma?"

"Who knows? But the killer used *something* to bash in his head."

"A rock? A lamp?"

"Could've been either, I suppose. It was a furnished rental. But…"

"What?"

She looked around as if double-checking that they

were alone. "Gertie had to go through the place this morning and take inventory, poor thing."

"Was she able to do it?"

"With her sister's help."

"Was anything missing?"

"Just an electric can opener."

Vivian backed up a step. "*That's* the murder weapon?"

"Used with enough force, an electric can opener can crush a skull as easily as a bat or a rock, I suppose."

Sickened by the thought, Vivian bit her lip. Poor Pat. Had The Crew done this to him? If so, would she be able to find out before it was too late?

"Did Larry say if the sheriff has his eye on any particular person?" She needed a hint of reassurance, something to tell her she was overreacting.

But she didn't get it.

"They have no motive and no witnesses," Vera said, "which means they have no suspects and very little chance of tracking down the culprit."

9

The motorcycle vibrated beneath Vivian as she clung to the man driving it. Sheriff King seemed to be taking the winding road too fast. But maybe it only felt that way because she hadn't been on a bike in years. She wasn't used to the exhilaration, the sense of freedom and power, or the other feelings that arose as she wrapped her arms around his waist and pressed herself against him....

He'd given her a leather jacket and a helmet to wear. She hadn't asked where he'd gotten them but they were obviously closer to her size than his. She assumed they'd belonged to his late wife. It was too sad to imagine what Amber Rose must've gone through before she died, and what Myles and Marley must've suffered. So Vivian chose not to think about it. She told herself she was simply grateful that he'd been practical enough to bring them. Warm as the day had been, the temperature was dropping rapidly as they barreled through the mountains.

"You okay?" he yelled when she kept shifting.

Her gun, which she'd shoved into her waistband, was cutting into the small of her back. She'd been trying to ease the discomfort and put some space between them at the same time. The gun she could move. But with the bike leaning this way, then that, it required constant effort not to plaster herself against him.

Should she ask him to slow down? No. She'd come out with Myles tonight to convince him that she was tough enough to take care of herself. Learning that she was frightened of riding on a motorcycle would hardly boost his confidence, especially when he seemed so comfortable on the bike, as if it was merely an extension of his muscular body.

"Fine!" she assured him.

Apparently taking her at her word, he opened the throttle, and she squeezed her eyes shut as they flew around the next turn and the next.

After that, Myles didn't attempt to communicate with her. It was too difficult to hear above the engine. Vivian didn't want to talk, anyway. The noise created a buffer that distanced her from everything, even her cares and worries. For tonight, her children were safe and so was she. Not only that, she had the whole evening, and the longer they traveled, the easier it became to relax. Soon nothing mattered except the speed and roar of the bike and the man driving it.

After an hour or so, Myles turned off the highway and down a dirt path that led into the woods. She got the impression that he was taking her to a cabin—and he was—but there was also a small clearing that became a beach. It sloped down to a lake about the same size as the one they lived by.

"This is beautiful," she said when he cut the engine.

He barely grunted. He didn't seem to be in a talkative mood. But she didn't care that he wasn't Mr. Congeniality tonight. With the sun beginning to set and the weather so mild, she was content to revel in the moment.

After lowering the kickstand, he waited for her to get off before swinging his own leg over the seat. She hesitated a few steps away, tempted to ask how he'd found this place. But she didn't. They'd reached a tentative peace, and she didn't want that to change. Besides, she liked being here without feeling any pressure to entertain him.

He set his helmet on the seat and she handed him hers, which he put beside it. Then he got a sack out of his saddlebags and strode to the cabin as if he assumed she'd follow. He didn't beckon her or even turn around to see if she was coming.

Something had changed since he'd been at her house earlier. He'd made a decision. She could sense it. He'd been matter-of-fact, purposeful. For her part, she'd been so grateful he wasn't pressing her for information about her ex-husband or why she had a gun in the house that she'd been willing to discount his aloofness as preoccupation with the murder.

Maybe he wasn't pleased with the results of the autopsy or he was concerned about some aspect of the case, but so far he hadn't even checked to be sure she'd brought her gun.

When they got to the door, he pulled out a key with a tag that indicated this was a rental. That was when Vivian realized he'd come here with a very specific agenda, one that had nothing to do with the murder—or the target practice she'd been expecting.

"What's…" She swallowed hard. "What's this all about?"

His eyes riveted on hers, but he didn't answer. He just waved her into the cabin ahead of him.

With walls of half-sawn logs, antler light fixtures

and animal-skin rugs, the inside looked like a clean but rustic hunting lodge. They passed through a small mud-room with pegs for coats and a metal trough for snowy boots, which sat empty. After that, they encountered a small kitchen and dining area with a view of the lake. A family room—furnished with a gas stove, U-shaped leather couch and bookshelves crammed with books, magazines and games—took up most of the ground floor, along with a master suite at the back, a half bath and a ladder leading to a loft where, Vivian guessed, she'd find more beds, probably bunk beds for renters who had children.

So…why were they here?

Her palms began to sweat as she became more and more certain of his intentions.

Folding her arms, she backed up against the closest wall. "I don't understand." That was a lie; she understood very well. Too well. She just didn't know why he'd changed his mind.

He threw the keys on the kitchen table and tossed her the bag he'd carried in.

Vivian was almost afraid to open it. When she did, she barely resisted the urge to drop it and run outside. "You brought…*condoms?*" Her voice went up on the last syllable; she couldn't help it. There was other stuff in there, too. Lubricant. Lotion. A G-string. She could hardly breathe as she took the G-string out and held it up. "Really?"

A boyish grin curved his lips. "Put that on for me."

He couldn't be serious. When she merely gaped at him, he stood in front of her with one hand on the wall above her head. "This is what you wanted, right?" He ran a finger down the side of her face. "What you asked me to give you?"

Yes! But that was last night. She'd been drunk last night. Today she wasn't so sure. "I—"

"Don't worry." His thumb caught on her bottom lip, drawing his attention to her mouth. "I accept your terms. You can have it your way."

"My *terms?*" There was an air of mischief about him. This wasn't what it seemed. And yet…

His eyes met hers again. "No repeats. No strings attached. Tomorrow, we'll go our separate ways as if it never happened. But for now, you can have it as down and dirty as you want."

Down and dirty. He was trying to intimidate her, make her nervous. And it was working. "What about my, um… what about the gun? I thought—"

"You have it with you?"

"You said to bring it." She removed it from her waistband and he took it but only so he could put it on the table.

"We'll deal with that another day."

"Why not now?"

He grinned again. "You're stalling."

Breathing became as difficult as swallowing. "It's important, don't you think?"

"It can wait."

She twisted to be able to see her Sig. "How long?"

Cocking his head to the side, he blocked her view of anything else and gave her a look that taunted her sudden terror. "What's the matter, Vivian? You were sure talking tough last night. Been making promises you can't keep?"

Frantically trying to gain control of the situation, or

at least to stop panicking, she licked her lips. "You—you turned me down, remember?"

"You'd had too much to drink. I couldn't take advantage of my beautiful neighbor."

"That's the only reason you refused?"

"No," he said. "But you're not going to hold that against me, are you?"

She didn't know what to do. Shoving him out of the way so she could get to the door came to mind. She knew he'd let her go. But *beautiful neighbor* had her a bit entranced. And the way he was looking at her added to the paralysis caused by those words, made her feel as if she was melting from the inside out. "Your rejection was pretty humiliating."

She was teasing—and stalling—and he knew it. He toyed with the hair above her ear. "Good. Now you know how it feels."

"That's why, when someone turns you down, you don't ask again," she said.

"Unless you can tell they don't really *want* to turn you down."

What could she say to that? She already knew he'd noticed her acute interest in him. He'd mentioned it last night.

"So here's your chance to say yes," he prompted.

His warm breath carried the scent of spearmint gum. She liked spearmint.... "What if I stick with *no?*"

"Then you have to go out with me. Dinner in Libby. Once."

So that was his game. But if they went to dinner, they'd talk. He'd ask her where she was from, if she had any family, where her family lived, why she had no contact with them. She'd have to dance around the truth, one question after another. He'd think he was getting to know her when, in reality, he'd only be coming to know the fictional character she'd created. What was the point?

She hated the lies. That was the reason she didn't date, why she avoided social gatherings altogether, at least any that required conversation beyond the superficial, especially if she didn't have the buffer of her children. "And if I say yes?"

His smile disappeared. "You know what you'll get if you say yes." He'd been setting her up, forcing her into a corner this whole time, hoping she'd capitulate and date him. But he was aroused. Maybe he'd crept a little too close to the fire. Because if she said yes, she had no doubt he'd deliver. There'd be no talk. Only sensation. Like the ride on his bike. She could completely escape her life, her precarious situation. For however long it lasted, she wouldn't be touched by the fear that constantly plagued her. And then, after that, there'd be no contact.

"I'm not so bad to have dinner with," he murmured. Obviously he'd rented this cabin, purchased sex aids and put her on the spot because he believed that with her normal inhibitions back in place she'd chicken out. He was calling her bluff, trapping her into finally accepting his dinner invitation.

But she wasn't going to accept a date. She was going to call *his* bluff instead.

Standing on her tiptoes, she ran her tongue along his bottom lip. "Take off your clothes."

Those four words hit Myles's nervous system like a shot of heroin, or how he imagined a shot of heroin would feel. He'd heard druggies talk about the experience, heard them explain that first high was so spectacular it blew a person's mind—which was why heroin was so addictive.

He had a feeling he could get addicted to *this,* to Vivian. Which made the self-preservation instinct that'd carried him away from her house last night kick in again. But he pushed his better judgment aside. Vivian wasn't supposed to choose the way she had! He'd seen how skittish she was, how she'd hidden the sight of her braless chest from him earlier. She retreated from anything intimate, even from making close friends. He'd believed that, without the wine, she'd naturally refuse, and then...

Oh, hell. None of that mattered anymore. He was only human, and no single man he knew would be able to refuse Vivian, not with her hands up his shirt and her mouth on his. He was pretty sure he was harder than he'd ever been—

The memory of kissing Amber Rose for the first time suddenly rose up, and affected him almost like a physical shock. Surprised and shaken that such a vignette would appear in his mind *now,* he pulled back. Having sex with someone other than his late wife didn't necessarily feel like a betrayal. He knew Amber Rose would want him to move on, to find someone else, to be happy. It'd been three years since she died. It was the *amount* of desire flooding through him that was the problem. He wanted Vivian with a desperation he'd never experienced before. She wasn't just a stand-in because he couldn't have Amber Rose, and that jolted everything he'd come to believe about himself and his marriage.

Vivian glared defiantly up at him. She *knew,* he realized. She'd felt him jerk, understood he was suffering from some kind of hesitancy or regret, but she had no idea why. And he wasn't about to tell her. It gave her, basically an unknown entity and certainly an untrustworthy one with all her evasions and secrets, too much power over him. He wasn't sure why his feelings were so disproportionate to what they should be, given how little he knew of her, but that was the reality. She appealed to him on such a basic level that logic had no control.

"Apparently you're the one making promises you can't keep." Attempting to laugh off his withdrawal, she slipped out of his grasp and started for the door. He'd take her home if she insisted, but he caught her before she could leave the cabin.

"Don't chicken out."

She didn't turn. "Myles, you don't have to—"

Sliding his arms around her waist, he pulled her up against him and gently bit her neck. "I said don't go."

His voice sounded ragged even to his own ears. He pressed into her, making it obvious that he wanted her. But she didn't relax and begin to respond to him again until he reached under her jacket and unsnapped her bra.

"Nice," he whispered as her nipples hardened against his palms.

Although he hadn't removed his clothes, as she'd told him to, she allowed him to dispense with her coat and T-shirt. Her bra went next. He could see her bare breasts from his vantage point, which was slightly above and behind her, and cupped them more gently, more reverently, because rushing this early contact would be a terrible waste.

She was larger than Amber Rose. Taller, bigger-boned, bigger-breasted. He didn't want to make comparisons, had told himself he wouldn't. But this one was inevitable. Her long legs put her ass almost even with his groin and although she was still wearing jeans, her backside was a soft cradle for his erection.

"You're beautiful." He was about to bend his head to nuzzle her ear when she turned to face him. Judging by her expression, he'd said something wrong.

"Don't waste my time with meaningless remarks," she said.

She thought his compliment was meaningless? That couldn't have been farther from the truth. He found her stunning, gorgeous, which was going to be a problem. Forgetting about this afterward would be easier if he admired her less. He still wasn't sure how that part of the deal was going to work. Whenever he caught sight of Vivian, he knew he'd remember this heart-stopping image of her standing in front of him with her wary blue eyes, boyish haircut and bare breasts.

But there'd be time enough to worry about tomorrow and all the days after. "I wouldn't have said it if I didn't mean it."

He reached for her, but she held him off. "So…you don't hate my haircut?"

He almost laughed. Another challenge. And yet there was a hint of insecurity beneath her question that he found endearing, especially after all her rejections. "No, I don't hate your haircut. I wasn't sure at first, but…I like it."

She remained skeptical. "They've done studies. Most guys aren't attracted to women with short hair."

Was that why she'd cut it? She was so contrary, so ready to dismiss the whole world, daring him or any other man to like her.

"Then maybe they asked the wrong guys, because I think what you've done is sexy as hell." So was the rest of her. She was different, intriguing. She was also rebellious—but, oddly enough, that made him want to protect her. Convince her that she could trust him.

It also warned him that losing Amber Rose might not be the only painful thing he'd ever experience.

Myles eyed her as if he couldn't quite figure out what was going through her head. "So…are we fine?" he asked. "Is everything okay?"

Vivian wasn't sure. Rational thought was beginning to intrude, beginning to make her question why she was behaving so irresponsibly. "I'm reconsidering…"

"What?"

Everything, but she could only admit to part of it. "*This.* I've only been with two other men in my life. My husband and a steady boyfriend." Who was currently missing. "This situation is so…different, so reckless, so—"

"You're telling me you're not as brave as you pretend to be?"

"I don't want to make a mistake. I—"

Whatever she was about to say fled her mind as he took her face between his large hands and kissed her tenderly. "I'm going to take good care of you, Vivian. You believe that, don't you?"

She did. He was a cop. Taking care of people wasn't only his job, it was part of his nature. She liked that about him. The problem was that she wasn't taking good care of *him.* If, after this was all over, she couldn't replace the barricade she'd tried so hard to maintain between them, she could be putting him in harm's way.

"I believe you'll try," she said. "But…we shouldn't be

doing this. You don't…you need to pick someone else. You have a lot of options."

His hands dropped to the curve of her waist and held her in place as he lowered his head. "I don't want anyone else," he whispered, and drew the tip of her breast into his mouth.

The sensation of his tongue caused darts of pleasure to race through Vivian's blood, interfering with her ability to think. "You promise you won't ever call me again?" she gasped, trying to stand firm.

He looked up at her as though he might change the rules or question why it had to be that way. But when she unzipped his fly and began running her fingers over him, his chest lifted as if the contact had just kicked his heart up into his throat. "I promise."

His voice sounded strangled. She knew the way she'd exacted his agreement hadn't been fair. But she planned to hold him to his word. She had no choice.

"Good. Kiss me again," she whispered.

10

Vivian had never made love quite like this before. They stripped off his clothes and what was left of hers and joined instantly.

"Let's...slow down," Myles panted, his chest damp with sweat even though they'd moved from the wall, where he'd borne her weight, to the softest place in the vicinity—a bearskin rug. "I want...this to be good for you."

He seemed intent on achieving come control. But she wouldn't allow it. She believed she'd be able to forget him far more easily if they took a quick bow to lust and only lust. So she urged him to let himself go, told him she wanted it that way, and he obliged her. Hooking his arms beneath her knees, he drove into her with the abandon she craved, and the intensity and pleasure carried Vivian where she needed to be—to that place where thoughts don't exist, just sensation.

Their lovemaking ended almost as fast as it'd begun, which made her feel as if she'd won a victory of some sort. At least she hadn't enjoyed it *too* much. That some-how meant she couldn't miss it later. Or so she told her-self until, after a short nap, they woke up and started all over. Soon, they'd made love in the living room and in the bedroom as well as that first time in the hall, and each experience was better than the last.

It was three hours later when, too exhausted to expend any more energy, Vivian rolled away from Myles to check the clock on the wall above the dining table. Almost eleven. She'd been admiring his face while he dozed, but knowing she'd never see him this way again felt like such a loss she didn't want to think about it. "We've got to go," she whispered, giving him a slight nudge to wake him. "It's late."

His eyes opened but he made no move to get up. "Let's sleep a little longer."

"We have kids to worry about."

"One more time."

"What? Don't tell me you're not satisfied," she said with a laugh.

Instead of laughing with her, he sobered. "I'm not satisfied."

"How many times is it going to take?"

"You tell me."

"I don't know what you're talking about."

"You've been holding out on me. Why?"

Scowling, she glanced away. "I don't know what you're talking about," she responded.

"Yes, you do."

"I had fun."

"You encouraged me to let go and enjoy myself but you wouldn't. You hung on to your control so tight I couldn't pry you away from it."

"Stop."

He sat up. "I want to talk about this."

"Talk about what?" she said with exasperation.

"The way you wouldn't really connect."

"How do you know it wasn't *your* fault?" She felt terrible the moment she'd said it. It wasn't his fault at all. She just didn't want to address the truth.

Fortunately, he didn't let her get away with it. "Because I watched you. Every time you got close you'd simply...shut down."

And then he'd try harder. To no avail. "I just... couldn't, okay?"

"It's not a physical problem..."

The heat of a blush warmed her cheeks. "No."

"Then why wouldn't you share that moment with me? You knew I wanted it."

She started looking for her clothes. "You got what you wanted," she muttered.

"I got *half* of what I wanted."

Her shirt was on the floor. Where her panties had gone, she had no idea.

"Is it because of your ex?" he asked when she didn't respond.

"I don't think so," she said. She could blame Tom for a lot, but not for that. Guilt stood in her way, for stealing what she had no business taking. And bad memories— the people who'd been killed because of their association with her. She couldn't stand the fact that she was dragging Myles into the mess that was her life.

"What, then? You thought I wouldn't notice?"

She'd thought he wouldn't care. "I've got...issues. Surely that's no surprise to you." At last she found her panties, under his jeans.

He stood and watched her as she put them on, which made her more than a little self-conscious. "If you were going to hold out on me, why'd you want to make love at all? I thought a good climax or two, or maybe ten, was what you wanted."

So had she. She'd assumed she'd indulge her body and the cravings that'd become so troublesome would go away. But she hadn't realized that she wanted much more than a one-night stand, even a one-night stand with the man she'd been fantasizing about for well over a year. When she looked at Myles or touched him or kissed him…

Stop. She couldn't even *think* it. That acknowledgment would only make matters worse. "I'm fine, okay? You were fantastic. I'm sorry if I didn't moan loudly enough."

She was being flippant, hadn't really meant it, but it made him angry all the same. She could tell by the muscle that jumped in his cheek. "Don't patronize me," he growled. "I'm not looking for an ego boost."

She couldn't handle arguing with him. Not on top of everything else. She raised a hand. "Please, I don't want this to end badly."

"Neither do I. But I'm willing to go let that happen if it means I'll finally get some honesty."

"You want honesty?"

"That's exactly what I want!"

She held her shirt to her chest. "How about you give me some honesty first?"

"Fine." He put his hands on his hips, completely indifferent to his nudity. But he had no reason to be self-conscious. Every inch of his body was lean and well-toned. "What do you want to know?"

She hurried to finish dressing. She'd revealed too much, literally and figuratively. She should never have started this.

"Well?" he demanded.

Feeling safer once she had her clothes on, she whirled to face him. "Do you have any idea who murdered Pat?"

Rocking back, he threw up his hands. "You've got to be kidding me. The murder? That's what this is about? You thought you could trade a piece of ass for the insider scoop?"

"Quit making everything worse! I just...I need to know."

"We all need to know. But it hasn't been determined. I'm not sure we'll ever learn the answer. We're doing what we can and that's what we'll continue to do. There isn't enough to go on."

"The autopsy had to show something."

"If you call death by blunt-force trauma something. I could tell that much by looking at him."

"Have you found the can opener?"

He stepped toward her. "You heard about the can opener?"

"Yes."

"How?"

"Gertie's been talking about it."

"Damn it! That isn't information I want circulating around the community, Vivian. If I'm lucky enough to find the bastard who murdered Pat, that detail might've been helpful in putting him away, but it'll be useless if everyone knows about it."

"I understand why you'd be worried, but—"

"I don't think you do."

Curving her fingernails into her palms, Vivian drew a calming breath and lowered her voice. "I just said I did. Why are you so worked up?"

"Because I'm pissed off! And I'm not even sure I can tell you why."

She handed him his boxers. "If it's about the case, there's no reason to take it out on me."

"It's not the case. At least, it's not *only* the case."

"You're saying it's me."

"Yes! You gave me everything I could ask for tonight. And yet…forget it." Unable to explain further, he thrust one leg, then the other, into his underwear.

She brought his jeans next. "Do you always act this way after sex?"

He didn't bother buttoning his fly. Standing there without a shirt, his hair mussed from her hands, a five-o'clock shadow covering his jaw, he was pretty damn appealing. Maybe even *more* appealing than before they'd made love. And that scared her. What had just happened here was supposed to be enough to satisfy her. It *had* to be enough.

"Don't you understand?" he said. "Trying to reach you is like…grasping at smoke!"

She winced. He was right. She couldn't help it, couldn't change that without leaving him open to more pain and loss than he'd already experienced.

When he seemed to realize his words had stung her, he scrubbed a hand over his face and sighed. "I'm sorry. I know you've…you've been through something terrible. That you've been hurt. Is it too much to ask to get to know you? What do I have to do?"

A lump grew in her throat. This was a disaster, the worst thing she could've done. Instead of feeling better, liberated, free from all that pent-up longing and desire, she felt as if she'd rolled around on broken glass and was bleeding from little cuts all over her body.

She turned so he couldn't read the conflict in her eyes. "Just keep your promise."

"My promise?"

"Find someone else for your next encounter." Tears blurred her vision. She did her best to hide them while she put on her shoes. But he wouldn't let her withdraw that easily. He took her arm and pulled her closer.

"I don't understand you," he whispered.

She couldn't explain. Neither could she stop the tears from rolling down her cheeks. She wanted to bury her face in his chest, beg him to hold her until she felt strong enough to face the world again. She didn't need sex. She didn't need anything except a shoulder to cry on. But she couldn't even ask for that.

He used his thumbs to wipe her tears. "You think it was your ex-husband, don't you."

Stepping back, she pressed her palms to her eyes. "What are you talking about?"

"For some weird reason, you think he's here and he killed Pat. That's all I can figure. You've been acting so strange since the murder."

He was getting too close to the truth. "I don't think it's my ex."

"Then why do you need a gun?"

His mention of her gun reminded her that it was still on the table. Reclaiming it, she shoved it into the waistband of her jeans again. "Because there's a killer on the loose."

"But why would he be more interested in you than anyone else?"

"For all I know, he's not."

"Then it wouldn't be that big a deal if I confiscated your weapon."

"Sorry. You had your chance earlier."

His eyebrows shot up at her refusal. "If I decide to take it, you won't have any choice."

Frustrated with herself for crying, and for letting him see it, which was worse, she wiped her cheeks and threw back her shoulders. "Then you'll just have to do what you have to do."

Chuckling without humor, he shook his head. "Why does everything have to be so difficult with you?"

"It won't be difficult if you keep your distance."

He grabbed his shirt and yanked it on, but he didn't insist she hand over her gun—thank God. "Give me his name."

"Whose name?"

"Your bastard ex-husband's."

"No."

"I already have his initials. *TH,* right? That's what's on your arm. Or maybe it's *FH.* Tell me the rest. Let me check him out, see what he's done and where he's at. Maybe I can put your mind at rest."

"No one can put my mind at rest. This is over. I have to get back to my children," she said, and walked out.

No one can put my mind at rest. What did she mean by that? And why was she so damn secretive about her past?

The whole ride home, Myles wondered about those two questions. He could feel Vivian on the back of his bike, trying not to touch him, and it upset him—enough that he took the turns a little more sharply than usual just to make her cling to his waist. He hated that they'd argued, that the night hadn't brought either of them the satisfaction they craved. But he couldn't say this came as a surprise. She'd warned him not to get involved with her. Hell, he'd even warned himself.

You deserve this, asshole. He knew it was true. He'd dived in with his eyes wide open. But he'd said no last night and walked the floor for hours because of it, which hadn't felt a heck of a lot better. Problem was, there didn't seem to be any way to win with this woman. He wanted someone he should leave alone.

Shit... He'd been telling the truth when he said he was angry. He *was* angry—at her because she couldn't make what they were feeling as simple as he wanted it to be, at himself for not being able to avoid getting tripped up by desire and at her ex-husband because he had to be the reason she was so afraid to trust.

Tonight had changed one thing, though. Myles was going to find out what really happened in Vivian's past. Maybe she wouldn't tell him her ex's name, but he could start with hers and backtrack from there. He wanted to find the man who'd damaged her life, to hear what that man had to say for himself. Curiosity was quickly turning into a driving compulsion to reach the truth.

When he pulled into his driveway, Vivian hopped off the bike and removed her helmet. He got the impression that she would've put it on the ground and dashed off to her house with barely a goodbye if she could get away with it. But she had to collect her children.

He removed his own helmet. "You coming in? Or do you want me to carry the kids over?"

She nibbled on her bottom lip. "If they're asleep, maybe we could leave them until morning. Would that be possible?"

This surprised him. She never let her children spend

much time at his place, used any excuse she could to drag them away. "That's fine."

"They might get you up early…."

Leaning the bike to one side, he lowered the kickstand and got off. "Won't bother me. I have to get up early, anyway."

She scanned the street, then studied his house, which was dark except for the porch light glowing over the stoop like a full moon. "I'm sure they're asleep."

"It's after midnight."

"And they'll be safe here."

They were back to her obsession with safety. "I won't let anything happen to them." He wanted to tell her he wouldn't let anything happen to her, either, but he knew she wouldn't believe him.

"If they wake up and want me—"

He lifted the garage door and put the helmets away before rolling the bike inside. "They'll be fine. I know where to find you if they need you."

With a nod, she took off the jacket he'd lent her and gave it back to him. "Okay. Thanks. Bring them over as soon as you get up, no matter what time it is. I don't want to put you out."

He wished she'd stay over, too. Maybe then they could arrive at a sense of closure about tonight. They seemed to have so much unfinished business. But even if he could talk her into it, which he doubted, he wasn't ready to sleep with another woman in the house where he'd lived with Amber Rose. That would be too strange, something he wouldn't risk with Marley home, anyway. And yet it felt odd when Vivian thanked him politely and edged away as if they hadn't made love several times.

"Hey!" he called.

She stopped at the edge of the grass. "Yes?"

"You might as well tell me, you know."

"Tell you what?"

He scratched his neck to make his words seem more casual, less like a threat. "About whatever it is that has you so scared."

"There's nothing to tell."

"You're even afraid for your kids."

"Having them stay with you tonight is for practical reasons, that's all."

"That's *not* all."

She didn't reply. She just kept walking.

"I'm going to find out," he called after her, but she didn't turn around again.

11

Now she'd done it. She'd made the sheriff so determined to learn more about her that he might actually dedicate some time and resources to it. Which was the last thing she needed...

How was she going to get him to back off?

The obvious answer would be to move out of state without a forwarding address. But that wasn't any more appealing now than it'd been before. She didn't want to live anywhere else. She had her kids in a place she loved; she had a business that was beginning to thrive—or soon would be. She *deserved* to be able to stay here, to continue building her life, didn't she?

Even if she didn't, she wasn't leaving.

That meant she had to do something about the sheriff.

Or maybe not. What if she simply avoided him for a while? There wasn't any way he could find out who she really was. He had her ex-husband's initials. So what? That wasn't enough to go on. He wasn't like The Crew, who knew Virgil and Rex so well and were familiar with her background—who'd been tracking her for four years. If Myles tried to dig up any details about her past, it would only lead to one dead end after another, because he didn't know what to look for. Besides, he had Pat's murder investigation to worry about, which was much more important than filling in the details of her past—

She froze as she reached her house. The front door stood slightly ajar.

She'd locked it; she was absolutely certain of that. Had Jake or Mia come home for a toy or a treat?

They were asleep, so she couldn't ask. And since she'd already parted company with Sheriff King, she planned to do everything she could to avoid further interaction. Hopefully, time would take care of the mistakes she'd made, allow all those confusing emotions she'd stirred up to dissipate so their relationship could return to what it had been before, what it had to remain.

Besides, if The Crew *was* waiting inside, Vivian couldn't think of a better time to confront them. At least her children weren't with her. No other innocent bystanders could be hurt. It was just her—and them. And she had a gun.

Come on, you bastards. I'm done. Let's finish this here and now.

Taking the Sig from her waistband, she removed the safety and crept silently across the porch. She imagined the sheriff hearing a series of gunshots, knew he'd come running, but by the time he showed up, whatever was going to happen could well be over. Either the men who were trying to kill her would be dead, or she would, at which point she hoped The Crew would flee without hurting anyone else.

If only her shooting skills weren't quite so rusty. Could she hit a man? Especially one who might be moving? And, if so, could she fire fast enough and absorb the recoil of each shot in time to aim and shoot again?

They did it all the time in the movies. But this wasn't

a movie. She could be confronting three or four men, maybe more. The one called Ink still appeared in her nightmares. She'd seen what he could do, what they could *all* do. They killed with no remorse.

But Ink was in prison, and he was the one who frightened her most. She wouldn't have to deal with him.

Calm down. If she could pull this off, she'd be doing Virgil and his wife and son, even the new baby, a huge favor. She'd be freeing the people she loved, including— and perhaps most of all—her own children. That made it worth the risk, didn't it? She was so tired of running, so tired of living in fear that someone she loved would be hurt.

Besides, she no longer wanted to be the person The Crew had twisted her into: *Trying to reach you is like... grasping at smoke!*

She hadn't chosen to be that way....

The door creaked as she gave it a gentle push.

Moonlight streamed across her living room floor in elongated squares. The landlord she'd just bought the house from hadn't provided blinds for the old heavy-paned windows. Not in the front rooms. And she'd never gone to the expense of getting them herself. Her neighbors weren't close enough to be able to see in, and thanks to the bears there weren't many people walking around the lake after dark. With all her family's other needs, blinds hadn't seemed like a high priority, not when she did the majority of her work in the basement once the kids went to sleep. That was where she had her workroom.

The rattle of her own breathing spooked her. Holding her breath, she slipped through the door, then paused to listen. If there were people in her house, they weren't ransacking the dressers and cupboards. She couldn't hear a sound....

Maybe The Crew had come and gone. Or maybe they hadn't come at all, and she was worked up over nothing.

She was just beginning to chide herself for being paranoid, when she spotted two footprints on the hardwood floor framed by one of those ethereal-looking squares. Someone *had* come in, and it wasn't her children. Those footprints were too large. They had to belong to a man. And they were fresh. As meticulous as she was about keeping this wood floor polished, she would've noticed them earlier.

A hard lump formed in the pit of her stomach. Was her intruder alone?

Fortunately, she saw only one set of prints. But that wasn't conclusive. Maybe his companions wore different kinds of shoes, ones with soles that didn't pick up enough dust to stick to the polish.

A bead of sweat rolled from her hairline. This was it, all right. She'd soon come face-to-face with the end, one way or another.

Praying she'd survive, she swallowed hard and forced her legs to carry her forward. The adrenaline that was supposed to come in so handy during a fight was actually sapping her strength, making her light-headed. With her heart chugging a mile a minute, and her body slick with sweat, she couldn't even hold the gun steady.

But she so badly wanted this to be over that she didn't give up and turn around. Eyes as wide as possible, so she could take in every bit of light, she made herself move farther inside. She studied the darker recesses, searching for any indication of where her visitor had gone.

The footsteps led to the kitchen. At least, they seemed to. Was someone waiting for her?

Swinging doors, which she'd almost removed a million times because she thought they were so ugly, kept her from being able to see what lay beyond. But she was more familiar with the layout of the house than anyone else. That gave her an advantage.

She did what she could to steel herself for the worst, then quietly pushed through.

The kitchen was darker, and she blinked several times so her eyes could adjust. Then she saw it. A shadow. Outside. Moving fast.

Hoping to catch a glimpse, she rushed to the windows only to realize it was Marley's cat, who made himself at home in both yards. But just as she sagged in relief, she heard a creak.

Chills rippled down her spine as she whirled, ready to defend herself, but she didn't get off a single shot before a pair of strong hands wrenched the gun from her grasp.

A child's voice interrupted Myles's sleep. Positive that he'd only gotten to bed a few minutes ago, he didn't want to open his eyes, but when he did he saw a change in the color of night that indicated it'd been hours. He also saw a little boy's face a few inches above his own.

"You awake yet, Sheriff King?"

He was now, not that he was very happy about it. "What time is it?" he croaked.

"Morning time."

Looking for something a bit more specific, he rolled over to check his alarm clock, which confirmed his initial suspicion. It was barely five. Damn, when he'd told

Vivian he wouldn't mind if her children woke him early, he hadn't been referring to predawn hours.

"Jake, buddy, I'm *really* tired." He cleared his throat in an effort to speak in his normal voice. "You need to go back to bed, okay?"

No response.

"Okay?" Myles prodded.

The boy slouched onto the edge of the bed. "I can't."

"Why not?"

"I'm afraid it'll be too late."

He sounded so dejected that Myles had to ask, "Too late for what?"

"For the fish! They'll go bad, won't they?"

"What fish?" he asked. Then the memory of Vivian's son asking him to gut some trout right before he took Vivian out last night helped him make sense of the boy's words. He'd put Jake off, said he'd do it first thing in the morning. But he'd never dreamed he'd have to fulfill that promise before the crack of dawn.

"You think another hour's going to make a difference?" he mumbled, burying his head beneath his pillow.

"I'm afraid it's already too late. Aren't you supposed to gut them *right away?*"

The answer to that question was yes. They would be inedible if it didn't happen soon. And it was the boy's first catch. Myles didn't want to ruin that for him. He also felt a little guilty for procrastinating just because he'd hoped to get lucky with the kid's mother and didn't want to smell like fish guts. "That's true. How many are there?"

"Three," he said proudly.

"Not bad." Myles pulled his head out from under the pillow. "And you put them...where, exactly?"

"In Nana's cooler."

"Which is…"

"On your back porch."

Of course. He was all prepared. Myles had to drag his tired ass out of bed. He planned to, but when he didn't move quickly enough, Jake leaned closer. "I'll give you one if you help me. You could have it for dinner."

That was just too damn cute. Myles couldn't hold out any longer, no matter how reluctant he was to start his day after another short night. "Fine." He motioned to the jeans he'd tossed over a chair. "Hand me my pants."

Jake hurried to do as he asked. "How tall are you?" he asked as Myles climbed out of bed.

"Six-two." He accepted his pants. "You?"

"Dunno," he replied with a shrug.

"We can measure you when we go downstairs, if you want."

The boy's gaze slid around the room, over Myles's gun, the uniform hanging from the open closet door, the electric razor Myles had left on the dresser, some outdoor magazines that passed the time when Myles got bored with the big-screen TV. Even the wallet and change on the nightstand seemed to interest him.

"I like your bedroom," he said when he'd surveyed it all.

"You do?" Myles was tempted to laugh but didn't want to embarrass the kid. He hadn't really looked at his surroundings since he'd boxed up Amber Rose's things and carried it all to the attic. She used to take great pride in their home, decorated every room, but he only cared about functional, not beauty. Especially now that she was gone. She'd taken the joy she'd brought to such activities with her. "What does your room look like?"

"It's got some stupid football stuff painted on the walls."

Myles felt his eyebrows go up. "Football's cool, isn't it?"

"Oh, yeah. I love it. Every guy likes football, right?"

Guy? Myles stifled another laugh. Vivian's son was something else.

"It's just that it has bears with helmets, stuff like that," he explained. "It's for babies."

And he definitely didn't view himself as a baby. "I see. Maybe your mother will let you paint over it. Have you asked her?" He reached for a clean T-shirt. "I could help."

"Really?"

"Sure."

He seemed hopeful for a few seconds, then his shoulders slumped. "I don't think she'll let us. She always tells me not to bother you. She says you're too busy. Even if you tell her you're not, I don't know if she'll believe you. And she says paint costs money."

Sidestepping Vivian's reluctance to include him, he tackled the money issue instead. "It can get expensive with all the rollers and stuff."

"Yeah, it's just…I hate those bears." He edged closer to the dresser. "But I probably wouldn't care about them if I had a TV like this."

The kid was nine going on nineteen; he wanted to be a grown man more than any boy Myles had ever known. What was his hurry? Was it that he felt he had to take his father's place? "Maybe you'll be able to get one when you're older," he said, digging his shoes out from under the bed.

"How tall do you think I'll be when I'm all grown up?"

"Hard to guess." Myles sat down so he could tie his laces. "Are you big for your age?"

"Not really." He seemed disappointed.

"Well, everyone grows at a different rate. And you don't have to be big to be tough."

"Football players are big."

"Fishermen don't have to be."

He seemed to consider this. "I guess that's true. Hunters don't have to be big, either."

"No. Anyway, you should be plenty tall. Your mother's got some height."

"So does my uncle Virgil. He's huge!"

Myles froze while picking up the Swiss Army knife he'd left on the nightstand. "Virgil? Is that your mother's brother or your father's brother?"

"My mother's." He pointed at what Myles was holding. "Is that a *knife?*"

"With a few tools attached. Want to see it?"

"Sure!"

Hoping it would preoccupy the boy enough that he could learn a bit more about this Virgil person, Myles handed it over. "So where does your uncle live?"

"My mom hasn't told me." He held up some needle-nose pliers. "What do these do?"

Myles showed him how they worked. "How long has it been since you've seen him?"

"Uncle Virgil?"

"Yeah."

Jake hesitated. "A long time."

"You don't have any contact with him?"

"No."

"Look, here's a little screwdriver." Myles pulled that out to show him.

"Cool!"

"What about your father?"

Enthralled with the small pair of scissors he'd discovered, Jake didn't seem to be listening. "Can I have one of these someday?"

"We can certainly suggest it to your mother. Or maybe your father. Do you ever see him?"

Instantly wary, Jake looked up and Myles tried to mask his eagerness to hear the answer. He had to act as if this discussion was no big deal, as if he was just passing the time, or the boy would clam up. "No. He never gives me anything. He doesn't even call."

The heartbreak in those words hit Myles like a right hook, made him realize how much Vivian had been coping with. "Where does he live?"

"Don't know, or I'd go see him." He kept opening various tools on the knife.

"How long has it been?"

"Since before I saw Uncle Virgil."

Myles helped Jake close a serrated blade. "Why's that?"

He returned the Swiss Army knife. "I guess he doesn't love me anymore."

His response showed how badly he missed his father, which was sad. Had Vivian's ex been as abusive with the children as he'd been with her? If not, why weren't they allowed to see him? Was she *that* scared of him?

From all indications, she was. But what was that business about someone being shot that he'd heard from Chrissy? "Are you named after your father, Jake?"

He scuffed one sneaker against the other. "Sort of."

"How can you be 'sort of' named after someone?"

"My dad's name is Jacob. But everyone calls him Tom," he said without lifting his head.

This was the first time the boy had shared the smallest detail about his father. Myles had tossed out a few questions in the past, but they'd met with monosyllabic answers, or shrugs where monosyllabic answers weren't possible. "So your dad's name was Jacob Thomas Stewart?"

Jake glanced at the door. "You ready?"

The question had made him uncomfortable; Myles had pushed too hard. "I just need to brush my teeth."

"Okay." He headed toward the hall. "I'll wait on the porch."

Myles muttered a silent curse as he watched the boy go. He'd been so close to a full name. It couldn't be Stewart. Vivian wouldn't be able to hide very easily if she'd kept her ex-husband's name. And Stewart didn't match the initials on her arm. Myles had merely been hoping Jake would correct him.

At least he knew more than he did before. Vivian had an uncle who was in prison, an ex named Jacob Thomas or Tom H, and a brother named Virgil—not a very common name. She also had a gun that might have a serial number he could trace. And since he'd caught her carrying a concealed weapon without a permit, he had the legal right to do it.

It wasn't a lot, but it was a start.

Besides all that, thanks to the ungodly hour, he'd have a bit more time with Jake. Who knew what the kid might say? Especially with a few more carefully constructed questions…

12

When Vivian opened her eyes, she wasn't staring at her bedroom ceiling, as usual. She was looking up at the high plaster ceiling of her living room. Why? She never slept anywhere except her bedroom. Not unless she dozed off at her design table downstairs. That happened occasionally during her busiest season. She wasn't quite as far along as she wanted to be. There was a lot to do, but she had a few weeks before she had to finish her designs for next spring. They didn't go to the wholesalers until September.

Then the reason everything was so different came to her—Rex. He'd been in her house, waiting for her last night.

She rolled off the couch and landed hard on the floor before she woke up enough to move with any coordination. But the thump brought no reaction from anyone else and that made her frantic. Where was he? She hadn't dreamed that he'd shown up, had she?

After the stomach-churning worry of the past few days, she thought maybe her mind had been playing tricks on her. Maybe it'd fooled her into believing he was okay, that they were all safe for the time being, so she could get some rest....

Only when she spotted the blanket she'd given him, cast aside near the easy chair he'd sat on while they talked, did she know it'd been real.

"Rex?" she called.

No answer. Surely he hadn't left without saying goodbye.

"Pretty Boy?" She switched to the nickname he'd had while he belonged to The Crew. That was how she preferred to remember him because it hailed back to the good feelings they'd had for each other before everything fell apart. Besides, his nickname fit him well. He didn't look anything like the other members of the gang, most of whom prided themselves on their tattoos and over-muscled physiques, even their scars. Rex was on the tall side—and thanks to a metabolism that ran like a turbine engine, he was lean and lithe. He had trouble keeping weight on even when he wasn't using drugs. He had no tattoos or injuries that hadn't healed perfectly, despite all the fighting he'd been involved in over the years. But he had other scars, on the inside. And they were deep, so deep Vivian didn't think he'd ever be completely whole, which was why she couldn't be part of his life.

The muted sound of someone speaking elsewhere in the house reached her ears. He was here, all right. On the phone. Probably talking to Virgil. Although her brother hadn't picked up, they'd tried to call him last night.

Following Rex's voice, she located him in her basement. He'd left the living room so he wouldn't wake her. But she needed to get up. They had some decisions to make before her children came home.

"What's going on?" she asked.

His green eyes shifted toward her. Those eyes could be so vulnerable, so innocent despite all he'd been and done.

But they were simply matter-of-fact now. "I'm sure.... Yeah, your sister's here.... I'll tell her.... Got it.... Right. Bye."

"My brother didn't want to talk to me?" She sat in her work chair but swiveled to face him.

"He said he'd catch you later. He's got stuff to do."

"Like..."

"Researching what's happening inside The Crew." Slouching on the small secondhand couch she'd placed in the corner, along with some toys and a TV for when her children joined her down here, he rubbed his bloodshot eyes. Had he slept at all last night? Didn't look like it. Didn't look like he'd slept in days. But he'd always lived on the edge, as if he could outdistance the ghosts that chased him merely by running his ass ragged. Vivian felt certain that the past few years would've killed a lesser man. She was afraid his choices would take him yet. The past week hadn't been easy on him; she could see it in his rawboned, hollow-eyed face.

"You're using again," she said.

He regarded her from beneath half-lowered lids but didn't respond.

"You have to stop. You know that. You have to pull your shit together, or...or you're going to die, Rex. You'll get in a shoot-out in some bar, or screw the wrong man's woman, or go back to prison. Or overdose." Her voice went low on those last two words because an overdose was what she feared most. She guessed there were times when he considered death a better alternative to living. That had to be the case, or he wouldn't have spent so much of the past few years trying to destroy himself.

"I'm not using. But that's beside the point." Lying

back, he slung an arm over his face. "You lost the right to bitch at me when you blew up our relationship."

If it wasn't drugs, it had to be alcohol. He claimed they hadn't been able to reach him since he left for L.A. because he'd lost his phone charger, but if he'd been sober, he would've remedied that problem. "*I* blew up our relationship?"

"That's right."

"You broke up with me just as many times as I broke up with you."

"But you knew I loved you."

"I loved you, too. You—" Biting back the rest, she counted to ten before continuing. "I don't want to argue about who's to blame for what anymore. You have to come to terms with what happened to Jack or you'll never have any peace." Vivian couldn't believe she'd just said that. Jack was such a taboo subject. His ghost had stood between them all along, because it stood between Rex and happiness. But maybe the time had come to speak the truth, no matter how painful.

He raised his arm so he could see her, his eyes taking on that glittery look she'd seen only when he was at his angriest. "Don't start on Jack."

"Pretty Boy, look—"

"Don't call me that," he said with a grimace.

He couldn't identify with his old gang persona, or his new legitimate persona, either. He was lost in between, which was almost worse than being in prison. At least then he'd had some structure in his life.

She took a deep breath. "Fine. Rex. But *someone* has to get through to you. Your little brother—what…what happened to him—is at the root of all your problems."

"Stop with the psychoanalysis. Prison's enough to screw up anyone's life."

Virgil had gone to prison, too, but he'd been able to recover. Pretty Boy could've made good, if not for what was eating him up inside. He had a brother who was a doctor, another who was a chemical engineer. It wasn't as if he came from a poor or underprivileged home. He would've ended up with an education and a good job if not for that one afternoon at the river, cliff diving with his youngest brother. "You didn't mean for him to get hurt."

"I challenged him!" The veins in his neck stood out as he shouted. "I told him I'd made that jump."

She refused to allow her voice to rise with his. "You were just a kid."

"So was he! Barely twelve years old. I knew he thought I could walk on water, that he'd believe me. I just..." Tears filled his eyes as he fell back. "I never dreamed he'd do it, and I never dreamed it would really hurt him even if he did."

"Exactly. It was one of those freak accidents that happen sometimes. You screwed up, but you didn't mean for him to die. Had he landed differently, he would've been fine. You have to let it go. You're out of prison now, yet you're throwing away any chance you have."

Except for the anguish reflected in his eyes, he seemed to grapple with his emotions, finally gaining control. "Give it a rest, will you?"

She didn't want to give it a rest. She wanted to rant and rave and stomp her feet just to relieve the tension. "I'm worried about you!"

"After what I told you last night, you should be worried about yourself."

She hadn't forgotten. He'd come to Montana because he'd heard she was in danger. He claimed he'd run into an old friend at a party in L.A., someone loosely affiliated with The Crew, who'd confided that Horse had been bragging to everyone who'd listen that he was about to get even with Virgil and his sister.

But Rex couldn't tell her any more than that. And she suspected at least part of the reason he'd come was that he was hoping for some peace where she was concerned. Hadn't she been hoping for the same thing?

"So…are you going to start packing?" he asked.

Did he expect a different answer than the one she'd given him last night? "No."

"You're joking, right?" He sat up. "I came all this way to warn you, to convince you, to help you get out of here before it's too late."

"You haven't told anyone where I live—"

"You think I'd do that?"

She felt bad for offending him, but he had a substance-abuse problem that made him suspect. She still couldn't imagine how The Crew could've traced her here without him. "They'd have no other way of finding me."

A dark scowl etched lines in his face as he got to his feet. "How can you say that?"

After everything he'd done for her, she felt guilty enough to avert her eyes. "Or maybe Horse was drunk when he said he was poised for revenge. Maybe it was idle bullshit."

"Horse doesn't drink. He's a serious man, a businessman. He's methodical and thorough."

"That doesn't change my mind," she insisted. "I won't leave here, won't let them chase me from place to place for the rest of my life. Don't you understand? That would mean they've won. We want to stay put."

He studied her for several seconds. "You've met someone."

Her thoughts reverted to the sheriff, to his naked body moving against hers, and she felt…she wasn't sure what she felt. Embarrassment? Remorse? "That's not it. I want a life. And this is where I've chosen to live it."

"What am I supposed to do with that?"

"Whatever you want. You've warned me. You don't have to stay. But I know the kids would like to see you. Now that you're here, you can hang around for a day or two, can't you?"

"You want to treat this like a standard visit?"

"Why not?"

"Because you're in danger, damn it! You're all in danger!"

"I've got a gun, Pretty—Rex," she corrected. "And I'm not afraid to use it."

"You mean the gun I took away from you last night?"

"You snuck up on me from behind!"

"Because I didn't want you to blow my head off! But if you think they'll announce their presence, you're crazy. They'll come here with two, three, maybe more. Be realistic, for Christ's sake!"

She covered her face for a moment before dropping her hands. "I'm telling you, I can't move. I can't do it again. This is the end of the line for me, one way or another."

With a curse, he shoved his hands in his pockets and began to pace.

"So what are you going to do?" she asked after he'd made a few passes.

"Stay and try to take care of you, I guess."

"They could've followed you."

His razor stubble made a rasping sound as he rubbed his jaw. "They didn't have to. They already know you're here."

The beating of Vivian's heart thudded in her ears. He thought she was making a mistake. Was he right? Would she die in this house?

Jake, calling to her from upstairs, interrupted.

"M-o-o-o-m? Mom, where are you? I have something to show you!"

"Think of them," Rex whispered.

She thought of how much Jake loved it here, how close he'd become to Nana Vera. And Mia, so happy in her ballet class and elementary school, despite Chrissy's catty little girl. This was home to them. It was home to them all. And home was a place worth fighting for.

"That's what I'm doing," she said.

There was a woman in the kitchen. Ink could see her through the window. When the tow truck driver couldn't tell them where Laurel lived, said he didn't know her, they'd had to decide what they were going to do until they could find her. And first on the agenda was securing a base. They needed regular beds, food, a shower. Hell, even a toilet seemed like a luxury after the past several days. He knew they might have to resort to camping again at some point. If they didn't collect the truck, and they couldn't, the sheriff would know he had a problem, and he'd most likely start looking for them. But Ink couldn't imagine his first thought would be to check all the cabins scattered in these mountains. There were too many of them, most of them rentals. Unless he got a distress call of some kind, he'd probably assume they'd hitchhiked into town, Libby if not Pineview, or left the area.

"You think she's alone?" L.J. whispered.

They'd been watching the woman for more than thirty minutes, had cased the house and yard. This seemed like the perfect solution, just what they'd been searching for. It was within a few miles of where the truck had broken down, so they'd been able to walk here. It was remote, but not so far from Pineview that they'd have much of a drive to get to town when they wanted.

There were other attractive features, as well. The extra refrigerator in the garage suggested the place was well-stocked. An SUV sat in the driveway, so they'd have the transportation they were currently lacking. And it looked comfortable. Since they couldn't pay for a motel room, couldn't show any ID even if they'd had the money, Ink was going to get what they needed another way. "I'd say so."

The grass rustled as L.J. crept a little closer. "But you never know. Someone could come home at any minute."

"Then we'll kill them, too."

L.J. grimaced and shook his head. "I say we move on. This doesn't feel right to me, and it must not feel right to you or we'd be inside that house already."

In typical L.J. fashion, he couldn't stay put for long. "Don't give up too soon. This place has promise." Why walk any farther? His back hurt like hell. Besides, the other cabins they'd come across were empty, which meant there'd be very few groceries, if any, and definitely no car. If they weren't empty, they were filled with the suitcases and backpacks of outdoorsmen. The last thing he and L.J. needed was to break into some place that would have five or six men returning to it at nightfall—most toting a gun or a knife.

"There'll be others," L.J. muttered. But it didn't hurt him to keep walking.

Ink tried to ignore him, but snapped, "Chill out," when L.J. tugged on his sleeve.

"There're toys in the yard, man." *Now* they were getting to the real reason behind his reluctance. "That's obviously a mom."

"So? We knew it was a family when we saw that wooden plaque over the doorway." The Rogers Family. What had L.J. thought when he saw that? Or had he thought at all?

"Kids live here. I don't want to do no kids, man. You know what happens to guys who do kids once they hit prison. We'll be in the hat for sure."

Ink wasn't going back to prison. He'd put a bullet in his own brain first. So what did he care about any kids? They were nothing to him. Less than nothing. It was the parents he was thinking about. Adults could be so unpredictable, especially when they were trying to protect their children. "I just want to be sure her husband's not home. Our only other choice is to take on a bunch of hunters, and I promise this middle-aged bitch will be easier. You don't want to get shot, do you?"

"No, but I don't want to get caught, either." L.J.'s scowl darkened as he stared across the clearing. "If this woman has a husband, we're going to have to kill him, too. We'll have to do it now if he's home. Later if he's not. And if either one of 'em goes missing, someone's bound to come looking. That'll lead the sheriff right to us. And that's not smart, not if we plan on sticking around for a while."

They were sticking around, all right. Ink wasn't going

anywhere until he found Laurel Hodges or whatever she called herself these days. But he hated to pass up an opportunity for immediate gratification. "This woman's home alone." He couldn't get beyond that.

"For now!"

L.J. had a point. Part or all of a local family would be missed far sooner than a group of hunters who were visiting from out of state and weren't expected home for a week or two. And hunters would be just as likely to have a vehicle and groceries. If they didn't have enough food, a little shoplifting could fill in the gaps. Ink had already stolen a couple hundred bucks' worth of snacks from the gas stations they'd visited since they escaped the California Men's Colony, not to mention all that fishing and camping stuff. They'd even held up a liquor store in New Mexico and walked away with two hundred and eighty-four dollars in cash.

"What about that last cabin we came across?" Ink asked.

"What are you talking about?" L.J. was no longer following the conversation. A girl had come out onto the deck, proving that the woman inside wasn't as alone as they'd thought. Her daughter was home, too. And what a daughter she was. With long dark hair, porn-star boobs and a tiny waist, she was curvy and cute, and she was wearing a skimpy bikini while talking on a cordless phone.

Just seeing her up close, within reach, made Ink crave much more than food. He was so sex-starved he could smell her from behind the screen of trees, and he could tell L.J. was equally affected. He was standing there like a statue, no longer trying to drag Ink away.

"Maybe I spoke too soon," L.J. murmured. "I vote we get a piece of that before we do anything else."

Ink wanted her, too. He'd never seen tits that could compare to those. His injury meant he couldn't get an erection anymore, but that hadn't diminished his desire. He'd find some way to satisfy the craving, even if it was only by watching L.J. ride her. The sight of her made him feel young and strong again, more like himself than he'd felt in a long, long time.

But he had to think this through, figure it out. Could they drag her into the woods without her mother hearing? And if they succeeded, then what?

"I don't know..." he said.

"What do you mean you don't know?" L.J.'s voice was tight with desire. "We could take turns. Maybe keep her for a while."

"And then what?"

"Let her go when we get outta here."

"No. We can't. You're not thinking straight."

L.J. whirled on him. "What? You gotta throw me a bone. I helped you bust out. You wouldn't be here without me."

Ink didn't like acknowledging that, so he didn't. "But if we rape her, we'll have to kill her. Otherwise, she'll be able to testify against us."

"Maybe not. Maybe—"

"No maybes. Leaving her alive would be stupid. And, like you said, these people are people who'll be missed. If she disappears, the sheriff will come knocking on every door up here. Hell, the whole damn community will start combing the area."

L.J. didn't respond. His attention had swung back to the girl with the razorlike focus of a mountain lion who'd spotted his first meal after a long famine. A moment before, he'd been so reluctant to harm this family. But the sight of Betty Big Boobs had thrown some sort of switch in his brain, given him fresh incentive to take what he wanted, and nothing else seemed to matter anymore. Not even the kids. That concerned Ink. If L.J. raped this girl, there'd be consequences. They'd have no choice but to run. And he hadn't found Laurel.

Ink nudged him. "You listening to me?"

"We don't have to kill her if we cover her head." He groaned as she bent over to arrange a towel on the chaise. "Her other end is all I care about. Look at that tight, sweet ass."

There was too much testosterone flooding through him. Ink sensed that he was losing control of his companion. "You think she's just going to spread her legs and let you have your fun? That she won't report what happened? Rape will bring the sheriff out here as fast as murder. We gotta let her be."

"It won't be rape. She wants it. I can tell. Look at the way she's teasing us. I bet she knows we're here. And it won't take long. It'll work out, you'll see."

This was crazy. Pulling the gun from his waistband, Ink pressed the tip of the barrel to the younger man's head. "You'd better talk yourself down, little brother."

"What the hell?" L.J. jerked away.

At his raised voice, the girl looked up, but if she'd heard him she was too engrossed in her telephone conversation to investigate. If Ink had his guess, she'd never had to fear anything in her life, didn't know she had reason to be scared now.

"I said we're going to leave her alone!" Ink whispered.

A sulky expression claimed L.J.'s face. "And do what instead?"

"Head back to the last cabin we passed."

"But we counted the bags in that place! There are three or four guys staying there."

"Yeah, well, with any luck, some of 'em won't be guys, right?"

L.J.'s hand covered his heart, as if what he felt was more than lust. "If there's a woman in the bunch, there's no way she's going to look like *that!*"

"Sometimes you have to take what you can get."

"When you're old and lame, maybe," he muttered, and Ink nearly hit him with the gun. He would have, if he didn't have to worry about noise.

"I'm going to forget you said that. For now."

The threat in those last two words finally seemed to give him some leverage. "Oh, come on," L.J. said. "It was a joke. You can take a joke, can't you? I'm not going to take any risks."

"You better not."

"I won't! But I don't know if breaking into that other cabin is any smarter. It's bad odds. Two against four. Or worse."

"We'll have the element of surprise on our side. No one gets back after a long day of hunting expecting an ambush."

13

A motorcycle sat parked against the side of Vivian's house. Myles spotted it as soon as he started over with Jake and Mia. While the kids ran in to talk to their mother, he stood outside wondering where the hell that bike had come from. It'd obviously seen a lot of miles. And it was far too big for a woman....

Before long, Jake appeared at the door to the little antechamber that led to Vivian's kitchen. "Hey, you coming?"

"Looks like you have company." Myles motioned to the bike.

He grinned. "My uncle Rex. You gotta meet him."

Myles had heard about an uncle Virgil. Just this morning. Now there was an uncle *Rex?* Vivian had more family than he'd thought. Yet she'd gone two years without an out-of-town visitor. Why hadn't either of these brothers come to see her?

"Sheriff King?" Jake prodded when he didn't move.

Despite his curiosity regarding Vivian's family and her past, Myles felt oddly reluctant to go inside. But he climbed the stairs and followed her son into the kitchen, and there he saw a wiry man about his own height and age sporting a little too much razor stubble to be making a fashion statement. Dressed in a torn T-shirt with the sleeves cut out, some holey jeans and unlaced boots, he was leaning up against the counter and laughing with Mia, who was hugging his leg. When he saw Myles, his eyes narrowed. And that was when Myles knew—this was no family relation.

Vivian had said she'd only slept with two men in her life—her ex-husband and a steady boyfriend. This wasn't the ex; that was plain. Myles didn't want to believe it was the boyfriend, either. Not after last night. But the way Vivian refused to meet his eyes suggested otherwise.

Trying to squelch the jealousy that sprang up, Myles forced a congenial smile as Jake ushered him across the room.

"Uncle Rex, this is Sheriff King."

Determined to be polite, Myles extended his hand. "Nice to meet you."

Rex glanced at Vivian before responding with a half-hearted shake. "Same here."

"The sheriff helped me gut my fish," Jake announced as if Myles had just done something incredible.

Rex considered Vivian's son. "The law helps with that sort of thing these days, does it?"

"The *law?*" Mia wrinkled her nose in confusion.

Jake tried to explain that a sheriff was "the law." He caught on to a lot more than most nine-year-olds. But no one else bothered to clarify. From what Myles could see, Vivian was too uncomfortable having him and Rex in the same room to allow herself to be distracted—another indication that Uncle Rex held special, and most likely romantic, significance in her life.

"Least I could do, for a neighbor," Myles replied with a shrug.

Rex poured himself some coffee. "Nice of you to take the time. Especially since I hear you're in the middle of a big murder case."

The underlying accusation—that he should be at work—caused Myles to bristle. Vivian reacted, too, by attempting to defend him.

"He has his investigators on it," she said, but Myles kept his focus on Rex.

"You know what they say. You want something done, give it to a busy person."

"They say that, do they?" Rex blew off some of the steam rising from his coffee before risking a sip.

Myles let his gaze range over the other man, all the way down to his untied boots. He didn't care who this guy was. He wasn't intimidated by him and he wanted "Uncle Rex" to know it. "Maybe only among the working segment of the population."

Rex surprised him with an outright laugh. "That so? Guess I know how I missed it, then."

"What do you do?" Myles asked.

Lifting his cup in a taunting salute, he sobered but a faint smile remained. "Whatever I want, Sheriff."

"I figure whatever you've been doing must've been important. Otherwise, I'm sure you would've shown up long before now, given the fact that Vivian could use a hand around here."

That mocking smile finally disappeared. "You know, I'm not particularly fond of anyone who wears a uniform. You might've noticed."

"Oh, yes, I've noticed. And I'm guessing it comes from past experience." He turned to go, but Jake grabbed his hand.

"Wait! You're leaving?"

"I've got to get to work, buddy."

"But you're coming to dinner tonight? So we can cook the fish? You said you would."

One glance at the stone-faced Rex and embarrassed Vivian, and Myles decided he should've listened to his better judgment yesterday. Whatever he'd felt when he was with Vivian last night…he must've been confused or looking for an escape from the tedium that'd become his life. Vivian was beautiful; there was no question about that. And there was something about her that stirred him on a very deep level. But he wasn't about to get involved in some kind of love triangle. If Vivian wanted this guy, who was obviously *not* a productive member of society, she could have him.

"Actually, I'm afraid I'll have to pass. I've got a busy day ahead of me and I'll probably have to work late." He mussed Jake's hair, hoping a bit of affection would soften any disappointment. "But I'm sure Uncle Rex will be happy to help out."

It was small consolation that Jake didn't seem enthusiastic about the substitution. "I don't think he cooks," he said with a frown. "He doesn't even eat much."

Myles wanted to say that drug addicts rarely do but bit his tongue.

"Anyone can fry a fish," Rex muttered, and Myles accepted that as the end of it.

Without acknowledging Vivian, he offered Jake and Mia a quick goodbye and left. Then he sat in his car for several seconds before starting it, wondering why he felt sick.

Vivian cradled her head in her hands. "That went well," she groaned.

Rex continued to nurse his coffee. "What is he to you?"

Jake dragged his precious cooler to the fridge. "I told you, he's our neighbor."

"Friendly guy."

Vivian couldn't resist the urge to defend Myles. "*You* started it."

"So? I didn't like the look of him." Rex watched her with heavy-lidded eyes. He was sexy—she had to give him that, even when she was angry with him. The pretty face that'd earned him his nickname was so appealing, so arresting. It didn't matter that he was haggard and spent after doing God knows what to himself for the past few weeks, months, years. He was as much a danger to her peace and well-being as The Crew. She couldn't love someone who was so broken. She was too broken herself.

"It was the *look* of him that made you so unfriendly?"

"Maybe it was the way he looked at you."

Distracted from his catch, Jake's attention shifted between them as if he was watching a Ping-Pong match. No doubt he could feel the undercurrent, and Vivian didn't want that. She lifted one hand. "Let's just…let it go."

Rex opened his mouth to argue, seemed to realize he had no right, and finished his coffee instead. But she could tell he understood that Myles was a bit more than the average neighbor. And he wasn't happy about it. She wasn't sure how she felt about the situation, either. Especially because, when she was with Rex, the comfort of the familiar engulfed her, made her want to slide down the mountain she'd climbed, right into his open arms.

Hoping to dispel the sudden gloom that hung over her, Vivian stood and tried to infuse her voice with some enthusiasm. "Who wants pancakes for breakfast?"

"The sheriff already made us pancakes." Jake moved

his fish into the fridge before taking his cooler outside to empty out the water and ice.

During his absence, Mia twirled around in the middle of the floor. "He made my pancake look like Mickey Mouse."

"He's a regular father figure," Rex drawled.

The phone rang, giving Vivian an excuse not to respond. But once she picked up, she wasn't sure this conversation was going to be any easier than the confrontation she'd avoided. It was Virgil. And he started by saying he had bad news.

"What kind of bad news?" she asked.

Hearing this, Rex came forward. She could feel him, standing directly behind her.

"Ink broke out of prison a week ago."

Vivian felt as if the floor had just dropped out from under her. Ink was the man she feared more than any other; it was his face that appeared in her nightmares and woke her in a cold sweat. "Out of Corcoran? How?"

"Out of the California Men's Colony. The details are sketchy but I was told they cut through the fence around the yard."

She blinked, battling a sudden welling of tears. "I've never heard of the California Men's Colony."

"It only goes up to level three. It's known as the country-club prison because of all the programs they've got down there."

Lowering her voice, she turned away from the children and right into Rex's chest. She thought he might put his arms around her, but he didn't. "Ink's a murderer! Why would they move him to a cushy place like that?"

"Because of his handicap. He wasn't deemed a threat. He can't get around like he used to. He came across as withdrawn, penitent, always in pain. And he didn't seem to be active in The Crew anymore. Word has it he's become a bit disenchanted with the brothers."

"That could be good news, couldn't it?" she asked. "If he's disenchanted, why would he carry out their business?"

"I'm not sure he considers us 'their' business. For him, it's personal. He hates all three of us. Rex most of all, but he'll take the easy prey first, if he can."

She closed her eyes. Since Rex hadn't returned to the society of his former friends, she'd decided she was fine. That she had no reason to fear. She'd wanted to believe it so badly. And now this. What did it mean? Was Ink using his time out of prison to enjoy all the things he'd missed?

Or was he coming after her?

Suddenly Horse's words, as shared by Rex, took on a whole new meaning. Something was up inside the gang. What was it, exactly?

"How'd you find out about Ink?" she asked her brother.

"I called Jones."

Jones was their handler, the U.S. marshal who'd helped protect them until they could get moved to Washington, D.C.

"And?"

"They would've notified us if they could. They didn't know how to find us."

"By design. But…wouldn't a prison break have been on the news?"

"It's not big enough to make the national news. From what the marshal told me, they still don't consider Ink much of a threat."

Then they didn't know him the way she did.

"Neither is the guy he busted out with," Virgil continued.

"What was he in for?"

"Dealing."

"What's going on?" Rex murmured.

Vivian raised a finger to tell him to give her a little longer.

"Is something wrong, Mommy?" Mia had stopped dancing and was looking concerned.

She covered the mouthpiece. "No, honey, it's fine. It's just…business stuff."

"The purses?"

"Yeah."

Rex gave Mia's ponytail a playful tug. "How about you show me your room? Then Jake can show me his."

"I don't wanna show you mine," Jake said. "It has these stupid bears painted on the wall."

"You have something against bears?" he teased.

"You should see 'em. They're for babies!"

"Let's take a look." Tossing Mia over one shoulder, Rex prodded Jake to lead the way.

"Hey, put me down!" Mia squealed, even though it was quite apparent that she loved being right where she was.

Their voices dimmed as they passed through the living room. After they were gone, Vivian carried the phone to the table, where she sank into a chair. "It's not easy to break out of prison. Maybe a level one, but…level three? Where were the C.O.s?"

"In the tower, where they were supposed to be. Some of The Crew created a disturbance while others blocked the closest tower's line of sight, and Ink and his cell mate slipped out in the confusion."

"What do you make of the escape?"

"It could be a coincidence that Horse has recently been talking tough, but…"

"You don't think so." Neither did she. Not anymore. All that unease she'd been denying, that was intuition, warning her that her life was about to change.

"No. No one's seen Ink. Unless it was a quick pass-through, he hasn't shown up in L.A. Rex would've heard about it if he had. Rex was just there."

Virgil didn't add that Rex was there "partying with old friends," but Vivian knew what he meant.

"He heard what Horse has been saying, right?" he went on. "Stands to reason he would've heard about Ink, too. This is bigger news."

"Ink scares me." Vivian would never forget Colorado, how he'd attempted to kill her and her children. How close he'd come to succeeding. To her, he represented everything evil and depraved.

"Rex is with you now. That makes me feel better."

She lowered her voice. "He can't stay here, Virgil."

"Why not?"

Because she didn't want to fall prey to old habits. They'd gained some distance from the heartbreak that'd taken such a toll on them both. She couldn't survive a relapse, didn't want to watch Rex suffer any more, either. "He's using again."

"He says he isn't."

"Then it's alcohol. It's…something. You should see him."

"It's only been two weeks since he was here, Laurel."

"Add two weeks of sleepless nights to that and you

might have some idea. He's lost a lot of weight during the past year, maybe thirty pounds. And he wasn't heavy to begin with."

"I know. We need to get him some counseling."

Judging by his voice, Virgil felt out of his depth—and so did she. No one could change Rex's life if he wasn't willing to fight the good fight, and she didn't get the feeling he'd make that kind of commitment.

Hearing a sudden noise, Vivian glanced up. Rex was standing in the doorway, staring at her with an inscrutable expression. He'd heard some, if not all, of what she'd said about him.

"Okay, well, Rex and I will talk about it," she said into the phone.

"Keep me posted," Virgil responded.

"Virgil." She stopped her brother before he could hang up. "They could be coming after you and Peyton instead, you know."

"I've thought of that."

"You're not worried?"

"I'm worried, but like I said, if I know Ink, he's going to want to kill you first."

Dimly, she realized how different their conversations must be from those of normal people. "Why?"

"Because his revenge won't be complete unless I know about it."

A dial tone sounded in her ear; Virgil was gone.

Although she didn't look up again, Vivian could feel the weight of Rex's gaze as she returned the phone to its base. "Where are the kids?"

"Setting up a game I promised to play if they gave me a few minutes to speak with you."

Feeling guilty that she'd even thought he might've let

her location slip, she turned to face him. "Ink busted out of prison."

He didn't seem all that surprised, and yet she didn't get the impression he'd already known. "Nice."

"But...he couldn't find us."

"Do you really believe that?"

It was what she *wanted* to believe. That they were safe. That they could continue with what they'd created since the last move. That Pat's murder was unrelated. "No."

After crossing to the opposite counter, he refilled his coffee. "There are too many ways to narrow it down."

"But I've been so careful."

"How careful?"

"*Very* careful."

He arched an eyebrow at her. "Have you reached out to *anyone* from your former life?"

She couldn't quite claim that. "You're the only one I've called from here."

"That's not what I asked."

His hand trembled as he lifted his cup. She wished she hadn't noticed it. She couldn't deal with seeing him like this, not in addition to everything else. "Okay...yes. I've called others. But—"

"What phone did you use?"

How was he still functioning? She'd never met anyone whose body could take such abuse. She'd bet he hadn't been lucid since he left New York. "A pay phone. There are several in town." She preferred to leave it at that, but her guilty conscience dragged out the detail she'd been hoping to ignore. "And...once, just once, I used the phone at the Golden Griddle."

"What?"

She repeated it, louder, and he scowled. "What's the Golden Griddle?"

"A restaurant in town. They serve breakfast."

"Shit."

"You're not going to get mad, are you? Because that would be ironic. As a matter of fact, I think that would be about as ironic as anything I've ever heard, considering what you've done to yourself since we broke up."

He gave her a look that warned her away from the subject but didn't respond to that statement. Instead, he asked, "Why that phone?"

"Because it seemed safe. My friend Leah works there. She asked me to help get her car into the shop, but when I showed up to follow her over, she wasn't quite ready. So I sat in the back while she cleaned. The kids were with a woman who's become a surrogate grandmother to them, the restaurant was closed and the phone was right there. I liked the privacy, the chance to say something that couldn't be overheard by Jake and Mia or people on the street. This is such a small town."

He blew out a sigh and leaned against the counter. "Who'd you call?"

She was embarrassed to admit this. If he'd been Virgil, she couldn't have brought herself to tell him. Because she'd called the one person she shouldn't even want to talk to—someone she often claimed she *didn't* want to talk to. "My mother."

When he didn't say anything, she added, "But if The Crew traces the call, it won't matter. It's a restaurant."

He shook his head. "Babe, a restaurant in Pineview, Montana. Population one thousand or less. If Ink comes here, you don't think he'll be able to find you?"

Of course he would. So where were all the justifications she'd used the day she'd called? "As far as he'd know, I was just passing through."

"Not if you made calls from that restaurant over a period of time."

"I didn't! I called only once."

He stared through the window, at her backyard. Maybe he was noticing Myles's yard, too, and how they adjoined each other without so much as a fence to separate them. "Actually, I'm betting even the location of the pay phones would be traceable. If you called from this area code in December and then again in…I don't know…May, that would make anyone believe you've settled down."

She'd thought of that. But she'd been so lonely, so unwilling to lose everything from her past, that she'd convinced herself the chances of The Crew finding out about those calls were too slim to worry about.

"And what did you say to your mother? What does she know?"

"Not much. Anyway, she wouldn't sell us out. Not again."

His eyes jerked back to her. "Bullshit."

"When Virgil went to prison, she was choosing between her brother, who'd been trying to help her, and her son. She feels terrible about what happened."

"As if that could make up for destroying Virgil's life! And, to a certain extent, yours." He sipped his coffee. "You've forgiven her?"

Not completely, but she was too busy playing devil's advocate to explain. "What good would it do to hold a grudge? It'd just isolate me further. People make mistakes, right?"

He lowered his voice. "And they tend to make the same ones over and over."

There was no point in arguing with that. He was the perfect example.

"So what do we do?"

"Will this grandma figure you mentioned be willing to watch Jake and Mia for a few hours?"

She rubbed her eyes. "What day is it?" She'd lost track of time.

"Friday."

"She should be. She doesn't have to work."

"Give her a call and see. Then we'll head to a neighboring town and use a pay phone to reach Ellen."

"Why do we need to go a neighboring town? The entire state has the same area code."

"In case they can trace the phone, farther would be better. Anything that extends their search parameters will help."

"And what do we say to my mother once we reach her?"

Straightening, he poured the rest of his coffee down the drain. "We ask if anyone's contacted her looking for you, and hope to hell she tells the truth."

14

Rex wasn't sure he could do this. He'd just spent two weeks in self-imposed exile from the rest of the world, lying in the empty bathtub of a cheap motel room in Los Angeles, so he'd be close to the toilet, sweating and shaking and feeling like he was going to die. He knew going off drugs with no one else around was a dangerous way to detox. He could've had a grand mal seizure or some other serious complication. But he couldn't afford a clinic, and there was no way to taper off OxyContin. Not on his own. One high only led to the next. And he didn't want to burden anyone. As far as he was concerned, he'd gotten himself into this mess; he needed to get himself out.

"You're ill. You should see a doctor." Laurel, or Vivian, as everyone else around here knew her, sat in the passenger seat. She'd been silent for the duration of the drive, all thirty minutes of it, but she'd been studying him. He could tell she'd wanted to say something almost since they left.

"I'm fine." He'd insisted on driving, but he wasn't anywhere close to fine. He'd been crazy to show his face in Pineview. He wouldn't have if he'd felt he had any other choice. Besides, by the time he made the decision to come here, he'd been starting to feel better for periods of time. He'd been able to come out of the bathroom and lie on the bed to watch TV. At that point, he'd believed the determination that'd kept him clean for ten days would enable him to soldier on.

But OxyContin still had a strong hold on him. His hands trembled, bouts of nausea threatened to bring up what little he'd forced himself to eat for breakfast and his craving for the euphoria he remembered so well overwhelmed him when he least expected it. There were moments when he felt certain he'd go mad if he didn't find a source.

He should've kept himself sequestered until he'd recovered—or at least maintained a safe distance from Laurel. Facing her and all the feelings she dredged up compounded the difficulty of what he was going through, made it even more hellish. The regret, the guilt, the longing—they all worked as triggers. They were the very emotions he'd hoped to escape by taking OxyContin in the first place.

But someone had to come to Pineview to protect her, and he knew it couldn't be Virgil. Virgil had a family now. Peyton was just about to give birth to their second child. So Virgil needed to stay in New York, run his business and take care of those he loved. Rex had already screwed up so badly, he didn't have anything left to save. Except Laurel. Whether they were together now or not, she'd been the best thing in his life to date.

"You want me to drive?" she asked for the third time.

"No." Perspiration caused his T-shirt to stick to him despite the air-conditioning blowing from the vents. He hoped she wouldn't notice. He had enough other things to worry about. Like the cramping in his stomach. It felt as if someone was tearing his organs out with an ice pick, but stopping wouldn't ease the pain. Nothing would. It was just there, and he didn't know how long it would last. Going to a hospital wouldn't help. All they could do was monitor him. And he refused to be put out of commission now, especially when there was no remedy except determination and time.

"Don't push yourself if you're not up to it."

He wanted to be able to do this much. He hated that she was seeing him at his absolute worst. But he couldn't have delayed his visit, not without leaving her at risk. As much as she didn't want to believe The Crew had found her, he trusted Mona Lindberg, the friend who'd told him otherwise, mostly because she had no reason to lie.

Laurel slid on a pair of sunglasses. Unfortunately, he couldn't hide his eyes as easily. He'd left his shades at a hamburger stand somewhere in the middle of Missouri during his cross-country motorcycle odyssey from New York to Los Angeles. It was on that odyssey that he'd made the decision to turn his life around. Foreboding had ridden with him for those first few days, telling him that if he went back to L.A. and didn't give up the OxyContin, he'd either fall in with the men he hated or others who were just as bad. If someone didn't kill him along the way... If he didn't give it up, he'd lose the only relationships that really mattered—his friendship with Virgil, Virgil's wife and Laurel.

"Can we talk about what happened in L.A.?" she asked.

She wanted details about his stay there, but he wasn't interested in providing them. The past two weeks were nothing more than a painful blur. "What do you want to know?"

"Why would you go back there? You know what they'll do if they find you."

"That isn't true for every member of The Crew. Just certain ones."

"Any of them could try and impress Horse by bringing him your head on a platter."

"I was willing to risk it." When he'd started out, he'd sort of hoped the trip *would* end that way, that he'd go out with a bang instead of wasting away on dope.

"For what? What'd you do while you were there?"

He hadn't been partying quite as much as she assumed. But he wasn't going to say that. He couldn't cope with her skepticism. This wasn't the first time he'd tried to clean himself up. "Nothing, really."

"You had to be doing *something*. You were gone for fourteen days, and you wouldn't even pick up your phone."

He clenched his jaw against another cramp, had to wait until it passed before he could answer. "I already explained that."

"You didn't explain why you couldn't use someone else's phone."

And he wasn't going to. "Let it go."

"You were that strung out?"

She had no idea what he'd been through, how hard he was trying, but he couldn't fault her for her disgust. He was just as disgusted with himself. "I guess so."

"Who were you with? You don't know anybody there except Crew."

"I grew up in L.A. Trust me, I know plenty of people." None of whom were very good for him, which was why he hadn't looked many of them up.

"So you renewed friendships from the past."

"That's right."

"If you weren't socializing with your old gang buddies, how'd you find out they know where I'm living?"

"From Mona. I told you when we talked last night."

"Shady's girlfriend."

"*Ex*-girlfriend. They broke up before he died."

"Are you sure she's not holding a grudge for *how* he died?"

"I'm sure."

"And yet she still hangs out with his buddies."

Thanks to drugs, she probably always would. "The Crew keeps her supplied."

That was why he'd tracked her down. He knew Mona would be able to replace the pills he'd thrown away or, failing that, get him some heroin. He also knew she'd be willing. So he'd contacted her sister, who was in the phone book, and her sister had put him in touch with Mona.

But he hadn't taken the drugs she brought. Seeing what her addiction had done to her was too much of a jolt. He didn't want to be like her. Instead of succumbing, he'd flushed the pills down the toilet and crawled back into the tub to suffer some more.

"But if they find out she told you, they'll kill her," Laurel said.

"I did her a favor once, okay? She felt like she owed me."

When Laurel closed the air-conditioning vent closest to her, he considered turning off the AC. It wasn't so hot that he needed to run it. But the cool air distracted him from his misery just enough that he could drive another mile and then another. Right now, that was the best he could do.

"What kind of favor did you do for her?" she asked.

"It's not important."

"I want to know."

"I gave her a ride once. That's all."

The way she watched him suggested she could tell there was more to it. "You helped her even though it put you at risk?"

It was a guess. But it was close. "Not so much. I'd already assumed the risk by being where I was when I found her. I just took an interest when she needed it, gave her a shoulder to cry on and another chance to escape, and she was grateful. You must remember some of this. I've told you before."

She didn't respond to that last part. "Did you sleep with her?"

He shot her a glance. "Why do you want to know?"

"I'm curious."

"No. Not when I helped her out, and not when she helped me out, either." Mona had been used by so many men there was no telling what diseases she carried. Besides, he'd never found her appealing. He'd just felt sorry for her because of the crappy way Shady and the others treated her.

Laurel kneaded her forehead. "But you've slept with other women since we've been together. Haven't you?"

He didn't answer. He knew she wouldn't like the truth. Maybe they weren't together anymore but certain feelings lingered.

"Wow. Where did that come from?" She gave an awkward laugh. "I'm sorry. I don't know why I asked."

He did. She'd asked because it wasn't a lack of love or attraction that'd driven them apart, and that made it difficult not to fall back into bed. Not until the morning after, or maybe several mornings after, did they figure out they couldn't get along. But it was his shortcomings that came between them, not hers. "What's going on with you and your neighbor?"

She winced. "Don't ask."

"You're sleeping with him, aren't you."

"No, not 'sleeping with him.'"

He wished he could see her eyes. "It's not like you to lie."

"I'm not lying, exactly."

"So do you want to explain why you went bright red the moment he walked into the kitchen?"

She fidgeted with her purse. "We spent a few hours together at a cabin once. That's all."

He lowered the volume of the radio. "When?"

"Last night."

"Oh, God. No wonder he hated me on sight," he said with a laugh.

She turned accusing eyes on him. "I believe *you* were the one who started that little power struggle."

Allowing his smile to persist—at least this subject distracted him from his illness—he gazed out at the velvet-green pine trees, the clear blue sky, the black ribbon of road. Laurel had been living in a good place the past twenty-four months. He liked knowing that. Imagining her and the kids happy here made him feel less guilty for letting them down in D.C. "Maybe you're right."

"You're going to admit it?"

"I don't see any reason not to."

She adjusted her seat belt so she could turn a little more toward him. "Why didn't you like him?"

He cocked an eyebrow at her. "Why do you think?"

"You're jealous."

"Damn right."

He saw a hurt expression on her face and felt a fresh twinge of pain himself, pain that had nothing to do with his withdrawal from OxyContin.

"Will we ever get over each other?" she whispered.

The memory of making love to her, one of many such memories, filtered through his mind. "I hope not completely."

"But our relationship is so…complicated."

"*Life* is complicated, in case you haven't noticed."

"Can you be attracted to two people at once?"

"Hell, yeah."

"When I see you, I wish things could've worked out."

He reached across the seat and took her hand, and suddenly the terrible cravings for OxyContin and the cramps he'd been feeling subsided just enough that he could relax for the first time since he'd arrived in Pineview. "We don't have to be together to love each other."

A tear slid down her cheek. "You helped me through a terrible time, Rex. You showed me what love could be like after the bastard I married made me feel I never wanted to be with a man again. I'm grateful to you for that."

More guilt reared up—that he couldn't continue to be what she needed—but he wasn't going to let guilt or regret ruin this moment. After two years, he had her fingers entwined with his, felt a measure of forgiveness, and that was all he could ask for. He hadn't experienced peace without the aid of chemicals in months and months. Maybe he wasn't the man who'd become her husband and the father to her children. But he wanted her to be happy, even if it meant seeing her with someone else. "Just…let me ask you this."

"What's that?"

He scowled. "Does the man who replaces me have to be a cop?"

Releasing his hand, she gave him a playful slug. "I'm not getting together with the sheriff. Last night was a…a fluke. I hadn't been with anyone…well, since *you*."

That created quite an image. And not an entirely pleasant one. "So? How was it?"

A blush rose to her cheeks. "I can't believe we're talking about this."

He lowered his window so he could put his arm outside. "Does that mean you're not going to tell me?"

Her chest rose as she drew a deep breath. "It was good. It was *really* good," she said with an embarrassed laugh.

"I wish I was happier to hear it."

"If you're not happy, why are you smiling?"

Because he was free. Because it felt as if he had a second chance at becoming the man he wanted to be. He wasn't sure where this moment of contentment had come from or how long it would last. He didn't know if he'd be able to maintain it, or if the OxyContin would try to regain control. But for now, he was happy just to be with her and have everything right between them. He was in charge of his own life for the first time in months, was exactly where he needed to be, doing exactly what he needed to do. One small victory for Rex McCready. "Beats the shit out of me," he said.

She grabbed his hand again. "It feels great to have you back."

He hoped he could stay "back." That being part of each other's lives wouldn't get too painful to endure, like it always had before. Maybe, as close friends, they could finally achieve some stability.

They drove, windows down and hands clasped, music playing loudly until they reached Libby. Then Rex spotted a pay phone at the edge of a video store parking lot and pulled over. "There you go."

Laurel's smile disappeared as her mood shifted. "You believe Mona."

"I believe Mona heard Horse talking about you. Whether or not he really knows where you are…" He shrugged. "That's what we're hoping your mother can tell us."

A click sounded as she released her seat belt. "What if they showed up at her house?"

"We need to know."

She opened her door, but turned back. "But what if she gave them the numbers I called from?"

He pulled his bottom lip between his teeth as he considered her. "You won't know until you ask."

Myles stood in the opening of Jared's cubicle. "Grab Linda and bring her to my office."

Jared's eyebrows rumpled as he twisted around. "Right now? I'm still pulling my notes together." He tapped the cheap combination calendar and clock near his phone. "See this? Our meeting isn't for an hour."

"I don't care. I can't wait any longer." Like yesterday, Myles had spent most of the morning on the phone with the concerned citizens of Pineview, repeating himself, mollifying, placating, soothing and promising to find a killer he wasn't sure he could catch. He and his investigators certainly weren't going to solve this case on what they knew so far. And the more time that passed, the weaker their chances grew. He had to have fresh information, and he had to have it right away. He also needed to keep his mind fully engaged. Even with the pressure he was under, whenever he stopped moving or had half a second to himself, he began thinking about Vivian.

He didn't like that, mostly because he couldn't come up with a consistent reaction. One minute he was reliving last night. The next he was picturing the rough-looking character who'd been in her kitchen this morning and wondering if their time at the cabin had been some sort of game.

Rex acted as if *he* belonged in Vivian's house.

But a woman who just wanted a quick lay didn't hold back the way Vivian had done....

"You're a little uptight these days, Sheriff," Jared complained. "If you don't settle down you're going to have a heart attack."

"I'm thirty-nine."

"Doesn't matter. I'm talking about an hour. Sixty minutes. I can't have sixty minutes?"

"I don't need a typed report, okay? For right now, let's bypass your meticulous but time-consuming process. I just want you to sit down in my office and tell me what you've got."

"What's the rush?" He rummaged around inside his drawer for a pen.

Myles spotted a pen on the floor and picked it up for him. Jared's desk was no cleaner than his car. How he could create such orderly reports and detailed investigations out of this chaos, Myles had no idea. He obviously didn't feel he could be bothered with the mundane details of life.

"I've got everybody and his dog blowing up my phone," Myles told him. "And in three hours, I have to meet with the mayor and tell him that we haven't got a clue who killed Pat. Needless to say, I'm not looking forward to that. I want to be able to offer more than what I've been telling the people who've checked in with me already."

Wearing a put-upon expression, Jared jotted a few notes on the outside of a manila folder. "Fine. Give me ten minutes."

"You got it."

Myles planned to spend that time reading the coroner's report, which the M.E. had faxed over a few minutes earlier. Instead, he received a call from Chrissy Gunther, who wanted to find out what he'd done with her tip about Vivian's gun. He tried to convince her to trust him with the information, but she was having none of it, so he was infinitely relieved when Jared and Linda knocked on his open door. Waving them in, he told Chrissy he had a meeting. Then he hung up without even waiting for her to say goodbye.

"Sit down." He eyed the files his detectives were carrying. Several were quite thick—a sign that they'd been doing their interviews. "So?" He rubbed his hands. "What have you found?"

Frizzy dark hair with a sprinkling of gray framed Linda's face. The only way to tame it was to wear it in a ponytail, which she did, every day.

Dropping her stack of files in the middle of his desk, she slouched in her seat and met his gaze through a pair of glasses that always sat a little crookedly on her nose. "We don't have a lot, but we're making progress."

That was a fairly standard answer. One he'd given himself at least a dozen times this morning. It wasn't enough.

"Be more specific."

She glanced at Jared, who nodded for her to continue. "What do you see here?" she asked, opening the top file.

Myles stared at a picture of the shoe impressions he'd already seen on the linoleum of the vacation rental. "Looks like the perpetrator was wearing athletic shoes." Which he'd surmised when he saw them the first time. He hoped Linda wasn't going to suggest that this was some kind of breakthrough.

"Correct. Do you notice anything unusual about them?"

He picked up the photographs so he could study each one. "No."

"Look at the wear on the soles."

"There is no wear."

"Exactly," Jared said. "All the nicks and gouges and wear patterns that make a pair of shoes unique to their owner are missing."

The lack of imperfections suddenly jumped out at Myles. "They're new?"

"They'd have to be, right?"

Linda seemed pleased by this conclusion, but Myles couldn't imagine why. New shoes would only make it harder to tie a suspect to the crime scene. "And this is good *why?*"

"Hang on," she said. "What else do you see?"

Tired of playing her guessing game, Myles put down the pictures. "I don't see anything unusual. Tell me what you're driving at."

She set two pictures side by side. "We didn't spot it at first, either. It wasn't until we tried to figure out the size of those shoes that it became apparent."

"*What* became apparent?"

"Pat had more than one assailant."

Grabbing the two pictures again, Myles held them close. "That would mean two different pairs of shoes. But...every shoe impression here looks *exactly* the same."

"Because they're all from the same *type* of shoe. Both pairs are new. The only difference is size. Give me your ruler. I'll show you."

Myles searched through his top drawer. It wasn't as messy as Jared's, but he'd stuffed too much inside it.

Eventually he came up with a ruler and Jared measured.

"See? One is a size eleven. The other a twelve and a half."

"You've verified this?"

"More than once."

"You're saying two men bought the same shoes at the same time." Myles thought of the guys he'd found on the side of the road. They'd entered his mind so many times. Maybe it was worth stopping over at Reliable Auto to see if they'd picked up their vehicle. If not, maybe he could get hold of them, talk to them again....

Linda smiled. "They probably even bought them at the same place."

Now they were making progress. "Where?" If they could find that out, maybe they could get the store's surveillance tapes for the two weeks prior to the murder, see who came in to buy athletic shoes.

"According to the database, they're Athletic Works Brand, which are sold at Walmart."

They didn't have a Walmart. The closest one was in Kalispell. There was no guarantee they were even bought at that location, but Myles was willing to try anything.

"Have you spoken to the manager of the Walmart in Kalispell?"

"Yes. We're going out there this afternoon."

"Good," he said, but his brief flash of hope had already dimmed. He tried to focus on how the shoe details fit with all the rest. "The odd thing is…this information contradicts everything we've established about the murder."

Linda blinked at him from behind her thick lenses. "What do you mean?"

"If two men bought shoes to avoid leaving prints that could be traced back to them, they were planning a crime. Yet everything about the scene indicates that Pat's murder wasn't premeditated, from the choice of weapon to the lack of any effort to conceal the crime or dispose of the body."

Resting his elbows on his knees, Jared clasped his hands together. "Maybe the *murder* wasn't premeditated. Maybe it was meant to be a *robbery*."

"You do that much planning? Get your buddy to go with you to buy shoes, then call up a Realtor and ask to see a house, just to grab a guy's wallet?"

"Why not? It's the perfect way to have a stranger meet you at a private location."

"But a guy like Pat isn't likely to carry much on him. Hitting a gas station would probably net you more."

"They could've taken his car."

"They didn't."

"I know. I haven't quite figured that out," Jared admitted.

"Maybe Pat fought them, like you were saying earlier," Linda said. "Maybe he hurt one, and it really pissed him off."

"If someone else was hurt, there should've been some evidence of it at the scene." "Ron Howard" and his sidekick hadn't been sporting any scratches or gouges. At least not that Myles could see. But maybe there were marks he *couldn't* see. The lame guy had been covered from head to toe. His excessive tattoos had reminded Myles of prison inmates. Did they have a couple of violent ex-cons on their hands?

Jared jumped in again. "Not necessarily. Maybe the injury didn't bleed. And they didn't take the car because they knew it would link them to the murder."

That made some sense. Myles rocked back. "What about the partial thumbprint on the door?"

"Turned out to be Gertie's," Jared told him. "After Pat died, she wasn't thinking straight. Instead of using the phone right there on the counter, she stumbled outside and ran down the street to C.C.'s. Or so she said. I can't imagine walking away from a phone that's right in front of you, but…there you have her side of the story."

Myles could imagine Gertie doing precisely what she'd said. He remembered how disoriented he'd felt when Amber Rose passed away, and he'd been expecting it, watching death's inexorable approach, for months. "Her husband had just died in her arms, Jared."

Jared cleared his throat and Linda shifted as if his words had reminded them both why he'd know about this particular situation, and he clenched his jaw, trying to contain his irritation. He hated dealing with the discomfort his loss created in others. That made it so hard to ever be normal, to carry on without feeling as if he was constantly being examined under a microscope. If the good citizens of Pineview perceived him as acting too distraught over Amber Rose's death, they whispered things like, "He's got to pick up and go on, for the sake of that little girl. You can only mourn for so long." And if it seemed to them that he didn't care enough, as if he *was* putting her death behind him as so many suggested, they began to doubt that he was being honest about his grief or that he'd ever really loved Amber Rose to begin with. Her death was bad enough. The extra attention he'd had to suffer over the past three years made it worse.

Or maybe, given that he'd made love with someone else for the first time last night, he was especially self-conscious today. Did the fact that he'd wanted Vivian so badly, that he'd thought of Amber Rose and yet that hadn't lessened his desire, somehow take away from what he'd felt for his wife? Was he capable of moving on in an emotional sense? Had he finally reached that point after all the lonely months since he'd buried her? Or was it only hormones?

Trying to regain his focus, he thumbed through the rest of the files they'd brought until he came to the diagram of Pat's many injuries. He'd already seen it, briefly, in the autopsy report, but this reminded him of the missing can opener. "Any more news on the murder weapon?"

"A little," Jared replied. "The wounds Pat sustained are consistent with the electric can opener that's missing."

"You mean *a* can opener. You haven't found *the* can opener."

"No. But Gertie took me to the store to show me the brand, and I bought one. The dents in Pat's skull match perfectly."

"Could there be other objects that match?"

"I doubt it. I took a short video of the coroner's demonstration—" Linda searched through her purse and withdrew a very small video camera "—if you'd like to see it for yourself."

When she had the camera powered up and ready, she passed it across the desk to him, and he watched the coroner use the can opener like a rock against a Styrofoam head to simulate what had happened to Pat. The indentations clearly matched the protruding magnet.

Poor old guy, Myles thought. Pat didn't deserve to die, especially like this. It was even more tragic that he'd been killed for less than fifty dollars. "Does Gertie know you're investigating her?" he asked as he returned the camera.

"She knows I'm doing all I can to find out who killed her husband," Jared said, "and she appreciates it."

She'd probably appreciate it a lot less if she knew he'd been snooping around in her personal affairs, looking for a motive. Investigating her added insult to injury. Feeling protective of her, Myles was somewhat offended by Jared's attitude. "I can't believe there isn't any blood at the scene belonging to someone other than Pat," he mused. "Could we have missed something?"

"No."

"No trace evidence under his fingernails?"

"No."

"What about that smear on Pat's shirt?"

"That was his," Jared said.

Myles decided he was definitely going to Reliable Auto. He wanted to find "Ron Howard" and Peter Ferguson. They'd given him a bad feeling, and all those clothes "Howard" had been wearing seemed even more suspect now. "Damn, I'd like to think Pat got in a swipe here and there."

"Against *two?*"

Myles rolled his eyes at Jared's heavy skepticism. "You can't allow me the comfort of one harmless fantasy?"

Puzzled by his response, Jared leaned forward. "How does it bring you comfort if it isn't what really happened?"

"Forget it." Myles gave Linda a look of exasperation, but he knew she wouldn't necessarily agree with him. Although she used to complain about Jared all the time—the mess that surrounded him, his obsessive tendencies, his literal nature—she'd gained a great deal of respect for him over the past two years. Since he had no wife or children with whom to spend his evenings, and would work 24/7 if left to his own devices, she and her husband invited him over for dinner probably twice a week. Other times, she brought him leftovers for lunch.

"I must be hanging out with him too much," she admitted, "because what he just said actually makes sense to me."

Myles threw up his hands. "Fine. Let's face the bitter truth, shall we? Pat had no chance from the beginning. Now tell me about your interviews."

When they exchanged a questioning glance, Myles had to acknowledge that *he* was the one acting strange today. He was as tense as Jared had accused him of being, and had been ever since he'd seen Rex standing in Vivian's kitchen only hours after he'd made love to her at the cabin.

"No one in the other rentals saw anything," Jared explained. "C.C. is the closest neighbor, but there are trees secluding both residences. And she was vacuuming, had no idea Pat was even showing the cabin."

"Wouldn't you know it? With all the folks in Pineview

who pay a little too much attention to their neighbors, our murder occurs next to someone who pays no attention whatsoever."

"It's a rental. One of several in the area. She sees a lot of people come and go," Linda said.

"Did anyone along the drive to the cabin spot a vehicle that didn't belong? That seemed to be going too slow or too fast?"

Jared shook his head. "'Fraid not."

Myles glanced longingly at his coffee cup. After being amped up on adrenaline for so many hours, he was hitting the skids, but he'd had enough caffeine for one day. "Delbert called me yesterday. Said you already talked to him."

"Yes. A few times," Jared said. "He's been very cooperative."

"He has an alibi?" Myles hadn't wanted to ask Delbert where he'd been at the time of his stepfather's murder, not when he didn't really consider Delbert a suspect and he had investigators who could do it for him.

Linda took over. "He was at work. Several people have confirmed his presence there, including his boss. But he let me take pictures of his bare torso to show there isn't a scratch on him."

Myles rearranged the piles of paper on his desk as he digested what he'd been told. "What about Gertie?"

"No alibi."

"She's still in the running for number-one suspect?"

Jared stood. "Why wouldn't she be? I don't rule anyone out until I have a reason."

Myles massaged his temples. "I know."

"So…do you have what you need for your meeting with the mayor?"

He'd hoped for more. "If that's all you've got."

"That's it for now."

Jared reached for the files, but Myles said to leave them. He wanted to read the interviews himself, get a feel for what people were saying.

He was alone in his office and in the middle of Jared's notes about his first conversation with Delbert when Deputy Campbell appeared. "Hey, you got a minute?"

Myles looked up. "Sure, what do you need?"

"Trace over at the auto shop wants to know what to do with that Toyota truck Harvey brought in."

Myles had been planning to go there. "The owners haven't shown up?"

Campbell popped the top of the soft drink he'd carried in with him. "Trace hasn't heard from them."

Myles closed the folder. "Didn't they ride back with Harvey?"

"No. They said they had a friend picking them up."

What friend? When he'd been there, they acted as if they were going to ride with the tow. Damn. Had they slipped away already?

"Thanks." Once Campbell left, Myles went out to retrieve the pad of paper he kept in his car. He'd found "Ron Howard" and Peter Ferguson suspicious enough that he'd written down their registration information. Maybe he could contact them through Quentin, Peter's older brother....

It took minimal time and effort to access a reverse directory. Soon he had the phone number for the residence in Monrovia and a man on the phone who claimed to be Quentin. But, judging by his voice, he was at least fifty years older than Peter.

This couldn't be the *brother* Peter had referred to, could it? Maybe it was his father.

Myles explained who he was and what he wanted, but he didn't get any farther before the man said, "You must've run across the fellows who stole my truck."

The hair on the back of Myles's neck stood on end. "What are you talking about? It didn't come up as stolen when I ran the plates."

"Because I don't drive it much anymore. I didn't realize the damn thing was missing until this morning."

15

Vivian's hand shook as she used a prepaid calling card Rex had in his pocket and dialed Ellen's number. She'd agonized over every call she'd placed to her old home since Virgil went to prison. Partially because she couldn't decide if her mother was as complicit in her stepfather's murder as she suspected. Partially because reaching out to Ellen felt disloyal to her brother. And partially because any contact increased her desire for resolution, which always seemed to be just one step away—no matter how many steps she took in order to achieve it.

But none of her earlier anxiety could rival what she felt now. Before, the worst she had to worry about was how well she'd be received, and she'd felt fairly confident her mother would, at a minimum, be cordial. Ellen was always cordial, to everyone. Soft-spoken and unconfrontational, she was too indecisive to stand up and fight, even for her children.

Still, the image she projected created an appealing illusion, one of a loving mother wrongfully accused. At times, Vivian was so tempted to believe in Ellen's innocence, so tempted to reunite and rebuild what they'd lost, that she doubted every decision she'd ever made concerning her mother. Ellen claimed that, at the time

Virgil was arrested, she believed the police because of
his temper and the fact that he'd threatened more than
once to kill Martin if the abuse didn't stop. He also didn't
have an alibi for the night it happened; he was downstairs
in his bedroom, sleeping, and the gunshot didn't even
wake him up.

Vivian hadn't been home, so she had no idea what
happened.

Once Uncle Gary's marriage fell apart years later, his
ex-wife's conscience finally got the best of her—or she
was looking for revenge. Either way, she came forward
to tell what she knew and the police began to realize
what Vivian's heart had insisted all along—they had the
wrong man. Almost as soon as Gary fell under scrutiny,
he confessed that Ellen had asked him to do it. He told
detectives that she came to him, insisting Martin would
kill her or one of the kids if he didn't step in. He'd also
said she'd offered him half of the insurance money if
he'd make Martin disappear for good. Because he was
in debt and losing his house, he felt this provided a way
out for both of them.

But it was impossible to prove what he'd said. Ellen
did give Gary a sizable portion of the money. Was that a
payoff for murder? Or because she wanted to help him
keep a roof over his family's heads, as she claimed? It
could be either, but Ellen had chosen to give Gary the
money rather than hiring a better attorney for Virgil,
and that was something Vivian simply could not understand. Considering how often she'd heard her mother tell
people what they wanted to hear rather than the truth, she
couldn't trust Ellen. Especially when, instead of being
beside herself with worry, Ellen had seemed almost...

relieved. Relieved to have a scapegoat, even if that scapegoat was her own son.

When Ellen quickly got involved in yet another romantic relationship, Vivian left home, at sixteen, and had been taking care of herself ever since. But that didn't mean she never looked back. There were times she sorely regretted the loss of her relationship with her mother. That she was still in contact with Ellen proved it. If she didn't need to be so careful about her whereabouts, she might've called more often.

Now that Virgil was out of prison, holding a grudge felt pointless. The older she got, the more Vivian wanted to purge the anger that'd been trapped inside her for so many years. It was too dark, too negative; sometimes that darkness seemed about to overtake everything else.

And now, just when she'd been closest to forgiving her mother, the doubt was back. Had Ellen let The Crew threaten her or bully her into putting her own children and grandchildren, as well as Rex, in danger? It wasn't as if Vivian thought Ellen would call Horse or any of the others. She knew her mother wasn't out to hurt her or Virgil. She just didn't believe that Ellen would go to much trouble to protect them if her own life or welfare was on the line.

"What's the matter?" Rex called.

She'd misdialed and hung up. Shoving her sunglasses higher on her nose, she waved him off and tried again.

This time the phone rang. Then her mother's voice came on the line, but it turned out to be the recorded message.

Vivian hung up and almost walked back to tell Rex they'd have to wait until later. As long as she didn't know for sure, she could continue to hope that her mother wasn't the reason she was once again in danger.

But if Ellen *had* heard from a member of the gang, not knowing could cost Vivian one or both of her own children. She couldn't be a coward.

"She's not home?" Rex called.

"No."

"Can you call another family member?"

"My cousins have moved around so much I've lost track of them." Uncle Gary was in prison. His ex had testified against him, then washed her hands of him *and* his extended family. But Ellen still lived in the house on Sandalwood Court where Vivian and Virgil had grown up, so Vivian knew quite a few of the neighbors. Were any of them still around?

She'd once had a terrible crush on Junior Ivey, the next-door neighbor's son. Could she remember the number to his house? She'd certainly called it often enough, much to his annoyance, since he was four years older and in high school when she'd been mooning over him.

She racked her brain for the number but couldn't come up with more than the prefix, and that was only because it was the same as her mother's. But she remembered Junior's father's name and that meant she could get the rest from directory assistance.

The phone rang so many times Vivian thought she'd wind up with another recorded message, but the breathless voice of the woman who answered told her she had a live human being.

"Mrs. Ivey?"

"Yes?"

Vivian pushed her sunglasses up again. "This is Vivi—er—Laurel Skinner."

"Laurel! My goodness. Hang on a sec. I was downstairs doing some ironing. Needless to say, I'm not as fit as I used to be."

She'd been overweight even back then. "Take your time."

After an audible breath, she said, "I'll be okay in a minute. How are you?"

"Fine, thanks."

"It's been years and years since we've heard from you."

"It has been a while."

"Too long. Your mother tells me you have two children now."

"Yes."

"She'd love to see them, you know. It's a pity you live so far away."

The disapproval in those words told Vivian that Sonja Ivey had forgiven Ellen for the murder, if she'd ever held her accountable for it in the first place. Ellen could be quite convincing. That was part of the reason she hadn't been charged for Martin's murder along with Gary. The police believed Gary was telling the truth, but the D.A. didn't have enough hard evidence connecting Ellen to the killing, and he felt she came across as too genuine to try with what he had.

"Maybe someday I will," she said to avoid discussing why she hadn't visited so far.

"How's your brother?"

"Good."

"Terrible what happened to that boy. So hard to believe."

"Yes." Hard to believe Ellen didn't have a hand in it, or do more to stop it. "How's Junior?"

"Fabulous! He's a doctor."

"That doesn't surprise me. He was always a smart kid."

"But we don't like his wife much," she murmured.

Vivian would've laughed, except she was too anxious to get to the point of her call. "I'm sorry to hear that. Adjusting to in-laws can be difficult." No one knew that better than she did. Instead of having an ounce of sympathy for what Tom had put her through, his parents had spent most of the time they were together trying to convince her that he wasn't really a bad person. Never had they taken her side. Instead, they'd acted as if she must be provoking him into acting the way he did. They didn't care that something as innocuous as making the wrong dish for dinner could set him off.

"She's a spoiled little prima donna from the rich side of town," Sonja said.

"Hopefully, Junior is happier with her than you are."

"I don't think he is, but...what can you do? It's not my place to get involved."

Vivian glanced at Rex, who made a motion that said to hurry up. "Listen, Sonja, I'm really sorry to interrupt your ironing, but I'm calling because I can't reach my mother. You don't know where she is, do you?"

"She should be home. I'm standing at my kitchen window, looking out at her car right now."

"I just tried her. She didn't answer."

"She's been pretty depressed lately. Randall left again, you know."

Her mother's latest love interest. She hadn't married

this one, but they'd been together for a couple of years. "When?"

"Maybe two weeks ago? Found someone else."

That must've been a blow to her mother's self-esteem. It was usually Ellen who became dissatisfied. She was only interested in the initial wining and dining part of a romance and grew bored as soon as the mundane intruded. "Would you do me a favor, Sonja? Do you think you could walk over and see if you can rouse her?"

"Sure, honey. Here, call my cell. I'll take it with me and let you talk to her."

Vivian had the feeling that Sonja suspected Ellen was simply ducking her call. They'd had so many problems, almost anyone would think that. She didn't try to disabuse her of the notion. Instead she wrote down the number Sonja rattled off, hung up and dialed again.

"It's raining," Sonja complained when she answered the second time. "Let me grab a coat."

Vivian covered the mouthpiece to signal Rex that she was making progress. Then she waited while her mother's neighbor trudged next door. She heard the knock, heard Sonja calling Ellen's name, but she couldn't make out any response. Several seconds later, Sonja confirmed that there hadn't been one.

"Can you see inside?" Vivian asked.

"'Fraid, not. The blinds are pulled. I told you, she's in a real funk."

What now? Her mother was retired and living on social security and what she'd been able to glean from her many divorces. If her car was there, she should be, too. "Could you go around back, please? Something isn't right."

"Sure."

Vivian listened to the swish of Sonja's clothing as she moved. Then Sonja's voice came through loud and clear. "Oh, boy."

"Oh, boy?" Vivian straightened. "What does that mean?"

"Looks like the door's been broken."

Tendrils of fear slithered around Vivan's stomach and squeezed until it hurt. That was when she knew her ulcer was coming back. She'd been too anxious this week; it was bound to happen. But that was the least of her worries right now. "Broken as in…someone forced their way inside?" She almost didn't recognize her own voice….

"I don't want to scare you but…"

She sounded scared herself. "Maybe you shouldn't go in. Maybe you'd better call 9-1-1."

That brought no response.

"Sonja?"

"Wait a second. There's a terrible stench. And I see something."

Vivian bit her lip and gripped the phone even tighter. "What is it?"

"Oh, God!" Sonja wailed. "Someone's stabbed her. She's dead."

"They didn't even lock the door. That means we're basically invited in, don't you think?" Ink chortled as he let himself and L.J. inside the cabin they'd come across earlier.

L.J. didn't answer. He hadn't said a word since Ink dragged him from the edge of the clearing where he'd been watching the pretty teenager sitting on her deck.

Attempting to ignore his partner's sour mood, Ink visited the kitchen. "Hey, they've got enough beer in here to last us a month." He opened the refrigerator door wide, so L.J. could see for himself. "Look at this."

L.J. didn't bother to glance over. Slumping onto the couch, he stared straight ahead.

Ink closed the fridge. "Quit pouting about that little bitch, will ya?"

"I'm just wondering why we always have to do what *you* want. You can threaten people, kill people, whatever. First you killed that lady in L.A. Then—"

"*I* didn't kill her."

"You told Horse she had information. You knew he was sending a couple Crew over there. What did you think they were going to do? Dance with her?"

"They did exactly what I expected. And, just like I told you, she *did* have information."

"A phone number that goes to a restaurant?"

"It's what brought us here, ain't it?"

"Yeah, and I bet that old guy at the cabin's glad we came."

Ink didn't want to think about the old guy at the cabin, but L.J. brought it up all the time. "Listen, you can have that sweet young thing when we're ready to leave the area. Then it won't matter what you do because we'll be gone before the sheriff can come after us."

"And when will that be?" L.J. grumbled.

"I've told you. After I kill Laurel Hodges and her kids and send their heads to her brother."

L.J. grimaced. "That's sick, man. Are you really gonna cut off their heads? Even the kids?"

"Why not?" Searching for clues that might tell him how many men they'd soon be facing, and what those men were like, Ink limped into the living room and began snooping around. He found a pair of waders, an extra fishing rod, a paper sack with a few pennies, a receipt for bait and a bag of chips.

A joint lay on top of the entertainment system. Ink thought that might come in handy.

L.J. watched him circle the room. "Getting that woman killed was bad enough. But the old guy? After seeing that shit, I wouldn't put anything past you."

"What's the matter?" He grinned. "Can't handle the violence?"

Two grooves formed between L.J.'s eyebrows. "That's not it. It's just…we been here a week and you still don't know where this Laurel woman lives. Unless she's dumber than dirt, she's changed her name, so it's not like we can just ask around. And it hasn't done any good to stake out the Golden Griddle. How will we ever find her? Ask everyone we meet to see if they know a woman who's tall and thin with long blond hair? That could describe lots of women. And she could've gained a ton of weight or changed her hair color."

"Maybe she can change her hair color and her weight, but she can't change her height. She's got to be five-ten. That doesn't describe as many women as you think."

"Oh, yeah? You might be surprised." His sulk more pronounced, he folded his arms.

"Besides, I've seen her," Ink said. "I'd recognize her."

"That might work if she ate at that restaurant, but we haven't spotted her there."

"We could spot her somewhere else."

L.J. barked a laugh. "What're the chances? You gotta be realistic, man. All you got is the phone number Horse's men forced out of Laurel's mother. That's not much. Maybe if they could've gotten the kids' names, we'd have a chance, but the old lady wouldn't give that up."

"I'm going to remember the daughter's name myself. You'll see."

"That's what you've been saying since I met you, bro."

"I will. I heard Laurel say it once. I was right there in her living room."

L.J. waved him off. "So we got nothin', like I said. We're just wastin' time."

Ink gritted his teeth. As far as he was concerned, L.J. didn't deserve to call himself a member of The Crew. The Crew didn't whine like this kid. That was the problem these days. They were letting in guys who had no balls whatsoever. "You'll see. I'll think of the name eventually." But he didn't have a lot of hope. He'd been racking his brain for the past four years to no avail. All he knew was that it was short and unusual....

God, it drove him nuts. At times, it was on the tip of his tongue. And why would she change it? She probably didn't even remember using her daughter's name in front of him. He'd only been at her house for one or two minutes. "Pineview ain't that big," he pointed out.

"So? Maybe she doesn't live in town. Maybe she lives out here, in the mountains. These cabins are so spread out we couldn't find 'em all even if we wanted to."

"She has to go into town sometime."

"Who says? Maybe she lives like a freakin' hermit."

Tired of the complaints, Ink began to fondle the trigger of his gun. It would be so easy to blow L.J.'s brains out.... "She has kids. That means they gotta go to school."

"Not during the summer."

"They have to get groceries, dumb shit."

L.J. shot to his feet. "Stop calling me that! I'm tired of

it, you hear? I'll leave your sorry ass to limp around this place on your own if you don't keep your mouth shut!"

Ink nearly raised the gun. L.J. needed to learn some respect, needed to see how a real Crew member behaved. The Glock he held was all they'd been able to bum off their brothers on such short notice, so it wouldn't be hard. L.J. didn't even have a weapon.

But Ink wasn't about to sabotage his own success, not after getting this far. Once he had what he wanted, he'd cap L.J. Then he'd steal a car, sneak over the Canadian border and get lost in a whole other country. Until then, he had to have someone who could go into town and ask about Laurel, someone who didn't stand out the way he did. Who else could he trust?

"Calm down before you ruin everything." Picking up a *Playboy* from the coffee table, he stared down at the blonde bombshell on the cover. According to the issue date, it was a recent purchase, which meant the guys who were staying here must've brought it with them. "We've got a nice place to stay, plenty to eat and drink. We even have some naked girls to enjoy." He tossed the magazine at L.J. "We keep our cool, we can have ourselves a party, once we whack the guys who rented this cabin."

L.J. let the magazine fall to the couch. He had such a sullen look that Ink wondered if L.J. was contemplating the odds of overpowering him. Ink was fifteen years his senior and couldn't stand straight anymore but L.J. didn't have as much experience, or enough nerve to kill a man. The way L.J. had puked up his breakfast after Ink beat the crap out of that Realtor convinced Ink that half the shit L.J. claimed to have done wasn't true. Ink thought he could beat L.J. despite his handicap, and was eager to do it—but he had other plans for the time being, so he adopted a more conciliatory tone. "What do you say?"

At last the kid sat back down. "If you know where Laurel's brother is, why don't we just go there, shoot him and be done with it?"

"Because I *don't* know where he is. That's what she's going to tell me in order to save her kids."

"You just said she's met you before. That means she'll realize that nothing can save her kids."

"Then something in her house will give it away. Virgil and his sister were always close. She'll have his phone number, letters, emails from him, some way to find him."

L.J. pulled a piece of gum from his pocket and shoved it into his mouth. "What about the other guy?"

"Who?"

"What'd you call him—Pretty Boy? We're going after him, too, right?"

Just the mention of Pretty Boy made Ink clench his jaw. "You know we are."

"You haven't said anything about him lately. It's been all about the bitch."

"Doesn't mean I've forgotten him. She's first. Virgil and his wife are next. Pretty Boy's last. The order's important."

Muttering something that sounded like, "You're crazy," L.J. turned on the TV, but Ink grabbed the remote and turned it off again.

"What are you thinking? They hear that shit, they'll know they got company. You want to face the business end of five rifles?"

"There're fishing poles in here."

"That doesn't mean they don't do a little hunting, too."

"Black bear's the only thing in season. How many black bear hunters can there be?"

"Enough to have a season, right? Who told you it was bear season, anyway?"

"That guy at Walmart. I distracted him while you lifted our shoes, remember?"

He gazed around the cabin again. "So they could be hunters, like I said."

L.J. scratched his neck. "They could also be a bunch of yuppies who wouldn't know how to use a gun even if they had one."

"Like I told you before, it's safer to assume the worst."

"Fine. We'll assume the worst." With a sigh, L.J. got up and helped himself to a cold beer. "So what do we do until these bear hunters come back? It's barely noon."

"We wait until they drag their sorry asses home. They'll be here for dinner, if not before. With all the food they got, I'm betting they're planning a barbecue."

A *snick* sounded as L.J. popped the top of his beer. "That could be five or six hours, man. I hate waiting."

Ink whirled on him. "Could you quit complaining? I mean, you got any better ideas? Where else are we gonna stay? How else are we gonna get food?"

When he didn't reply, Ink gestured at the *Playboy*. "Why don't you go look at that magazine if you want some tits and ass? Take it into the bathroom. The way you're actin', two minutes should take care of your problem."

"At least I can still get it up," he snapped.

L.J. was guessing, but he was right. It wasn't just his ability to have an erection that Laurel, Virgil and Pretty Boy had taken away from him. He wasn't half the man he used to be. But they'd pay for what they'd done. They'd pay for everything. Soon.

He opened his mouth to tell L.J. the dick he was so proud of wouldn't work very good if he shot it off when he heard a car pull up outside. "They're early!"

L.J. checked the window while Ink got behind the couch.

"How many are there?" Ink asked, his voice barely audible.

"Four."

"They have rifles?"

"Not unless they left 'em in the truck. They're carrying cameras. Looks like a bunch of dads getting together for some kind of reunion." At that point, L.J. glanced back as if he wanted to ask Ink not to go through with it. But it was too late. Ink didn't have any choice. He had to get rid of these guys; it wasn't like they'd walk away and keep their mouths shut just because he and L.J. asked them to.

The door swung inward. Then L.J. dropped to the floor, and Ink began to fire.

16

Rex had his arms around her. They were standing beneath a tree in Libby in some park she'd probably passed by once or twice but never noticed, and he was crooning words of comfort in her ear. "It'll be okay, I promise. Don't worry about anything."

Vivian heard what he was saying but his words held no meaning. Her mother was gone. *Murdered.* And Vivian wasn't even sure she'd loved her. Not at the end. Was it possible to love someone you couldn't trust? Someone you blamed for so much heartache?

She'd *wanted* to love Ellen. All along. But...

God, she'd thought her feelings involving her mother were complicated before this happened, but she'd had no idea how confusing they could get. She needed to find herself in all of this, to at least grab hold of an emotion she could understand. An emotion that would make her feel normal. But she couldn't manage it.

"What's going on, Laurel?" Her real name seemed as foreign as everything else at the moment. She was no longer Laurel. He wasn't Pretty Boy anymore, either. He'd told her that himself. Too much had changed.

She missed him, missed her old self, too. And yet she wanted more power than she'd had before. She wanted to take charge of her life and refuse to let The Crew control her through the threat they posed.

Rex pulled back to look into her face. "You haven't said a word since you dropped the phone."

The way she'd grabbed the pedestal in order to keep from sagging to the ground had told him something was wrong. He'd dashed out to catch her, hung up the handset and helped her back to the car. Then he'd brought her here, where there was no phone and no busy street, only green grass, green trees, gold and orange flowers and a wide blue sky.

"I don't know what to say," she said. "I don't even know what to *feel*." She was pretty sure there should be something besides emptiness inside her. What about sorrow? Regret? Relief? Vindication? She could justify any of them, and yet they weren't there. A void filled her heart where the pain should be.

He removed her sunglasses and lifted her chin, forcing her to look him in the eyes. "Start with what you're thinking."

"Nothing." She gave her head a quick shake. "I'm numb."

"Come on, don't shut down." Setting his hands on her shoulders, he squeezed them for emphasis. "Talk. It'll make this easier. You can trust me, remember?"

She could trust him to care about her, but she couldn't trust him to take care of himself. And that meant she couldn't risk loving him. And yet she did love him. Not like she used to. Not in a romantic sense. But as a good friend, someone who'd always be special.

Even that frightened her.

"Laurel?"

She had to get him to stop calling her that. "Vivian."

"Fine. Vivian. You're scaring me. You're white as a ghost and I could feel your pulse a second ago. Your heart's racing like a rabbit's. Will you let me know what's going on inside that pretty head of yours?"

She studied the crushed grass between them while she tried to isolate a single ingredient from the stew of her thoughts. She wanted to ask what Ellen's death signified. But he wouldn't know. Did it mean The Crew had paid Ellen a visit and she *wouldn't* give up what she knew?

That possibility made Vivian wince. Had she misjudged her mother after all?

Or...had Ellen told as much as she could about Vivian's calls?

The mere fact of her death didn't provide the answer. The Crew could've killed her even if she cooperated.

"Hey!" He gave her shoulders another squeeze.

Talk. She needed to talk. "Who's going to see to her burial?" she asked. "I can't expect Virgil to do it."

"You're right. He can't leave Peyton. Not while she's so close to having the baby."

It was more than that. Her brother was absolutely convinced that Ellen had conspired with Gary to murder Martin and let him take the blame for it. He wouldn't attend Ellen's funeral even if it was right across the street and there was no danger.

"So?" She reclaimed her sunglasses and put them on. They provided a shield of sorts—a small one, granted, but that was better than nothing.

"It's a homicide, so there'll be an autopsy," he replied. "That may take several days, maybe a week or two."

"She's already been dead awhile. Who knows how long? Sonja Ivey was so upset she could hardly speak. She was too busy gasping and crying." Images of the murdered marshal in Colorado loomed, but Vivian shoved them away.

"The police will get whatever information they can about the way she was killed. But my point is this—you don't have to make every decision right this minute. Let's deal with the shock first."

The shock was exactly what she was attempting to overcome. She felt as if she'd been dumped into some kind of arctic wilderness. If she didn't force herself to keep thinking, keep planning, keep moving, she'd freeze and be unable to do anything. "But I have to worry about her burial at some point, don't I? Some point soon."

She stepped out of reach. Being so close to him had once felt right, but not anymore. He'd been *Laurel's* crutch, *Laurel's* love, not Vivian's. Vivian was too infatuated with the sheriff to be able to fall back into a relationship with Rex. Not that she could pursue what she felt for *him,* either. "At the very least, I have to tell the police who's responsible for her death. I won't let The Crew get away with this."

The empty place inside her was filling up—with anger and outrage. It threatened to make her reckless because she was beginning to care less about her own safety and well-being than achieving justice.

Or maybe it wasn't justice she wanted so much as revenge. Was she becoming less like ordinary people and more like the men who hunted her? It wouldn't surprise her. They'd made her live in their world, made her look over her shoulder every second, for nearly four years.

"You might have to let the police handle the investigation on their own," Rex said.

"No."

He gripped her elbow. "Look, I know what you're feeling. I feel the same. But it's a war we can't win."

She knocked his hand away. "We won't win if we don't fight."

"Don't you think Virgil and I have considered that? We have. Lots of times. But there are too many of them. We could pick off one or two, maybe even three or four. But we can't get to the most powerful members. They'll just keep sending more foot soldiers until we screw up or get too tired to run. Then they'll get us."

She didn't want to hear that. As logical as it was, it pushed her into a corner. "Maybe that's a chance we have to take. Maybe we have to risk our lives to make our lives worth living."

"That sounds fine and good for us," he responded. "*I'm* willing to take that risk. But what about Jake and Mia? And Virgil's kids?"

"That's exactly what The Crew's counting on, that we'll offer no resistance, play it safe."

"Or, by killing your mother, they could be trying to coax you out of hiding. Which is why you can't contact *anyone,* least of all the LAPD."

She threw up her hands. "Oh, come on. The Crew can't have moles everywhere."

"They can in L.A.! That's their home turf."

She couldn't even go to her mother's funeral? "Then who'll bury her?"

"Natalie."

Ellen's sister. "You think she'd bother to interrupt her life, to put herself out for us?" Natalie lived in Texas with her husband, who'd been in the air force for most of his career. She'd been very careful to keep her distance, didn't want the taint of what had happened to ruin her life, too.

"If there's no one else," he said. "She remained loyal to Ellen throughout it all, right?"

Natalie believed that Gary had killed Martin as a favor to Ellen, but that Ellen had no foreknowledge of it. According to her, Gary only implicated Ellen because Ellen didn't give him more of the money, and his ex supported this theory, which was another reason Ellen had never been charged. But letting Natalie take over the funeral arrangements meant conceding yet another battle to The Crew. "She was my *mother*. That makes her funeral my responsibility."

He raked a hand through his hair, which was longer than she'd ever seen him wear it, longer than hers. "Doesn't matter. You can't go back to L.A. The Crew could be watching and waiting for you to do just that."

Or they could be here in Montana. That was the problem. She didn't know.

"I've…had it," she said. "I don't know how else to explain what's going on with me."

He sat on the edge of the closest picnic table. "You don't have any other choice, Laurel—Vivian," he corrected before she could protest. "You have to do what you have to do in order to survive."

"No. I could fight back. I have that choice."

"But do you know what fighting means?"

"It means I'll endanger my children, like you've already pointed out. But what if you took them to Virgil?"

He got up again. "That's crazy. I'm not leaving you here alone."

He had to. He wasn't well. "If I don't have to worry about my kids, I'll be able to defend myself."

His expression said he didn't think she stood a snow-ball's chance in hell. And he was probably right. But she had to at least *try* to break free, didn't she? Running wasn't necessarily any safer. The Crew could find her again. And maybe next time she wouldn't have the warning she did now.

"Against how many?" he asked. "One? Two? Don't you remember what happened in Colorado?"

She'd never forget. But she couldn't allow the fear inspired by that event to define her whole life. She could no longer live behind the boundaries of that fear, not anymore. "However many they send."

Instead of arguing with her, he pulled his cell phone from his pocket and dialed. No doubt he was hoping Virgil could talk some sense into her.

"Bad news," he said into the phone. "She's okay. But… she's talking crazy. And she has something to tell you."

At first Vivian refused to take the phone. She knew what Virgil would tell her. But Rex insisted they wouldn't leave until she had this conversation, and she had no hope of getting the keys from him, even in his weakened state.

"Tattletale," she muttered to Rex, then gave him a dirty look when he grinned at her. "Hello?"

"What's going on?" Virgil demanded.

Tilting her head back, she stared up at the sky and breathed in the scent of pine. "Mom's been murdered."

His response, when it came, was so low she could barely hear it. "I'm sorry, Laurel."

Suddenly the tears that'd been so conspicuously missing began to burn behind her eyes. Determined not to shed them, she blinked rapidly. She was done crying. She was done allowing herself to be frightened and intimidated, too. This was *her* life, damn it. She was taking it back.

"How'd it happen?" he asked.

"She was stabbed. Sonja Ivey found her on the floor of the laundry room."

"The Crew got hold of her?"

"Who else? With Ink out of prison, that has to be it." Tears leaked out despite her efforts to dam them, so she simply squeezed her eyes shut and relied on her glasses to hide them.

"I haven't told you this, but…I tried to warn her."

This took Vivian aback. "*You* called Mom?"

"I went to see her. Right after we left Washington, D.C."

Her eyes popped open. If he'd contacted Ellen, he hadn't been as impervious to the doubts that had plagued her as he'd pretended. "What did she have to say?"

"Nothing more than she always said. She didn't know Gary was planning to kill Martin. She'd never be party to such a thing. She only thought it was me because of what the detectives told her."

"And you said?"

"What could I say?"

"You could've said you believe her."

"I tried. It just…wasn't there."

Vivian understood. How many times had she hovered on the brink of forgiving Ellen? Too many times to count. And yet, even when she *wanted* to believe, when she made up her mind to trust, Ellen's story rang false. "Weren't you afraid that showing up there might be exactly what The Crew wanted you to do?"

"I was careful to minimize the risk."

"Meaning…"

"I flew into Phoenix, rented a car and drove from there. Then I returned the car in San Francisco and flew out."

"Why didn't you tell me about this trip?"

"I don't know."

Because their mother was a hard subject for both of them. Because the visit hadn't changed his mind, as he'd probably hoped it would. Because it was easier to pretend, as he had for years, that he didn't care.

"You could've taken me with you."

"I needed to meet with her alone. Give her one last chance."

Ellen hadn't realized it had been her last chance. She'd been trying to convince Vivian as little as six months ago that they could still be a family. But that was so typical of her.

"I told her about The Crew," he said. "I explained why I joined them and why they wouldn't let me go. I made sure she understood that they'd use any means available to find me, including her, and that they weren't going to give up anytime soon. I suggested she leave the area."

"Advice she obviously ignored."

"Yes. She felt safe since she didn't know where I lived or how to contact me. We haven't been part of her life for so long…I guess she thought they'd continue to assume she was out of the picture. And she met Randall the day I left. After that she forgot about everything else."

Suddenly the irony of the situation became clear to Vivian. Ellen cared more about the men in her life than she'd ever cared about her kids. Her many romances always came first. Yet, in the end, she'd been alone.

Not only that, but if Ellen had instigated Martin's murder, it was her fault that Virgil had gone to prison.

And it was because he'd joined a gang in order to survive that Ellen had lost her life. What she'd set in motion nearly twenty years ago had come full circle.

Too bad there wasn't more satisfaction in knowing that. No matter what Vivian believed, she could never wish this kind of death on her own mother. "So why would they kill her now, after all this time?" she asked. "They could've gone after her four years ago."

"They knew we didn't have any contact, so they didn't see any point in it. But enough time has passed that… they must've decided to take a chance."

She watched a cruiser drive slowly past, knew the cop inside was probably wondering if they were doing a drug deal. They were standing in a park, just the two of them, and they didn't have kids, a dog or a picnic basket. "It's not only that."

"What do you mean?"

"It's Ink."

"You think he killed her himself?"

"If not, he's behind it." Which meant her worst fears were becoming a reality. "Question is…how close is he?"

"That depends on what our mother told him."

"She couldn't have told him much. Maybe she jotted down the numbers I called from, and passed that along, or turned over her phone records. But that's it."

"So we have to assume Ink knows you live in Montana. Maybe, through Horse or some other contact, he even has a cop on the payroll who's been able to trace one of those numbers to Pineview."

It was chilling to hear Virgil say that. His acknowledgment of how easily Ink could find her made it that much more real. He could be waiting at her house right now. "That's why I need Rex to bring Jake and Mia to you until this thing plays out."

"Are you crazy?" he snapped. "No way do I want you there alone."

"It's better than having me here with the kids. What if I can't protect them?"

"What if you can't protect yourself? Come *with* Jake and Mia. You can start over. One more time. This is a great area. I'll pay for the move, whatever you need."

She wished it could be that simple. She missed Virgil and Peyton. But she didn't want to leave Pineview, especially because she had no assurance that this would be the last time she'd have to flee. "And when they find us in New York?"

"We'll deal with that when we come to it."

The cop appeared again, slowed and parked next to her Blazer. He didn't get out, but he distracted Vivian, irritated her. The police were present and available when she *didn't* need them, but she had no confidence she'd have help when it mattered most. They'd never been able to help her before. "No. I'm finished running. I won't move again."

"Then I'll have to come there."

"You can't leave Peyton unprotected!"

"I can't leave you unprotected, either."

"This is my choice."

"You must not be thinking straight."

Rex wasn't comfortable having that cop so close. He eyed the cruiser as he leaned against the picnic table. He was shaky, not feeling good. Vivian could tell. But he was trying hard not to show it. "I'm making perfect sense. And that's what has you so angry. You don't have a better plan."

When he didn't immediately reply, she knew she had him. "Tell me the truth," she said. "What would you do if you were me?"

"I'm *not* you. I spent fourteen years fighting with men in other gangs. I've had to kill to save my own life, Laurel. Even if I thought you could defend yourself, I don't want you to experience that. It's too much. You never forget it. Listen, Peyton's not due for two weeks. Let me come out there and—"

"No. She could go into labor at any time. Gestational diabetes makes it a high-risk pregnancy. I know how worried you are. Are you really going to leave her? What if she loses this one, too?"

No answer. He was weighing his options, trying to decide, so she gentled her voice and tried to persuade him. "Stay, Virgil. Take care of your family. I'm guessing Ink's already here. That means I need to deal with it."

"Why not send the kids but have Rex stay with you?" he asked.

Vivian shot Rex a sideways glance. "Because Rex needs help himself."

"What kind of help?"

"You know what kind of help. Get him into rehab as soon as he walks off the plane."

"That's bullshit," Rex said. "Give me my damn phone. Rehab can wait."

She stepped out of reach. With a cop watching, he wouldn't force the issue. "We have no idea how long this situation might take to resolve itself. One week? Two? A month?" she said to Virgil. "Rex is barely hanging on. He won't admit it because he's a stubborn fool but he needs help."

"Now you're really pissing me off," Rex growled. "I'll take the kids to Virgil, but I'm coming back."

"He will, you know," Virgil said. "He won't let you face this alone."

He'd probably try. But she didn't think his body could handle much more. "We'll talk about that once you have the kids."

She had a feeling it would all be over by then, anyway.

17

The digging seemed to go on forever since Ink couldn't do much of it. L.J. was young and strong, but it took one man with a shovel several hours to dig four graves, even in the soft, loamy earth of the forest. Ink would've skipped burying the bodies; he was anxious to return to town now that they had a car. But he couldn't leave his victims in the house. The stench would soon be unbearable, even if they shoved them into a closet or a back bedroom. And they couldn't just dump them in the forest in case someone stumbled across them. Provided no one realized these men were missing, quite some time could pass before anyone came looking for them. Certainly long enough for him and L.J. to finish their business here in Pineview.

That meant they had to bury the dead.

Ink was glad they'd made that decision, out of sight, out of mind. While L.J. toiled in the forest, Ink had been swabbing up the blood in the living room—as much as he could reach. He'd been so determined to shoot every man before that man could react he'd slaughtered them all before they knew what hit them. And it'd created quite a mess.

Relieved to be done with the cleaning, he stood and watched L.J. work.

"This is bullshit." L.J. rested against his shovel and wiped the sweat from his forehead. "It's hotter 'n hell this afternoon, and here I am doing manual labor."

"So? At least you won't have to sleep on the ground tonight." Ink tossed the camera belonging to one of his victims into the grave that would soon hold another of the bodies. "No more going without a shower, either." He took the beer he'd carried out under his arm and popped the top. "There's another one of these waiting for you in the fridge."

"You gotta be joking! You think I care about having a beer right now?" L.J. motioned to the blanket that covered the only man he hadn't yet pushed into the ground. "This guy's blood's all over me." He held out his arms to show Ink the pink rivulets where the dead man's blood had blended with sweat.

Ink merely shrugged. He'd seen and done a lot worse than shoot a few guys who happened to be in the wrong place at the wrong time. After he'd killed his sister for getting him in trouble with the cops because he'd robbed a liquor store, he'd stood by her casket and cried along with his mother, all the while smiling inside that he didn't have to deal with the bitch anymore.

"So? Someone had to carry him out," he told L.J. "It didn't hurt you." He took a long drink of his beer, found it as refreshing as he'd hoped. "Just be glad you're not him, huh?" He pointed at the dead guy and laughed but L.J. didn't join in.

"You scare me, dude." This wasn't a casual statement. Ink had been the kid's idol in prison but L.J. no longer seemed impressed, and Ink wasn't all that surprised. No one liked him once they really got to know him, and that bothered him more than he wanted to admit. Pretty soon, every person who encountered him looked as horrified as L.J. did now. His own sister used to stare at him as if she'd never seen a bigger monster. That was another reason he'd killed her. She was his first murder, not that anyone had been able to pin her death on him. Not yet, anyway. The police were still working on that one. Had been for fifteen years and probably always would be. He'd done it as a drive-by while riding along with some of his more violent friends and she was walking home from school. Everyone assumed a rival gang had made the hit.

"That's good." He told himself the change in L.J.'s feelings about him didn't matter. L.J. wasn't going anywhere until Ink was done with him. "You *should* be scared. Because if you ever cross me—" he grinned "—you know what'll happen."

L.J. gaped at him as if he'd never seen him before.

"Why so glum, huh? Now that we've got a cabin and a car, the fun's just starting." Ink lifted his can in a salute and hobbled back to the house. He'd taken eight hundred bucks off the men he'd killed, four cell phones that didn't work, thanks to the remote location, the keys to their vehicle and several credit cards. He didn't understand why L.J. was so shaken. They were set.

Now all they had to do was head into town and find Laurel.

Myles put out a Be on the Lookout, or BOLO, on the two men he'd found with the Toyota truck. Then he spent the afternoon and evening driving around Libby and Pineview, asking everyone he met if they'd seen anyone fitting either description. "Ron Howard" and his younger companion seemed to have disappeared into thin air, but they had to have gone somewhere. When Harvey left them on the side of the road, they'd been on foot, which gave them only three options. They'd walked. (Which meant they couldn't have gone far.) They'd stolen another car. (There'd been no reports of that—at least, not yet.) Or they'd hitchhiked. Surely, anyone who'd picked them up would remember.

Bob, down at the Gas-n-Go, told Myles they'd been in to get gas yesterday. Based on his estimate of the time, Myles figured it was right before he'd found them on the road. He hoped their images had been captured on the security tape; he planned to create a flyer. A picture would be a far better search aid than mere descriptions.

But the tape was so old and overused he couldn't differentiate one customer from the next, let alone capture images clear enough to print. He told Bob to buy a new tape, just in case they came in again, and left disappointed. He wanted to find out who these men were, what their backgrounds were and why they'd driven a truck stolen on the outskirts of a farming community in central California all the way to Montana. What business did they have here? Unless they had family in the area, the backwoods of Lincoln County was a bit out of the way for a random visit.

He checked the frozen lasagna he'd put in the oven when he got home. Not done. Those things took forever. Judging by the frozen lump in the center he wouldn't be eating until midnight. But it didn't matter. It wasn't as if Marley was waiting for supper. He'd let her go to Elizabeth's more than six hours ago. He didn't like that she was outside his protection, but he believed she was safer there, with adults, than staying alone while he worked, especially after dark.

Thinking it might help him find "Ron" and "Peter" if he put a notice about them in the paper, he called Chester. Chester was already in bed, but his wife woke him and he immediately agreed to do a write-up. Myles hung up just as the timer went off on the lasagna.

"Now that I'm too tired to eat," he grumbled. He'd been going on very little sleep for the better part of a week and had pushed himself extra hard today. He was determined to solve Pat's murder. Keeping his mind occupied also stopped him from obsessing over Vivian. The jealousy that'd reared up this morning hadn't gone anywhere. It simmered in the background, making him glance out his kitchen window every so often to see if Rex's motorcycle was still parked where he'd seen it earlier.

As of two seconds ago, it was. Two minutes before that it'd been there, too. The same held true for ten minutes earlier and so on. Myles was pretty sure, at this point, that Rex was staying the night.

Did that mean he'd be sleeping on the sofa?

Myles was staring into space as he contemplated this question when the doorbell rang. Turning off the timer, he retrieved the slow-cooking lasagna and sat it on top of the stove so he could answer the door. It was late, too late for regular guests. So he hoped Vivian had come to talk about last night, or at least explain her relationship with her unexpected visitor.

But it wasn't his neighbor. It was his neighbor's guest.

A fresh spurt of dislike caused Myles to stiffen. Despite Rex's shabby appearance, most women would find him attractive, Myles had to admit. He had a reckless, rock-star air about him that, unfortunately, extended to his not-so-well-hidden drug habit. Myles didn't want to notice the sheen of sweat that made Rex's T-shirt cling to him, the clammy pallor of his skin or the slight trembling of his hands. Myles had enough going on without worrying about some out-of-towner's addiction. In fact, he wished he could forget Rex *and* Vivian, but that wasn't going to happen anytime soon. Not after making love to her at the cabin.

"What can I do for you?" he asked.

A toothpick dangled from Rex's mouth. He chewed on it, apparently in no hurry to respond.

"Well?" Myles prompted.

Rex moved the toothpick to one side with his tongue. "Can I come in?"

Myles gave him a somewhat hesitant nod—his agreement stemmed more from curiosity than anything else—and held the door. "If you want."

After a quick glance at the light glowing in Vivian's kitchen, Rex frowned and stepped inside. Then he looked around and gave a grudging nod. "Nice."

Oddly enough, Myles got the impression that compliment was sincere. But a bitter note also rang through what Rex had said, and that stopped Myles from offering any kind of thanks. "I assume you didn't come over to check out my place."

"No." He shoved his hands in his pockets, probably to hide the shaking. "I came over to ask you a favor."

Myles had to catch his jaw to keep it from dropping. "You want something from *me?*"

The facade created by Rex's I-don't-give-a-shit attitude and that tough-guy toothpick routine cracked when he had to reach for a wall to steady himself. Myles almost felt sorry for him. Vivian's friend, or whatever he was to her, was too proud to be in this position. "You need a doctor," he said. "You know that, right?"

"Don't worry about me. I can take care of myself."

"Doesn't look like you're doing a very good job."

A self-deprecating smile twisted his lips. "Yeah, well, not all of us can be like you."

"If you hate me so much, or what this uniform stands for, why are you in my living room?"

"To tell you this." He grimaced, whether from pain or a general reluctance to continue, Myles couldn't tell. Humility didn't come easy for this guy. The only reason Myles could imagine he'd come over was that he had no other choice.

"I'm waiting."

"Vivian needs you. I can't...I can't protect her right now." His eyes grew watery, another sign of weakness he no doubt despised, but it was this subtle evidence of caring that evoked enough respect to temper, somewhat, Myles's previous opinion of him. At least Rex was sincere. At least he was worried about someone other than himself.

"What is she to you?" Myles wished this question wasn't so transparent, but...there it was.

Rex studied him before responding. "I'm a friend. We used to be more, but..." He shook his head. "We're no good as a couple. *I'm* no good for her," he clarified, being more honest. "She needs someone like you, someone who could be the father her children deserve, someone with a decent job and a house." He waved at the trappings around them. "You care about her, don't you?"

There was no arguing that she meant *something* to him, but Myles wasn't willing to examine what, not in front of Rex. Nor did he appreciate the idea that he might be some sort of consolation prize. "I don't want to see her hurt, if that's what you're asking."

"Then you're going to have to do your part."

Myles rested his hands on his hips. He'd taken off his utility belt. That thing weighed about twenty pounds and he didn't like lugging it around the house, but he hadn't changed out of his uniform yet. "What is my part, exactly? Is this where you tell me about her abusive ex-husband?"

Rex wiped the sweat beading his upper lip. "No, this is where I tell you that someone's trying to kill her."

He was serious. *Dead* serious. Suddenly Vivian's bringing that gun home from the bank made a whole lot more sense. So did her fear after hearing about Pat's murder. "And it's not her ex?"

"No."

"How do you know?"

"The threat isn't new. We've been in WitSec for four years. Well, we were in for two, until we left D.C. When The Crew found us there and came after us again, we figured there had to be a leak. So we abandoned the program and split up, hoping we could finally shake them."

"Who are The Crew?"

"They're members of a relatively new prison gang in California. Her brother and I used to belong."

"That doesn't tell me much. Why do they want *her* dead?"

"Payback. It's a long story, but basically they're determined to avenge a couple of deaths they blame us for, as well as a few convictions that wouldn't have been possible without information we provided."

"And how did *she* get involved in that?"

"They were trying to get to us through her and the kids, and some shit happened."

If he thought he could get away with such a short summary, he was mistaken. "Maybe you could explain *what* shit."

Besides being ill, Rex was clearly anxious, agitated and eager to get back to Vivian. "Shots were fired. People died. Others were hurt permanently and will never forget."

Myles couldn't imagine Vivian associated with any of that. But he'd never expected her to be associated with someone like Rex, either. "And how did you and her brother come in contact with this prison gang?"

Rex's chuckle held no mirth. "How do you think?"

It was as he suspected, then. "You're an ex-con."

He didn't confirm or deny it, but he didn't have to. His silence spoke for him. "She'll have to tell you herself. I can't stay. She won't be happy that I came over here. I just…couldn't leave town without knowing I'd done all I could for her."

"You're leaving Pineview?" Myles couldn't believe how glad he was to hear this. Evidently he felt more threatened by Rex and Vivian's history than he wanted to admit, even to himself.

"Yeah. Tomorrow morning. I'm taking Jake and Mia with me. They'll be staying with their uncle for a while. They're not safe here."

"If The Crew's trying to kill Vivian, she's not safe, either," Myles pointed out.

"She won't leave. That's why I'm depending on you."

"Why won't she go?"

"This place matters to her." Rex's gaze flicked over him again. "She's not willing to give it up."

Was Rex intimating that he thought Myles played some part in Pineview's appeal? And, if so, was it true? "So...let me get this straight. She's planning to defend herself?"

"She'll have to if she stays. And she's aware of that. She knows what these people are capable of. She's seen it before. I gotta go."

Myles followed him to the door, stopped him at the last minute. "But you still love her, right?" In the midst of everything else, Myles wasn't sure why he wanted to know this, but he did.

"I wouldn't be standing here if I didn't."

At least he was honest. Myles had guessed correctly, but that only confirmed everything he'd been telling himself. He'd been stupid to get mixed up in Vivian's love life. For his own good, and Marley's, he needed to stay out of it in the future. But now that The Crew had come to his community, there was a lot more at stake than protecting his heart. "Where does her brother live? How will I be able to reach you?"

"You won't."

"You're asking me to look out for her, but you don't trust me enough to tell me where to find you?"

"The less you know, the better. Just in case."

Myles shook his head. "You don't have much confidence in me."

"I could say the same."

There was no answer to that. They regarded each other with equal distrust.

"You're a small-town cop who's probably never come up against people like this," Rex added. "The odds aren't in your favor."

Myles stopped him once again. "Before you walk

away, tell me what you know about the men who're coming after her."

"I'm guessing there're two. They busted out of a California prison ten days ago."

"What makes you think they're coming here?"

"That Realtor dude who was killed, for one."

"What connection does The Crew have with Pat?"

"None. Except for how senseless the killing was. Whoever did it was probably looking for a place to stay or money or something else and negotiations didn't go as planned."

"You said, 'for one.' What else makes you think they're coming here?"

"Besides the fact that they've sworn to see us all dead?"

"Yeah."

"They've already started to make good on that promise. They stabbed Vivian's mother to death sometime in the past week."

Myles felt his eyebrows jerk up. "They killed her *mother?*"

"Neighbor found her."

Shit... This was serious, all right. "And Vivian knows?"

"About her mother? As of this morning, she does."

How was he supposed to react to that? Vivian was caught up in something bigger than he could ever have imagined. "And the names of the men who broke out of prison are..."

"I only know one of them. He's called Ink. Spent a lot of time with him back in the day but don't remember his real name because I never used it. All I know is that he's a crazy son of a bitch."

"What does he look like?"

"He's got tattoos—"

With a scowl, Myles pulled his shirt out of his pants in preparation for removing his uniform once Rex left. "Let me guess. Those tattoos are all over, including his face. Lightning bolts for eyebrows?"

Rex stopped trying to make his escape and actually advanced toward him. "You've seen him."

He recalled the uneasiness he'd felt in the presence of "Ron Howard" and his younger buddy. "Yesterday. With a kid maybe nineteen, driving a stolen truck. Only I didn't know it was stolen at the time, or I would've arrested them."

This news seemed to infuse Rex with enough adrenaline to overcome the physical symptoms of his addiction. He quit shaking, became extremely focused. "Were you alone?"

"Yes."

"Then it's a good thing you didn't try. Where are they now?"

That was the million-dollar question. "I wish I knew." Especially because he was pretty sure that Rex was right. These escapees had killed Pat. Two men fresh out of prison would need to buy some regular shoes. They might even buy the same shoes. And those shoes would likely be cheap, common and brand-spanking-new.

Rex cursed, paced and cursed some more. "You have to find them before they find Laurel. You realize that."

"Who's Laurel?" This was getting more complicated by the minute.

He waved impatiently. "Vivian. Of course I'm talking about Vivian."

"Her real name's *Laurel?*"

"Used to be. Laurel Hodges. At least, that was her married name."

TH. Those were the initials of her husband. His name was Tom Hodges. Myles finally knew, but that was little consolation. The woman he'd slept with at the cabin wasn't even the person he thought she was. No wonder she'd been so secretive, so hard to know. Understanding brought a touch of comfort because it explained so much. And yet...he'd already lost Amber Rose. Only a fool would get emotionally involved in this.

Myles thought of a dozen additional questions he needed to ask. But Rex wouldn't wait any longer. "She'll have to tell you the rest," he said. "She's got enough going on over there packing up her kids' stuff. I don't want her to realize you know until after I'm gone. It'll only upset her that I told you." He paused. "There's just one more thing you need to understand."

"What's that?"

"You can't trust *anyone*. Especially anyone from California or the Federal Bureau of Prisons."

Myles frowned. "Don't tell me you've concocted some conspiracy theory. You were just gaining a little credibility."

Rex didn't like that response. He came over and got right in Myles's face. "Listen to me. This gang is more powerful than you think. They bribe, threaten, coerce, do whatever they need to do in order to gain information. If you put Laurel's location out there, they'll access it, and they'll show up long before the cavalry. Or they'll wait until she's supposedly safe, and then they'll make their move."

Myles refused to back away. "I can't let anyone know she's here. Is that what you're saying?"

"If you do, she'll wind up dead."

And with that he walked out, letting the screen door slam behind him.

Myles blew out a sigh as he tried to take in everything he'd just learned—the fact that it was Vivian who'd brought Pat's killer to Pineview, that she must've suspected and hadn't told him, that she was probably too scared to trust anyone but should've trusted him....

Sometime later, he sat on the couch and leaned his head back as he continued to think. He must've fallen into an uneasy sleep because that sleep was disturbed the following morning when he heard car doors opening and shutting outside.

Leaning up to peer out the window, he saw Jake and Mia standing in Vivian's driveway while Vivian—or Laurel—and Rex loaded her car.

"How long will we be gone, Mommy?" he could hear Mia ask.

"For a few weeks. It'll be a great vacation. You'll get to play with your cousin, see the new baby after she's born, be with your aunt and uncle." Vivian's voice sounded unnaturally high, too high to be as excited as she was pretending.

"I can't wait!" Jake seemed genuinely enthusiastic. "It's been *so* long since we've seen Uncle Virgil. I'm going to tell him about the fish I caught."

Vivian said something Myles couldn't quite hear; he guessed it was about how proud his uncle would be. Then Mia spoke up again. "Will we get to see Daddy when we're there?"

The slight delay in Vivian's response suggested this wasn't an easy question to answer. "No, sweetheart. I'm sorry. Not this time. Maybe later. Daddy doesn't live anywhere near Uncle Virgil."

"Will we get to see Dad for Christmas, then?" Jake asked.

"Maybe," she replied. "I'm working on it."

By trying to stop the men who were trying to kill her so she could come out of hiding? Was that what she meant?

"I'm going to ask Santa to bring Daddy to our house for Christmas," Mia said, which obviously meant it *had* to happen because Santa would never disappoint her the way mere mortals would.

Neither adult argued with her. Rex kept loading the luggage; Vivian got Mia and Jake buckled into their seats.

"You have everything?" Myles heard Rex ask.

"I think so," she said.

Rex grabbed her arm before she could climb behind the wheel. "Are you sure you won't change your mind and go with us? *Please?*"

She slipped out of his grasp. "I can't," she said, and Myles could tell she was weeping.

18

"You look worried."

Virgil glanced up to see his pregnant wife at the door to their home office. "I don't know what to do."

"She won't come?"

They'd discussed Laurel before, lying in bed last night, whispering so they wouldn't wake Brady. "No."

"Do you feel you need to go to Montana?"

The strain in her voice let him know she wouldn't be glad to see him do that. She was scared of losing him. He was equally scared of losing her. After all he'd been through in his life, he was happy, whole, at last. But he wouldn't be happy or whole without her.

"I'd go if we weren't so close to having the baby. I hate leaving Laurel on her own. But...this has been such a difficult pregnancy."

Peyton came over and sat on his lap, and he rested his forehead on her shoulder as he wrapped his arms around her. "Are you sorry you married me yet?"

Her hands covered his. She knew he was teasing, but she answered seriously. "I could never be sorry about that."

He rubbed her big belly, trying to get his baby to move. There was nothing more reassuring to him than feeling their tiny daughter shift inside Peyton's womb. Peyton had endured so many fertility treatments and dealt with so many complications since those treatments had worked—gestational diabetes, water retention, early cramping. He couldn't wait to cradle this latest addition to their family in his arms and feel he had half a chance of protecting what they'd fought so hard to create. Fifteen months ago, they'd lost a little boy to a very late miscarriage, and it was worse than anything he'd ever experienced, mostly because the pain wasn't just his. Peyton had been devastated.

"Why'd this have to come up *now?*" he grumbled. "Right before the baby?"

"It wouldn't be any easier afterward," she said. "You wouldn't want to leave me with Brady and a newborn."

True, but what about Laurel? She'd always been so close to him, so loyal, and regardless of what she thought she could do with that gun he'd given her, she wasn't capable of defending herself. Not against The Crew. They were determined, brutal, relentless. Ink, especially, had no conscience. He'd rape and torture her before he killed her, if he ever got the chance. Rex had called from the airport in Montana to say he'd alerted local law enforcement to what was happening. The sheriff lived next door to Laurel. But was that enough?

It was so hard for Virgil to rely on anyone else, even the police. In the past, they'd had the protection of federal marshals and it hadn't helped.

"No, I guess I wouldn't be able to leave then, either," he admitted.

"How are you feeling about the murder of your mother?"

This question surprised him. Other than what Ellen's

murder said about The Crew and what they might or
might not be doing, he'd put it out of his mind. He'd never
wished her dead, but her death was easier to take than
her betrayal had been. "The same," he said. "As far as
I'm concerned, she was a complete stranger to me."

"Her murder hasn't changed *anything?*"

"Nothing." Maybe Martin had been a lazy, selfish,
abusive asshole who deserved what he got as much as
anyone could. But Ellen's compulsion to save herself
at any cost, even at the cost of her own children? That
wasn't a mother to him. What made her actions even
more reprehensible was that she'd waited so long to take
responsibility for what she'd done. She'd lied and lied,
and she'd kept lying, forcing him and Laurel to writhe in
uncertainty for years. Ellen had waited so long to come
clean that, when she finally told him, it made very little
difference in his life.

Peyton twisted around to see his face. "Are you ever
going to tell Laurel what you learned two years ago?"

He'd had the opportunity when he'd talked to his sister
on the phone and hadn't taken it. He wasn't sure why.
When Ellen was alive, he'd justified keeping her confession to himself because his silence gave Laurel the best
possible chance of establishing a relationship with her,
which was what he thought Laurel secretly wanted. But
now? Their mother was dead. He could no longer use
that excuse, and yet he was *still* reluctant to divulge the
ugly truth.

Why? Was it due to some inexplicable urge to protect
his mother by hiding her true nature from Laurel? Or
was he trying to protect his sister from the disappoint-

ment he'd felt? He wasn't convinced she needed to learn at this late date. Would it help her in any way?

He couldn't see how. Not knowing was torture, but so was facing the harsh reality. Maybe it would be different if Ellen had been innocent. But she'd been guilty as hell. And there'd been nothing to redeem her, even in her confession. She only told him when she did because she'd been between boyfriends, was getting older and feeling lonely, and she'd hoped she could use her children to fill the emptiness in her life.

"Well?" Peyton prompted when he hesitated.

Virgil rubbed his eyes. He hadn't slept last night. He'd tossed and turned, worrying about Laurel, Peyton and Brady, the new baby, Rex. "Eventually. Maybe. But not yet. She's going through enough right now."

"You should've turned Ellen in."

"Why? She was my mother. Besides, I'd already paid the price for her crime. There wasn't anything to be gained by sending her to prison."

"Some people would argue with that."

He cocked an eyebrow at her. "Some? Like my deputy warden wife?"

"*Former* deputy warden. And, yes, I would like to have seen her charged."

"My testimony might not have made a difference. You know that. She didn't give me any damning details. She just told me she asked Gary to 'take care' of Martin, like he claims. That was all I could get out of her."

"You believe she might've denied what she told you? Later on?"

"If the police came calling? Sure. Why wouldn't she, after everything else she did?"

Peyton tucked her long hair behind her ears. "I guess I wouldn't put it past her."

Deciding whether or not to turn his mother in hadn't been difficult for Virgil. It was deciding whether to tell Laurel that'd been tough. And it still was. He didn't want to give his sister another emotional hurdle to clear. Maybe, with Ellen gone, it would be easier for both of them to leave the past in the past. As much as Virgil hated to admit it, they were both better off without her in the world. There was no manual on how to act when you had a selfish, lying murderer for a mother. Ellen was always so soft-spoken and nice. Pretty, too. Dealing with her was confusing as hell. Should they sympathize with the desperation that'd made her resort to murder? Chalk up her behavior to a few months of insanity and then too much fear to ever attempt to right her wrong? Assume she was sorry, that she'd changed even though she'd never taken responsibility for her actions?

Peyton stood. "So what are you going to do?"

"Maybe I'll tell her later. When we have a chance to be together." *Maybe* being the operative word...

"I'm talking about The Crew."

Pursing his lips, he rocked back in his chair and said what had been going around and around in his head since he'd first learned of Ellen's murder and realized what it meant. "I'm going to call Horse."

His wife's eyes latched onto his. "You can't mean that."

"I have to do *something*."

"And this is what you've come up with? What on earth will you say to him?"

"Mommy, what's wrong?"

Brady stood by the door, frowning at the tension in the room. He wasn't used to seeing them at odds.

"Nothing, honey," she responded, but the fact that she didn't so much as glance back at him told Virgil she was completely involved in their conversation. He understood why. Calling Horse was a huge risk. But doing nothing could prove to be an even greater one.

Spotting his father, Brady scampered past Peyton. Virgil wouldn't let Peyton lift him up, not while she was pregnant, so these days Brady relied primarily on Virgil to carry him when he wanted it. He snuggled with his mother only when she was sitting on the couch or lying down. "Can we throw the baseball, Daddy?" he asked as he climbed into Virgil's lap where Peyton had sat just seconds before.

"In a minute, bud." For now, Peyton still had him pinned beneath a disapproving stare.

"I asked you a question," she reminded him.

Virgil drew a deep breath. "I'll explain that he'd better not pick this fight."

"Or..."

"I'll finish it."

He was transferred several times before he spoke to someone at California's Department of Corrections and Rehabilitation who could help him, but it wasn't long before Myles had the information he was looking for. The mug shots for the inmates who'd broken out of the California Men's Colony had come through the fax machine and, sure enough, he recognized them. One was "Ron Howard." Nickname Ink. Real name Eugene Rider. The kid who'd claimed to be Peter Ferguson was Lloyd Beachum, age nineteen. Lloyd had three priors for drug possession and grand larceny, but Eugene's arrest record made Lloyd's look like child's play. Rape. Armed robbery. Arson. Several counts of murder.

With a curse, Myles dialed the number he'd just gotten from the CDCR.

A woman answered. "Warden Wright's office."

To avoid the noise two of his deputies were making as they reported for work, Myles got up and closed his office door. "Is the warden in?"

"He is, but I'm afraid he's not available. Can I take a message?"

"This is Sheriff King in Pineview, Montana. Tell him I spotted your boys and believe they're still in this area."

"Excuse me?"

He returned to his seat. "The two convicts who cut a hole in the fence and slipped out ten days ago? They're in Montana."

"Oh, dear! Um, in that case, hang on. I'm sure he'll want to speak with you sooner rather than later."

Two or three minutes dragged by before a male voice boomed across the line. "Sheriff?"

"Yes?"

"Thanks for calling. You have something to report on our escapees?"

Propping his elbows on the desk, Myles smoothed his eyebrows with a finger and one thumb. "I wish I had more than I do, but I'll give you what I've got. They stole a red Toyota truck from a Quentin J. Ferguson in Monrovia, which they drove here. A leak in the radiator stranded them on the side of the road. That's where I found them yesterday."

"Tell me you have them in custody."

"I'm afraid not." Myles explained what had happened, then mentioned Pat Stueben's murder.

"Eugene Ryder should never have been transferred from Pelican Bay. He's a level-four prisoner if I've ever met one." The stress in the warden's voice revealed just how much he wanted to get these particular inmates back where they belonged.

Myles had wondered what someone convicted of so many counts of murder was doing in anything less than maximum security. But it happened sometimes. Due to good behavior, time served, overcrowding or myriad other reasons, their points dropped. "Considering his long list of offenses, why'd they reclassify him?"

"Four years ago, Ryder tried to kill a woman who was going into WitSec. Murdered the federal marshal who was protecting her, but he took a bullet that night that nearly severed his spinal cord. He was never supposed to walk again. He's done much better than the doctors predicted, but he's in constant pain. No one dreamed he'd leave his free and ready supply of codeine and head for the hills. When his back gets bad, he can barely limp around. And it's bad almost all the time."

Was the warden joking? Prison doctors didn't have a corner on the painkiller market. "But there are plenty of alternatives to codeine available on the street. Including some drugs, both legal and illegal, that are a lot stronger."

"He spent two years in Pelican Bay after the shooting, seemed like a different man. And they're so crowded up there."

Myles read over Ryder's arrest record again. They thought he was a different man? This was obviously a screwup, and the warden didn't want to admit it. So Myles changed tactics. "Who shot him?"

"Don't know. Until ten days ago, he was just another inmate to me. Now all I care about is dragging his ass back here."

Myles remembered the stories Mia had shared with her friend at school. Had she witnessed the shooting that'd injured Ryder? Or the slaying of the marshal?

Rex had mentioned that The Crew had been out to get Vivian and her brother for a long time, that they'd been in protective custody. "Was it the woman he was trying to rape who shot him?"

"Could've been. I haven't looked into those details. They don't matter. All that matters is what's happening now. We gotta get these boys back in prison before they hurt someone else."

But they'd have a far greater chance of catching their "boys" if they could figure out where they might be going and why. And that could be linked to their pasts. "What can you tell me that might help me locate Eugene? Does he have family in Montana? Friends?"

"No. His family lives in San Diego, and he lost touch with them years ago. This guy's a career criminal and not right in the head. His family's as scared of him as everyone else, especially his mother. When he was only twelve he tried to set her bed on fire while she was sleeping."

Nice son... "So he won't be reaching out to them anytime soon."

"They certainly hope not. But we've been in touch, just in case."

"What about the guy who escaped with him? Beachum? Where's his family?"

"He's from Modesto, here in California. We're in contact with his family, too, or what's left of it. He was born to a crack addict who lost him to Child Protective Services when he was eleven. From there he bounced around the foster system for three or four years. Finally wound up on the street. Mother claims she hasn't heard from him, but she's still on the pipe so who knows if she'd even remember."

Myles groped for some other way to track Eugene Ryder. "*Someone* had to help these men escape. Someone on the outside. A girlfriend. A family member. A buddy. Isn't that how it usually works?"

"More often than not."

"Have you figured out who that might be?"

"No. They have a lot of friends, Sheriff, but not the type who'll help us. Ryder and Beachum belong to a gang called The Crew."

That was the problem, not the answer.

"They must've had some wire cutters smuggled in so they could cut the fence," the warden was saying. "But we could drag every member of that gang into my office and interrogate the hell out of them for hours and not a single one would talk, because nothing we're at liberty to do can compare with what'll happen to them if they rat out a fellow member."

"But you've tried to talk to them? Maybe there's a weak link. Someone who really hates Ryder and would like to see him get caught. Someone who, down deep, wants to do the right thing."

Laughter crackled over the phone. "I can see you've never worked in a prison."

That told him they hadn't called in any of Ryder's or Beachum's "buddies." "Look, I already have one dead man here, thanks to your escapees. I expect you to do all you can, no matter how futile it may seem."

Silence greeted this response. Myles had been speaking out of frustration more than anything else, but he didn't apologize. When Ryder and Beachum drove that beat-up Toyota into his town and killed Pat, California's problem had become *his* problem. And he didn't appreciate it.

"We *are* doing all we can, Sheriff." His manner, suddenly wooden and overly polite, indicated any camaraderie had come to an end. His next words confirmed that the conversation had, as well. "Thanks for calling."

"Wait!" Myles tried to catch him before he could hang up. There was no response, but he didn't hear a click so he barreled on. "Tell me this. Why would these men come to Montana?"

"Sheriff, I didn't even know they were in Montana until you told me. But it's as good a place to hide as anywhere else, I suppose."

The California authorities knew nothing, just as Myles had suspected. Laurel Hodges had left WitSec, so she didn't even have that conduit to people who might know where she was and inform her of this escape. That tempted Myles to open their eyes, despite Rex's warning. "You need to check out the shooting incident that damaged Ryder's spine," he said.

"Why?"

"Because maybe these two cons aren't looking for freedom. Maybe they're looking for revenge."

"Against whom?"

"Whoever was involved in that shooting!"

The way the warden cleared his throat and deepened his voice reminded Myles of his father. "Do you know something you're not telling me, Sheriff?"

Was he going to tell what he knew? *All* of it?

Myles tapped his fingers on the desk while he tried to decide. He wasn't sure he believed what Rex said about The Crew being able to find out everything the authorities knew. That would require too much corruption, or too many girlfriends working in too many government offices. But…Los Angeles, where he'd been told this gang was largely based, wasn't Pineview. Maybe he was being too naive. "I know they're not out for a joyride. That's what I know."

Long after he hung up, Myles sat staring at the phone. Should he have explained that Vivian was Laurel Hodges and her life was at stake? That she was a mother of two children? That she'd already been through far too much and deserved to feel safe for a change?

He could've tried to enlist their support, offered to collaborate. Most sheriffs would've done so; he'd certainly considered it.

But he couldn't ignore what Rex had said. Apparently he trusted Vivian's ex-boyfriend more than he wanted to admit. Or maybe he just didn't want to see what might happen if he disregarded that advice. Either way, he'd told the warden that Ryder and Beachum were here. Let them come look for their escapees without knowing any more about Laurel and her whereabouts than they did now. He'd make sure she was safe.

Speaking of safe… Myles glanced at the clock. He needed to head back to Pineview. He didn't want Vivian returning from the airport in Kalispell to an empty house.

He'd just scooped up his keys and started for the door when one of his deputies—Ben Jones, his most recent hire—intercepted him.

"Ned Blackburn's on the phone for you," Jones announced.

Ned was an insurance salesman who was also on Myles's softball team. At their last practice, Myles had mentioned that he'd like to increase his life insurance. But now was not the time. "Tell him I'm busy. I'll have to call him back when things slow down around here." He tried to circumvent Jones, but Jones caught his arm.

"I think you're going to want to talk to him, Sheriff." Myles hesitated. "Why's that?"

"He says he saw those two men you're looking for. Gave 'em a ride yesterday."

At last. Maybe Ned was the person who'd picked up Ryder and Beachum after Harvey left them on the side of the road. Or he'd given them a ride since. The way word spread in a place like Pineview, he knew it couldn't be long before he heard *something*.

"Where is he?" Myles asked, suddenly far more interested than he'd been before.

"Line one."

"Can he show us exactly where he dropped them off?"

"Says he can. Told me he'd drive you there right now if you'd like to go."

He did want to go. But he wanted to make sure Vivian was okay first. "Tell him to hang on, that I'll be with him in a second."

Myles returned to his desk and called Vivian's house. No answer. He hated to leave her at risk for even a minute, but he had no guarantee she was coming right back. For all he knew, she was spending the day in Kalispell shopping. It wasn't as if they'd talked before she left.

"Sheriff? Ned's waiting," Jones called out.

"I know, I know," he muttered, and glanced at his

watch again. It was only eleven. If he hurried, he could take that drive with Ned and get back to Pineview by noon.

Pressing the button with the flashing light, he brought the handset to his ear. "Ned? Where can you meet me?"

19

Vivian had made a commitment to this place. After moving around for most of her life, searching for her niche in the world, she'd finally found what she wanted, and she was determined not to abandon it. She'd painted and repaired this house herself. She'd spent hours looking for the right cast-off furnishings—unique and eclectic pictures, rugs, window coverings and furniture. She'd planted her garden. Tomatoes, eggplant, zucchini, watermelon, strawberries. Pumpkins for fall. If she left now she'd never see any of it come to fruition.

But sending her children away hadn't been easy. She didn't know if or when she'd see them again. And that caused all kinds of doubts. Was she making a mistake? Taking an unnecessary risk? Being too stubborn for her own good?

So many times she'd almost turned the car around and gone back to Kalispell to board a plane for New York. But it was the fact that she had no guarantee that they'd be able to stay there, either, that stopped her. A life on the run was no life at all.

Virgil and Peyton would raise Mia and Jake if anything happened to her. But that was small consolation, because her kids meant everything to her. She just couldn't envision finding another town or city where they'd be as happy as they were here. It wasn't the beauty of Pineview that convinced her, or her house, much as she prided herself on being a homeowner at last. It was the promise of what the future here might hold. It was Nana Vera. The women in her Thursday-night book group. Herb Scarborough at the bank. Mia's ballet instructor. Claire and all the other people she'd tried so hard not to love. They'd worked their way into her affections despite her resistance, and she wanted to stay and embrace them fully. To truly become who they thought she was and let go of the fear that had been driving her for so long.

She'd survived the abuse she'd suffered at Tom's hands, become a designer, even without a formal education, gotten over Rex when it would've been so much easier to continue wallowing in the mess they were together, and built a company to support her family. And she'd done it all on her own. She was established and successful and she wasn't going to let anyone take that away from her.

As she drove around the lake, her eyes gravitated to the two-story house next to hers. Her night with Sheriff King hadn't ended as well as she'd hoped. She couldn't imagine he was too impressed with her at this point. But she'd been able to act on the feelings she'd had toward him for so long and, regardless of what happened, she'd always treasure the experience.

Her gaze shifted to her own home. The coming days, maybe weeks, were going to be so strange without Mia and Jake. The place looked different already, empty and forlorn with Mia's tricycle on the grass and no little girl to come out and ride it.

How would she manage to live in a house where every noise, creak or rustle would be suspect?

She couldn't even guess. But she had to try.

After pulling into the driveway, she grabbed her gun from under the seat and got out, but she didn't walk around the car right away. She studied the place, searching for any sign that someone had been there while she was gone.

She couldn't see anything. So when a figure emerged from her porch, she nearly jerked up the Sig and squeezed off a round.

Claire had been sitting deep in the shadows, hidden behind a pillar. She must've walked over because there was no car nearby. She did that sometimes, even though it was nearly two miles. She liked the exercise. But if she hadn't called out when she did, Vivian might've shot her.

"Where're the kids?" her friend asked, raising a hand to block the glare of the sun.

Rattled by what she'd almost done, Vivian shoved the Sig in her purse, which just happened to be the biggest purse she'd ever designed. She hoped Claire hadn't seen the gun. It didn't look as if she had. Vivian was carrying Jake's jacket, which he'd left in the car when he got out, along with her purse, and the jacket had been partially covering her hand. Besides, Claire would never expect her to be carrying a weapon so she wasn't likely to assume anything, unless it was very obvious.

Still, the incident made Vivian wonder if she knew what she was doing. She'd decided what was best for her family, but what was best for the people of Pineview? They didn't deserve to get caught in the cross fire between her and Ink or whoever else The Crew had sent, and that could easily happen if Claire continued to show up here unannounced. Look at poor Trinity Woods. She'd been shot and killed on Vivian's doorstep in Colorado.

Vivian forced a smile. "They're visiting relatives out of state."

"Your sister?"

"Um, yeah." She'd made up a fictional family who lived in Denver. She felt guilty every time Claire mentioned them: *Have you talked to your parents? How are they doing? When's your sister's baby due?*

The subject seemed to come up again and again. But she'd had to provide *some* history. Everyone came from somewhere. To be able to share her excitement over Peyton's pregnancy, she'd created a sister named Macy who was recently married and expecting her first baby. She'd also made up parents who were retired schoolteachers and gone so far as to say her mother suffered from adult-onset diabetes, which was why Claire constantly asked after her health.

Was it time to tell her best friend the truth?

That was something she'd never dreamed she'd be able to do. Just considering it made her feel freer than she'd felt in four years. She could be honest again. Not only that, considering the danger, she had a moral obligation to be honest.

She just wasn't sure how to go about breaking the news, or how Claire might react. Claire had shared her deepest, darkest secrets, had trusted Vivian completely. How would she respond when she heard that Vivian hadn't been doing the same? That she'd pretended to be someone she wasn't from the very beginning?

Claire would feel betrayed. Hurt. Vivian didn't think she could cope with that right now, not in addition to the pressure and worry she was already experiencing. But she wouldn't be able to live with herself if anything happened to Claire, and that meant she had to warn her.

"So you're looking at some time off from the kids?" Claire waited on the porch steps. "How long will they be gone?"

"Possibly all summer." That sounded like an eternity to Vivian but she had to accept that it could take a while to solve her problem. If she was lucky, the police would find Ink and put him back in prison before Ink ever found her, and Horse would be busted along with him. Maybe they'd take down several more Crew members, and all the ones who felt so strongly about exacting revenge would be locked up.

If she was lucky it could happen. But she'd quit counting on luck years ago....

Fearing The Crew might come careering around the corner at any moment and gun them both down, she beckoned Claire to the car. "Let's go out to dinner."

Claire didn't move. "Right *now?*"

"Why not?"

"It's only three o'clock."

"I missed lunch." She'd missed breakfast, too. Feeling as unsettled as she did, she couldn't imagine stuffing food in her mouth, doubted she could keep anything down. It'd been too hard to say goodbye to her kids. But she had to get Claire out of here. "And...I have something to tell you."

Obviously concerned by her ominous tone, Claire came to meet her. "What is it?"

"Can we talk at the Chowhound?"

She smoothed her blouse, then wiped her hands on her khaki capris. "I guess. If that's what you want."

"It's what I want." Vivian watched the street, guarding Claire until she climbed into the passenger seat. Then she got behind the wheel.

"What's going on?" Claire was trying to work out how worried she should be, but Vivian couldn't prepare her. She was too busy rehearsing her part of the conversation....

"You'll see."

"Is it bad?"

"Yes."

She offered Vivian a weak smile. "Great. I love bad news."

Vivian had already started the engine. With a quick check in the rearview mirror, she peeled out of the drive, and Claire grabbed for her seat belt. She'd been too preoccupied by Vivian's references to impending disaster to put it on.

"Whoa! Be careful. You live next door to a cop, remember?"

How could she forget? She watched and waited for the sheriff all the time. She hadn't realized what a habit it'd become until the past couple of days. With Rex around, she couldn't gaze out the window or sit on the porch listening for Myles. Her fixation would be too noticeable, and that made it all the more apparent to *her*. "He's at work."

Claire seemed to understand that Vivian was gathering her thoughts. She studied her for a moment as if she could decipher the problem without words before attempting to move past her curiosity. "I bet Sheriff King's been busy."

"Very." The comment was innocent enough, but Vivian's mind immediately returned to the cabin where they'd made love. Claire would freak out if she knew. She'd been after Vivian for a long time to give the sheriff a chance. Like everyone else, she seemed to believe he could walk on water. If she wasn't still struggling to get over David's death of a few months earlier, Claire might've been interested in him herself.

"But you've talked to him, right?"

"Now and then." She'd tell Claire that she was really Laurel Hodges, but she wasn't going to mention her encounter with Myles King.

"Has he said anything about the murder?"

Now Claire was guessing at the bad news. "Not really."

As they reached the highway, Vivian noticed a car she didn't recognize turning down her street. She tensed— but there was an old woman in the driver's seat. Definitely not a member of The Crew.

"You okay?" Claire asked.

"Fine." Breathing easier the more distance she put between them and the house, she tried to calm down so she could handle the coming conversation as carefully as she needed to.

"So…the sheriff didn't tell you *anything* about the murder?" Claire pressed.

"It has nothing to do with what happened to your mother, Claire."

"You don't know that," she responded. "No one does."

Apparently, hearing that Alana had been murdered by some deranged killer was better than continuing to live with the mystery of her disappearance.

It broke Vivian's heart to see how deeply the past still affected the present. But she couldn't blame Claire for being so determined and steadfast. From what Vivian had heard, Claire's mother had been as devoted to her children as Ellen had been selfish.

"What does your stepfather have to say about it?" Vivian asked this as if she was merely making conversation, but she was more than a little curious.

"He thinks my mother's disappearance might be related to Pat's murder. I mean, he hasn't ruled it out. Until we know who killed Pat, and if they ever had any connection to our family, no one can say."

"Including your stepfather?"

"Right."

If anything, Vivian thought Darryl O'Toole, Tug as he was called, might know more than he'd ever admitted. He'd been the last person to see his wife alive, and he'd certainly benefitted from her death. "Did he get that snow-removal contract he was hoping for?"

"He did."

"Great." Not that Tug needed the money. He'd inherited a couple of million dollars, thanks to his wife's wealthy family. He'd bought a nursery and the bowling alley in Libby with the money, so he owned other businesses besides his snow removal company. But these days he was mostly retired and enjoying the good life, which included a luxurious home in the mountains with the woman he'd moved in with only six months after Alana went missing. "How's Leanne?"

"Her business is growing. Have you seen her latest?"

Vivian hadn't asked about her business. She'd asked about *Leanne,* but this answer was typical of Claire. Claire didn't like to discuss her sister. From all outward appearances, they got along fine. But they were so different…. "What's she working on?"

Leanne made stained-glass windows and lamps and

sold them to stores around Montana or on the internet. She did incredible work, had even been commissioned to do windows for several churches.

Vivian thought Claire should leave Pineview and pursue her dream of becoming a famous hairstylist in New York or L.A., even if that meant leaving her sister behind. She'd married at twenty-six, then lost her husband after only four years, before they chose to have kids. Although her stepfather and her sister were all that kept her in Pineview, Claire wouldn't consider leaving. Vivian had never heard the details behind the sledding incident that'd broken Leanne's back—Claire wasn't willing to talk about it—but she suspected Claire felt guilty for being the one who made it to the bottom of that mountain safely. Otherwise, she would've left town long ago.

"She's doing a piece for the new library in Kalispell," Claire explained.

"They commissioned her?"

"Are you kidding? They have no money."

"So she's donating it?"

"Yeah."

"How nice of her. That's a lot of work."

"She can be surprisingly generous."

It was the *surprisingly* that made Vivian wonder if their relationship was as loving as it seemed.

The Chowhound came up on their right, just past Chrissy Gunther's Nice Twice store and the bank. When Vivian flew past the restaurant, Claire rapped on the window with her knuckles. "Hey, didn't you want to turn there?"

She did, but first she had to see who was in town. She eyed all the people she could see, searching for anyone who looked out of place, or who could be Ink or another thug. Only when she'd driven all the way past Gina's Malt Shoppe did she whip around and return to the window-less Chowhound.

Claire took her by the arm as they met up at the door. "You're acting so strange."

"You'll understand in a minute." Squaring her shoulders, she motioned her friend in ahead of her.

At night the Chowhound became a strip club. On dollar dance nights it gave the Kicking Horse Saloon a run for its money. Some locals hung out here, but most of the nighttime traffic came from the men who poured through the area on their various hunting and fishing trips. During the day it served breakfast and lunch. It was always much less crowded then, even though it served some of the best burgers in town.

Today, because they were wrapping up after the lunch rush, only a handful of patrons sat inside. One was Tony Garvey. He had his work boots on and a pair of jeans that were as dirty as his T-shirt. Tony owned Garvey's Sand and Gravel, but he wasn't afraid to dig in and work alongside his employees.

He nodded as they passed and Claire stopped to say hello. She knew everyone in town. Tony had been one of her husband's best friends.

"Tony and his wife are getting a divorce," she whispered afterward as they found a booth.

"I'm sorry for their son." Although Tony's wife wasn't part of Vivian's book group, that was where she'd learned about Mrs. Garvey's affair with her chiropractor. The gossip in Pineview was usually pretty reliable, but Vivian didn't like that aspect of the community, so she tried to ignore the rumors. She certainly hadn't wanted anyone talking about her. She'd had far too much to hide.

"I feel bad that they've had trouble. No matter what happened, I've always liked them both," Claire said.

The smell of cigarette smoke permeated the carpet, the vinyl booth, the dark paneling. Smoking hadn't been allowed inside, even in taverns, for some time, but George Johnson, the owner of the Chowhound, was a heavy smoker and probably smoked as much as he wanted before and after business hours.

"Afternoon, ladies. Can I get you a drink?"

George himself had come to wait on them.

"Just water for me," Claire said.

Considering the state of her nerves, Vivian thought she might want something stronger, but it wasn't a good idea to consume alcohol while toting a gun. Besides, alcohol upset her ulcer.

"So…what do you have to tell me?" Claire asked the minute he walked away.

Vivian had kept her in suspense long enough, but she didn't know how to begin. Baring her soul would relieve her of the burden she'd been carrying, the need to pretend and lie and evade, but it would also be a terrible risk. What if Claire couldn't forgive her? What if she stayed in Pineview but lost the relationships that were important to her? "It's something you're going to find… unpleasantly surprising."

Claire's curious smile faded when she realized Vivian wasn't fooling around. "How upset will I be?"

"Pretty upset."

"At you? Or someone else?"

"Me."

"What's the worst it could be?" she said with a doubtful laugh.

Vivian reached across the table to take her hand. "Claire, everything I've ever told you is a lie."

Again, Claire seemed tempted to make light of it, until the intensity on Vivian's face convinced her that this really wasn't a joke. Then her eyebrows knitted together and the worry Vivian had glimpsed earlier reappeared. "Maybe you should be more specific."

"I'm not who you think I am. I'm not Vivian Stewart."

How often did someone hear that from her best friend?

She seemed to gulp before grabbing the table. "What are you talking about?"

Vivian didn't want this to hurt their friendship, but she didn't see how it wouldn't. "That's an assumed name, one I picked myself. I don't have a mother who suffers from diabetes and my parents aren't retired schoolteachers. I don't have a sister, pregnant or otherwise. I have one brother who's married and has one and a half children, and that's it. They're all I have in the world, besides my own kids. And I can't even see them. We've been on the run and had to split up for safety."

Letting go of the table, Claire sat back. "You don't mean you're wanted by the police."

"No." Vivian struggled to decide what to tell her next. Now that she'd started, she wanted to get it all out as fast as possible. "There are some…men. They—they tried to kill me once. In Colorado. They're coming after me again. It's really my brother they want, or at least that's how it began. Now…they hate me as much as they do him."

"They tried to kill you?"

"Yes. They murdered the U.S. marshal who was guarding me and then they came for me."

"Wow." Other than in the movies, Claire had probably never heard of anything like this. It wasn't the kind of thing that happened in Pineview. Neither did murder, yet Pat was dead. Neither did kidnapping, yet Claire's mother was missing. Was that what she was thinking? That maybe nothing was what it seemed?

Vivian did her best to explain about Ellen and her uncle and her murdered stepfather and what'd happened to Virgil and how he came to be associated with The Crew. The more she talked, the more unbelievable it sounded, even to *her* ears. Did Claire think she'd lost her mind?

She didn't act as skeptical as Vivian had thought she would. When Vivian finished and looked up at her help-lessly, waiting to see how her friend would take the news, Claire glanced around them, then leaned in close. "What do these men look like?"

That wasn't the response Vivian had been expecting. "Ink has tattoos everywhere, but he broke out of prison with a guy I've never seen before. He's likely got plenty of gang tattoos, too." She thought of Pretty Boy and re-vised that statement. "Then again, Ink's partner in crime could look as clean-cut as a Mormon missionary."

Claire's face drained of color, but the question that came out of her mouth wasn't, "How could you do that to me?" or "Why couldn't you trust me?" There was no recrimination, no accusation or anger that she'd been misled. Instead, her voice urgent, she asked, "What was your name before?"

"That depends," Vivian replied. "I've had to assume two different identities over the past four years."

"The name these people would have. What is it?"

"My real name. Laurel Hodges."

Her jaw dropped and she brought a hand to her chest.

"Oh, God. I saw them at Mailboxes Plus not more than an hour ago. Two guys. One sat outside in a white truck. I couldn't see him too well. But the other guy approached me. He said he was looking for his sister, who was adopted out at birth. That she was supposed to live in this area. And he told me her name was Laurel Hodges."

Vivian's blood ran cold. She'd been afraid The Crew had come to Pineview.

Now she knew for sure.

20

"This is it? You're sure?" Myles stood with Ned in front of Allen Biddle's house east of town. It wasn't a likely place to drop off a couple of hitchhikers. There was no bus stop, no pay phone, no café and no gas station, just one residence—the lodgelike home of a middle-aged bachelor who split his time between Montana and Alaska, and hired out as a hunting guide.

"Positive, Sheriff. I knew they wouldn't want to continue on with me."

"Why not?"

"Because I wasn't going all the way into town." About forty years old, Ned had lived in Pineview most of his life and, when he wasn't on the ball diamond, dressed like an old cowboy. He hitched his Wranglers a little higher as he talked but couldn't fasten them around the big belly that hung well over his belt. "I came from Libby, had to pick up a few things there," he said. "Saw them when I was coming back and stopped, but explained I wasn't going all the way to Pineview."

"And they said…"

"To take them as far as I could, and that's what I did."

Myles scratched his head, trying to determine whether the two had walked into town, found another ride or headed into the mountains. He doubted they'd gone into the mountains. He'd checked on their Toyota before leaving Pineview. All the camping and fishing equipment he'd spotted earlier was still in the bed. "Where were you going?" he asked Ned.

"I bought Leland's Christmas tree farm a few months ago, so I was on my way up there."

Myles hadn't heard this. "Insurance business must be good."

"Same as always. Good enough. But I was looking for something I could do on the side, and when this opportunity came along, I decided to take it."

For all his cowboy attire, Myles couldn't see Ned as a farmer. "Do you know anything about growing Christmas trees?"

"Not much." He produced a rueful grin. "But I'm learning."

Myles hoped he was better at farming than softball. "So you were going to the farm when you picked up these boys."

"Yeah. Turnoff's right there." He pointed. "Ain't nothin' up that road but trees so I figured they'd have a better shot of reaching town if I dropped them here."

"They didn't try to persuade you or…coerce you to take them any farther?"

"No, sir."

Squatting at the side of the road, Myles examined the dirt for any sign of the shoe imprints they'd found at the scene of Pat's murder but didn't see any. "Did it look as if they were armed?"

"Not that I could tell. They didn't have a rifle or anything obvious."

Myles raised one hand against the glare of the sun. "What *did* they have with them?"

"Nothing but the clothes on their backs."

"They tell you where they were hoping to go?"

"Pineview."

He stood. "I mean once they got there. Did they mention a motel, a campground, some place to eat?"

"No."

Myles kicked a pebble across the road. "They had to give some reason for needing a ride. There aren't a lot of hitchhikers around here."

"Said their truck broke down a ways back. That's all."

"You didn't ask why they didn't ride with the tow?"

"I didn't know they'd been able to call one."

Of course. How would he know Myles had found them on the side of the road and called Harvey? "What did you talk about while they were in your truck?"

"The weather, mostly. After we were driving for a bit, I brought up Pat's murder. They asked me if the police had any leads on who did it and I said no." He spat at the pavement. "But you suspect they killed Pat, right? That's why you've been passing out flyers like the one I saw at the coffeehouse this morning."

"That's right. I'm pretty sure it's them. Did you happen to notice the shoes they were wearing?"

"Tennis shoes."

"What brand?"

He shrugged. "Couldn't tell you. Didn't pay close enough attention. They all look the same to someone who prefers boots." With a proud gleam in his eye, he lifted one bowed leg to show off his fancy snakeskin boots.

"Nice," Myles said, but scarcely glanced at them. He

was too intent on what he was doing. "Did they both have on the same kind of tennis shoes?"

Ned's eyebrows slid up. "Now that you mention it, I think they did."

Would it do any good to search the area? It'd been yesterday afternoon that Ned had seen them....

Myles figured he'd check with Allen at least, and take a peek in his outbuildings. "Is there anything else you can tell me, Ned? Anything that might give me some idea where to search?"

He spat again and shook his head. "Wish I could. They pretended to be searching for someone themselves, and I stupidly believed them."

"What do you mean?"

"The young guy told me he'd come to town hoping to reunite with his biological sister, who was adopted out at birth. Woman by the name of Laurel...something. Asked me if I'd heard of her. I told him I hadn't and that was about it."

Vivian... Because this was taking much longer than planned, Myles called the office and asked Deputy Campbell to ride over to Pineview and sit in front of her house until he could get there himself. "What'd they look like?"

"The one guy had tattoos everywhere, just like it says on the flyer. He didn't say much. His younger friend did all the talking."

"They give you their names?"

"Ron Howard and Peter Ferguson. Seemed like nice guys. I never would've guessed they were wanted by the police." He offered Myles a grim smile. "Or that I was lucky to get away with my life."

"Thanks for coming forward," Myles said.

As Ned left, Myles knocked on Allen's door. But he didn't learn anything new. Allen insisted no one had stopped by. He hadn't seen two men rambling around, and he doubted there was anyone on his property, but he helped search just in case.

"Where else do you think they might've gone?" Myles asked when they were done.

"Who knows? If it were me, I'd make my way to town. A man's gotta eat."

"Yeah." Frustrated that he'd come up empty, Myles let Allen go on about his business, but he was reluctant to leave. There had to be some way to find Ink and the little asswipe who was with him before anyone else got hurt. He just needed to think like they would. There wasn't much out here for two people without even a tent. Not only would they need food, they'd need shelter. It was easiest to come by those things in town. Town was also where they'd have a better chance of locating Vivian. And yet…this was where their trail had gone cold.

He drove around to a few cabins in the area but could document no other sightings. By the time he called it quits, it was getting dark and he felt like a bloodhound who wouldn't give up on a scent.

Deputy Campbell checked in by radio just as he was getting into his car.

"How's she doing?" Myles asked.

"Don't know. She hasn't come back."

"What?"

"I've been sitting here all afternoon but haven't seen a soul. I'm thinking she spent the day in Kalispell."

That was a possibility. Lord knew anyone would be hesitant to return to the situation going on here.

"Let me know when she arrives."

"Will do," Campbell promised.

Myles looked at the clock. He needed to get back and relieve his deputy, who had a young family waiting eagerly for him. He was on his way. But he was close to where Marley was staying, so he decided to swing by and pick her up first.

Music blared from the house as he approached the front door. He had to ring the doorbell three times before he managed to rouse anyone, but eventually Alexis, Elizabeth's sixteen-year-old sister, answered. Dressed in a spaghetti-strap T-shirt and the shortest shorts he'd ever seen, she smiled up at him as if her chest wasn't all but falling out of her shirt. "Hey, Sheriff."

Myles avoided looking anywhere below the neck. As far as he was concerned, she was still a child. "Hi, there. Looks like you've gotten some sun." Her red face contrasted sharply with the circles of white around her eyes, giving her an owl-like appearance.

"A little." She pressed her cheek to show him just how bad it was. "I spent the morning on the chaise. I didn't realize I was getting burned because it wasn't that hot."

"Some aloe vera should help."

She shrugged away the suggestion. "I'm not worried about it. It'll turn into a tan by tomorrow."

"Hope so. Hey, can you grab Marley for me?"

A frown tugged at the corners of her mouth. "I was afraid you were going to ask me that. She's not here. The girls went to Kalispell with my mom."

"For what?"

"Shopping."

Marley had left town without telling him? She knew damn well that she was supposed to ask. She'd say she "forgot" to call—how many times had he heard that excuse?—but she'd probably decided to ask forgiveness instead of permission. She always wanted to go with Elizabeth's mom. Those excursions meant more to her than any others. He suspected being with Janet reminded her of being with her own mother.

Wondering whether to leave word that Janet should bring Marley home, since she'd taken her out of town without his permission, or come back and pick her up, he cleared his throat. "What are they shopping for?"

"School clothes."

"But it's only June. School just got out."

"My mom starts early," Alexis said with a laugh. "And I think they wanted to get away, have a girls' day out. They talked about seeing a movie, too."

That meant it could be late when they returned. He'd have to ground Marley for disobeying him, but no doubt she'd think it was worth the sacrifice. "Why didn't you go?" he asked, still trying to figure out what to do about this.

"I already had plans with my boyfriend."

That would explain Jett Busath's truck in the driveway. He and Alexis had been an item since Christmas. Their relationship had so captured Marley's imagination that it'd been all she could talk about for weeks.

"Your father home?" Myles wanted to alert him to what was going on, tell him there were people running around who'd busted out of prison and were very dangerous, but he suspected Henry was gone, and Alexis confirmed it.

"No, he's on a business trip. That's why Mom wanted to get out. He's been traveling, and she's been stuck here doing laundry and dishes."

"I see. So you're babysitting?"

"No, my brothers are at camp this week."

Alexis was home alone, wearing next to nothing and spending the evening with a boy who, at sixteen, probably had more hormones than brains. Myles's father-instinct was buzzing like crazy, urging him to warn her to be careful. He knew her parents would freak out if she got pregnant. They were hoping she'd win a scholarship for softball, had big plans for their oldest daughter. But as protective as he felt toward everyone in the community, especially Elizabeth's family because he knew them so well and they had so much influence over Marley, it wasn't his place to get involved.

"What time will the girls be home, do you know?" he asked.

She shook her head. "No. Sorry."

Resting his hands on his utility belt, he turned to look out over the front yard. He liked this property. The cabin was more modern than rustic, but the convenience of having a big, gourmet kitchen and plenty of bathrooms added to its appeal. The Rogers family got to live out in the wilds without missing any of the conveniences of city life—except when it snowed. Then it was hard getting out to the main road, but they always managed.

"If I know Marley and Elizabeth, they're going to call you up and beg to have Marley stay over again," Alexis said. "Why don't you just pick her up in the morning?"

Myles preferred she come home tonight. He hated having her out of his sight when there were dangerous men floating around. But after what he'd learned about Vivian—or Laurel—maybe it was for the best if Marley wasn't at home while he tried to track down the fugitives. Surely she'd be safer here, sequestered in the mountains with her friend's family, than sleeping next door to the woman The Crew had come to kill.

"Okay, that's fine," he said. "Tell her to call me when she gets home, and we'll make arrangements for tomorrow."

A voice issued from somewhere inside the house. "Alexis? Where are you?"

Jett was growing impatient. "I'll let you get back to your, um, company," Myles said.

"Thanks." She sent him a fleeting smile and closed the door.

Trudie's Grocery was a mom-and-pop establishment with elevator music playing in the background, the kind of place that sold homemade pie and jellies and reminded L.J. of the store his grandparents used to own when they were alive. He lived with them during the summers between his fifth- and seventh-grade years. Those six months before he went into foster care were the happiest of his life, so he liked the feel of this place, the neat rows of cans and snacks, the freezer section at the back with the ice cream and frozen foods. He used to help stock that stuff.

This was one of the rare occasions he'd been away from Ink since Ink was transferred to the California Men's Colony and became his cellie. Because he really needed the break, he took his time meandering through the aisles before approaching the birdlike woman perched on a stool behind the cash register.

Preoccupied by a show on the small TV behind the counter, she barely looked at him. "That all for tonight, honey?"

"Yeah, that's it. Thanks."

She wore a badge that read Trudie and although he'd never met another Trudie her name somehow fit. With her hair dyed an awful orange color and teased up the way his grandma used to do hers, she wore a purple smock and bright red lipstick with matching nail polish. She wasn't bad-looking despite the terrible dye job, not for someone in her seventies. He liked that she took care of herself. He could smell her perfume from the other side of the counter. It didn't smell particularly expensive, but he thought if he ever got married, he'd like to be with a woman who always tried to look her best.

The cash register beeped as she scanned his chocolate milk, pork rinds, whiskey and condoms he threw down at the last second.

He glanced out the window to see Ink sitting in the white Dodge Ram that had belonged to the men they'd killed. Ink had taken to driving. He stayed behind the wheel and left the engine idling while L.J. ducked into one place after another to ask about Laurel Hodges. At this point, L.J. was in as much of a hurry to find her as Ink was. He wanted to finish whatever they had to do in Montana and get the hell on the road. Pineview was so small, he felt they stood out, especially with Ink tatted up the way he was.

Seeming anxious not to miss a minute of her program, Trudie handed him his bag with an absentminded, "Thank you. Come again," and returned to her stool.

It was time to launch into his spiel. "Excuse me, but… I'm hoping you can help me."

She looked at him for the first time.

"I'm searching for my sister," he began. "She's about five-ten and—"

He didn't get any farther before Trudie's gaze flicked

toward a flyer taped to the side of her register. Then her eyes widened and she nearly fell off her stool.

Almost as surprised as she was, L.J. checked the flyer to see what was wrong—and saw a picture of him and Ink beneath the heading Sheriff's Notice. A phone number and an explanation had been printed on there, as well, but he didn't take the time to read it. He didn't need to. He knew what that flyer was, just as he knew Trudie had recognized him.

Leaving the snacks and the condoms, he bolted out the door and jumped into the passenger seat of the truck. "Go! Go! Go!"

Ink didn't pause to question him. Evidently the terror on his face was enough to get an immediate response. Heedless of any back pain he might be suffering, Ink shoved the gearshift into Reverse and launched the vehicle backward, only to shift again before they could even come to a stop.

Positive that they were about to have an accident, L.J. closed his eyes. He knew Ink couldn't be watching for oncoming traffic. He was too busy putting some distance between them and that store. L.J. was more afraid of getting arrested than crashing, anyway. He'd bought and sold drugs, and he'd beat up a few people, but he'd never considered doing the shit Ink had gotten him into. Shooting those hunters. Beating that real-estate agent to death. Getting that woman in L.A. killed. If they got busted, he'd go down for all of it.

Rocks smacked the undercarriage like machine-gun fire as their backend fishtailed and their tires spun gravel. But once they reached the pavement, they had traction and lurched forward with greater power. Miraculously, Ink managed to bring the truck under control, and they hurtled away from the little grocery store without hitting anything. But only because the road was clear.

Grabbing the rearview mirror, L.J. turned it so he could see if Trudie had come out of the store. He didn't want her to jot down their license plate number. Then the sheriff would be able to trace the plate and figure out it belonged to the men they'd killed.

All he could see was a big cloud of dust; that was probably all she could see, too.

"What happened in there?" Ink asked once Pineview had disappeared from sight.

"She recognized me!" He hadn't bothered with his seat belt. He braced himself with one hand on the door and the other on the dash, eyeing the rearview mirror to see if a cop car would come racing up from behind.

Ink smacked the seat between them. "How? What the hell happened?"

L.J.'s heart seemed to be chugging harder than the pistons in the engine. "How should I know? I went in and asked about my long-lost sister, like usual. At first the woman seemed fine, but then she stared at me as if she'd swallowed a marble. I wasn't sure what was going on until I saw the flyer."

"What flyer?"

"A sheriff's bulletin with my picture on it. Yours, too."

Ink cursed. He was so worked up he didn't seem to be slowing down.

Now that they were safely away, L.J. felt there was no reason to draw attention by speeding. Getting pulled over would put an end to their freedom, possibly for life. "Hey, can you take it easy?"

"You want me to take it easy?" Ink snapped.

The wildness in his eyes frightened L.J. and he let go

of the armrest long enough to motion for his partner to calm down. "Whoa! We need to blend in, not stand out, right?"

Ink didn't like being told what to do. L.J. had never seen anyone get angry quicker or for less reason. He was always looking for a fight. But he seemed to see the logic in L.J.'s words because he eased up on the gas. "We're going to find her."

"Of course we will." L.J. just hoped they'd find her soon. Because until then, his own safety was in jeopardy.

Ink commandeered the rearview mirror and checked it every few seconds. "So what did you do when she recognized you?"

"What do you think? I ran out before she could call the cops."

"Why didn't you shoot her? Dead people can't talk."

The thought hadn't even crossed his mind. Murder wasn't his answer to everything. "I wasn't the only shopper in there, that's why. There was a mother and two kids."

"There weren't any other vehicles outside."

"They must've walked."

Somehow Ink knew he was lying. "You can't be too scared to use that gun, man."

"I'm not scared," he grumbled. "I just don't see any reason to kill people unless I have to."

"You should've put a plug in her."

Bullshit. That was only going to get him into more trouble. He had to escape from this psychopath. The sooner, the better. He just wasn't sure how to go about it. If he left now, Ink would find Laurel, kill her, then come after him. And if Ink ever caught up with him…

"Do you have a death wish or something?" he asked.

"Because they're gonna go for the death penalty when they get hold of you."

"They won't get hold of me." He must not have seen anything worrisome coming up from behind because he made the turn that led to their cabin and they rode in silence for the next twenty minutes.

Once they pulled into the drive, L.J. stared out at the growing darkness. He was thinking about the men Ink had shot and the stomach-churning process of burying them. He wondered about their families, whether or not they had children. This was all so senseless. His life was turning into a nightmare. He didn't feel big or bad, like he thought he would. He just felt like shit. Worse than shit, because he knew how ashamed his grandfather would be.

"What are we going to do?" he asked. "We can't go back into town. Not with all those flyers everywhere."

"We'll wait until it's too dark to see us clearly."

He had an answer for everything. They hadn't shaved since they left the California Men's Colony, but his beard growth hadn't stopped Trudie from recognizing him. "And what if it doesn't work? In another day or two, everyone in town will have seen that flyer."

"That's why we've got to go back tonight. But we'll wait another hour or so, let things die down."

Bile rose in L.J.'s throat. "Are you joking? We can't go back there."

"We have no choice. And we need to do it soon, or you're right—it's only gonna get harder."

It was already hard enough. "That's asking for trouble. We're screwed, you know that."

Ink shut off the engine. "No, we're not."

L.J. didn't move. He'd pissed himself rushing out of

that damn grocery store, and there was no way he wanted Ink to see the wet spot on his jeans. He'd never live it down.

Fortunately, it was getting darker by the minute. In a little while it would be too dark to see that small detail, especially way the hell out here. "How can you be so sure?"

Ink met his gaze. "I remembered her name."

L.J. didn't immediately follow. "What are you talking about?"

"Laurel's daughter. I remember her name!"

This wasn't exciting news. L.J. had been a fool to come to Montana with Ink, but…now that he was here, he had to get through it the best he could until he found a way out. He'd been so set on becoming a Crew member. Now he couldn't imagine why. If they were anything like Ink, then Ink was right. He wasn't cut out for it. "How?"

"Don't know. When you came out screaming, it just popped into my head. Can you believe it?"

Frankly he couldn't. What if Ink only *thought* he knew the name? It didn't make sense that he couldn't remember it for so long and then suddenly there it was. Was Ink bullshitting him? "You're dreaming."

"Dreaming?" Ink echoed. "You mean lying, don't you? But I'm not. And even if I was, it's not your place to question me."

Question him? What was he, L.J.'s father? L.J. had never had a father, and he didn't want one now, especially a freaking psychopath only fifteen years older than he was. "We almost got caught back there!"

"I'm telling you we're going to be able to find her now. Then we'll get the hell out of here."

Finding her wouldn't save the day. Too much shit had

already gone down. L.J. was pretty sure he was headed for death row no matter what. "But she might've changed her daughter's name, too. Or given her up for adoption. Or maybe she…she died of a childhood disease. This solves nothing. Let's leave Montana. Get out. Revenge isn't worth spending the rest of our lives in prison. Or worse."

"You gotta be kidding me."

L.J. had the impression that Ink would kill him right here, right now, if he did or said anything more to defy him. "All I'm saying is…we're taking a risk." He hated himself for backing off, but Ink was too unpredictable, too volatile.

"That's what I thought." Ink opened his door. "Anyway, you'll see. She wouldn't give this kid up. And she didn't change the kid's name—that would confuse the little bitch. Laurel isn't the kind of mother who'd want to cause her precious babies any pain."

"How do you know?"

L.J. couldn't believe he'd dared ask another question. He wanted to kick himself when Ink's attention swung back to him and those cold eyes riveted onto his face, but Ink seemed to have snapped out of psycho mode.

"I've seen how hard she tries to protect them."

With a sigh, L.J. thrust a hand through his hair. He was as trapped as he'd ever been in prison, maybe more so. In another hour, they'd be cruising through town, risking their futures again. "But is her daughter's name different enough that people will know who we're talking about?"

When Ink smiled, it was the coldest smile L.J. had ever seen. If he'd needed proof that Ink was crazy, there it was. Jack Nicholson in *The Shining* had nothing on him. "People will know who we're talking about. How many little girls in this town are called Mia?"

Not many, as L.J. soon learned. When they returned to town, they found a woman who was just locking up Chrissy's Nice Twice store. Afraid his usual spiel would only alert her to trouble, especially after what had happened at that grocery store, L.J. approached with a frown. "Darn, you're closed?"

The woman pivoted to face him. "We closed several hours ago, actually. Why, is there something you need?"

"I was hoping to buy a gift for my niece, Mia. Maybe you know her?"

"Vivian Stewart's daughter?"

He had no idea, but he figured it'd be smarter to play along. "Yes."

She hitched her purse higher on her shoulder while juggling a box of files and an armful of clothing he guessed she was taking home to wash or mend. "Oh, I know the whole family. Mia goes to school with my daughter."

"Can I help you with that?"

Smiling in relief, she allowed him to take the box. "What did you have in mind?"

"Maybe a pretty dress? You know, just a nice surprise since I'm visiting from out of town and haven't seen her in a couple years."

"Did you want a present for Jake, too?"

He felt a rush of relief and foreboding at the same time. He had the right person. Ink had mentioned that Mia had a brother. But he knew what that would mean…. "Of course. That'd be perfect."

"I can help you. Come on in." Pleased to have a paying customer despite the late hour, she reopened her store and did exactly as she'd promised. She helped him choose a dress for Mia and some sporting equipment for Jake, whom she admitted liking better than anyone else in the family. Then, as he stood at the register to pay, he said he was afraid he might have trouble finding the address, since he'd never visited before.

So she drew him a map.

21

When he saw Vivian's Blazer turn down their street, Myles breathed a huge sigh of relief. Arriving home to find that she was still gone at nearly eleven o'clock had left him with a growing sense of panic. He'd asked the deputies he had on duty to look for her or her vehicle, but when no one was able to spot it, he couldn't help wondering if Ink and Lloyd had bumped into her after tearing out of Trudie's Grocery—and dragged her into the woods.

With such terrible thoughts churning in his mind, he'd been cursing himself for not going with her this morning and sticking with her all day. That would've been the only sure way to protect her. He'd briefly considered doing so when he saw her packing up. But Rex was there, at least for half the trip. Myles had decided his own time would be better spent in Pineview, trying to catch these guys. But he hadn't made as much progress as he'd hoped.

While she parked, he waited on the porch steps so she'd see him. He didn't want her to be frightened. He also didn't want her to shoot him.

"Where've you been?" he called as she got out. He couldn't hide the concern in his voice, but he figured he was allowed to feel concerned. He was the sheriff. It was his job to care about the people in his jurisdiction. The fact that he was more worried about her than he would've been about anyone else made him wish he could've left Campbell here, or assigned someone else to keep her safe through the night. But he lived right next door; he was the obvious choice.

She checked to make sure the street was clear before hurrying toward him.

"It's true, you know," he went on. "The Crew is here. Two guys. They killed Pat, and now they're looking for you. A few hours ago they went into Trudie's Grocery, asking for Laurel Hodges. I got the call on my way home, and rushed over there, but we couldn't find any trace of them."

Her shoulders slumped. "Did Trudie get their license plate number at least?"

"No, she fell when she was trying to hurry outside. They were gone by the time she made it."

She reached him and jogged up the porch steps. "Is she okay?"

"Bruised and a little spooked but otherwise okay."

"Claire saw them, too," she said. "So now you understand why you can't stand out in front of my house. It's like painting a red bull's-eye on your chest. These people won't care that you're a cop. They'd rather kill a cop than anyone else. Except for me—or Virgil, Peyton and Rex." She brushed past him, fumbling with her keys, and nearly dropped them in her rush to get the door open.

"And now you know why I was so worried." He could hear the edge to his own voice. But it was the relief flowing through him, and the way his body reacted whenever she came close, that bothered him.

"Hang on a sec." She was so focused on getting inside

that she couldn't concentrate on anything else. Her hands shook as she tried to put the key in the lock, so he insisted on taking over.

The second the tumbler fell, she pulled him inside with her. Then she locked the door and sagged against it. "Welcome home, huh?" she said with a weak grin.

He understood so much more about her behavior now, and he had to sympathize. She'd been living in fear all the time. Hiding. Watching. Worrying. Dodging the kind of relationships that might threaten her cover. No wonder she was so guarded. And yet, even after all that, the people she'd been hoping to escape were coming after her again. That she fully believed she might not survive the next few days was apparent from the pallor of her skin. Just coming home had been a terrifying ordeal, knowing she could be shot walking to her front door.

But he didn't want to feel sorry for her or admire her courage or anything else. He wanted to do his job, professionally, unemotionally. That was all. If the way he'd felt since seeing Rex in Vivian's kitchen had taught him anything, it was that he wasn't ready to care again. Not that much.

Although they hadn't turned on any lights, he could see her in the moonlight streaming through the side windows. "So where have you been?" He'd already asked, but he wanted an answer. "With Claire?"

She nodded. "I was reluctant to come home. And she was pretty reluctant to let me."

"You should've stayed at her place."

"And have them track me there instead? No."

"Does she know what's going on?"

"Yes, I told her."

"What'd she say?"

"She couldn't believe it, but she wasn't angry, like I expected. She probably would've been, except she'd just seen Ink and whoever he's with."

"Where?"

Vivian seemed so weary. He wished he could do something to bolster her strength, to reassure her that this would end well, but he had no guarantee. "At Mailboxes Plus. They were in a white truck. But you don't need to rush over there. They're gone now."

"What I need to do is set up some surveillance on this place. But with summer vacations, I'm short-staffed. Tomorrow's the earliest I'll be able to pull that together."

"I assume we're okay for tonight, anyway," she responded. "If they're still asking around town for me, they don't know where I live. And that close call at Trudie's should've rattled them a bit, made them less likely to approach people. Most guys would keep their heads down for a while, wouldn't they?"

He frowned. "There's no way to be sure. I'd start surveillance tonight if I could. I just don't have the manpower and keeping you safe is my priority. I'm having a deputy drive by every hour or so. It's not a lot, but…"

"At least we know what Ink and his friend are driving," she said. "That might come in handy later."

"Except white trucks are probably the most common vehicle around here. I didn't realize that until I started looking for them." He noticed that she kept rubbing her stomach. "Are you okay?"

She dropped her hand. "I'm alive. That's about all I can hope for right now."

"You should've told me before."

"About…"

"The Crew."

"And how would that have changed things?"

He didn't have an answer. He just felt she should've trusted him.

Closing her eyes again, she rested her head against the door. "I can't believe this is happening."

"Why didn't you call me tonight, let me know where you were? Didn't you realize I'd assume the worst if you didn't come home?"

She reached for her hair, seemed to remember there was nothing left to tuck behind her ears and shoved her fingers through it instead. "No. I was too busy trying to convince Claire that we weren't going to flee town."

This distracted him. He'd known Claire practically since the day he'd moved here, liked her. But she could be as evasive as Vivian. "She wanted to go with you?"

"She's not happy here. There are too many memories. She's wanted to leave for a long time."

"Why doesn't she?"

"Leanne." A speculative expression settled over her face. "Do you think her stepfather killed her mother, Myles?"

He was surprised she'd ask in the middle of her own crisis, but he supposed it was a distraction of sorts, easier to deal with than the danger she faced. So many people had asked him the same question since he'd come to Pineview. For Leanne and Claire's sake, he'd always said no. He didn't want the truth to get back to them, to make their lives any more difficult—especially because he could be wrong. "I can't answer honestly. And I think you know why."

She tilted her head. "You thought I should trust you with my identity, my life."

And yet he wouldn't trust her with something as small

as his opinion on this matter. "Fine. Just between you and me?"

She nodded.

"I think it's more likely than any other scenario."

She chuckled without mirth. "It's always the husband."

"*Almost* always," he corrected.

"That's especially sad in this case. Claire worships her stepfather."

"If she suspected him, she'd lose both parents, because then she couldn't love him. It's classic denial."

"I've had a bit of experience with that. Some people are capable of terrible things."

He wanted to shed the weight of his utility belt, get out of his uniform, but he hadn't decided how he was going to handle keeping her safe. He knew what he wanted to do, but he wasn't sure Vivian would cooperate. "How'd Claire let you out of her sight?"

"I insisted. And then Leanne came over and needed her."

"That's about the only thing that would do it. She puts Leanne above all else. But she cares about you."

"She has to stay away from me until this is over." She finally seemed recovered enough to move. "Shall we go upstairs or down?"

"Excuse me?"

"We have to get off the ground floor." She waved around them. "We'll be safer without all these windows."

"Up would be better." Then he could see out, but whoever was looking in couldn't get to them without coming up the stairs.

"Up, it is."

He followed her to her bedroom. Decorated in beige and black, it contained a canopy-style bed made of iron and surrounded by sheer black fabric held back with big, drooping beige ties. Aside from the bed, there was the kind of chair usually found in a garden, paired with an antique dresser. Probably twenty old clocks covered one wall. But it was the elaborate chandelier hanging from the ceiling that somehow brought it all together.

As different as it was, he liked it. "I'm surprised Rex was willing to leave you here alone." He stood in the doorway because he wasn't too sure about venturing inside.

"You saw him." She put her gun on the bed before kicking off her shoes. "He had no choice."

"What's wrong with him? Besides his drug addiction?"

"Nothing's wrong with him, other than that." She held up a hand in the classic stop position. "And don't judge him, please. He's had a hard life. I…I owe him a lot."

"Are you still in love with him?" Myles couldn't believe he'd asked that question. He'd told himself he wouldn't go anywhere near her relationship with Rex, because it didn't matter one way or the other. She wasn't the right person for him. He needed someone with whom he could feel a bit more…indifferent. Someone nice, pleasant, a reliable companion but no one who could steal his breath with just a look.

She seemed intent on formulating her answer. Sitting on her bed, she crossed her legs. "Maybe a little."

He wished he hadn't asked. Her answer was too honest not to hurt. And how she felt was none of his business, especially since he still didn't know whether he was ready to let go of Amber Rose to the point that falling in love with someone else would require. "He needs to get some help."

"My brother will take care of that, if Rex will let him. If he won't, there's nothing anyone can do. Trust me. But I wasn't finished answering your question."

"You said yes," he reminded her.

"I said *a little*. I think I'll always feel *something* for him. If you knew what we've been through, what he's done for both me and my brother, you'd understand. But I'll never go back to him. What we had is over."

"Getting serious with someone like that would be trouble. But that's just a piece of friendly advice." He leaned against the door frame. "It doesn't matter to me one way or another."

Her forehead creased. "Is that so?"

Unable to meet her gaze, he bent to pick up a penny he saw on the carpet. "Yes."

"You're putting me on notice that you're no longer interested?"

"Just keeping the promise you made me give you at the cabin."

"To find someone else for your next sexual encounter."

He knew the reason she'd required that promise was no longer valid. Her secret was out; as far as he knew she had nothing left to hide. But that was just the point. Now that she had no reason to deny him, he was afraid of how hard he might fall if she started saying yes. "If you want to spell it out."

"Fine." She cleared her throat. "You—you're not why I stayed, in case you were wondering. There are a lot of other things here in Pineview. Good things."

"I agree."

A hard lump had formed in the pit of his stomach, but he forced himself to move on. "So what's your plan?

Don't tell me you're just going to hang around and wait for the worst."

"That's about my only option, isn't it?" She shrugged but there was a tension in her body that hadn't been there before. He could see it in the way she held herself. "I'm the bait that'll draw them out."

He felt his eyebrows shoot up. "And then what?"

"As far as plans go, it's not complicated. I try to kill them before they kill me."

"Have you ever killed anyone before?"

"No. But I've seen men killed." Her voice fell until he could scarcely hear her. "And I've been the reason others have died."

As terrible as that must have been, it wasn't the same. That was outside her control. This wouldn't be. She'd have to squeeze the trigger herself. But he didn't see the point in trying to differentiate. "That doesn't matter. If you think I'm going to let you go it alone, you're crazy."

"You don't have any choice. I don't want you involved. These men…nothing deters them. I couldn't take it if someone else was killed. Maybe you don't think much of me after everything that's happened, but I…I don't want to see you hurt."

He ignored her reference to what he thought of her. He thought more of her than she realized, but it wouldn't help him maintain any emotional distance to admit it. "No one's going to get hurt. Not on my watch. Grab whatever you're going to need. Tonight we're staying at my place."

She hopped off the bed. "I can't do that!"

He finally came inside the room. "Why not?"

"For the same reason I wouldn't stay with Claire. If

you're not worried about your own safety, what about Marley?"

"She's not home. She's with a friend."

She reached out to grab his arm, but caught herself before making contact. "Please, don't. Every time I think of you trying to stop them, I see…I see the U.S. marshal who…" She choked up so much she couldn't finish.

He wanted to relent and hold her. But he couldn't, not without rekindling the desire he'd experienced at the cabin. And doing that would only make the rest of the night too difficult to get through. Not to mention the rest of the week, the month, the year.

Shoving his hands in his pockets, he told himself he didn't want to feel her against him. "It's going to be okay," he promised. "You're tired, overwrought. You need some rest."

"I'll be fine. I know what I'm up against."

"Vivian…Laurel—God, I don't even know what to call you anymore."

"It's Vivian," she said softly.

"Why choose that persona?"

"Because that's who I am to you. That's who I've become even to me. At least for now."

He had a feeling those words held more meaning than their easiest interpretation—that he was most familiar with that name—but he refused to examine it. He had to convince her to stay with him; if he wanted to keep her safe, he had no choice about that. "Vivian, then. Let me take care of you for a little while."

Her eyes, so pretty and yet so haunted, pleaded with him to understand. "But what if—"

"I'm not going to be hurt." Suddenly angry, he scowled at her. "Stop turning down the help you need, okay?"

He started taking clothes out of her drawers. He didn't care what they were; he figured if she wouldn't cooperate he'd gather up as much as he could hold, and that would have to be good enough. There was no way she was staying here even if he had to carry her out. "Tomorrow we'll put you in a safe place, somewhere no one else in town knows about and—"

"No." She grabbed his arm. He meant to shake her off so he could continue, but he turned and stared at her instead and the memories he'd been fighting flooded through his mind—the taste of her kiss, the softness of her skin, the moment he'd first buried himself inside her.

Surprised by whatever she'd seen in his face, she let go.

Frustrated with himself for wanting her so badly regardless of all the reasons he should leave her alone, he went back to collecting her clothes. "Work with me here. Just until we can find these men. They're strangers in Pineview. And we have their pictures plastered all over town. They can't remain hidden forever."

He didn't get the impression she believed it would be that easy. But, with a resigned nod, she got a bag and helped him finish packing.

After what seemed like an interminable silence, Virgil checked the minutes he'd used on the prepaid cell phone he'd purchased for this call. Fifteen. Already. Shit. He thought he'd bought more than enough. How long did it take to threaten somebody? He should've guessed it wouldn't go smoothly. Nothing involving The Crew ever did....

Pivoting in front of the windows overlooking the parking lot at his office, he waited for the guy who'd answered his call to bring Horse to the phone. He'd never actually spoken to Horse before. He knew his real name was Harold Pew, but he'd never actually used it. As with most prison gangs, everyone went by nicknames—and Virgil didn't have to think too hard to guess how Horse had gotten his.

At least he had *something* to offer the ladies. From what Virgil had heard, Horse was a big, pockmarked ugly son of a bitch—and a mean one, too. Since Horse had taken over leadership of The Crew's foot soldiers living in Los Angeles, the power had gone to his head.

"Is this some sort of joke?" A deep, raspy voice barked this question into the phone. Since Virgil had asked for Horse, he could only assume it was him.

Finally. Virgil had been about to hang up, return to the store to load the phone with more minutes and call back. "Surprise!" he crooned. "Must be your birthday, eh?"

"Is this *really* Virgil Skinner?"

"Do other people call you up and impersonate me?"

"Considering how I feel about you, no one would be that stupid."

"Then you've answered your own question." Turning his back to the view, Virgil eyed his office. There were times when he woke up expecting to see the cell he'd lived in for fourteen years instead of the beautiful home he owned with Peyton. He still couldn't believe he'd been able to change his life, that he had so much he cared about when he'd started with absolutely nothing. He was happy. Why did *this* have to keep cropping up?

"You have some balls, you know that?" Horse said. "What do you think you're doing, calling me up as if we're friends?"

"I could've sent an email saying, 'I'm going to fuck you up if you don't stop what you're doing' to dirtbag@gangbangers.com, but I was afraid you'd discard it as just another idle threat."

Horse laughed a bit too loudly and a bit too long. "But it *is* an idle threat. There's *nothing* you can do to me."

"I wouldn't bet on that."

"Why not?"

"I have one advantage."

"You don't have shit."

"I know where you are. You can't say the same about me."

"But to reach me, you'd have to come through fifty other Crew."

Virgil manufactured a laugh of his own. "That's a bit of an exaggeration, wouldn't you say? Day to day there are maybe…five guys around at any one time." The Crew couldn't hang out with Horse all day. They had prostitutes to pimp, debtors to rough up, dope to pedal. "Five to one. Those were *good* odds where I learned to fight."

"You mean four *years* ago? Before you settled down and became a *family* man? I'm guessing you're a bit rusty."

Apparently Horse didn't know Virgil owned his own bodyguard service. The Crew must've missed that detail when they came after them in D.C. All they cared about was an address, and they'd come up with Laurel's somehow. Virgil would never forget the call he'd received from her after the attack. If not for Rex, she'd be dead.

But Horse wasn't entirely wrong. In the four years Virgil had been protecting others, the worst he'd had to do was shove someone out of the way or toss a few drunks out of a club, and even that was before he'd hired others. Now he had a team of eight, not counting the three who did background checks and other searches, and his clerical staff of two. "What I might've lost in technique I've gained in motivation," he said.

"And you think I care? Come on—blood in, blood out. You know how the game's played. Winner takes all, Skin."

Virgil winced at his old nickname. It reminded him of the years he'd been driven by rage, rage not so different from what he was feeling right now. "Call Ink off and let bygones be bygones, or I'll bring the fight to your front door, and then it'll be too late for peace."

"Ink? *That's* what this is about? You're worried about that broken-down crazy bastard? I couldn't call him off even if I wanted to. You know he's certifiable, right? Payback. That's all he cares about."

That broken-down crazy bastard had already caused too much damage. "He's one of yours. You need to do something about him before this goes any farther."

"There's nothing I can do. Your sister's probably already dead."

Fighting a sudden impulse to break something, Virgil returned to the window and let his forehead fall against the glass. "For your own sake, you'd better hope that's not true."

"I'm not scared of you, Skin. You want me? Come get me. If you show up here it'll save me the trouble of finding you." He lowered his voice. "Because I *will* find you. No matter how long and hard I have to look. I bet Laurel's giving Ink your address right now. But when I come for you, I won't kill you immediately. First I'm going to destroy everyone you've ever loved." He chuckled softly. "Just like I did your mother."

Something inside him snapped. Whirling, Virgil threw the first object he could grab, which happened to be his stapler. It landed against the wall, creating a sizable dent and a loud thud. "You won't touch anyone else. You won't have the chance," he said, and hung up.

Sandra, his administrative assistant knocked at the door. "Hey, is everything okay?"

Covering his face, he stood perfectly still, grappling for control before he threw something else. She knew his background, his real name. He'd told her so she'd be extra careful about releasing any of his personal information to people who called, but she'd probably never really believed the threat he lived with. Most people couldn't even fathom what it was like.

"Can you hear me?" she asked, louder.

Breathe... "It's fine, Sandra. Everything's fine." He choked out those few words.

"Oh. Good. Okay. Well, did you want to go over those contracts with me now?"

"No." He couldn't think about business. He couldn't think about anything except the fact that he'd have to leave right away, despite the impending birth of his daughter. He had to stop The Crew before anyone else got hurt. It might mean he'd miss the delivery, but he had no choice. Neither he nor Laurel was in a position to run again. If he couldn't convince Horse to bury the hatchet, he had to stop him some other way, even if it meant putting a bullet in his head.

His assistant knocked again. He'd assumed she'd gone back to her desk. "What now?"

There was a brief hesitation. No doubt she was surprised. He never treated her rudely.

"Have I done something wrong?" she asked.

He cursed under his breath but managed a solid, "No, it's me. I'm sorry."

That seemed to make it better. Her voice sounded more strident when she spoke again. "Mr. Winn is here. He'd like to see you."

Mr. Winn owned a liquor store and wanted to beef up security beyond the single guard Virgil provided on weekends. "Tell him I'm dealing with a family emergency and won't be able to meet today."

There was a pause and then a drawn out, "Okay…"

"And, Sandra?" he said before she could move away.

"Yes?"

"Clear my calendar. I'm going to be gone for a couple of days."

At this she opened the door and peered into the room, her face flushed with excitement. "Is it the baby? Is your wife in labor?"

He prayed Peyton could manage on her own and that nothing would happen to their daughter. Or their son. Or anyone else he loved. As soon as he dropped off Laurel's kids, Rex would be flying back to Montana to look out for Laurel, and Virgil would be in L.A. He'd have to move Peyton, Brady, Jake and Mia into a motel until he could get back. They could order room service and swim in a heated pool. That was the upside. The downside was that he didn't know how long he'd have to be gone. "Not yet."

Sandra's smile faded as she glanced at the damage the stapler had done to the wall. "So…where are you going?"

"I have a job to do."

"A protection job?"

"Yes."

Nonplussed, she let go of the handle and the door

swung wider. "But we don't have any jobs scheduled for out of town. You haven't accepted one of those in weeks."

"I can't get out of this."

"Is it what you were telling me about before? About… the people in L.A.?"

With a nod, he grabbed his keys, left the stapler where it had fallen and walked right past Mr. Winn before taking the stairs two at a time and hurrying into the parking lot. Breaking the news to Peyton wasn't going to be easy. But he had to get on the next available flight.

22

While Myles went upstairs to change out of his uniform, Vivian walked around the main floor. Except for the section of living room visible from the front door, she'd never seen the inside of his house before. The coziness of it, the family portraits, the ceramics and drawings Marley had created, reminded her of what so many women wanted—a home and family, a steady relationship, a place to call their own, safety and security. Even the expansive, unused deck out back appealed to Vivian because it symbolized a man's love for his wife—Myles's commitment to Amber Rose as he cared for her in those last months.

Vivian wanted the same kind of love and commitment. And from the same man. Sure, she'd stayed in Pineview because of Claire, the gals at the Thursday-night book group, Myles's daughter, who was so willing to babysit, Nana Vera and all the others. She'd also stayed because she loved her home, and her children were happy here. But all these things wouldn't have been enough, wouldn't have motivated her to take the risks she was taking now. It was Sheriff King she hadn't been able to leave. She was afraid she'd never meet another man like him, one who so closely fit her ideal of what a husband and father should be. If not for him, she probably would've gone to New York and considered herself lucky to have escaped The Crew yet again, lucky to be reunited with her brother.

But living near Virgil didn't hold the same attraction if it meant living without Myles. She'd fantasized about the sheriff far too many times to walk away from the hope that'd taken root inside her, especially after making love with him at the cabin. Maybe she'd chased that desire into a corner, but it was still there. Despite all her denials, she'd allowed herself to believe, at least on some level, that they had a chance of becoming a couple. She was fighting for that chance, fighting to establish the family she'd always wanted. That went beyond a house. After finding him on her doorstep when she returned, she understood that he was what she'd been looking for all along.

Only now he'd taken a giant step away from her. Had she been crazy to send her children to New York, to take a gamble on trying to have it all?

"You hungry?"

Startled by the sound of his voice, she turned away from a portrait of Amber Rose to find him standing at the foot of the stairs. She hadn't heard him come down because she'd been studying the photograph of his wife with such intensity. He had pictures of her all over. Not that the house was a shrine, exactly. Far from it. She figured these pictures were the same ones that'd been up when Amber Rose was alive but they still made Vivian a little uncomfortable. She'd been so worried about her own problems, her own reasons for being unable to sustain a relationship, she hadn't really considered whether or not she could compete with someone like Amber Rose.

In death, Myles's wife only became more perfect. While Vivian had to live with whatever life threw her.

"No, I'm fine." She was too exhausted to eat. And she was afraid, that if she ate the wrong thing, her ulcer would act up again. Her stomach had been burning all day.

As his gaze moved over her, she realized she wasn't looking her best. Knowing how much she was going to miss her children, she'd cried the whole way back from Kalispell and hadn't bothered to repair her makeup. And she was wearing loose-fitting jeans with holes down the legs, sandals and a simple T-shirt, nothing that would impress him.

He was dressed in jeans and a T-shirt, too, but after a shower, he looked fresh. Smelled good, too. The scent of his shampoo brought back the night she'd pressed her face into his neck and breathed in the same scent she was enjoying now.

"Did you ever have dinner?"

They'd been staring at each other. Slightly embarrassed by the appreciation that must've shown on her face, she blinked. "No, I had a late lunch with Claire."

"It's midnight. Even a late lunch would've been hours ago."

"I'm fine," she repeated.

He started to move past her but hesitated. She could sense him behind her, large and solid, and wished he'd place his hands on her shoulders, her arms, anywhere. With so much at stake, she needed him to reassure her that she'd put her hope in the right thing. But he didn't. After a pause, in which it felt as if he wanted to say something but didn't, he skirted past her into the kitchen and opened the refrigerator.

"I make a mean omelet. Will you eat one if I cook it?"

Her stomach burned enough already. "Thanks, but I don't think so."

"What's wrong?"

She adjusted her position to try to ease the discomfort. "Nothing."

"You keep rubbing that spot. Does it hurt?"

"A little," she said with a shrug. "I have an ulcer that gives me trouble every once in a while. Nothing big."

"An ulcer."

"It comes and goes. The wine I drank the other night might've caused it to flare up again. I don't do well with alcohol. And stress makes it worse."

"What can I feed you that'll help?"

He seemed genuinely concerned, but after what he'd been through with his wife, she couldn't imagine he wanted to deal with any kind of illness, even if it wasn't cancer. "An omelet will be fine." She smiled as she said it.

The comforting sizzle of eggs in a frying pan filled the kitchen as she wandered to the windows overlooking his back porch and that elaborate deck. From where she stood, she could see straight into her own kitchen. She wondered if he'd ever noticed that—or been tempted to watch her as she moved about. She certainly glanced over here often enough.

"Will you tell me about your ex-husband now?" He opened a drawer and the utensils rattled as he came up with a spatula.

Leaving the windows, she sank into a seat at the circular booth that served as his kitchen table. She wasn't that impressed with the decor in his house, thought Amber Rose's taste had been mundane. But Amber Rose hadn't been known for her decorating ability. She'd been known as a wonderful wife and mother. So saintly it was probably crazy to hope Myles could ever get over her.

"Why do you want to know about my ex?" she asked.

"Was he abusive? Or was that a front for everything else that was going on?"

As Tom's face appeared in her mind, Vivian grimaced. "He was definitely abusive."

"In what way?"

"Is there anything I can do?" she asked.

"No. I've got it. In what way?" he repeated.

She would rather have chopped vegetables or grated cheese. It would be easier than watching him. "In every way."

He put two slices of bread in the toaster. "How old were you when you married him?"

"I'd just turned eighteen."

"Wow, that's young."

"Too young."

Opening the cupboard closest to him, he took out the salt. "Where'd you meet?"

"At the doughnut shop where I worked."

"He came in?"

"Pretty regularly. I didn't notice him at first. He was just another customer, someone who was quite a bit older than me. It was his persistence that eventually caught my attention. I worked at the doughnut shop in the mornings and waited tables at a Mexican restaurant in the evenings. Once he learned I had a second job, he began to show up there, too."

Myles twisted around to look at her. "Sounds like a stalker."

"He has emotional problems. I wish I'd been smart

enough to realize it then. But I had to work night and day just to get by, and that left me with no social life. I was really lonely, angry at my mother and worried about my brother. Tom stepped up to help me through it."

"And I'm sure he did that for your benefit."

She recognized the sarcasm in those words but didn't attempt to justify her actions. Hindsight made her mistakes so clear. What she didn't add was how desperate she'd felt for a little love, how long it had been since she'd experienced anything like that. "Everything started out okay," she went on. "It wasn't until I was pregnant with Jake that he got so possessive."

Myles didn't seem to like this story. A muscle jumped in his cheek and his movements grew jerky, at odds with his typical athleticism. Yet he was engrossed enough that he'd all but forgotten his cooking. "Where were your parents?"

She pointed to the pan behind him. "I think the eggs are going to burn."

He shook on some grated cheddar and flipped the omelet. "So, where were your parents?"

"My dad abandoned us shortly after I was born. My mother went from relationship to relationship. Each new 'love' was all that mattered to her. I moved out at sixteen, shortly after my brother went to prison. He was what made home bearable for me."

"You're talking about Virgil."

"Yes. He's my only sibling."

"Prison was how he met The Crew."

"Did Rex tell you that?"

"Yes, but not what Virgil did to land himself in prison. And…didn't you say you have an uncle in prison, too?"

"I'm getting to that." She propped her chin on one fist

as she recited the rest. "They charged Virgil with killing my stepfather, but he was exonerated fourteen years later, after my uncle's ex-wife came forward with what she knew about the night in question."

He put the first omelet on a plate and started another one. "What took her so long?"

"Loyalty. It wasn't until they broke up and some of that love and loyalty faded that she was willing to reveal what she knew. After all, she'd benefited from it, too—at least, financially. When he fought her for custody of the kids, she got so angry she went after him with everything she had."

"Bet that was interesting."

"It was. She said he'd gone out the night Martin died. That when he came home, he had blood on his clothes and was visibly shaken. Then the insurance money arrived, and they could finally pay their bills. That sort of thing."

"So it was your uncle who killed your stepfather."

"That's right."

"With what?"

"My stepfather's own gun, if you can believe it. He kept it in the house for protection." She laughed at the irony that seemed to pervade her whole life. "The police knew that much when they arrested Virgil. The gun was on the floor near his body. Whoever shot Martin fired the weapon, dropped it and ran."

"Not the smartest killer in the world."

"Definitely an amateur but he did wear gloves. There were no fingerprints on the gun. And thanks to my mother, he nearly got away with murder."

Myles took out another plate. "Wouldn't your mother

be the one to get the insurance money? How come the uncle was named beneficiary?"

Vivian thought about the autopsy the M.E. had likely performed on her mother today, or would perform in the near future, depending on how many bodies awaited his attention—and in L.A. that could be quite a few. What had the police discovered? Did they realize it was a gang hit? Did they have any hope of tracking down Ink without her help?

She doubted they'd be able to. Now that The Crew had found her despite her efforts to remain hidden, she could call the LAPD and offer what she knew. She planned to do it in the morning. She still wasn't sure she'd be able to attend the funeral, though.

"Vivian? The insurance?"

"Oh, yes. My mother split the money with him. Uncle Gary claims she put him up to the murder in the first place. She claims—*claimed*—she was just trying to help him out of a financial mess, since he'd lost his job."

His hand froze over the pan as if he was wondering whether or not to broach the subject of her mother's murder; she was glad when he kept their conversation to the story. "What kind of job did your uncle lose?"

"He was a service manager at a Toyota dealership. With the state of the economy, other dealerships weren't hiring, and he was struggling to find a way to support his family."

Myles whistled as he slid the second omelet from the pan. "I see. Your mother was behind it all and yet she let your brother go to prison."

Vivian rubbed her face. "Sick, isn't it? I couldn't stay with her after that."

"But…now she's gone."

Vivian didn't answer.

"Are you okay with that?"

She wasn't okay with any of it. "I don't want to talk about how I feel. It's too complicated."

"I understand." He bent to see the gas flame beneath his pan as he lowered the heat. "So where'd you go when you left home so young?"

"I tried living with a friend. But her parents were about to divorce, and I was so worried about making things more difficult for them that I rented a room from a stranger, dropped out of school and went to work."

He buttered the toast. "Did you ever go back? To school, I mean?"

"Never had the opportunity. I met Tom, got married and had Jake. And Tom hardly let me out of the house. I think he was afraid I'd meet someone my own age, and he'd lose me."

"How much older was he?"

"Twenty years."

Probably thinking of his own daughter, already in her teens, he shook his head. "Two decades is a big difference, especially when you're only eighteen."

"I'm lucky I got away from him when I did."

"How long were you together?"

"Six years."

He pulled a carton of milk out of the fridge. "When did he cut his initials in your arm?"

"After the first time I tried to leave him. He got drunk and showed me what would happen if I ever tried that again." He'd done a lot more than cut his initials into her arm. He'd also tied her up for eight hours. She'd never forget how badly her hands and feet had hurt once she got her circulation going again.

"Did he drink often?"

"Toward the end, all the time."

He'd finished the second omelet. After turning off the stove, he carried both plates to the table. "What did Tom do for a living?"

"He was a stockbroker. He was educated, established, successful."

Myles set the plates on the table. "And he was determined to keep you. How'd you ever get away from him?"

She laughed ruefully. "It was like trying to escape The Crew. After he went to work one day, I packed up the kids and left the state."

He crossed the kitchen and returned with two forks. "Did your mother help you with finances or anything?"

"No. We weren't speaking. When she got the insurance money and split it with her brother instead of putting some toward Virgil's appeal, it upset me so much. I couldn't believe she'd do that. My brother was the one person I loved, the one person I felt I could trust, and she'd taken him away from me."

"Did she understand what you were going through with your husband?"

"Not really. I tried to talk to her, but she'd always gloss over it by telling me some men were more possessive than others. She said at least I had one who earned a decent living and wanted to be a good father. Bottom line, she didn't care, didn't want me to become her problem. That wouldn't have gone over very well with Terry, her latest boyfriend, who didn't want anything to do with me or Virgil."

He must've realized he'd left the milk on the counter because he got up and poured them each a glass. "She sounds very childish and selfish."

"She was." As much as Vivian wanted to remember her in a more positive light, she had to be honest enough to admit that.

"So what happened? How'd you get by?" He nodded for her to start eating while they talked, and she did her best to take a few bites.

"There was a woman by the name of Kate Shumley who ran a woman's shelter in Tucson, Arizona. I'd driven there, hoping to eventually make my way to Colorado, where they'd moved Virgil, but couldn't go any farther. I had no more money for gas, no money to feed my kids. I'd hoped to get a job, had looked in every major city we passed through, but no one would hire me because I didn't have a permanent address. So I managed to find this shelter, and Kate took me in. With a state grant, she eventually paid for me to relocate to Colorado, where I'd wanted to go in the first place."

He added some Tabasco sauce to his omelet. "That was nice of her."

"A man had called the shelter, looking for me. She guessed it was a P.I., someone Tom had hired, and was afraid he'd figured out where I'd gone." She found she was enjoying the omelet; it tasted much better than she'd expected.

"How did Colorado work out?"

"Just being close to my brother helped. Especially because I'd been in touch with an organization called Innocent America, based in L.A., which was working to free him. The state had no forensic evidence. A jury had convicted Virgil on circumstantial evidence alone. Still, I didn't have high hopes that we'd be able to get him out, but they were trying, searching for evidence to prove it was—or could have been—someone else. Then my aunt came forward, and they had what they needed." She took a drink of her milk. "I thought the worst was over, that Virgil and I would finally get to build new lives."

"But your brother had joined a prison gang and they weren't willing to let him go."

"That makes him sound rebellious or irresponsible," she said with a grimace. "Or even stupid. But he didn't have any choice. He wouldn't have survived prison if he hadn't joined one gang or another. He was getting into a fight almost every day."

"There's always a price to be paid for safety."

"Yes, and he knew too much. They were afraid of what he might tell the authorities. Not only that, but once you join, you're in for life. If you try to leave, and they can't get to you, they go after your family."

Myles had already finished his omelet and pushed away his plate. "So you had to run and hide again."

"Only this time I had the government's protection. Virgil made a deal with them. If they'd put me in WitSec, he'd go undercover to help them bust another gang that was taking over Pelican Bay. He'd just come out of prison, so he was believable in the part. And he had the motivation."

"When was this?"

"Four years ago."

"He was trying to save your life."

"And my children's."

"It sounds rather opportunistic of the government."

She swallowed another bite. "The gang problem was getting so bad they were beginning to panic. They considered it a win-win."

"But they were gambling with his life!"

"Yes."

"I take it he came through."

"It didn't go as smoothly as we would've liked, but he did what he could. A lot of bangers in both groups—the Hell's Fury and The Crew—were brought up on new charges through his efforts."

He stretched out his legs and crossed them at the ankle. "So is anyone from the Hell's Fury after you?"

"I'm sure they'd love to find us. But it's The Crew that's been the most determined and successful. For them, what Virgil did was a personal affront. They're the ones who knew him so well, who'd basically lived with him as a brother for fourteen years. And when he left, Rex eventually went with him. That didn't go over too well with The Crew, either. The familiarity they have with both men has given The Crew an advantage."

"They managed to track you down, even in WitSec?"

"That's why we left D.C. two years ago."

He drained his glass. "How do you think they did that?"

"They had to have had someone on the inside or someone with access to insider information."

He nodded, then motioned for her to continue eating, and she dutifully raised her fork to force down a few more bites.

"So how well do you know the guy who's coming after you?" he asked. "Ink?"

"Well enough to know he's the most dangerous, *deranged* individual I've ever met."

"Are you the one who shot him?"

"No, that was Rex, but Ink blames me because Rex did it to save me."

"Did Mia see it?"

"Yes."

He cursed under his breath. "Poor thing." He leaned closer. "I guess you never really know who your neighbors are, do you?"

The conversation had been so serious it took her a few seconds to realize he was joking. "No. What dark secrets are *you* hiding?"

His mouth slanted to the left. "I'll never tell."

"Tell me about your family, then."

"What about them?"

"Are your parents alive?"

"Yes."

"And where are your siblings?"

"I have only one brother. He's in Arizona, too."

"How often do you see him?"

"Once or twice a year."

She remembered Myles and Marley packing up for vacation last summer. They'd gone to Disneyland for a few days but spent at least a week with his family. Marley had told her all about it when she'd come over to babysit Mia and Jake for a couple of hours one afternoon. Marley had also stayed with her maternal relatives at the end of the summer, and Myles had been home alone. Vivian had definitely noticed that. It was probably about the time he'd first begun to return her interest.

"Here, I'll take that."

Somehow, she'd managed to eat all her food. And she actually felt better because of it. "Thanks. It tasted great."

He took her plate to the sink. "Make yourself comfortable while I change the sheets on Marley's bed, okay?"

After he'd rinsed off the dishes and put them in the dishwasher, he headed upstairs.

Vivian tried to wait, but she was so full and so sleepy

she couldn't keep her eyes open another second. She wandered into the living room, where she sat on the couch, and the next thing she knew Myles was carrying her up the stairs.

23

He'd found her. At last. After all the months of sitting in prison and planning this moment, it had arrived.

Ink almost couldn't believe his good fortune. Her house was right there, just like L.J. had been told.

But that wasn't all he saw. Ink knew he wasn't the only one who'd noticed when L.J. grabbed his arm and motioned to the house next door. "Look, a cop!"

A cruiser sat in the driveway. But Ink wasn't worried about it. There was no one inside. The cop who normally drove it wasn't even on duty. He had to be in his house, asleep, like the other neighbors on the street. "He probably lives there. No big deal."

"No big deal?" L.J. looked as if he was about to have a heart attack. "This is crazy, man!"

"Stop! He won't even know we're around."

The kid was so nervous he kept glancing behind them, shifting from foot to foot, sighing aloud or doing any number of other irritating things, like hocking a loogie every five seconds. Ink was about to tell him to go wait in the truck, which they'd hidden behind some trees partway around the lake. He didn't want L.J. to ruin his victory. But he needed a wingman, someone to help if the situation got out of control, especially with a cop possibly living next door. He didn't want to risk getting caught before his revenge was complete. He still had Virgil and Rex on his list.

Fortunately, he wasn't too worried that he'd run into problems. If he played it smart, he'd be in and out of her house without creating a disturbance, and be long gone by morning. It wasn't as if she lived all that close to her neighbors. The cop wasn't far away, but the other three homes were strung out like pearls falling from a broken necklace—like that one of his mother's he'd once broken, on purpose.

She'd been so sorry to lose that strand of pearls....

Remembering her tears, he smiled. He'd kept a handful of those milky-white globes in his pocket for days, so he could reach in and touch them whenever he wanted. They'd been a gift from her father, all she had from him, and he'd taken that away from her.

He was going to take more than a string of pearls from Laurel, although he liked the idea of using a necklace to choke her. He could creep into her room and find something like that, the belt of a robe or a pair of panty hose, maybe. She'd wake up when he slipped it around her neck, but she'd be disoriented and groggy and, before she was lucid, he'd yank the necklace or belt so tight she wouldn't be able to breathe. Her eyes would fly open and show him the terror he wanted to see.

Then he'd tear the clothes from her body....

Imagining her utterly and completely at his mercy, unable to even scream, sent a shudder of pleasure through him as powerful as any climax he'd ever experienced. Sex had never been easy for him. He'd never felt what he was supposed to feel—no tenderness, no sense of connection, no relief of tension, ever. Violence, on the other hand, came as naturally as breathing. Maybe, if he was lucky, he'd get his first boner since the shooting. That would be fitting, wouldn't it? He'd punish Laurel for crippling him by tying her legs apart and raping her.

Nothing but the best for Virgil's sister.

And if he couldn't get an erection, he could be creative, use the most painful objects he could find. One way or another, he'd be satisfied, and she'd be sorry.

Sorry she ever met him.

Sorry she'd tried to defy him.

Sorry she'd ever been born.

Drawing a deep breath so he could handle the excitement, he gazed at the stillness of the lake gleaming like a mirror beneath the half-moon overhead. He'd tossed the electric can opener he'd used to bludgeon the old guy into the lake, but he didn't let that bother him. He wouldn't let anything ruin this moment. Not only did he finally have Laurel, she was the key to all the rest. The key to finding Virgil, who thought he was so damn great. And the key to finding Rex, who owed him more than any of the others.

"Come on, man, let's get this over with," L.J. muttered.

Ink nearly whirled on him. "Shut up! You're not going to ruin this for me, you hear?"

Scowling, L.J. backed up a step. "What's wrong with you? We're in a hurry. She lives next door to a cop, man. Why else would that cruiser be there? We need to get this over with."

"I don't want to get it over with. I want to take my time."

"Oh, my God, you're loving every second."

There was that disgust again. It infuriated Ink. L.J.

had no right to make him feel inferior. L.J. was just a kid; he could never do all the things Ink had been able to accomplish.

But Laurel and her children came first. "Damn right," he said from between gritted teeth, "and it only gets better from here."

Whispering for L.J. to stand guard at the front door and to shoot anyone who came through it, he made his way around to the back of the house, where he used his elbow to break out the small square of glass closest to the door handle.

The noise reverberated around him like a symphony of promise but not loudly enough for anyone else to hear. He watched the cop's house for a couple of minutes, searching for any response, any change, and there wasn't one.

Then he stepped inside.

Too worked up to relax, Myles paced the hallway outside Marley's room. He'd deposited Vivian on his daughter's bed at least fifteen minutes ago. Despite her protests that he'd hurt his back if he didn't put her down, he'd managed without so much as a twinge. She was tall but didn't weigh much. Now she was tucked in and fast asleep.

But he couldn't seem to forget about her and go to his own room. He wanted to slip under the covers with her, curve his body around hers. If he was being honest, he wanted to make love to her, too. But he was tired enough that sex was a secondary consideration, less important than just holding her against him. If he could feel her chest rise and fall as she breathed there'd be no question that she was okay and he could rest easier himself.

He doubted she'd kick him out if he tried to sleep

with her. Still, considering how difficult it'd been not to touch her since he'd brought her home, he knew where it would lead. And he'd just decided that he'd play it safe, use some caution before giving his heart away. He'd taken an emotional beating when he lost Amber Rose. Why ask for more?

He didn't want to get serious about anyone right now, not so soon and not so fast. Vivian least of all. Because he instinctively understood that a relationship with her would not only be intense, it would move at the speed of light. They'd been in a holding pattern too long already, first refusing to acknowledge the attraction, then refusing to let it take its normal course.

Which had left them waiting, watching and wanting. The way they felt about each other was kindling, just waiting for the lighted match, and he wasn't going to be the one to throw it on.

So why was he standing here in the hall? Tempting himself to start that fire?

Because I'm being an idiot. Determined to control himself, he went to his own room but stayed there only briefly before coming back out. He couldn't stop his mind from churning. Pat's murder. Vivian's mother's death. Virgil, the previously unknown brother. Rex, the previously unknown boyfriend. The kids. The responsibility he felt to find the bastards who'd already caused so much heartache.

He needed a sleeping pill but couldn't take one. He didn't dare dull his mind. Ink and Lloyd were driving around in a truck that looked almost identical to the majority of trucks in Lincoln County, which meant they could pretty much come and go as they pleased despite the flyers posted in every establishment. He had to remain cautious and ready to act, just in case....

A cup of tea was about the strongest sleep aid he could use.

With another glance at the closed door that separated him from Vivian, he headed downstairs. He was haphazardly digging through the cupboard above the stove, looking for the box of tea he'd purchased on his last trip to the grocery store, when he suddenly felt that something was wrong.

His scalp prickled as he turned. Then he knew what the problem was. A light burned in Vivian's house—a light that hadn't been on when he'd made breakfast for her only thirty minutes earlier.

Shit! Lloyd and Eugene had found Vivian's address. That had to be it. The sons of bitches had come for her in spite of the incident at Trudie's store just hours earlier, in spite of the fact that they must have realized everyone in town was looking for them.

God, they were brazen. Fearless.

Feeling as if he had a knot in his windpipe, Myles crossed to the switch plate and turned off the light in his own kitchen so he could look out without being seen. He'd asked his deputies to drive by every hour or so, and he was sure they'd been doing that, but even if they'd made a pass recently, this couldn't be spotted from the street. It was an upstairs back bedroom.

He was so afraid Ink and Lloyd would get away, he didn't want to take the time to call for backup. But he didn't want to be stupid, either. He had a daughter to raise. So he grabbed the phone and dialed 9-1-1 regardless of his desire to get over there as quickly as possible.

"Operator. What is your emergency?"

It was Kimberly Hannah. He knew all the people who worked dispatch.

He told her he'd found the suspects they'd been looking for and asked her to send two squad cars to the house next to his.

"Haney called in sick. Only Botha's in the area and he just took off to deal with a brawl at the Kicking Horse, but I'll get him over there as soon as possible," she said. "Sit tight and wait for him, okay?"

She was scared for him. Their little county didn't see many homicidal maniacs. But he couldn't wait another second. If he let these men escape, it would endanger the whole community.

"Just tell him to hurry," he said. "And call the others." Then he hung up and dashed upstairs to get his gun.

Virgil's eyelids felt like sandpaper against his eyeballs. The flight from Buffalo had been cramped and hot and sleepless. His head pounded as he managed to retrieve his carry-on from the overhead bin while wedged between all the other people standing in the aisle. That one bag was all he'd brought. He didn't plan on staying in Los Angeles more than a day or two—just long enough to finish what he should've done four years ago.

With any luck, he'd be on a flight home by morning.

If he wasn't lucky, he'd be going back in a box.

"Excuse me."

A soft, female voice came from behind him. A woman wanted to get to the same bin he'd used. He stepped aside to accommodate her, but her bag was too heavy for her to lift, so he got it down for her.

"Thank you." She smiled at him with enough appreciation to let him know she found him attractive, but he wasn't interested. Since he'd found Peyton, he never was. His wife, son and his other loved ones were all that mattered to him.

With a curt nod, he put his back to her and turned on his cell, which rang almost as soon as he hit the Power button. "Yeah?"

"Rex is here with the kids. I just wanted you to know."

It was Peyton. She'd dropped him off at the airport, then had to wait another hour before she could pick up Rex and Jake and Mia.

Head bent, he lowered his voice so he wouldn't disturb the other passengers. "How are they?"

"The kids? Great. Excited. This is a party for them."

"And Rex?"

She took a deep breath; he could hear it through the phone. "I think he needs a doctor."

Virgil would've cursed if he'd had any space to himself. This wasn't a good time for Rex to be ill. "It's that bad, huh?"

"It's that bad."

"God, if anything happens to him..." Rex was the brother he'd never had. The only person he'd ever really trusted, other than Laurel and Peyton.

"He'll be fine. I just... I wanted to tell you that I'm not letting him go back to Montana. Not if I can stop him. I'm going to take him to the hospital."

Peyton didn't need any additional worries. The pressure of everything already going on was bad enough. "Laurel tried to tell me," he said.

"She was right. But if he won't cooperate, there won't be a lot I can do."

Virgil imagined the concern on her face, feared what

the stress of this was doing to her and the baby. "Pey, don't let any of this upset you, okay?"

"How can I avoid that with you in L.A., heading straight back to the people who want to kill you?"

Hearing the tears in her voice, he began to knead his forehead. He wished he could be in two places at once.

"I don't even know if you'll survive," she added.

"Have I ever let you down before?"

"You'll come through if you can, Virgil. There's no question about that. It's just—"

"Quit thinking the worst," he broke in. "I need you to have faith."

There was a brief moment of silence during which she seemed to muster her strength, and he prayed she'd be able to hang on—and keep all the children safe. "Okay. I can do that. I'm with you. You know that, don't you?"

"You're always with me, babe. Just take it easy until I get back."

"I understand."

"Can I talk to Rex?"

"Hang on."

Rex's deeper voice came across the line a second later. "Hey, buddy."

"You're sick, huh?"

"Hell, no. I'm fine."

"Let her take you to the hospital."

"What? No way! I'm going back to Montana as soon as I can get a change of clothes and buy a ticket. I left all the shit I took to L.A. at some motel."

They'd opened the plane door. The line was finally beginning to move. Virgil could feel the balmy evening air so distinctive to this part of the country waft into the aircraft.

Hefting his bag over one shoulder, he nodded at the flight attendant who wished him a good night. "You must've been out of your mind in L.A.," he murmured to Rex.

"Sort of," came the response.

"Listen, I really need you to do something."

"What's that?"

"I need you to let Peyton take you to the emergency room and get you some help."

"No. I just told you—"

"Rex, please. Will you do it? For me?" Virgil couldn't remember a time when he'd ever had to plead with Rex about anything. They always understood each other. He knew about Jack, doubted he could've handled what had happened himself. So he gave Rex a lot of latitude and tried not to ask for much. But he was pleading with him now.

It obviously set Rex back on his heels, made him go silent.

"You still there?" Virgil asked at length.

He made a sound of frustration. "Yeah, I'm here. I'm trying to decide what the hell to do. I can't leave Laurel alone. Not against Ink and whoever else he has with him."

"I'm going to cut off Ink's support and direction just as soon as possible. That way he'll be left without reinforcements if he fails and no one to report to for praise or promotion. I doubt it'll remove all his incentive, but if Laurel and the sheriff can take care of what's happening in Pineview, we'll make it through this. All of us. Peyton's about to have a baby, one that's been trying to come early. She can't look after all three kids and worry about you, too, not if she goes into labor. So I need you to step up, and the way you can do that is to get yourself some help so I can rest assured that she and the kids are in good hands. You feel me?"

There was another long silence.

"Rex?"

"But this town. Pineview. You should see it. It's not prepared for what Ink is capable of doing."

"Just stay in Buffalo with Peyton until I call. Then one of us will go to Pineview. Laurel means as much to me as she does to you, but this has to happen in a certain way or we're all screwed."

Rex's response, when it finally came, was grudging. But an agreement from him was an agreement. Virgil trusted him to stand by his word. "Okay."

The terminal opened up ahead of him, wide and cavernous, with people flowing in both directions, and he lengthened his stride. "Thanks," he said, and he meant it.

"So what are you going to do now?" Rex asked.

"First thing? I've got to buy a gun. I couldn't exactly bring one on the plane."

"From where?"

"A few bucks spread around the right neighborhood, and I should be able to come up with something."

"I've got a friend," Rex said. "He'll fix you up if you call him."

"Can I trust this guy?"

"Completely. He doesn't even know any of The Crew."

Which meant Rex's contact with this guy came before his gang involvement, before he went to prison. "What's his name and number?"

As Rex gave it to him, Virgil put the information in his phone.

"And once you have…what you need?" Rex said.

"It'll be time to pay Horse a little visit."

Rex's voice, which was muffled now, told Virgil he'd turned or moved away from Peyton, and for that, he was grateful. "What you're planning—it's suicide, you know that, right? You don't have a prayer of pulling it off. Not alone."

"Yeah, I know," he said, and pushed the End button.

24

Myles checked outside his front windows. He saw no truck parked at Vivian's, no vehicle at all, except for hers, which was in the drive. From what he could tell, there were no lights on in the front of her house, and no squad car rolling down the street. The view looked exactly like it did every other night. The houses sat dark and quiet, the lake glimmered, placid, beneath the moon, and the stars dangled like Christmas ornaments above.

Because he doubted Ink and Lloyd would've approached Vivian's house from the front, and he figured they'd probably come out the same way they went in, he hurried through his kitchen and exited onto the deck. There he paused to listen. He could hear his heart pounding with urgency, maybe even fear despite the gun in his hand, but he couldn't hear voices or movement.

Had he already missed them?

That upstairs light didn't allow him to see in the first-floor windows. Maybe when they found her gone they'd left without bothering to turn it off. Or they were ransacking her house right now, looking for clues or leaving surprises....

Guessing they'd be too disappointed and angry at finding her gone to simply go away, he walked as quickly and quietly as possible through Vivian's garden. He had no idea what vegetables he happened to be trampling, but he wasn't worried about it. If he could arrest Ink and Lloyd, send them back to prison where they belonged, it'd be worth a few smashed tomatoes.

Although Myles had put on his bulletproof vest along with his utility belt, he hadn't taken the time to change into his uniform. He wore the vest over his T-shirt, knew it probably looked a little ridiculous, but he had what was necessary. That was all that mattered.

When he discovered the broken door, which stood slightly ajar, and the glass on the floor inside, he was especially glad he'd had the presence of mind to put on some shoes.

Someone had been in her house, all right.

Hinges squealing as he pushed the door wider, Myles stepped over the shards of glass and stopped again to listen. He couldn't hear anything, couldn't see anything, either. There was no light whatsoever in this room. The moon slanted into the front of the house and didn't filter to the back. Myles had brought his flashlight, but he didn't dare use it. He wanted to find Ink and Lloyd before they realized he was there, so he felt his way through instead, hoping he wouldn't knock something over in the process.

He hadn't even made it out of the laundry room and into the kitchen when he heard footsteps pounding down the stairs. Whoever was here seemed to be leaving.

Without seeing where he was going, he couldn't move fast so he snapped on his flashlight and charged through the swinging doors between the kitchen and the living room.

The shifting glow of his flashlight landed on the back

of a man who was opening the door. Ink. He turned at that second, giving Myles a glimpse of his face. Then Myles spotted a second man, Lloyd, standing behind Ink across the threshold.

Lloyd had a gun. Ducking behind the sofa, Myles called out, "Hold it right there or I'll shoot!"

They didn't stop. Myles hadn't really expected them to. Ink shoved Lloyd to the side, and attempted to shut the door behind him, so Myles squeezed the trigger. He felt the familiar recoil travel up his arm and hoped to God he'd hit something. He was peering around the sofa to see, when someone flung the door open again. It crashed against the wall with a bang that reverberated through the house just before the sound of a second shot, this one coming from the bad guys.

Ink had taken control of the firearm. Blinded by Myles's flashlight, he was shooting into the dark, but he'd come darn close. *Too* close. When Myles heard the bullet whiz past his ear, he tossed the flashlight into the living room so it couldn't give his location away and dropped to the floor. But there wasn't any time for the *Oh, shit!* that was going through his mind. He had to act and he had to act now.

Lifting his Glock, he fired once, twice, three times.

And he hit someone. He heard the grunt of pain, the curse.

Hoping the squad car he'd ordered would come and hem them in at the front, he waited. Without his flashlight, he couldn't see them anymore. "Ink?" he called out. "Drop your weapon!"

"Go to hell!" came the reply. Then someone started to run.

It had to be Lloyd. Myles didn't believe Ink could

move that fast, not with his handicap. That meant he had a good chance of apprehending Ink, even if Lloyd managed to escape. But he wouldn't get anyone if he stayed where he was. He had to sacrifice the cover of the sofa in order to advance.

First, he wanted to reload. The clip he'd been using wasn't out of bullets, but he didn't want to be down to two or three shots if he got into another exchange. So he changed clips by feel alone, then rose cautiously to his feet.

His abandoned flashlight painted a steady white circle on the wall. It was the only thing he could see as he darted for the door. He reached it without incident, but as soon as he stepped through it he heard another blast.

This one wasn't from his gun, either.

Then he felt the pain.

The sound of gunshots woke Laurel from a deep sleep. She blinked against the darkness, wondering if she could've dreamed the sound. Had she been reliving that night in Colorado as she so often did?

She didn't think so. After a few seconds of trying to catch her breath and sort out the thoughts and feelings bombarding her from all sides, she heard another shot.

That was when she knew it was real.

"Myles?" she called.

No answer. It felt as if she was completely alone in the house, but she knew he'd never leave her without someone else being there. Not in her current predicament. And not without good reason.

"Myles?" she called again.

The familiar influx of adrenaline began to pour through her. Something was wrong. Something terrible.

Where was her gun?

She had to rack her brain to remember. It was in her purse. But she hadn't fallen asleep in this room, hadn't brought it upstairs with her. The last she remembered was that she'd had it in Myles's kitchen while he was cooking her meal.

"God, please," she mumbled. She wasn't praying for anything specific. Nothing she could identify in this hellish moment. She was praying for all of it. Safety. For herself, for Myles, for everyone in Pineview. For Virgil and Rex and the children. She didn't want to find the sheriff dead. She couldn't take that. Not after what she'd seen that night in Colorado.

More shots rang out. Whatever was going on hadn't ended. She had to get out there and help, if she could. But she didn't even have her jeans. After Myles had carried her to bed, she'd shed them for the sake of comfort and curled up under Marley's blankets.

Where were they? Probably on the floor somewhere, but she was already in the hall and wasn't willing to waste so much as a second going back.

Running down the stairs, she rushed into the kitchen to get her gun. She could see a light burning upstairs at her house, but that didn't surprise her. What did was that she didn't hear any sirens or police activity out front.

Where was the rest of the police force? Had Myles gone over there by himself? If so, what had motivated him to do that?

She found her purse on the table, where she'd left it, and pulled out her gun. Then she ran through the living room and out the front door. There'd been no new shots since she'd left Marley's bedroom, but she didn't hear Myles making an arrest, or coming back home, either.

Why not?

"Myles? Where are you?"

"Get back…in the house…and lock the door!"

Relief flooded through her as she recognized his voice, but she didn't turn back as he asked. It sounded as if he was in pain, as if he could hardly talk, let alone yell.

She imagined him bleeding on her front porch.

She glanced around, looking for danger, but saw nothing and hurried closer. A series of dark, amorphous shapes surrounded her, but she realized those shapes were her car, her chairs, her hibiscus plant, the columns on her porch. Whatever had happened was over.

"Myles?"

"Didn't you…hear me?" he said hoarsely. "I have a deputy…on the way. He'll…help me. Get…inside. Now!"

If Ink and his partner were around, they would've fired again. At her, if not him. But she wasn't sure it would've stopped her. She had to get to Myles right away, before it was too late. That was all she cared about. So she lowered her gun and ran hell-bent for her porch.

She found him lying, alone, on her welcome mat. "Have you been shot?"

"Just…in the leg. I'm…okay."

He was okay if the bullet hadn't struck a major artery. She stepped over him to turn on the porch light and saw that he'd actually been shot twice. Once in the leg and once in the neck.

"Turn that off!" he growled, but she didn't. She could hear a siren now. The deputy was on his way. Ink and his partner were gone. She had to stop the bleeding.

Tears streamed down her face as she ran inside to get a clean sheet she could cut up and tie around his leg. This was exactly what she'd been afraid of. She'd brought The Crew to town, and now they were hurting the people who meant the most to her.

She returned as a parade of cop cars drove down their street. The neighbors closest to the corner had been roused from sleep. They stumbled out of their house and stood in front, rubbing their eyes and yawning as they watched to see what was going on. A few began to walk over. But she ignored them. In situations like this, seconds mattered.

Using a pair of scissors, she cut the sheet and tied a strip above Myles's thigh, where he'd been shot. The leg injury looked worse than the wound in his neck, which appeared to be a simple grazing. She was wiping the blood away when she felt his hand slip beneath her underwear and cup her ass.

"What are you doing?" She sniffled, surprised. The porch railing blocked any view of her from the oncoming cop and the neighbors, but that would change within seconds.

His teeth flashed as he gave her a lopsided grin. "Hey, stop crying. I don't think I'd want to touch you so badly if I was about to die."

Laughing, she pushed his hand away and laid her head on his chest. The bulletproof vest wasn't the most comfortable thing in the world, but nothing had ever felt better than the tenderness he showed her by running his fingers through her hair. "It's going to be okay," he murmured. "I'm fine."

And that was when she knew. He might be fighting it—might be as scared of falling in love again as she was—but he cared about her every bit as much as she cared about him.

* * *

"What the hell's wrong with you? Run!" L.J. whispered harshly. They didn't have time for Ink to limp along. They were dead if they didn't get out of Pineview fast. It seemed as if the police were coming from every direction. The flashing lights on top of their cruisers made L.J. dizzy with their strobe effect.

He moved deeper into the forest, into the welcoming shelter of the trees, but the red of those lights seemed to reflect all around him, and the sirens were deafening. The cops were too close....

"I'm...coming," Ink gasped, but he wasn't making great progress, and L.J. didn't want to wait. Why should he? Ink was nothing but a crazy old gimp. The heartless son of a bitch had dragged him into some deep shit, and now it was all going wrong, just as he'd known it would.

Ink could go down for it alone. No way would L.J. be caught with him, not if he could help it.

Once he'd made that decision, L.J.'s path seemed so ridiculously obvious he almost couldn't believe he hadn't broken away from Ink sooner. He'd leave his old cellie; Ink would never know where he'd gone. Then he wouldn't be tied to this nightmare, this...this violent nut job. After the gunfight that had just occurred, Ink wouldn't make it till morning before they dragged his ass off to jail.

Picking up speed, L.J. put more distance between them. But it wasn't that much easier for him to run. He'd been shot in the left shoulder. He had no idea how bad his injury was, but he knew it hurt more than anything he'd ever experienced before. Pain radiated through his whole chest, and blood flowed down the front of his shirt, causing the fabric to stick to him. With his luck, he'd lose too much blood and be unable to continue moving at all. Then Ink would catch up and kill him for trying to get away. He was already making guttural threats as loudly as he dared.

"You leave me behind, you little prick, and I'll kill you. I swear to God I will. If I have to hunt you across the entire country, I'll be there someday when you least expect it."

Those words terrified L.J., which only made him run faster. He'd seen what Ink could do, how casually and carelessly he killed whoever stood in his way. Ink was so twisted he made L.J., who'd always been the badass of his neighborhood, feel like a choirboy.

He wanted to turn around and scream, "You can eat shit and die, sucker!" and continue charging through the forest. But as they left the highway behind, with all those headlights zipping past, it was getting too dark to see. There was no telling what he might run or fall into; his legs were already wobbling.

Besides all that, Ink had the keys to the truck, and the truck was an absolute necessity. They couldn't escape on foot. Even if the cops didn't find them, they couldn't travel fast enough, wouldn't have enough food and water to reach a safe place, especially with him bleeding all over. It wasn't as if they could stumble into a gas station and ask to use the bathroom so he could clean up, or go to a hospital. Their future well-being hung on getting to the truck before the police discovered it, and driving to their cabin where they'd have the privacy to recuperate and live until everything went back to normal.

Ink had him again. If he kept running, he'd probably die in the forest. Or the police would find him and send him back to prison. His only real hope was to head to the truck with Ink and try to reach the cabin.

Slowing to a stop, he bent over to catch his breath. The air rattled painfully in his lungs, and his heart pounded. It seemed to vibrate through his entire body, which shook uncontrollably.

"What the…hell were…you thinking?" Ink said as he came scraping up from behind. "You thought…you could…leave…my ass?"

He'd been thinking he'd risk almost anything to do just that. But this was not the time. "I wanted—" he dragged some air into his lungs "—to get farther…from the…the cops." He felt for the hole in his shoulder, found a small circle below his collarbone. "I've been…shot. Don't know how long…I'll be able to…keep running."

Ink was gasping, too, but this seemed to pacify him. "You were…hit? Where?"

"Shoulder."

Ink gave no indication whether that mattered to him or not. He grabbed L.J. by the back of the shirt and shoved him forward. "We have…to keep moving."

Dizziness threatened to overwhelm L.J. Even worse, the darkness of the surrounding forest suddenly seemed too forbidding, too impenetrable. He felt as if his feet were five times their normal size. He could hardly move. He wanted to lie down, to somehow rid himself of the anvil crushing his chest.

"Do you…know where…we're at?" Because he didn't. He couldn't remember. He could only feel the pain.

"Yeah. Truck's not…far," Ink said, "Get going," and gave him another push.

It was a nine millimeter, not the most powerful gun around, but that was the best Rex's friend could do on such short notice. And it could certainly be lethal, especially at close range. A nine millimeter wasn't going to stop someone as big as Horse, not unless Virgil hit him in just the right place. And it wouldn't be worth much if he wound up facing an army.

As he drove the car he'd rented at the airport past Horse's illegal club on sixtieth and Vermont, Virgil hoped he wouldn't have to confront The Crew en masse, but it didn't look promising. Although he'd hoped to arrive early, before the nightly activities really got under way, he'd spent too long getting here. He'd had to pick up the car, rendezvous with Rex's friend, who'd taken him to meet another friend, and buy the gun. Then he'd messed around trying to get a silencer, to no avail. And after that, he'd had an hour's drive on freeways that were almost as congested at night as they were during the day.

Already the club was packed. Cars, trucks and motorcycles lined both sides of the street; groups, mostly men with a few hookers thrown in, congregated on the sidewalks, some smoking weed, some buying harder drugs. Inside, he knew he'd find rooms where these men could take the girls for just about any activity they chose, including a gang bang. There'd be slot machines and other types of gambling, gun sales, whatever a guy could want.

He'd called Rex a few minutes ago, reaching him as he was going into the hospital, and gotten Mona's number. She was still cliqued up with The Crew, still one of them. But she liked Rex, and Rex trusted her. Virgil hoped to God he could trust her, too, because she'd agreed to be his eyes and ears tonight. According to her last text, he'd beaten her to the club, but when she eventually showed up she was supposed to scope out the place, report on who was inside, who else they were expecting, what they were doing, where Horse was and when Virgil might have an opportunity to get him alone.

His plan, simple though it was, sounded feasible in theory. But Virgil couldn't be sure Mona would provide reliable information. She could get high and forget the whole damn thing. He also had no guarantee she'd want the money he offered more than what Horse might provide if she turned on him instead. She could decide to tell Horse he was sitting outside, lure him right into a trap.

Trusting her was a high-risk venture. But he had to trust someone. Without intel, he'd have no chance whatsoever.

He didn't bother ducking his head or even looking away when he passed the men on the sidewalk. Chances were slim any of them would recognize him. He grew up in L.A., but he hadn't been a gangbanger until he went to prison. And thanks to tougher sentencing laws, he'd been dropped into the federal system, served his time in Arizona and then Colorado. Maybe a few of The Crew members he'd known had found their way to L.A. to live with the brothers and be a bigger part of the criminal empire, but acting suspicious would cause more of a ripple among this group than acting unafraid, as if he belonged right where he was.

The picture of Peyton hugging Brady that he'd put on the console stared up at him as he rounded the corner and parked. He was too anxious, didn't want to wait for Mona. Peyton could go into labor anytime. He hated the thought of her being alone, especially now, while they were dealing with so much.

If she lost the baby...

He couldn't even consider that. Neither could he get ahead of himself. Not if he hoped to see her again.

Taking the gun from the seat beside him, he checked the magazine while he called Laurel. He'd brought the prepaid cell phone he'd purchased so he'd have a safe way to communicate, something that wouldn't contain all his contacts if it fell into the wrong hands. So he hated to dial her number. It meant he'd have to destroy the phone before he went in. But talking to her might get him new information and shore up his resolve. If he had to kill Horse, he hoped it would save her, too.

But her voice mail answered. "You've reached the Stewart residence…."

Where the hell was she? It was two in the morning. She should be at home.

Worry tightened his stomach muscles. Had Ink gotten to her? Was it too late?

If so, The Crew had no idea what was about to happen to them. Because once he unleashed his rage—

The beep sounded, signaling that it was time to leave a message. He didn't really know what to tell her. What could he say after so much had happened?

Something. This could be his last chance to communicate with the sister, who'd stood by him through every problem and setback, even when the entire world, including their mother, seemed determined to break him.

"Hey, ah, it's me," he said into the phone. "I wanted to let you know that…that I'm sorry. I wish you'd never been dragged into any of this, wish I'd been able to find another way to manage my life so that there'd be no spillover on you. But…that doesn't help much, does it? We are where we are. Just know this—I love you. I've always loved you."

Another call came in as he was hanging up. After checking caller ID, he punched the Talk button. "Yeah?"

"It's me. I'm a block away."

Mona. The game was on. Either she'd give him the information he needed to kill Horse, or she'd give up the information Horse needed to kill him.

25

This wasn't going to work. They were making him wait forever.

Already nervous when he'd arrived, Rex eyed the crowd hoping to see an emergency-room doctor. A mother holding a sick baby. A teenager nursing a swollen, probably broken, ankle. A toddler wiggling in the lap of some exhausted father who was trying to keep a cloth pressed to the cut on his head.

He wasn't one of these people. He was here because he'd been stupid enough to get hooked on OxyContin, and he didn't want to go crying to someone about it now. So what if he was sick? He couldn't sit here while Virgil hunted down Horse, and Laurel faced Ink. What kind of friend would that make him? What kind of man?

He eyed the door. Peyton thought she'd done her duty. She wouldn't worry if he left because she wouldn't know about it. At his insistence, she'd gone to a motel with the kids. He could call her, tell her they were giving him clonidine, and that he was fine now, perfect and heading home to sleep. He wished he could get some clonidine. At least then he'd be able function in the short-term. It would stop the nausea, the coughing, the heart palpitations. His bones felt as if they were on fire, as if they were burning through his flesh. Clonidine should help that, but for how long? With a success rate of less than ten percent after one year of treatment, even a medical detox rarely worked. Either he quit, or he didn't. He'd believed that from the start. So why was he here?

"Fuck this," he muttered, and got up.

"Are you leaving?" The woman who'd sat next to him for the past two hours acted like he was committing a cardinal sin. She'd been staring at him as though there wasn't a TV to entertain her five feet away. She creeped him out. Maybe she recognized him as a fellow addict, thought they could become friends or allies or share needles or some shit. She didn't know he wasn't going in the same direction anymore. No one did, because he looked and felt worse than he ever had in his life.

"Hey!" She tried again to get him to respond. He didn't bother, but she'd spoken loudly enough to draw the attention of someone in authority.

"Sir? Excuse me, sir?" It was the nurse Peyton had spoken to when they first arrived. He didn't want to acknowledge her, either, but she caught up with him before he could reach the doors.

"Would you give me the respect of an answer, please?" She sounded pissed, but she had no idea how hard it was just to walk. His head felt as if it'd been cleaved in two.

"What can I do for you?" he asked, marshaling all his strength to be polite.

"You could take a seat. I don't think it'll be much longer."

He hung his head, took a few measured breaths. "What'd Peyton say to you?"

"Peyton who?"

She was playing dumb. He could read it on her face.

"The woman I came in with. You remember her. Had a belly out to here?" He held his hand in front of his own stomach.

Her mouth flattened, became a mere slash in her face. "She said you probably wouldn't stay. She was worried about it when she saw how crowded the waiting room was. She cares about you, so I'm doing my best to help her out."

The nurse thought Peyton's baby was his, that Peyton had to deal with an addict—that is, loser—for a husband.

"Come on, sit down," she coaxed. "I'll go see if I can get you in any sooner."

Before all the kids who needed to be treated? No way. He wasn't going to jump the line. He was a full-grown man who felt guilty for wasting resources that should go to other people, people who weren't stupid enough to get themselves into such an unenviable position. He could buy a few pills on the street—any kind of painkiller if he couldn't get OxyContin—enough so that he could be useful again. Then, after everything was over, he'd go clean.

"I'm okay," he said.

She grasped his arm. "Please? That woman you were with. She just about begged me."

Staring down at her hand, he took a deep breath and nodded. "Fine." He started back toward his seat, but as soon as she disappeared down the hall, he strode out and used his cell phone to call his street pharmacist.

The fury that seethed inside Ink felt like a separate living and breathing entity, one he couldn't control. No matter what he did, Virgil and his sister always remained just out of reach. Now L.J. was shot and looking as if he had one foot in the grave as he slouched against the door of the truck, and Ink couldn't even get him some help.

Why he was suddenly so set on saving L.J., Ink didn't know. For a few minutes in the forest, he'd believed that L.J. was going to abandon him. That deserved no loyalty. Just yesterday, he'd been planning on killing L.J., anyway. But not yet. He wasn't finished with him. Losing L.J. created another wrinkle in his plans and narrowed his chances of success. It was a victory for the other side.

"You okay?" He'd been barking this question every few minutes, and L.J. would grunt, but this time Ink got no response. L.J. had even quit wincing when the truck's tires hit various ruts and grooves as they bounced up the dirt road to the cabin.

"Hey!" When Ink shook him, L.J.'s eyelids fluttered open, revealing glassy eyes. Quite a bit of blood soaked his shirt. Was he dying?

"Shit!" Ink slammed his fist into the dash. What was he going to do? He'd always fancied himself as resourceful, capable of doing whatever needed to be done in a pinch. If that meant sewing up a gash in his arm or one of his comrades', he'd do it. If it meant digging out a bullet, he'd do that, too. He'd removed a slug from his own shin once. It'd been a grisly affair—he'd nearly passed out—but he'd been successful, and it'd made him quite famous among The Crew. They still asked to see the scar, and talked about the balls it took to do something like that.

He had the balls to do this, too. But as far as he knew, he didn't even have a first aid kit to work with. He hadn't seen one, anyway. It wasn't something the men who'd rented the place had thought to bring. Probably because they'd only been planning to do a little hiking and fishing, and take a few pictures, and couldn't imagine getting hurt. Or they couldn't imagine getting hurt and being unable to seek help in town. They'd had a vehicle, after all, and there'd been a group of them.

Ink, on the other hand, had no help. And he had to lay low until the heat was off.

But he could work without a first aid kit. He'd sedate L.J. with the last of his pain pills, then use hot water and bandages made from the clothes of the men he'd shot. He'd tossed their suitcases in the back bedroom, so he still had access to them.

"What—what are you…thinking?" L.J. was watching him through narrow slits, as if it was difficult for him to open his eyes.

"I'm thinking how I'm going to patch you up."

His Adam's apple bobbed as he struggled to swallow. "Patch…me up? But…I need a doctor. I think…I'm dying."

He had to feel like shit to be less concerned about getting caught than getting help. "You're not going to die," Ink told him.

"Just…drop me off at…at a hospital. There's got to be one around here somewhere. You can…you can still get away."

But he wasn't done here. Not by a long shot. Besides, running, especially in the vehicle they had now, would only get him arrested. A description of the truck must've gone out to every law enforcement agency in the area. The best thing to do was sit tight. They had a few days yet before anyone noticed that the men who'd rented the cabin were gone. That gave them time to get L.J. back on his feet, time for Ink to come up with alternate transportation and time to finish what they'd set out to do in the first place.

"You don't have anything to worry about," he told L.J.

"But the pain… Feels as if my heart can't beat…as if…as if it's filled with…with blood or something."

"I've been shot before. It always feels like you're dying," he said. "Just relax. We're home now, and I'm going to take care of you."

And if he couldn't? He'd bury L.J. in the forest with the other guys and figure out another way. Because he wasn't leaving Laurel alive. Not after coming this close. That small-town bastard sheriff was going to get his, too.

"Son of a bitch!"

Vivian startled awake to see that she'd fallen asleep in a chair at Myles's bedside. Despite the late hour, the hospital in Libby was abuzz with various noises and had been the whole time. The beeping machines, the conversation of the doctor who'd spoken to Myles as he cleaned his wounds and bandaged him up, the nurses who came in and out with blood pressure cuffs or medication or pushed carts past his open doorway. It should've kept her from dozing off. But she'd somehow grown accustomed to it. Or she'd been too exhausted to let it bother her. She'd drifted off almost as soon as she knew he was going to be fine. But this, coming from the sheriff's own lips, made her bolt from her chair.

"You okay?" she gasped before she could gather her wits enough to realize he'd just hung up the phone and looked more angry than hurt.

"They let Ink and Lloyd get away." Hitting his forehead with the palm of his hand, he drooped dejectedly onto the pillow. "I had half a dozen deputies swarming the area and somehow they couldn't get the job done."

This wasn't what Vivian wanted to hear. She'd thought

that maybe, *finally,* the nightmare would be over. There'd been a price. Myles's injuries had been frightening to her and painful to him. But the bullet that went through his leg hadn't hit a major artery or chipped the bone. The second bullet, the one that grazed his neck, had left a cut, nothing more.

"Get away?" she repeated dully.

He sighed as he scowled up at her. "They've scoured the area. They can't find them or their truck."

But they couldn't give up this soon. "Ink won't leave until he gets what he wants. That means he's still here."

"Where?" he demanded. "For the past three hours, my deputies have stopped every car and truck coming to or from our neighborhood at two different checkpoints. I've had a K-9 unit and a bevy of officers with heavy-duty flashlights combing the forest. There's been no sign of them. The dogs picked up a scent and chased it to where we found some tire tracks, but every white truck we've stopped hasn't been the one they're driving. Maybe they slipped through before we put up the blockade. But if that's the case, they could be a hundred and fifty miles in any direction, and we don't know enough about the make and model of the truck to expect other departments to do much more than be on the lookout."

"They haven't left," she said. "They've holed up. They're waiting."

"There've been no reports of strangers lurking about, no other incidents since Trudie called me earlier."

"Maybe they're still in the forest."

"If so, they won't be able to stay there long. I'm pretty sure I shot one of them. I definitely heard a scream and saw him fall."

Could she be lucky enough that Ink was dead? Without actually seeing his body, Vivian couldn't believe it. He seemed indestructible. "Have the deputies checked my house?"

"Several times. Harold Willis from Libby is there now."

"Then I don't know what to say, except—" she rubbed her eyes, noted the lines in his face that suggested he was equally exhausted "—we need some rest. We'll have to regroup in the morning."

He didn't like that answer, but there didn't seem to be anything more to suggest.

"Do you want me to call Elizabeth's house? Let Marley know you've been hurt?" She hadn't done so because she'd wanted to know the extent of his injuries before setting off any alarms. There was no point in upsetting Marley, not without good reason. Once the doctor came, and he and Myles began to talk, she didn't want to interrupt. Then she'd fallen asleep.

"No. There's nothing to be gained from waking the whole Rogers family. Getting dragged out of bed to hear I've been shot will only scare Marley. I don't want her to come home in the middle of this mess, anyway. I'll explain what happened in the morning. Hopefully, by then, I'll look less ragged so she'll believe me when I say I'm going to live."

"Are you in a lot of pain?" Vivian couldn't imagine he wasn't. Earlier, he wouldn't take anything except Tylenol, said he was afraid it would impair his ability to think and he was still trying to direct the search for Ink and Lloyd from his hospital bed. But he'd already done all he could. In her opinion, it was time to give him the Vicodin his doctor had left in a little paper cup so he could rest.

"My leg is throbbing like crazy," he admitted. "But it's not as bad as it could be. Will you talk to the doctor? Get me some crutches so we can go?"

She blinked in surprise. "Go? Where?"

"Home. There's nothing more they can do for me here."

"But you were shot at home."

"No, I was shot at *your* house."

"Because you went over there before you had backup." His deputy had complained about this when he came running up the walk to find his sheriff injured. She was angry at Myles for taking such a risk, too. He could've been killed—exactly what she'd feared from the start.

"Ink and Lloyd would've been gone if I'd waited."

"They're *still* gone," she pointed out.

He didn't seem to like that answer, but he took the time to cover a yawn before responding. "You really know how to kick a guy when he's down."

She refused to smile, wasn't willing to make light of this. She didn't want him returning to his house until they'd found Ink and Lloyd and any other Crew members who might be in the area. "*Someone* needs to kick you. With your cruiser in the driveway, I'm sure they realize you live next door."

"So? They have no reason to come after me. I'm the guy they want to avoid."

"They'll come if they suspect I'm with you. Unless you want to get into another shoot-out, you should stay here."

He arched an eyebrow at her. "And where will you stay?"

"I'll get a motel room for the next couple of nights."

She couldn't face going back home, not after Myles's close call.

"Good idea. We'll both stay at the Blue Ridge. Get the doctor."

She rattled the paper cup with his pills inside it. "Will you take the Vicodin if I do?"

"I'm a tough guy. I don't need any painkillers." He was teasing, but she got the impression he honestly meant to refuse—until he tried to move. Then he winced and fell back with a groan. "Shit, yeah. Give me those."

She laughed as she offered him a glass of water to swallow his meds. Then she went to find the doctor, but he called her back.

"Vivian?"

She turned to see him put the empty cup on his rolling cart.

"Were you really not wearing any pants when you knelt over me earlier?"

The memory of his fingers slipping beneath the elastic of her panties sent a tornado of warmth and excitement twisting through her. She checked the hallway to make sure their conversation couldn't be overheard. "I was covered. I mean, as well as I would be in a swimsuit. It was just that once I heard the gunshots and knew you weren't in the house, I didn't dare take the time to find my jeans, let alone put them on." As soon as the deputy had arrived to assist him, she'd dashed into the house to grab a pair of sweats, so it wasn't as if anyone else had seen her in her underwear.

"I remember." A dreamy smile curved his lips. "Your panties—they're thin and lacy, right?"

She rolled her eyes. "If I didn't *know* it was too soon,

I'd think the Vicodin had kicked in and sent you for a loop."

His smile stretched wider. "Some things transcend pain."

"Apparently so." She folded her arms in an attempt to control the delicious shiver his expression evoked. "Wait a second. It was only a few hours ago that you put me on notice."

"For what?"

"You told me you didn't want to get involved with me."

He sobered. "That was before."

"Before what?"

"Before I realized it was already too late."

Horse is in the back bedroom with Gully. As alone as he'll get. Do it now. I just unlocked the back door on my way to the bathroom.

This was it. The text Virgil had been waiting for. It had taken most of the night for Mona to do what she'd promised, but the situation wasn't looking a whole lot better despite that. He had no idea who Gully was or how he might change what was about to happen. And although the sun was coming up and the crowd on the street had dispersed, there were still plenty of cars and trucks parked along the curb, suggesting a full house. A lot of the guys who frequented Horse's illegal club simply crashed out on whatever they could find. With a girl in one of the back bedrooms. On a couch. Some even fell asleep on the floor, too high or drunk to realize they were lying in their own vomit.

So Horse wasn't nearly as alone as Virgil would've

liked. To top it off, Virgil was so groggy he felt as if he was underwater. He'd been up for twenty-four hours, been on high alert too long to be as sharp as he needed to be. This wasn't the condition in which he wanted to decide whether Mona's text was an invitation to be tortured and shot in the head—or the help he'd requested.

But he didn't have to decide, did he? He'd already made the decision to trust her when he'd first contacted her.

After bringing the photo of his wife and children to his lips for a quick goodbye kiss, he took out the lighter he'd picked up at the last gas station and burned it, along with all the other photos and business cards he hadn't even known were in his wallet. He burned the car rental agreement and anything else that could possibly help The Crew find his family, too. In case he didn't survive the next few hours, he didn't want to leave anything that could be traced behind. He hoped The Crew's revenge would be complete at his death, if things went in that direction, but with them, there was no way to tell. They were the most bloodthirsty group of men he'd ever known. Their unflinching willingness to perform the most brutal acts had served him well in prison, had put him on top right along with them.

But it'd created a hell all its own once he was exonerated.

Slapping his face to revive himself, he took a deep breath, slipped the gun into his waistband under the front of his shirt and got out. One shot. That was all it would take—*if* he could get in without being stopped, maintain an element of surprise and manage to get Horse in his sights without the others standing in the way. Ironically, he'd never used a gun until *after* prison. But running a bodyguard service gave him good reason to visit the shooting range. Maybe it was the only thing in his favor, but he was one hell of a marksman.

Of course, there was another problem. Even if he hit his target and killed Horse, as he hoped, the blast would bring everyone else in the house down on him. Other than making a run for it, he hadn't figured out how he'd get back to his car. He could only hope the answer would be apparent when the time came, because there was no telling what he might encounter once he got inside.

As he walked around the trunk of his rental car, his cell phone buzzed with another text message.

Mona again.

Are you coming?

He didn't bother answering. If she *was* baiting a trap, he didn't want her to know any more than she already did. He was, however, tempted to call Rex, to tell him to look out for Peyton and Laurel if anything happened to him. He would have, except he didn't need to; he knew Rex would do just that. At least, he would if he could. So instead of placing that call, he dropped the phone on the asphalt and smashed it to pieces.

There went his ability to communicate. It was down to sheer nerve, his gun and whether or not Mona was being truthful.

26

Myles had fallen asleep almost as soon as his head hit the pillow, but Vivian moved around the motel room, taking a shower, brushing her teeth—two, then three, times—and bolting, unbolting and rebolting the door. When they'd arrived, she'd called the LAPD, told them as much as she knew about the people she believed had killed her mother. They didn't seem too impressed with her knowledge, or even particularly willing to believe what she had to say, but the detective she'd spoken to wrote it all down and promised to look into it. She figured she'd check back with him in a few days. When she knew what was going on here, she'd be able to push the issue a bit harder.

Myles had sent a deputy by the name of Campbell to get him an overnight bag. Campbell had shown up with it over an hour ago and had brought most of the items she'd put in Marley's room, too. But if he'd found her jeans somewhere on the floor, he'd left them where they lay, so she was still wearing the sweats she'd donned after Myles was shot. For the moment, though, she was satisfied with the few personal belongings she had with her. She didn't want to return home to see Myles's blood on her porch, or face the fact that Ink had once again infiltrated her personal space. There'd be time enough to deal with that later, when they caught Ink and Lloyd. The best thing right now would be to get some rest.

If only she could relax. The nap she'd stolen at the hospital seemed to have taken the edge off her fatigue, and agitation made it impossible to unwind. Especially because she couldn't get hold of anyone in Buffalo, New York. Myles had been able to call Marley, gently break the news and make arrangements for her to spend another day with the Rogers family. But Vivian didn't even know if her kids had arrived at their destination. According to the call she placed to the airport, their plane had landed on time, but that was where the trail grew cold. Rex's cell went straight to voice mail. Peyton wasn't picking up; neither was Virgil. Yet it was three hours later back east, nearly eleven in the morning. They should definitely be up and around.

Maybe Peyton had gone into labor and they were all at the hospital....

That had to be the case. Taking the cordless phone from the nightstand, she stepped outside and kicked a small pebble back and forth while dialing Virgil's office for the third time in the past two hours.

"I'm sorry, I haven't heard from him." It was the same woman who'd answered her last two calls, and she didn't sound pleased to be bothered again.

"This is his sister, Laurel. Do you know when he might come in?"

"I'm sorry, I have no idea."

The receptionist had been trained not to give out information. Vivian could tell. The woman probably didn't even know Virgil had a sister. They'd kept their lives that separate since D.C. But she wasn't one of the bad guys, damn it. She needed to know what was going on. "Can you at least tell me if Peyton's in labor?"

"I'm afraid I haven't heard."

Completely neutral again.

"Can you have him call me if you hear from him?"

"Of course."

"The number is—"

"I've got the number. You gave it to me last time."

"Great. Thanks for nothing," she grumbled, and hung up. She needed to hear Jake's and Mia's voices, wanted reassurance from them more than she'd ever wanted anything.

What should she do? Go to Buffalo? She didn't even have a car at the motel. She'd ridden to the hospital in the ambulance with Myles, and then Campbell had dropped them off before going to get their things.

Shit. She wrung her hands as she gazed out over the parking lot, which was only half-full. She could see the motel manager moving around in the office, most likely setting out the breakfast included with the room. For other people, this was the start of a day just like any other. But it wasn't for her. As long as Ink and Lloyd were on the loose, there was too much at stake for anything to feel normal.

With a sigh, she let herself back into the motel room. She was waiting for something. She couldn't say what. Some word from Virgil or Rex. News that the police had found Ink, or, better yet, that he or his partner was dead, thanks to Myles hitting one of them when he fired. Either would be good news.

She didn't want to consider the bad news that could come. She just knew that the dawn felt heavy and ominous even though there wasn't a cloud in sight.

Was it her state of mind? Or some kind of premonition?

Returning to her vigil at the window, she spent the next several minutes staring out at the town, as much of it as she could see from this vantage point. Where could Ink and Lloyd have gone? Were they running or hiding? And why couldn't the police find them and put an end to her misery?

Would it put an end to her misery if the two of them went back to prison? Or would The Crew send someone else in Ink and Lloyd's place?

Knowing they could easily do that made her attempt to stay and fight for the life she'd established here feel hopeless. She'd been crazy to think she could escape the past. She needed to leave, to get on the next plane to New York and never look back—

"Hey."

Startled by the sound of Myles's voice, she pivoted toward him. "What are you doing awake?" she asked. "Last I heard from you, you were pretty drugged. And that was only two hours ago."

"At least I slept. Doesn't look like you've been so lucky."

"I'm too anxious," she admitted. "I can't get hold of Virgil or Rex or Peyton. It feels as if something terrible is happening, as if… I don't know. I can't put my finger on it, but it frightens me. And here I am, unable to do anything about it."

Eyes dark and shiny and unfathomable, he watched her for several seconds, then pulled back the blankets. "Come here."

She shook her head. With two beds in the room, they didn't have to lie down together. She wasn't even sure she wanted to be that close. Part of her did. Part of her wanted nothing more. The other part felt too guilty. Without question, she'd stayed in Pineview for the life she'd created and all the promise it afforded. She'd put a lot into this town and gotten a lot out of it. But it was her handsome neighbor that distinguished this place from every other. She could buy another house, find a new town, a school Jake and Mia enjoyed, a talented dance instructor for Mia's ballet. She could continue her business from anywhere. And she could maintain her relationships with Claire and Nana Vera from a distance. She just couldn't maintain a relationship with the sheriff, not if she left. She'd known that from the beginning.

Had she done what she'd sworn never to do? Had she put her romantic interests above the welfare of her children, the way her mother had always done?

She'd thought she was fighting for all of them, for what staying here could mean to them as a family. Jake wanted a father so badly. She knew how thrilled he'd be to have Myles permanently in his life. But now she feared that she'd hoped for too much and reached too far.

She should've packed up and left town with the kids immediately. No one could beat The Crew. They were too determined, too vicious.

"I wish I could offer you some reassurance," he said. "I wish I could say it'll all work out. But I can't guess what's going to happen. I only know that as far as I'm concerned you're where you should be."

"And how do you know that?" she asked. "I'm here because of you. You know that, too, right? I—I've had a thing for you for a long time. And now…"

"Now you're wondering if you've made a mistake."

She rubbed her face. "I'm pretty sure I have. I appreciate everything you've done. But...I've got to go."

His attention suddenly far more acute, he pushed himself into a sitting position. "Where?"

"To New York State to get my kids. Then...Salt Lake. Cheyenne. Denver. Anywhere but here. I have to keep Jake and Mia safe. I'm all they've got."

"Don't go."

Tears caught in her lashes before spilling down her cheeks. "I have no choice." She started for the door, but when he got out of bed and came limping toward her, she couldn't walk away.

"Rex wouldn't let anything happen to Jake and Mia," he said. "Or you wouldn't have allowed him to take them. And even if you relocate, there's no guarantee The Crew won't find you. They could show up in Salt Lake or Cheyenne or wherever just as easily as here."

"That's the excuse I've been using, but I should've packed up and gotten on the first plane out of Montana. I shouldn't have sent them away or put you in danger. I'm sorry."

"Vivian, you didn't put me in danger. Ink and his buddy did." He placed one hand on the door to keep her from opening it. "I can't promise you'll be safe here. I can promise I'll do all I can to protect you."

She wanted to hear that, wanted to believe it. But he was standing in front of her with two bullet wounds, and Ink and Lloyd were still at large. What if it had gone the other way? Just like it did with the U.S. marshal? Her mother was dead. Pat, too. If things didn't change, she wouldn't even be able to attend his funeral next week. "But don't you see? Even if you catch them, it might not be over. The Crew could send more and more—"

"Then we'll take them on, too. You don't give in to a gang. That only builds their power."

"But you have Marley to worry about. Why would you be willing to remain involved in this?"

He was the sheriff. He could've said it was his job. But he didn't. His voice deepened as he held her gaze. "For the same reason you risked staying."

He was doing it for her, for what could happen between them. "But it's because of me that you've already been shot."

Hobbling a bit closer, he took her chin, tilting it toward him. "It brought you out in your underwear, didn't it?"

When she smiled at his sexy grin, he threaded his fingers through hers. "Don't leave me," he murmured. "We have something here. I don't know what it'll turn out to be. But we'll *never* know if we let The Crew tear us apart."

He was right. There was no way to see into the future, no way to provide guarantees on either side. They could be hurt, physically or emotionally; they were taking a chance for love. She'd trusted her heart when she'd stayed. She'd pried it open and allowed herself to care about him and this place, despite what she'd been through. That was a victory in itself.

The rest she had to take on faith.

"Okay," she said, and let him lead her back to bed.

Two men stood on the dirt and weeds that served as a backyard to Horse's club. They huddled near the chain-link fence at the far corner of the house, speaking in low tones as they transacted some sort of business. Virgil had no doubt that whatever they were doing was illegal. Almost everything that went down here was. But they weren't worried about his sudden appearance. When he rounded the corner, they glanced up to see what he wanted but went back to their negotiations as soon as they realized he wasn't interested in them. Too many men came and went from here for his presence to alarm them. He was alone, which was hardly threatening, considering their numbers. And he looked as if he fit right in. He knew how to look that way; he used to be as much a part of The Crew as they were.

The fact that these men were along his escape route could become a problem, however. Once he shot Horse, they'd know he wasn't an ally. He made a mental note of the complications they could cause as he swung the door open and stepped into a hallway that smelled of pot and cigars.

Blinds covered every window in the house, judging by the darkness. Privacy was important. The Crew wouldn't tolerate strangers peering in—although the inhabitants of this neighborhood knew better than to get nosy. Too much interest could get them killed.

The only light Virgil could see came from a lamp in the living room at the end of the hall; there was also a bit of light drifting up from the club downstairs. The clack of balls told him some people were still awake down there, playing pool. If they were doing coke, they might not sleep for days.

Several doors lined the hallway—all of them closed, except the one leading to the stairs that went down to the club. Mona had mentioned that Horse was in *the* back bedroom. But there were at least three rooms and probably a bathroom and no way to tell the difference between them. Which room was it?

Leaning against the door closest to him, Virgil tried

to hear if anything was going on, but there was no sound. He was about to turn the doorknob, risk looking in, when a woman appeared at the end of the hall and drew his attention with a little cough.

Dressed in fishnet stockings, high-heeled black boots, a skirt that didn't quite cover her ass and a blouse tied open to reveal a set of sagging tits, she looked well-used and strung out. Women didn't fare well inside The Crew. Two years spent servicing these men was equivalent to ten on the street. They were that demanding and abusive.

He'd never met Mona before, but he knew her instantly. The anxiety on her heart-shaped face, pale in contrast to the dye job that made her hair jet-black, gave her identity away. He nodded once as their eyes met. Then she used the tip of the domination whip she carried as part of her sexy attire to point at the door across the hall from him, and that was it. She disappeared. When the front door slammed, he knew she was getting the hell away.

Probably a good idea to go while she could. Whether she'd played it straight or sold him out, life was about to get interesting.

Or over.

Taking the gun from his waistband, he checked to make sure the safety was off. Then he stood to one side and opened the door of the room she'd indicated.

Two men sat at a desk, counting stacks of money—the night's take. The closest one looked up, wearing a scowl, angry to be interrupted. But the expression on his face changed the second he saw Virgil's gun. As his mouth formed an O, his eyes cut to his own weapon, a pistol lying within reach on the shelf.

"Go for it and I'll shoot you," Virgil murmured, his voice low.

"You do, and you'll never get out of here." A large man stood behind the first, head shaved, cheeks scarred by acne. This had to be Horse. Although Virgil had never met him, Rex had said enough about The Crew's leader for Virgil to be able to pick him out of a crowd, especially a crowd of two. Not many men stood six foot eight and had such a bulbous nose, such bad skin.

"Horse." Virgil managed a congenial smile. "Nice to finally make your acquaintance."

Horse bared large yellow teeth as he laughed, and Virgil wondered if *that* was where he'd gotten his name. "You're crazy for coming here."

"A point I'm more than willing to concede." Crazy was one thing, but Horse hadn't expected such a brazen move and that was important. Virgil could read his surprise; the man wasn't prepared, which meant Mona hadn't double-crossed him, after all.

If this ended well, Virgil promised himself he'd thank her properly.

"Gully, if you'll step out of the way, I'll let you live," he said to the stout man still standing in front.

Gully smoothed the leather vest he wore without a shirt. More biker style than street gang, it wasn't a good look for him. He was overweight and his complexion was far too pasty to pull it off, especially during an L.A. summer. But it showed his tattoos, which was probably the whole idea. "How do you know my name?"

Virgil grinned. "I know everything."

"Then you should also know that I'm not gonna let you shoot a fellow Crew member."

"Your choice." He lifted his gun. He didn't plan on

shooting Gully. Horse was tall enough that he could drop him if he had to. But he'd have to deal with Gully grabbing that pistol as soon as Horse fell behind him and was trying to decide how he'd get out of the room without taking a bullet himself. As determined as he was to save his family, to be free of The Crew at last, the prospect of killing someone, even Horse, didn't sit well with him. He'd killed before, in prison. But he'd had no choice.

He felt he had no choice here, either. Yet it wasn't the same, wasn't two men coming at him with homemade knives.

"You leave me and my family alone, I'll let you live, too," he told Horse.

"I don't make deals." Horse made a move as if he was going to grab Gully's gun. He couldn't reach it, but Virgil couldn't tell that when he fired. The bullet hit Horse in the shoulder. A dark spot bloomed on his shirt. Then Gully went for the gun, as expected, so Virgil had to shoot him, too.

Aiming for the leg, he hit Gully somewhere in that region. Gully crumpled, moaning. Virgil had only seconds before everyone else in the house descended on him, a split second in which to finish Horse off. But Horse had ducked behind the desk, making it impossible to get the kind of shot he needed, and Gully somehow managed to squeeze off a round in the interim.

Virgil heard the bullet strike the wall behind him. Close, but not close enough. Gully was in too much pain to aim straight. Or he didn't know how to hit a target. Regardless, the noise had attracted attention. Footsteps pounded down the hall, coming toward them. From the shouts accompanying those footsteps, at least a hundred Crew members were rushing to Horse's aid—but Virgil knew that was panic talking. Realistically, it was probably five or six.

Still, he was already outnumbered. And now there'd be no going out the way he'd come in. The futility of what he'd tried to do struck him in that moment, but so did the memory of burning that picture of Peyton and Brady. He couldn't let his family down. Laurel or Rex, either. He *wouldn't* let them down, not as long as he had the breath to keep fighting.

Firing again, he hit Gully in the gun arm, and the pistol fell to the carpet. The fat bean counter was neutralized. But Horse was very much alive. In between cursing and calling for help, he tried to shove Gully out of the way so he could reach the fallen gun. When he couldn't do that without exposing himself, he pulled Gully in front and used him as a human shield.

"This is the leader you were willing to die for?" Virgil shouted.

Red-faced and gasping, Gully managed to wriggle out of Horse's grasp, leaving him unprotected for only a second.

That was all Virgil needed. Planning to crash through the window in order to get out, Virgil crossed the room while firing into Horse's corner again and again. Splinters and Sheetrock dust rained down on them but Virgil was moving too fast to see if he'd hit Horse. At this point, everything was a smoky blur.

At the last minute, he had the presence of mind to shoot the window. He thought that might make it easier to break. But he didn't get the chance to jump through it. He was on the bed just a foot away when the other Crew members began pouring into the room.

Although his gun was empty, bullets began flying—from *their* guns. It took only a split second for one, then another, to hit him in the back.

27

L.J.'s vision was blurry, but the pain was gone. Had he really been shot? Or was it just a bad dream?

He blinked, trying to make sense of the bright light directly above him and the fuzzy objects surrounding him, but once he saw the picture hanging on the wall, he knew getting shot had been no dream. He was inside the cabin those dads had rented, the ones who'd walked through the door and been shot to death by Ink.

His mind shied away from the rest of the memory, the process of dragging them outside and digging their graves, but there was no avoiding the replay. It cycled in a never-ending loop—until he was distracted by the odd smell around him, a smell he couldn't place, and the sounds of someone rummaging in the kitchen.

He wanted to call out, ask what was going on and why he felt so strange, but he was afraid it was Ink. Had to be, didn't it? He hadn't been with anyone else since he'd busted out of prison. Ink had been with him in Laurel's house. Ink had been with him when the sheriff appeared and started firing. Ink had been in the truck after they ran through the forest. And Ink had helped him limp into the cabin, said he was going to operate—

Oh, God. L.J.'s hand wanted to go to his chest, to de-

termine what might've happened to him while he was
unconscious. But he couldn't move. His wrists were tied
to something above his head.

What the hell was going on? Was this Ink's idea of
saving his life? Or Ink's idea of revenge for nearly leaving him in the forest?

"Hey, you're awake!"

It was Ink, all right. The last person L.J. wanted to see.
The last person L.J. wanted cutting into him. Ink didn't
know anything about removing a bullet or what other
damage he might cause by digging into a guy's shoulder.
Neither did he care. That was the most frightening part.
This would become just one more thing to brag about.

If L.J. lived.

Actually, if he died, Ink would still brag about it.

His mouth as dry as cotton, L.J. had to swallow before
he could answer. "I can't…move. Why can't I move?"
His voice sounded hoarse and panicky, unfamiliar even
to him.

"Sorry." Ink came around the table carrying a dish
towel, which he was using to wipe his hands. "Had to
tie you down. For all I knew, you'd wake up and start
thrashing around and hurt us both. You should've seen
the way you jumped when I cauterized that hole in your
shoulder."

"When you…*what?*" That was the smell. Burning
flesh. *His* flesh. The thought made him more nauseous
than he already was.

"Cauterized the wound," Ink repeated. "I used a metal
spoon. That was all I could think of. The only way to
sterilize it and get it to stop bleeding since I had no
needle and thread to try and stitch it."

"But who said you should—"

"Saw it in an old Western once," he broke in. "Worked great, too. You should thank me. We're out of the woods now." He laughed. "Out of the woods. That's a good one."

It was called a pun. But Ink wouldn't know that. Maybe he was cunning, but he wasn't educated. At least L.J. had graduated from high school. It wasn't until a cousin got him into boosting cars that he went to prison and met the likes of Ink and the rest of The Crew. "Pun intended," he muttered, hearing his grandmother's voice saying the same thing.

"What?"

Unable to explain, he shook his head. "Just something that…came to me."

"So? How do you feel?"

L.J. squinted at the bright light above him. "Where am I?"

"My makeshift operating table, aka the dining room table. Pretty clever, huh?" When Ink tapped his head, L.J. thought he would definitely be sick. For all he knew, Ink had taken out one of his kidneys. Ink liked to talk about such morbid things, used to entertain the other guys in prison for hours with stories of black-market organ transplants and doctors who supposedly made a bundle stealing kidneys from the poor.

L.J.'s lips were cracked and peeling. He made an effort to wet them so he could speak. "What'd—what'd you do to me?"

"I removed the plug that damn sheriff put in you. What do you think?" He held up a small, slightly flattened piece of metal. "See? Here it is."

There was smear of blood on Ink's arm. He'd washed his hands but he hadn't done a very good job, hadn't washed high enough to reach all the evidence of his "operation."

"Great. Thanks," L.J. said drily. "So…will you untie me?"

Ink stared at him for so long, L.J. was afraid he'd refuse. But then he grinned and shrugged and got a knife that was still stained with blood to cut the strips of sheet anchoring his hands to two different objects that wouldn't budge. When he sat up and rubbed his wrists, L.J. saw that Ink had used the wooden captain's chairs, one on each side of his head, which shouldn't have been all that heavy. He was just weak. Weak and sick and confused.

"How do you feel?" Ink asked again.

"Okay, I guess." L.J.'s hand went to his head as if that might help sort out his thoughts. "What'd…you give me?"

"The last of my pills. That's friendship for you, huh?"

Friendship? L.J. didn't even want to be here. He would've left if he could have. Ink was crazier than anyone L.J. had ever met. "What were they?"

"Maxidone. Or so I was told."

"Which is?"

Ink tossed the knife onto the table. "Who knows? And who the hell cares? They work, don't they?"

"Yeah." He couldn't feel any pain; they must've done their job. Ink had obviously taken some, too—more than usual, because he was in a better mood than he'd been in so far. Odd, considering their situation had fallen to shit. "And you got them from…where again?"

"Quit being stupid, huh? I got 'em from Wiley Coyote, and you know that because you were there. Jeez," he added with a chuckle.

Jeez? Ink was high, all right. He'd probably smoked

the joint that'd been on the coffee table, too. Or mixed drugs and alcohol.

"You remember Wiley, don't you?"

Dimly, L.J. recalled The Crew member who'd helped them get away from the prison and provided Ink with a container of tablets for his back. "Yeah."

"Time to get you off this table." Ink motioned for him to get up. "I'll take you to the bed. You need to rest."

L.J. had no idea how he'd walk from point A to point B. When he slid off the table, he had to bend over and take several deep breaths just to keep from throwing up or falling over. "Yeah, bed," he said when he could finally straighten.

Ink supported his weight as they made their way slowly up the stairs; Ink even helped him lie down and covered him with blankets. But the sickness L.J. had felt a few minutes earlier came back, worse than ever, and kept him from falling asleep.

Was he having an allergic reaction to Ink's pills?

He was about to call out, let Ink know something serious had to be wrong, when he began to doubt everything Ink had told him. Maybe it wasn't an allergic reaction. Maybe he'd lost track of time and Ink had kept him shut up in this cabin for days. It could be an infection….

He racked his brain to determine whether or not that could be possible. But due to whatever drug he'd been given, he couldn't arrange his thoughts, had no concept of time. Had he been tied to the table just for a few hours? Or had he been there for several days?

The last thing he remembered was getting out of the truck….

Rolling gingerly to one side, he tried to feel his lower

back, which ached terribly. Was it from the hardness of
the dining room table? Or had Ink stolen his kidney?

He wasn't sure. He couldn't reach all the way around
without tearing open the wound on his shoulder.

"Ink?" he called. But it was a halfhearted, feeble effort
to rouse him. One Ink didn't hear.

A second later the front door slammed and the truck's
engine roared to life.

It should've felt worse to get shot. The bullet entering
his leg had been bad. The hospital visit wasn't much of
an improvement. And losing out on capturing Ink and
Lloyd had been a real bitch. But Myles could certainly
think of worse things than lying in bed tucked up against
Vivian's soft, warm body.

He slipped his hand up under her shirt to cup her bare
breast—he'd been aching to do that ever since she'd lain
down with him—and his body hardened. He liked her
just as much as he'd feared he would. He could feel himself falling into that emotional abyss called love, knew he
might slide in so deep he'd never get out. And yet, somehow, that was okay. Caring risked loss, but *not* caring
guaranteed a lukewarm life, devoid of any great passion.
Why he'd believed that kind of existence would satisfy
him he suddenly didn't know. He wouldn't take back the
years he'd had with Amber Rose despite how they ended,
would he? No. So why wouldn't he embrace a second
chance to feel the same way about someone else?

Vivian stirred and turned to face him. When her eyes
opened, she smiled sleepily. "How you doin'?"

"Fine. You?"

"Better now that I've had a chance to rest. What time
is it? Do we need to get up?"

He caressed the rim of her ear. "Not yet. It's only been a couple hours."

"Then what are you doing awake?"

Her eyes looked so big with her hair that short. "Thinking."

"About…"

"You," he said simply.

"And?"

"I'm glad you moved in next door."

She hesitated, obviously considering his words. "You're kidding. What about your wounds?"

He offered her a lazy grin. "Mere scratches."

Although she smiled at his response, her manner remained serious. "I'm very different from Amber Rose. You realize that, don't you?"

How could he miss it? But he found it interesting that she'd come to the same conclusion, since she'd never known his late wife. "In what way?"

"I have my business, for one."

Having a business created a difficulty? "I admire what you've accomplished. And I'm willing to support you in it. How is that a drawback?"

"I'm used to being independent."

"Understood. I can work with that."

"But…Claire said Amber Rose has a brother who's a doctor."

He couldn't help chuckling. What did Amber Rose's brother have to do with this? "I'm not following you."

"*My* brother is an ex-con."

"Oh, right." He nodded to let her know it was all clear to him now. "But *exonerated* means he didn't do it."

"My uncle did. My own mother might have put him up to it. And Virgil hasn't come out of those prison years unscathed. You know The Crew might never let us live in peace. They might not let us live at all."

"They won't hurt you as long as I'm here to protect you. But I understand your concern. And, just to save you the trouble of bringing it up, I also understand that your children's father was an abusive jerk who may come into the picture at some point in the future. Any other warnings and disclaimers?"

She raised her eyebrows, as if what she'd already said should be more than enough to scare him off, but since he didn't concede the point, she barreled on. "I've heard how sweet Amber Rose was."

"You've heard a lot."

"You're a favorite topic among the ladies. It's Pineview, remember?"

"So…you're different, like you said."

"And…maybe not as good. I'm aggressive and stubborn and…and I can be angry. Besides all that, I have baggage."

"Beyond what you've listed?" he teased.

"Maybe."

With her legs between his and the softness of her breasts against his chest, the memory of making love to her at the cabin made his pulse leap. "What are you really worried about, Vivian?"

"You loved her so much." Her voice fell. "I don't see how I could compete with that."

He ran his thumb over her bottom lip. He craved the taste of her, the smooth texture of her bare skin. And it was *her* he wanted, not a substitute for Amber Rose. "You don't have to compete. I loved my late wife, will always love her, but that doesn't mean I can't love you just as much."

He bent his head to kiss her, but she resisted. She seemed hesitant to trust what he'd told her, and he couldn't blame her. She'd been through so much. But as he slid his hands up the back of her shirt, kneading her tense muscles and coaxing her to stop worrying, her lips parted and she began to respond.

"I won't let anything happen to you," he murmured as their tongues met and touched and met again. "All you have to do is hang on to me."

Making love to Vivian this time was a completely different experience, even better than at the cabin. Myles slowed everything down so he could memorize her body, enjoy it and let her enjoy his. As his hands skimmed over her breasts, her waist, her hips, coaxing her to become more pliable, to believe him—to believe *in* him—she closed her eyes and arched her back and didn't fight him when he brought her to the brink of climax. At that moment, her eyes flew open and latched onto his, and he silently pleaded with her not to deny him.

"I don't think I can—" she started, but he removed the hand she'd just placed on his chest and pinned it, along with the other one, above her head.

"Let go," he whispered. "All you have to do is trust me."

She must've taken him at his word because her legs tightened around his hips, telling him she was as committed as he was, and it wasn't ten seconds later that she gasped and her eyes drifted shut. He tried to make the pleasure last as long as possible, but before the final spasm disappeared, he found his release.

The pain made it difficult to move. But worse than the pain was the struggle to breathe. One of the bullets must've collapsed a lung. All Virgil could think about was Peyton and Brady and the new baby. How he'd never see them again, never meet his new daughter. Peyton would have to go on without him. Maybe Laurel was already dead. His past had gotten the best of him, despite everything he'd done to outdistance it.

Then, suddenly, anger came to his rescue. It seemed to grab his heart and throw it against his rib cage. That wasn't a pleasant sensation, but it lent him enough strength and presence of mind to dive for the gun Gully had dropped on the floor. Surprisingly enough, no one else had reached for it. Horse and Gully were trying to melt into the paneling so they wouldn't be hit by a stray bullet.

They thought it was all over for him. And it was. He needed all his strength just to take in the smallest breath of air. But he wasn't going out alone.

His whole body burned and the lack of oxygen made it difficult to hang on to conscious thought. If he could only catch his breath, he could tolerate the pain. Pain meant nothing to him, not if overcoming it would reunite him with those he loved. It was his damn lung. He could feel the darkness edging closer....

The weight of a solid object in his hand finally cut through his delirium and he realized he was holding the gun. How he'd managed to come up with it, he had no idea. The room was spinning, blurring the part of his vision that wasn't fading to black. He needed to act fast, before he couldn't see anything at all.

Raising the muzzle, he aimed at the door and fought to steady his hand. But there was no longer an army there. Every person he saw was now lying on the floor, except one. How had that happened?

A tall, blurry shape appeared to be creeping into the room, stepping cautiously, slowly. He had a gun held out in front as if ready to fire.

Virgil ordered himself to kill that man. One less Crew member... But if he was going to take someone with him, he wanted it to be Horse. Forgetting the other guy—some stranger who was irrelevant to him—he cursed as he rolled over to look for The Crew's leader.

Horse was trying to hide behind the smaller Gully again. Gully seemed to have a trickle of blood running down from a hole in his forehead, but Virgil thought that had to be an illusion. Virgil had shot him, but not in the head. He'd only meant to wound him. So why would his own men finish him off?

"No!" Horse cried when he realized what Virgil was about to do, but Virgil fired, anyway. He squeezed the trigger as many times as he had strength in an effort to eradicate the threat to his family before he was no longer capable of helping them. But he felt the recoil of the firearm travel up his arm only twice before he couldn't manage another round.

With one last attempt to draw in enough air to remain conscious, he slumped over and was about to give up the fight when two strong hands pulled him into a sitting position and he heard a familiar voice.

"Virgil, hang on. I'm getting you out of here."

Rex. Virgil wanted to say his name but couldn't. He didn't know how it was that his best friend was in California and not New York, but he'd never been more grateful to see anyone in his life.

28

L.J. was no use to him. Ink had had his fun digging around for that bullet with his unwashed hands and experimental prodding. Now he was content to let L.J. die—if that was what happened. If L.J. didn't die, he might try and hike out of the mountains, maybe get some medical help. More than likely he'd be hauled back to prison. L.J. didn't have the smarts to navigate the outside world as an escapee. He didn't have the nerve to do what an escapee had to do, either.

Ink, however, had everything he needed, including a better plan. He couldn't believe he hadn't thought of it before. Now that Laurel knew he was in town, she wouldn't return home. He'd have to start looking for her all over again. But someone who was trusted in the community would be able to help him find her much faster than his former cellie. Especially now that L.J. had been shot. And who would look more harmless, more trustworthy, than a member of the Rogers family?

He'd seen their pretty daughter and the mildly attractive middle-aged mother. They were quite a family. And they were only half a mile away, in the very next cabin. There might be a father. Ink realized that but could handle him the same way he had the hunters.

The mother would work best for his purposes, he decided. Now that he had Laurel's new name, he could send Mrs. Rogers into town to poke around. By keeping her daughter and anyone else at the cabin with him, she'd have the incentive to work fast and keep her mouth shut. Once she returned with the addresses of Vivian's closest friends and any extended family that might live in the area, he'd kill her and the rest of the Rogers clan so they couldn't report him. And then he'd be on his way— either to finish up his business with Virgil's sister here in Pineview, or follow her out of town, if she'd already left. There wasn't any point in staying if she wasn't here.

He checked the gun he'd used earlier when he got in that shootout with the sheriff. It was good to go. He'd reloaded it at the cabin. Now all he had to do was hide the truck in the trees and wait until dark, which wouldn't be long in coming.

The phone in the motel woke Vivian at five o'clock. She'd fallen asleep after making love with Myles, had slept for several hours, much more deeply than she had since this whole nightmare began. But reality intruded with the jangle of that phone, and the dread that'd overwhelmed her before came back.

"Do you want to get it?" She assumed it would be one of Myles's deputies, looking for him. No one else in Pineview knew where they were.

His hand ran over her skin, but his eyes remained closed. "Mmm…no. Still groggy. Go ahead."

She was glad to see he was getting the sleep he so desperately needed. But she was afraid neither of them would be able to rest much longer. She had to get hold of Peyton, continue to try Rex, somehow find out what was going on with her kids and her brother. And she had to field this call, which she hoped was good news and not bad.

"Hello?" She settled back into Myles's embrace but held her breath.

"This is Sandra with EZ Security. Is Vivian there?"

Recognizing the name of the company and the voice of the caller, Vivian sat up. It was the receptionist she'd spoken to earlier at Virgil's work. "This is Vivian."

"I have a number for you to call."

Vivian used the pad of paper by the phone and the motel pen to copy it down. "Where does it go?" She recognized the area code but not the rest of the digits.

"Mercy Medical Hospital in Los Angeles."

She bit her lip. "Why do I need to call a hospital in Los Angeles?"

"Your brother's been shot."

Vivian must've made a sound or a movement to give away the pain that converged on her heart because Myles shoved himself into a sitting position, suddenly alert. "What's wrong?"

She couldn't explain. Not now. She had to find out whatever she could while this woman was willing to talk to her. "Is he…is he going to be okay?"

"The doctors are hopeful. He's in surgery now."

"Then…who am I calling if Virgil can't talk?"

"Rex."

"Why didn't you just give him my number?"

"He can't make a collect call to a motel."

Rex was in L.A., too? Why? Where were her kids? "Do you know if Peyton's safe?"

"She's fine."

Obviously this woman knew their entire background.

Vivian was throwing around names Virgil, Rex and Peyton hadn't used since they'd adopted their first false identity and moved to Washington, D.C.

"Rex said to tell you Peyton has Jake and Mia in a motel room with Brady here in Buffalo," she went on. "Don't worry about them."

It was a relief to learn her children were fine and in good hands. But after what she'd just been told about Virgil, it was hard to feel much better. "Does Peyton know about Virgil?"

There was a slight hesitation. "No. That's why she's not making this call. Rex said not to tell her until…until we know whether or not Virgil's going to make it."

Laurel dropped her head in her hand. "How'd it happen?"

"I don't have any of the details. I just know that Rex wants to speak to you. His phone was damaged when your brother was injured, so he called me from the hospital."

She brought her knees up so she could wrap her free arm around them. "Rex wasn't hurt?"

"No. But he would've been if his phone hadn't been in his pocket."

"Why'd he go to L.A.?"

"I think you should ask him that question. He just checked in with me to see if you'd called here. I told him I didn't know if you were still at this number, but I'd give it a try."

"I see. Thank you," she said weakly, and hung up.

Myles sat with the sheet draped across his lower half. "What is it? Are the kids okay?"

"They're fine."

His face creased with concern as he took her hand and kissed her fingers. "Then what's wrong?"

"It's my brother."

When the page came, Rex hurried to the information desk, where he identified himself and a nurse smiled politely while handing him a phone.

"Hello?" The cord kept him in one spot, but he turned so he could speak with a modicum of privacy.

"It's me."

Laurel. Tears threatened when he heard her voice, even though he hadn't cried since he was a kid. She was alive; he'd made the right choice. "God, it's great to hear from you."

"I could say the same. You okay?"

"I've been better." He was so sick, so strung out. He hadn't been sure he could last as long as he needed to, and yet he'd made it—made it here, anyway. Each minute, each hour, proved to be a new challenge, but he felt good about all the minutes and hours he'd conquered so far. Now he clung to the hope that his presence and prayers might somehow make a difference to Virgil while the doctors operated. When he'd walked out of the emergency room in Buffalo all those hours ago, intending to buy whatever OxyContin he needed to get rid of the pain in his head and his joints and the terrible cramping in his stomach, he'd remembered the trip to Libby. Remembered driving the last part of the way holding Laurel's hand and feeling so at peace. That was what had made him realize that if he went back on the pills he'd never escape them. He couldn't relapse even once. Ever. For any reason. So instead of doping up, he'd paid his dealer to take him to the airport, and then he'd had to make one of the most difficult decisions of his life.

Did he go to Montana to try and protect Laurel?

Or did he go to L.A. to support Virgil?

Ultimately, he'd chosen L.A. He *knew* Virgil was walking straight into trouble; Laurel was at least trying to avoid it. And, as much as he claimed not to have any confidence in the small-town sheriff he'd entrusted with her care, he knew Myles King would do all he could to keep her safe—and was probably more capable than he wanted to admit.

She sniffled, evidence that she was wrestling with her own emotions. "How—how's Virgil?"

An old woman approached with a question for the nurse and talked far too loudly. In an effort to block out the noise, Rex covered his free ear. "Took three bullets. Two in the back, one in the arm. He was already a mess by the time I could reach him. It's a miracle he's alive." Question was, would he stay that way? Rex didn't come out and say that, but he knew Laurel had to be thinking it.

"What was he doing in L.A.?" she asked. "How could he leave Peyton?"

He studied the flecked pattern on the floor. "He felt he had no choice. That he had to put a stop to The Crew once and for all, or none of us would ever be safe."

"So he went to them?"

Wincing when her raised voice lanced through his aching head, he moved the phone to his other ear. "Yeah. To a club Horse owns."

"And you followed him there?"

"Unfortunately, he was ahead of me."

"Or you'd probably be under a doctor's care, too. Or at the morgue."

"Maybe. I was lucky. No one expected a latecomer. They were so busy trying to kill Virgil they didn't even notice when I walked in."

"And that's how you got him out?"

"That's how." After shooting at least five men.

"What happened to Horse?"

"Dead." He didn't specify that it was Virgil who'd hit Horse. He wanted to save her from the more graphic details as much as possible.

"And the other Crew members who were there?"

Rex wasn't sure if they were dead or he'd just wounded them. He'd gone in shooting, but there was no other alternative. It was the only way to save Virgil—and himself, since they would've turned on him next. Sick as he was, he still didn't quite know how he'd managed to pull it off.

"Are the police involved yet?" she asked.

Rex tried not to notice the way the nurse kept staring at him. He was sweating again and having heart palpitations. But he was determined to tough it out on his own. He braced himself against the counter. "I don't know. They might be there now. I didn't stick around long enough to find out. I didn't even wait for an ambulance. Some guy—a neighbor I roused—helped me load Virgil into my rental car and I took off."

"They'll get to you eventually," she said. "But it was self-defense."

"With as much as they've done—and tried to do—to us, I think that should be easy to prove."

"Virgil would be dead if it wasn't for you," she said.

"Thank you." Another sniff indicated that Laurel was losing the battle with her emotions.

"I would've been dead long ago without the two of you," he said quietly. As far as he was concerned, they'd saved one another.

"You have to get off the pills, Rex. Please."

Wondering when his withdrawal symptoms would finally abate, he drew a steadying breath. "I'm off, I swear it."

When she didn't respond, he nearly sank to the floor. His legs simply didn't want to hold him up anymore. "You don't believe me."

"Actually, I do."

He rubbed a hand over his face. "That helps. I'm there this time, Laurel."

"I'm glad to hear it." She covered the phone and spoke with someone else. Then she came back on the line. "Is there any way Ink might know that Horse is dead?"

"I doubt it. It happened too recently. And I don't think it'll stop him, even if he finds out."

"Then why did Virgil do it?"

The anguish in that question seared Rex to the bone. But he knew the answer. He understood it completely. "To cut The Crew off at the head. That's the only way to stop them for good."

"But do you think it'll work?"

He wiped the back of his hand across his forehead, felt the dampness of his sweat. "Only time will tell." The nurse eyed him as if he'd been on the phone long enough, but he averted his gaze. "So there's been no sign of Ink?"

"He came to the house last night."

"And?" Rex felt himself tense.

"Got away."

With a curse, he began to massage his temple. "Where was the sheriff?"

"Trying to stop him. He got shot in the process, but he's fine. It could've been a lot worse."

"I'm glad he's okay." Rex was pretty sure he meant that, despite how he felt about Laurel. "I gotta get off this phone. I'll call you when Virgil comes out of surgery, okay?"

She gave him the sheriff's cell number as well as the motel number and said goodbye. But when he handed the phone back to the nurse, he saw her lip curl as if she didn't approve of him, as if she knew he was some low-life addict and, for a split second, the craving for Oxy-Contin intensified.

But then he realized—it couldn't get any worse than what he'd already been through. Regardless of what this woman thought, what *anyone* thought, he'd overcome that craving for nearly three weeks. And three weeks was longer than most people could fight it.

He was going to make it. He just had to believe he could.

With a smile that said he didn't give a shit about her judgments, he walked away.

While Vivian took a shower, Myles called Janet Rogers. He'd spoken to her earlier. He'd gotten both her and Marley out of bed this morning to tell them what had happened and to warn Marley to stay away from home until Ink and Lloyd could be captured. But he was afraid his injury had scared his daughter and wanted to check in with her again.

"She's doing great," Janet said.

"I hope it's not too much trouble to have her there."

"Not at all. You know how much she and Elizabeth love each other. She's been worried about you, of course, but we've talked about it, and she understands that you weren't hit in a vital area."

After losing her mother, Marley probably wasn't taking the incident quite that well, but being with Elizabeth would distract her, and he appreciated Janet's attempts to reassure him. It wasn't as though he could collect his daughter and go home. With Ink and Lloyd on the loose, Vivian wasn't out of danger and neither was the rest of the community. He still had a job to do. "I appreciate your willingness, but…are you sure? I can make arrangements for her to stay somewhere else…."

"Are you kidding? With Henry out of town and the boys at camp, I like having the girls here. They keep me company."

Myles breathed a sigh of relief. That made things much easier for him, because he was eager to jump back into the search. "Thanks. I'm grateful for the help. Is there any chance I could speak with her?"

"You bet."

A couple of minutes later, Marley's voice came on the line. "Daddy?"

"Hi, honey. How are you?"

"Okay. But…what about you?"

He shifted to ease the throbbing in his leg. "I'm good as new."

"*Really?* After being *shot?* You'd tell me if you weren't, right?"

"I'd tell you."

She seemed to trust his response. "When will I see you, then?"

"I'll come by after work tonight."

"To get me?"

He stood just to test his ability to put pressure on his foot. He'd barely been able to remain upright in the shower, but it seemed to improve with use. "No, just to say hi. I need you to stay at least another night. I'm going to be very busy trying to catch these guys, and I don't want you home alone."

"You'll get 'em. If anyone can, it's you."

Wishing he had her confidence, he eased himself back onto the bed. "I hope you're right."

"It's scary, though, isn't it?" she said. "To think that there are escaped convicts in town? I mean, we never went through anything this dangerous even when we lived in Phoenix."

"I know. Hopefully, it'll never happen again," he said as he checked his bandages.

"Is Vivian okay?"

Vivian was better than okay. She was naked and in the shower, and the thought of that was distracting to him despite everything else. "She's doing great. You like Vivian, don't you?"

"Of course."

He took off the gauze on his neck, balled it up and threw it in the trash can. He didn't need it, and it was wet from the shower, anyway. "Good."

She laughed. "Why'd you ask that?"

Because he wanted Vivian to be part of their lives. He didn't know for sure if she'd become a permanent fixture. They weren't that far along. But everything he felt so far suggested it was a strong possibility. "Just wondered."

"That's a weird question," she said, and laughed again. "Why wouldn't I like her? She's our neighbor. Do you want her to come stay with us until you catch the guys who are trying to hurt her or something?"

"No, we live too close to where she does."

"Where else can she go? Are you guys still at the motel?"

"For now. She's…um…in the next room. But I think I'll have Claire pick her up."

"The lady who cuts my hair?"

"That's her."

"Oh, right. She and Vivian are best friends. She always has one of Vivian's purses."

"Vivian's been generous with you on that score, too," he pointed out.

"I know. I can't wait to see her latest."

He smiled at her enthusiasm. He wasn't sure how quickly his daughter might accept Vivian as his love interest but they had a foundation on which to build. That reassured him. "I'd better get to work. I'll see you later, huh?"

"Okay. I love you, Daddy."

"Love you, too," he said, and disconnected.

Steam rolled out of the bathroom as Vivian cracked open the door. "Everything okay with Marley?"

"Fine."

"Did I hear you mention Claire?"

He pulled on the shirt he'd taken from his bag when he got out of the shower. He didn't have his uniform with him, but he wasn't going to worry about that. Today it was just jeans and a T-shirt—and his gun. "I was thinking you might want to spend the afternoon there, since I can't stay with you. Might make it easier to wait for the news on your brother."

She came out, wearing a towel. "I don't know if anything will make that easier."

"But I have no idea how long I'll be gone. You can't go home. And you can't be seen in your car, not after Ink and Lloyd saw it parked in your driveway. What else are you going to do? I don't want you walking around town if I can't make it back in time to bring dinner."

Fluffing her hair to help it dry, she stared at the phone. "I just want Rex to call."

"It might be a while," he said gently.

She sighed. "Then I'll call the hospital with her number. I'd rather be with her than alone."

His leg hurt with every step, but he made his way over to her and pulled her into his arms. "He's going to make it, Vivian."

She didn't answer, but when she pressed her face into his neck, he could feel her tears.

"Give Claire a call. I'll check in with you later," he said, and kissed her on the forehead before he left.

It was even easier to get inside the house than Ink had expected. The doors were locked. He'd tried them, starting with the back. But locked doors were no problem when there was a key under the mat. He guessed that key was what the teenage daughter used when she came home late at night, or a present she'd left out for her boyfriend. He doubted the parents even realized it was there.

The door swung open without so much as a creak, and Ink smiled as he stepped across the threshold. Laurel must've been tipped off when he went to her house, but he'd get to her yet. And Virgil and Rex would be next. Not only would he have his revenge, he'd gain new stature with The Crew when he reported to Horse that he'd accomplished what no one else had been able to do.

A TV blared somewhere deeper in the house. He'd seen the flicker of the screen while watching from the back, so that didn't surprise him. He probably should've waited until later, when everyone went to bed, but he'd been too impatient. He'd figured he'd have a better chance of getting in if he did it before the parents locked up for the night. He wanted people in town to be awake, too, so that Mrs. Rogers would have plenty of folks to ask about Laurel....

He hadn't expected the house to be secured so early. Most people didn't lock their doors at eight-thirty. But he would've gotten in whether the key was handy or not, would've broken in if necessary. It wasn't as if they had neighbors he needed to worry about. And he'd already cut the phone line. What were they going to do?

"Knock, knock. Anyone home?" he called out cheerfully.

The daughter he'd seen with L.J. appeared first. She figured heavily into his plans, was precisely the person he hoped to use as a distraction from the impending wait. But he couldn't give that away just yet.

"Hi, there. Is your father home?"

She dropped the remote when she saw the gun. But he hadn't raised it yet, so she didn't seem too sure about how to react. "Who are you?"

"I guess you could say a friend of a friend. Do you know Vivian Stewart? And Mia and Jake?"

She stepped back as if she'd realized who he was, and that was when he lifted the gun. "I wouldn't move, if I were you."

"Alexis—" The woman he'd seen in the window

earlier rounded the corner and froze. She was drying a baking dish, but lowered her hands and the dish immediately.

"I think you need to call for your husband, or I'm going to shoot your daughter," he told her.

She gaped at him.

"I gave you an order."

One hand, the hand with the dish towel, went to her chest. "He…he—"

"He what?" Ink prompted. "You can do it. Spit it out."

"He's not home," Alexis supplied.

What she said came as a surprise, and he thought it could be a lie. A man was part of this household. It was apparent from the way the garage was organized, the number of tools, the NASCAR and Dallas Cowboy cheerleader posters, the deer head mounted over the fireplace, even the smell, which reminded him of leather and playing cards. "I think he must be. My guess is that SUV out in the drive belongs to him. So…I'm giving you five seconds to get him out here."

Mrs. Rogers whimpered. He still had his gun pointed at her daughter, and she didn't like it. "No! Please! Listen, he—he's out of town. He works out of town. That is his Esplanade, but I drove him to the airport."

Could this be true? Ink hadn't actually *seen* a man at the cabin either time he'd been here. And he doubted she'd risk her daughter's life. "When will he be back?"

Alexis answered, as if she was afraid her mother might not be able to form the words quickly enough. "Not for two more days."

"If you're lying—"

"I'm not lying!" Her face was as chalk-white as Mrs.

Rogers's, but the ponytail that held her hair back revealed bright-red ears.

"Good. Looks like I'm getting lucky everywhere I turn. Where are the kids?"

Mrs. Rogers's eyes widened. "What kids?"

To make his threat even clearer, he stepped closer to Alexis. "I could rape her in front of you, or take her to the back. Your choice."

"Don't hurt her!" Her voice had fallen to a whisper, but there was more pleading in that whisper than if she'd shouted.

"I'm talking about the kid or kids who use the soccer ball that's in the yard and the other sports equipment in the garage."

"The twins," Alexis said. "They're at camp."

"Hmm. Lucky again. Why don't we go into the living room and have a seat so I can explain what I need you to do for me."

Mother and daughter turned just as a voice issued from the second floor. "Mo-om! Can me and Marley have another dish of ice cream?"

Ink almost pulled the trigger right then. He thought one death would be quite convincing. But he didn't want Mrs. Rogers to get hysterical. He needed her to be able to think straight. "Trying to trick me? Huh? You're going to pay for that," he said instead of firing. "Now get them down here."

The girl from upstairs called out again when she received no answer. "Mo-om!"

Mrs. Rogers closed her eyes and her lips moved as if in prayer.

"Now!" he yelled, giving her a shove, but she didn't have to speak. The sound of his voice drew two young teens down the stairs to see what was going on. Once they saw him, they stood on the landing with their mouths agape.

"Guess you didn't realize you had company." Grabbing Alexis, he put the muzzle to her temple. "Now, let me make myself clear. Is there anyone else in the house?"

Alexis was shaking. He could feel it. She didn't dare move, but one of the other girls spoke up. "N-no." Judging by her features, she belonged to the family. She was the "me" part of "me and Marley." The other girl, tall and dark and slender, did not belong to the family. That made her the "Marley" part.

"You won't get away with this," Marley said, big brown eyes shining with defiance.

He had to admire her nerve. "Me" was already crying.

"We'll see." He waved the gun.

They marched into the living room. That was where he told Mrs. Rogers exactly what she was going to do in the next hour—or return to find her family murdered. And that was when she insisted she didn't have to go anywhere to be able to give him the information he demanded.

After using a slim, regional phone book, she wrote down the name and address of someone named Claire, who'd advertised her haircutting business in the Yellow Pages. Mrs. Rogers said she and "Vivian" were best friends, that Vivian would be there or Claire would know where to find her, and she was pretty convincing. Desperation did that to a person.

She might've given Laurel up, but she was stupid to think he'd leave them in peace. He'd knocked out their phone, but even if he took the keys to every vehicle they had, they could walk or ride a bike to a cabin or the highway for help. He had no doubt whatsoever that they'd figure out some way to go to the police the moment he left.

And that was why he had to kill them.

29

The fuzziness caused by the pills Ink had given him had started to clear about an hour earlier. L.J. was more lucid now, lucid enough to move without stumbling or falling, lucid enough to separate reality from imagination. The pain in his shoulder was excruciating, made him wonder what Ink had screwed up in the process of digging out that bullet, but it was comforting to know he wasn't walking around with a slug in his body. He had to acknowledge that.

With concerted time and effort, he'd managed to traverse the half mile or so of forest separating their cabin and that of their closest neighbor. He'd use the phone to call for help. He'd tell the police everything that'd happened and everything Ink had planned and hope they'd believe he hadn't killed anybody. He didn't want to be a gangbanger anymore. He wanted to get his life in order, even if it meant serving more time. Punishing the world for his shitty childhood only insured he had a shitty adulthood, and nothing had been worse than the past week with Ink. It'd shown him that he wasn't like Ink at all, and no longer aspired to be. He wanted to make his grandparents proud—because if there was a heaven, they were in it.

When he spotted the back of the cabin peeking through the pines, he felt a huge surge of relief. Not only was he tired, he needed a doctor, probably some antibiotics, as well, and he wanted to know he was safe from Ink's unexpected return. But then he came across the white truck they'd been driving since Ink killed those dads and realized that he hadn't gone far at all.

He was here at the Rogers cabin.

Why?

This couldn't be about that bit of fluff they'd seen on the deck. Ink didn't care about sex; he couldn't even get a good boner. The bullet that'd jacked up his spinal cord had made him impotent. That was part of the reason he hated Laurel so much—the only part L.J. could sort of identify with. He wouldn't want anyone to take his manhood away from him, either. But from what he'd seen, whatever happened to Ink, Ink deserved.

So what did his old cellie want here? A hostage? New transportation?

Knowing him, it could be anything.

But what Ink did now didn't matter to L.J. If Ink had left the keys in the ignition, he was home free....

Careful not to make any more noise than was absolutely necessary, in case Ink was on his way back for whatever reason, L.J. slipped around to the driver's side and opened the door. Sure enough, the keys dangled from the ignition. He could jump in and head for town. Get help. These past two weeks would finally come to an end.

He was about to do just that, but hesitated. With a twenty-minute drive, any help he brought would be pretty damn long in coming. By the time the police arrived, Ink could be done here and well on his way to Canada or somewhere else in the family's Esplanade, if it was still parked out front.

Unless he was crazy enough to go after Laurel again…

Did he let his old cellie do whatever he was going to do? Or did he try to stop him?

Ink was so dangerous, L.J. preferred to escape unnoticed. But if *he* was scared, he knew this family had to be terrified.

Deciding to check out the situation to see what was going on, he left the truck and crept around the side of the house, looking in every window that wasn't covered by a blind.

Most of the rooms were dark and empty. Maybe Ink had already boosted the Esplanade. If so, L.J. could get out of here. But when he came around the house, he realized that wasn't the case. Probably because they had no close neighbors, Mr. and Mrs. Rogers weren't too cautious about lowering their blinds. They were raised as high as ever on the front windows, plenty high enough for L.J. to see that Ink had two younger girls, the bikini chick and her mother in the living room and was brandishing that damn gun.

Where was the dad?

Maybe he'd already been killed.

Or he wasn't home in the first place.

L.J. hated Ink, wanted to help the Rogers family. But he didn't have a weapon. The best he could do was use the bat he'd seen in the garage the last time they were here. His left shoulder was hurt, not his right. Still…did he have the strength to swing it?

"That's crazy, man. A bat against a gun?" he whispered to himself. He started to turn away, to head back to the truck. But then he saw Ink grab the dark-haired girl by the hair and yank her up against him. The bastard was going to kill her.

Almost without thinking, L.J. picked up a rock from amid the plants at his feet and threw it at the window. He heard the shattering of glass as he ran for the cover of the garage. Then a gunshot rang out. Where that bullet had gone, he had no idea. Maybe Ink had killed the girl. Or maybe he'd shot in the direction of the rock.

The bat was where he'd seen it. He grabbed it and waited, hoping Ink would charge out of the house and head to the Esplanade so he could rush him from behind. But that didn't happen. Nothing happened. Until several more shots rang out.

"Son of a bitch." Had he killed them, anyway?

Now that he'd committed himself he was actually eager to fight. He'd wanted to stop Ink when Ink had attacked that real-estate guy. He'd wanted to step in when Ink had shot those four men walking into the cabin. He'd even wanted to keep Ink from going to Laurel's house last night. He'd had no stake in coming to Pineview, no reason to kill innocent people. It was time he put a stop to his old cellie for good.

Wishing the bat didn't feel quite so heavy, he lifted it over his right shoulder and peered around the corner. The front window had been shattered; he'd expected that. But as he crept closer, using the darkness and the trees for cover, he saw that the living room was empty. If Ink had killed this family, they were lying somewhere else. And if he hadn't killed them, L.J. had done all he could.

Tossing the bat aside, he gave up searching for Ink and began to run for the truck.

But he didn't make it. Another gunshot ripped through the night, pain flared in his head, then he landed on the ground, face-first.

L.J. had thrown that rock? Ink couldn't believe it. That was gratitude for you. He should've let him die instead of removing that damn bullet.

His former cellie was dead now. Ink had shot him twice just to be sure, but it brought little satisfaction. There was no repairing the damage the bastard had done. When he'd thrown that rock at the window, Ink had thought a S.W.A.T. team was coming after him. He'd turned and fired, but then Mrs. Rogers had hit him with a lamp and just about knocked him senseless. By the time he could think straight, everyone was gone—they'd scattered all over the house or run to the same room. He hadn't bothered to look. He'd fired a few shots in frustration, just to scare the shit out of them, and hurried out to catch L.J. before he could do anything else.

Now it was no use trying to chase them down. For all he knew, Mrs. Rogers had come up with her husband's hunting rifle or some other firearm and would shoot him if he tried to go back inside. It was best to disable the remaining vehicles and leave. Hopefully, by the time they found help, he'd be finished with Laurel and well on his way to Canada.

She was the one he wanted, anyway. The only one who mattered here in Pineview. And, if Mrs. Rogers had given him adequate directions, he had a good chance of finding her.

The doctors were taking forever with Virgil. Vivian had spoken to Rex two more times, but he had nothing

new to report. An hour ago, the nurse had said Rex was
asleep in the lobby and had refused to wake him. "He
looks like death warmed over, that one. I suggest you let
him sleep."

Apparently the nurse could tell he was going through
withdrawal. Earlier he'd complained that she didn't like
him, that she had a bad attitude about letting him use
the phone, but he must've won her over. Vivian could
hear it in the woman's voice—and had to smile regardless of her concern for Virgil. Not many women could
remain immune to Rex's charm. If she hadn't met Myles,
if Myles wasn't exactly what she needed and wanted in
a man, she feared she'd fall right back into the same old
situation with Rex. As it was, she was happy with what
she'd found, hopeful that she and Myles might be able
to build the kind of life she'd always dreamed of.

She was equally hopeful that Rex could stay clean and
find the happiness he deserved.

"Keep a close eye on him," she'd told the nurse. "He
might need some medical help himself."

"My thoughts exactly," came the reply. The woman
told her Virgil was still in surgery, and that was it—all
she'd learned after waiting the entire day.

"Can it really take this long?" she complained to
Claire. They were sitting on Claire's small porch, drinking herbal tea and watching the moths dance around the
porch light, the stars overhead brighter than ever. Excited as she was by what was happening between her
and Myles, it would've been a perfect night.

Except for the agonizing worry.

Myles had called once and claimed his leg wasn't even
bothering him, but Vivian knew that couldn't be true.
From what he'd said on the phone, he was no closer to

finding Ink than when they'd separated at the motel, but he refused to give up. She had no idea how long it'd be before he came to get her, but she was looking forward to another night at the motel.

"I can't believe you're with the sheriff now. I *knew* you'd be good for each other."

"Yeah, well, don't jinx it," she teased.

"I think you make a perfect couple."

"You've been telling me that for a while." Vivian had enjoyed discussing Myles, but the worry lurking underneath all the chitchat was starting to get to her. "Do you think I should call the hospital again?"

Claire pulled her gaze away from her sister's house, which was set back even farther than hers. It was just the two of them on this little lane. Most of the homes in the surrounding area were impoverished—this was the poor side of town, farther from the lake—but both their houses were unique and more artsy than ghetto. They were right next to the old city park. That park wasn't used anymore but it was a pretty piece of land, except for the ugly cement restrooms. "Does it matter what I say?"

"What does that mean?" Vivian asked.

"I think Rex will contact you when it's over. But that isn't what you want to hear."

"Because I can't rely on it. Maybe the nurse doesn't want to wake him. Or she went off duty and the new nurse isn't even aware of what's going on."

Claire reached out to squeeze her hand. "Go call. It might ease your mind."

Vivian had just slipped inside and picked up the phone when she heard the roar of an engine revved way too high, followed by the sound of squealing brakes. This was a dirt road that dead-ended into the old park; there

was no need to be traveling at such speed. She was about
to duck her head out to see what was going on when the
pop...pop of gunfire turned her knees to water.

The call Myles received came from dispatch. Nadine
Archer said she had Trudie Jenson on the phone, which
meant he was hearing from Trudie for the second time
in as many days. But this call wasn't because she had
Ink or Lloyd in her store. This was because Trudie's
Grocery was the first open business one reached when
approaching town from the east and Brett Hamerschlit
had stopped there to get help. According to Nadine, he
had Janet Rogers in his Suburban.

When Myles heard what Trudie passed along to the
dispatcher, it felt like someone had wrapped barbed wire
around his heart. It hurt just to breathe. "What'd you
say?"

Nadine repeated herself, slowly and distinctly, but
her earlier rush of words had nothing to do with why he
hadn't been able to understand her. He'd quit listening
after hearing the name *Rogers,* flipped on his cop lights
and floored the accelerator in order to get out there as
fast as possible. Marley...

Fortunately, he'd already been headed in that direction. Allen had called a couple of hours ago to report
seeing a white pickup turn down a dirt road about a mile
or so from his house. Myles wouldn't have thought much
of it. He'd been following up on calls from various citizens who'd spotted white pickups all evening. But there
was the coincidence of Ned Green dropping Ink and
Lloyd off in that general area. So once he'd exhausted
any leads he'd considered more promising, he'd decided
to have a look. Although there'd been no reports from

up the mountain, he'd begun to wonder if Ink and Lloyd might've broken into an empty cabin and simply holed up there. They certainly weren't in town. He'd searched everywhere.

"Where is Marley?" he asked.

"Home with Alexis. So is Elizabeth. Janet drove a four-wheeler to the road and flagged down Brett. He brought her into town. They need you up there, Sheriff. There's a dead man in the backyard and the place has been shot up. Everyone's rattled."

"But Marley's okay, right?" He needed to hear that part again. "Elizabeth and Marley—all of them—they're fine?"

"Everyone's fine, except the dead man."

Yes, she'd mentioned a body. "Who is it?"

"They don't know. Janet says he came out of nowhere to save them, and a tattooed guy, obviously the guy in the flyer you put out, must've shot him when he tried to get away."

Myles asked a few more questions, but Nadine said Trudie couldn't get any more out of Janet, who was crying and babbling hysterically. It was a miracle Brett, Trudie and Nadine had been able to piece together as much of the story as they had.

"I'm halfway there already," he said, and almost disconnected.

Nadine stopped him. "Hang on. Trudie's saying something. Sounds like Janet thinks Claire's in trouble."

That cold wave of terror he'd felt a moment before returned. He'd barely had time to let Marley's safety sink in. Now he had to worry about Claire?

No, not Claire. *Vivian*...

* * *

Claire was screaming. The sound scraped Vivian's spine like nails on a chalkboard because she didn't know what it meant. Had Claire been hit? Or was she just scared half to death?

She'd acted so casual all afternoon, as if she wasn't even worried. She probably couldn't imagine anything like this really happening, despite Vivian's insistence that it could.

The truck that'd come barreling up to the house had stopped in the middle of the natural landscape and cobblestone path that was Claire's front yard. The *hub-hub-hub* of a motor at idle filled the air and the door *cre-e-e-a-ked* open as Ink got out.

Vivian was crawling on the wooden floorboards of the porch, trying to get to Claire, so she couldn't see his face. Only his feet, clad in a pair of cheap tennis shoes, showed from underneath. But she didn't need to see the rest to know who he was. He'd found her. At last. This was the moment he'd been waiting for—and the moment that'd haunted her nightmares—for the past four years.

The dust and dirt kicked up by his tires when he skidded to a halt combined with the truck's exhaust to clog her nostrils. Coughing, she gasped for clean air as she grabbed hold of Claire.

Fortunately, Claire was finished screaming. "I'm okay. I'm okay," she kept saying as if she didn't quite believe it herself.

"I've got you." Vivian had her gun, too, and planned to use it, but she couldn't get off a good shot. She wanted to drag her friend into the house before Ink was upon them. She wouldn't put it past him to shoot Claire just because she was vulnerable. The only reason he'd missed with the first couple of shots was that the bullets had to go through his windshield. Now he was out of the truck, and the windshield wouldn't be there to deflect the next one.

"Hi, honey, I'm home!" he called.

Fearing she might not have a better chance, Vivian knocked over the chairs they'd been sitting on so she and Claire had the benefit of a barrier and fired before he could. The blast deafened her, but she knew instantly that she hadn't hit him. She'd seen the spark of the bullet as it struck the hood of the truck.

"Is this any kind of welcome from the girl I've been dreaming about since we met?" He added a taunting laugh to that question, but he didn't fire back and he didn't advance. He was crouching behind the truck, using it for cover. She figured he wouldn't have walked into the clear the first time if he'd expected her to be armed.

What was he hoping to do? Get her to waste all her bullets before he used his?

"Claire? Are you okay? What's going on?" The voice came from farther down the lane. Leanne, Claire's crippled sister, had heard the truck, the shots and screams, and was coming to investigate. Moonlight bounced off the metal of her wheelchair as she rolled toward them.

"Go back!" Vivian shouted. "Go inside and lock your doors! Now!"

Leanne must've recognized the urgency of the situation because she immediately reversed. But Ink wasn't about to let her go. No doubt he knew she'd call the cops. He fired in her direction, missed, then jumped into his truck to chase her down.

Or run her over…

"Oh, God!" Claire jumped up as if there was something she could do. But Vivian pushed her aside. She couldn't have Claire getting in the way. Her gun was their only hope of stopping him.

"Call Myles!" she yelled, and ran after Ink herself, firing at the back window in hopes of hitting him.

The window cracked and splintered. Even in the dark, she could make out the holes she'd made. A web of lines connected them. But she ran out of bullets before she could bring him to a stop, and she didn't have another clip. Virgil hadn't even given her one. They'd always imagined a close encounter, the chance to fire once or twice at most, had never dreamed she'd use so much ammunition.

There was a huge crash, then the grating of metal on rock as Ink plowed into what was left of the concrete restrooms. Leanne had managed to reach one of the openings before he could run her down, but he had her blocked in.

When he realized she wasn't going anywhere, he abandoned the truck, keeping her barricaded there, and started back.

That was when Vivian got her first real look at his face.

He hadn't changed much. One leg appeared to be shorter than the other, or his spine had been fused, because he had an awkward gait. A grimace revealed what it cost him to move so fast. But his tattoos were as grotesque as ever, both in their abundance and the macabre nature of the designs he'd chosen.

And his eyes were still as devoid of human emotion as a snake's....

He didn't seem afraid that she'd use her gun. Obviously he knew how many bullets a typical handgun could hold and had already guessed she was out.

Hoping he couldn't see her well enough to shoot her, she ducked behind any tree or shrub she could find. As she made her way back to the house, she was surprised he didn't even attempt to fire at her. Was he saving his bullets? Or did he have other plans?

Claire was already inside. Hopefully she'd managed to get hold of Myles or someone else who'd be able to help. Now that Ink was the only one who had a gun, they wouldn't survive for long.

"Leanne's okay. She's fine," she assured her friend as she hurried into the house. She didn't know how much of a chance they had, but she promised herself and God that she wasn't going down without one heck of a fight. Her children were in New York. She planned on seeing them again. And there was no way she'd let Virgil's sacrifice be in vain.

She shut the front door just as he began to run in earnest. He rammed it a second later. She yelped at the noise and so did Claire, who stood at the kitchen sink holding a butcher knife while talking on the phone.

After turning the lock, Vivian started pulling the furniture in front of it.

"Open up!" he yelled. "Open up right now or I swear I'll go back and put a bullet in her head."

Leanne... Vivian froze. He wasn't going to force his way in. He didn't have to.

"He's going to do it this time. He's going to kill her!" Claire was still trying to verify basic information with the 9-1-1 operator. She'd given her name twice, her address three times because she was so nervous she couldn't get it straight, and screamed that they needed help *now*. But she'd heard what Ink said despite all that, knew he meant it. And so did Vivian.

Leanne was stuck out there in her wheelchair.

She couldn't even run.

30

Myles had sent every deputy in the area to Claire's house. Two had already arrived. When he drove up, he could see their squad cars parked haphazardly, red and blue lights flashing. He could also see a white Dodge Ram that had crashed into the old Pineview Park restrooms. His headlights landed directly on it, showed him the window that'd been shot numerous times.

But that was it.

Where was everybody?

After driving like a madman to get here, for one foreboding second he didn't even want to get out. He was too afraid of what he might find. He'd lost Amber Rose three years ago, had spent more than a thousand days trying to figure out how to make sense of his life again. And now that he'd moved on, found Vivian and wanted another chance at everything he'd once had, this...

Closing his eyes, he took a deep breath and got out. The house stood open, the light from within falling on two deep ruts in the yard, suggesting a vehicle had recently driven right up to the front door.

He heard crying....

Something cold and hard filled him as he approached that sound because he knew in his heart it wasn't Vivian.

Deputy Campbell glanced up when he crossed the threshold. He was on his radio, calling for an ambulance. A scratched-up Claire leaned on the table. She was the one in tears. Leanne sat, dry-eyed, in her wheelchair, which was smashed on one side, looking a little dazed. Vivian was gone.

"Where is she?" Myles asked.

"He dragged her into the woods," Campbell replied. "Peterson's gone after them, but…" He shook his head and let it go at that.

He didn't need to finish. Myles understood what he meant. He didn't think they'd find her alive.

Vivian fell several times as Ink pushed her through the trees. It was too dark to see much more than vague outlines. When she walked out of the house to save Leanne and he didn't shoot her instantly, she'd hoped she might have the chance to escape him. He wasn't the same man who'd shown up in her living room four years ago. This Ink was handicapped and in obvious pain. But he was still freakishly strong. And he was even more ruthless and determined.

"What is it…you want from me?" Occasionally a glimmer of moonlight streamed through the trees to illuminate a portion of his face or body, but she felt his presence more than she saw it. He had an iron grip on her shirt and was half shoving, half dragging her along with him.

"I want to make you pay. I want to make you *all* pay."

She stumbled while trying to look at him, and he kicked her. Fortunately, he was too close to land a solid blow. Her leg hurt despite that, but she refused to whimper or groan. Her pain and misery was what he wanted. She was pretty sure he'd put his gun in his waistband. It was close at hand, should he need it, but he didn't want to go that route. Making her death quick and easy wouldn't be enjoyable enough for him.

He wanted to relish the process.

"You're going back...to prison," she said. "I hope... you know that." She was trying to engage him, to stall him so the police could catch up, but he kept moving.

"They won't take me alive."

She listened for other sounds in the forest. Far off, she heard sirens. Myles was coming to her rescue, but how would he ever find her in time? There was too much land out here, and it was so dark.

"That's your out?" She prayed to catch a glimpse of a flashlight beam shining through the trees, proving that there were other deputies looking for her—deputies who were closer. But the immediate area remained dark and damp and quiet, except for the sounds of their own labored breathing.

Ink didn't answer.

"You're going to—" her leg burned from where he'd kicked her, making it difficult to walk "—to let them shoot you? Or...shoot yourself? Because even if you kill me...you won't get out of this."

Nothing.

"And Horse is dead," she said.

He stopped. "What'd you say?"

"He's dead. Virgil killed him." She didn't admit that The Crew might've killed Virgil, too. She didn't want to face that possibility, was still hoping it wasn't true.

"You're lying!" He clubbed her on the side of the head with his gun and nearly dropped her in her tracks. Her knees buckled as stars exploded onto her vision. But she shook off the pain.

"No. You can…" She blinked, trying to remain alert. "You can check. It happened…last night."

"Then he's dead, too."

Her ears were ringing when he hit her again. Apparently his desire for violence and punishment was overtaking his fear of discovery. Or he felt they'd come far enough. If he was going to stop somewhere, she preferred he do it closer to the houses, anyway. Maybe it would give Myles a better chance of catching up, of finding her.

If only she could survive the onslaught…

"Virgil will be sorry," he ground out.

The next blow split her lip. Blood flowed into her mouth, tinny in taste. He was really letting go now, planning to beat her to death right here. There was always the possibility that he'd shoot her, but she didn't think he'd resort to that unless he was forced to. This was far more personal, far more satisfying to him.

Briefly, she remembered Pat and the rage that'd been expended on him. That was what Ink had in store for her, if she let it happen.

"You bitch! Look at what you and your brother have done!" he growled. "You've ruined my life."

She would've responded that it'd been ruined long before she ever came along, that she hadn't involved herself in his world at all and never would have. But she knew he wouldn't understand that. He'd never been rational enough to accept responsibility for his own problems. She couldn't speak, anyway. He pummeled her with his fists, again and again until one monstrous blow sent her sprawling on the ground.

For a moment, paralyzed by pain, she felt certain he'd broken her jaw. She whimpered for Myles, but he wasn't coming. It didn't matter what damage Ink had already done to her, she had to stand up and fight on her own—or die. And this was the first time since he'd dragged her away from Claire's that he'd actually let go of her.

Staggering to her feet, she tried to run. If she could get away, hide in the trees… She had to stop the blows somehow, couldn't sustain many more. But her legs wouldn't carry her quickly enough. He grabbed hold of her shirt.

When he started kicking her, she couldn't help crying out. She tried to kick and hit him back, but she felt completely defenseless. He was like a vicious animal bent on tearing her apart. He felt nothing, heard nothing, cared for nothing except her demise.

Her only chance was to slip in close and get the gun.

"You won't…win!" She wanted to show him that she could still talk, that she could still function. He hadn't bested her yet. But her voice sounded so odd. It echoed through the forest. Or maybe it only echoed through her head. Had she said anything at all?

His hands found her throat, and he began to shake her. "I hate you!" he cried, muscles bulging beneath the short sleeves of his T-shirt. "I hate you and your brother. And I'm going to kill you both!"

He sounded like a child, she realized distantly. He *was* a child, emotionally. Almost everyone else matured as they grew older, but Ink had been stuck in the tantrum-throwing toddler stage for all of his thirty-something years. She wanted to laugh at this, to laugh at *him*. She would have if she could draw breath, but he was choking her, and he seemed to have more upper body strength than she would've believed possible.

She surprised him by going limp before he expected it, and that forced him to catch her if he wanted to keep them both from falling.

He instinctively tried to do just that and twisted something in his back. She heard a pop as if a twig had snapped, but from his screech she thought it might be a bone.

"You…bitch!" he wheezed. His breathing was as strained as hers, but he'd landed on top of her and was still gripping her clothes.

He clearly had a high tolerance for pain, could function with it because he was accustomed to it, but his injured back also gave her an opportunity. She could wrestle him for the gun, she told herself, and was determined to try.

"You're *nothing!*" she screamed back, and head-butted him in the nose.

She must've hit him just right because the blow stunned him. There was a pause during which he couldn't seem to do anything. Then he released her clothes in order to wrap his hands around her neck again. He was going to kill her now; she could tell. She felt his fingers dig into her skin as he tried to get a good hold when she sank her teeth into his forearm.

The salty taste of his sweat hit her tongue as the rank odor of his body filled her nose. But when he screamed like a little girl, she clamped down even harder, hard enough to break the skin. Then it was his blood and not hers she tasted.

Sickened, she wanted to recoil in disgust, to vomit, but she locked her jaws and held fast.

Gasping, he tried to grab her by the hair so he could yank her head back, but his fingers slipped through her short locks and, for a brief moment, he had no hold whatsoever. That was when she felt the gun. She didn't try pulling it from his pants. She knew he'd only take it away from her if she did. She barely had a second, just long enough to squeeze the trigger.

The blast seemed to ricochet off the trees and bounce back at them from the sky. He jerked, his scream a paroxysm of agony, and that was how she knew she'd hit whatever the gun had already been aimed at.

Judging from his position, she was pretty sure she'd just shot him in the balls.

The gunshot that gave Vivian and Ink's position away turned Myles's stomach. They weren't far. Had Ink just killed her? Had he missed reaching her by that little?

Deputy Peterson, who'd gone into the woods ahead of him, beat him to the scene. When Myles came upon it, Peterson was standing over Ink, who lay prostrate on the ground. Peterson had his foot on Ink's chest and his revolver pointed at his head.

"Kill me! Kill me, you bastard!" Ink screamed. "Pull the trigger."

Peterson kept his flashlight pointed right into Ink's eyes. "Sorry, buddy. I'm not like you. You're going back to prison for the rest of your life."

Myles took that in while using his own flashlight to scan the ground immediately surrounding them. He saw blood. Lots of it. Where was Vivian?

Then he found her. Although badly beaten, she'd managed to drag herself several feet away and sat shivering in stunned silence, watching the interplay between officer and felon as if she feared there might still be a chance that Ink could escape.

Afraid she was in shock, he lowered his flashlight and hurried over to her. "Hey, are you okay?" he asked as he knelt beside her. He prayed she wasn't too badly hurt.

Her eyes shifted from Ink and locked with his. Then tears began to stream down her face.

"It's over," he said, and gathered her gently in his arms. "He'll never be able to hurt you again."

"What about—" she winced as she tried to speak "—Virgil?"

Myles couldn't believe that was her first question. He'd never known a sister to care more about her brother. "He's fine. He's going to make it. And so are his wife and baby."

She dabbed at the blood on her busted lip. "You know about Peyton?"

He wiped away her tears. "Rex called me with the good news when he couldn't reach you. Peyton had the baby this morning—a girl, weighing nearly seven pounds."

"Both are healthy?"

She was obviously in a lot of pain, didn't seem fully capable of grasping what he'd said. "Perfect."

The tears came faster. "And my kids?"

"They're fine. Rex said they're so excited about the baby that's all they can talk about."

"Does Virgil…know about the…the baby?"

"I'm sure he does." He lifted her into his arms. "Come on. Let's get you out of here."

Epilogue

It rained ten days later at Ellen's funeral. Which was fitting. Nothing about her mother had ever been easy, but Laurel—she'd gone back to her old name, after all—was glad she could be there. She wanted to do the right thing, and that included taking responsibility for the person who could've made such a difference in her life, who *should have* made a difference, but had let her and her brother down so badly.

Myles stood on one side of her, Marley on the other. Sometimes Marley was a bit shy with her, but Laurel could tell Myles's daughter liked her. They were taking things slow, giving her time to adjust, but Laurel had been seeing both of them a lot. Marley smiled up at her now, and Laurel put an arm around her slim shoulders.

"Are you okay?" Marley whispered. She knew how it felt to lose a mother, but she had no idea that Laurel felt very different about Ellen than Marley had about Amber Rose.

Laurel couldn't talk for the lump in her throat, so she leaned over and kissed the girl's forehead, and that brought an even sweeter smile.

Myles noticed this exchange and squeezed her hand. Mia hugged one of his legs while she watched Rex toss

dirt on the coffin. They'd all thrown a shovelful, except
Virgil. He stood across the grave with Peyton, Brady
and the new baby, but he'd just been released from the
hospital and wasn't supposed to be on his feet quite yet.
Peyton and the kids had come to be with him during his
convalescence. Now they were ready to take him home.
Laurel had told him he didn't have to attend the funeral,
but he'd insisted. He said it was time to bury the past
along with the woman who'd raised them, that this ceremony was important for everyone involved, and she
agreed.

"Mom, do you want me to go back to the car and get
the umbrella?" Jake asked.

"No, honey. I'm fine."

Her son hovered close to Myles, as usual. He'd scarcely
left his side since he and Mia had returned from New
York. Laurel couldn't help being pleased that he was so
happy to have a good man, a good role model, in his life.
They had a camping and fishing trip planned for next
week. The girls were going to stay together and have
some fun of their own.

Peyton smiled as Laurel caught her gaze, and Laurel
smiled back. The baby was wrapped up tight, well pro-
tected by a large umbrella that Peyton held over herself
and Virgil, who was on crutches. Their new baby symbolized the fresh beginning they all needed. There was
something special about seeing little Anna there, at her
grandmother's graveside.

The ceremony didn't last long. The minister who performed the service wasn't too happy with the weather.
And that was fine with Laurel. Myles took the kids back
to the car to get them out of the rain; Peyton took Brady

and the baby. Soon, it was just the three of them—Laurel and Virgil and Rex.

"I wonder if she did it," Laurel said to them. "Wouldn't you like to know, once and for all?"

Rex shoved his hands in his pockets. His withdrawal symptoms had left and his color was returning. "And if she did?"

"Then we haven't lost anything, have we? That means she never really loved us as a mother should."

"And if she didn't do it?" he asked.

"Then I let her down. Then I should've forgiven her." She looked at Virgil. "We both should've forgiven her."

Rex and Virgil exchanged a meaningful glance.

"What?" Laurel said. "Do you two know something you're not telling me?"

"It's time," Rex murmured, and Virgil hobbled close enough to take her hand.

"We haven't lost anything," he said, and pulled her into as much of an embrace as he could in his current condition. "But you'll always have me."

She'd have him, Rex, Myles and the kids. And she'd have her freedom. At last. Ink was currently in the hospital under heavy guard, but he'd soon be heading back to prison. And after what he'd done, he'd never get out. The bodies of four men had been discovered behind the cabin where Ink had been hiding. She couldn't believe she'd survived his visit to Pineview.

It might take some of her friends and family a while to get used to calling her Laurel instead of Vivian, but she'd earned the right to go back to her original identity, to meld all the separate people she was into one complete person. She felt lucky to be able to do it.

As Virgil and Rex moved back to the cars and the loved ones who were waiting, Laurel tilted her head back and twirled in the rain.

* * * * *

Come back to Pineview, Montana, soon!

You've met Claire O'Toole. Now get

IN CLOSE

to her story....

As you know, Claire's mother, Alana, went missing fifteen years ago. That was big news in Pineview, the kind of town where nothing much ever happens. Then, last year, Claire's husband, David, died in a freak accident—after launching his own investigation into Alana's disappearance.

Is Alana dead? Or did she simply abandon her husband and daughters? Claire is determined to find out—and her former boyfriend, Isaac Morgan, wants to help. Although their relationship didn't end well, he still has feelings for her. But it isn't until he starts to suspect David's death *wasn't* an accident that he's drawn back into her life....

Look for In Close *by Brenda Novak.*
Available in November
from
MIRA Books.

MIRABRB312444

Check out all three *THE SEARCHERS* books
by *New York Times* and *USA TODAY* bestselling author

SHARON SALA

| Available now! | Available now! | Coming October 2011 |

The truth will set you free—
if it doesn't get you killed.

Available wherever books are sold.

New York Times and USA TODAY Bestselling Author

CARLA NEGGERS

When Emma Sharpe is summoned to a convent on the Maine coast, it's partly for her art crimes work with the FBI, partly because of her past with the religious order. At issue is a mysterious painting depicting scenes of Irish lore and Viking legends, and her family's connection to the work. But when the nun who contacted her is murdered, it seems legend is becoming deadly reality.

For FBI agent Colin Donovan, the intrigue of the case is too tempting to resist. As the danger spirals closer, Colin is certain of only one thing—the very interesting Emma is at the center of it all.

SAINT'S GATE

Available wherever books are sold.

REQUEST YOUR FREE BOOKS!

2 FREE NOVELS
FROM THE SUSPENSE COLLECTION
PLUS 2 FREE GIFTS!

YES! Please send me 2 FREE novels from the Suspense Collection and my 2 FREE gifts (gifts are worth about $10). After receiving them, if I don't wish to receive any more books, I can return the shipping statement marked "cancel." If I don't cancel, I will receive 4 brand-new novels every month and be billed just $5.99 per book in the U.S. or $6.49 per book in Canada. That's a saving of at least 25% off the cover price. It's quite a bargain! Shipping and handling is just 50¢ per book in the U.S. and 75¢ per book in Canada.* I understand that accepting the 2 free books and gifts places me under no obligation to buy anything. I can always return a shipment and cancel at any time. Even if I never buy another book, the two free books and gifts are mine to keep forever.

191/391 MDN FEME

Name _____ (PLEASE PRINT)

Address _____ Apt. #

City _____ State/Prov. _____ Zip/Postal Code

Signature (if under 18, a parent or guardian must sign)

Mail to the **Reader Service:**
IN U.S.A.: P.O. Box 1867, Buffalo, NY 14240-1867
IN CANADA: P.O. Box 609, Fort Erie, Ontario L2A 5X3

Not valid for current subscribers to the Suspense Collection
or the Romance/Suspense Collection.

Want to try two free books from another line?
Call 1-800-873-8635 or visit www.ReaderService.com.

* Terms and prices subject to change without notice. Prices do not include applicable taxes. Sales tax applicable in N.Y. Canadian residents will be charged applicable taxes. Offer not valid in Quebec. This offer is limited to one order per household. All orders subject to credit approval. Credit or debit balances in a customer's account(s) may be offset by any other outstanding balance owed by or to the customer. Please allow 4 to 6 weeks for delivery. Offer available while quantities last.

Your Privacy—The Reader Service is committed to protecting your privacy. Our Privacy Policy is available online at www.ReaderService.com or upon request from the Reader Service.

We make a portion of our mailing list available to reputable third parties that offer products we believe may interest you. If you prefer that we not exchange your name with third parties, or if you wish to clarify or modify your communication preferences, please visit us at www.ReaderService.com/consumerchoice or write to us at Reader Service Preference Service, P.O. Box 9062, Buffalo, NY 14269. Include your complete name and address.

SUS11

BRENDA NOVAK

MIRA | HARLEQUIN®
www.Harlequin.com

MBN0911BL